# Allie and Bea

# Also by Catherine Ryan Hyde

# Allie and Bea

## Catherine Ryan Hyde

*A Novel*

LAKE UNION
PUBLISHING

Text copyright © 2017 by Catherine Ryan Hyde
All rights reserved.

Published by Lake Union Publishing, Seattle

www.apub.com

Amazon, the Amazon logo, and Lake Union Publishing are trademarks of Amazon.com, Inc., or its affiliates.

ISBN-13: 9781477819715
ISBN-10: 1477819711

Cover design by Shasti O'Leary Soudant

Printed in the United States of America

# PART ONE

## BEA

# *Chapter One*

## *Rude Checkbook*

For perhaps the twentieth time that morning, Bea narrowed her eyes at the checkbook sitting on her kitchen counter.

"Stop looking at me that way," she told its blue vinyl cover.

Then her face flushed, and she looked around the tiny room as if someone might have overheard that embarrassing outburst—a second act of instability all in itself. Other than her friend Opal, nobody had so much as stepped foot into her trailer since the passing of her husband, Herbert. And Opal wasn't here now.

She hadn't meant it literally, what she'd said to the checkbook. It had been something of a bitter joke. But, in truth, she had been *mostly* joking rather than *completely* joking. That was the trouble right there.

She did feel mocked and threatened by its presence. There was no denying that.

"They put people away in weird places for making comments like that," she said out loud. Then, as an afterthought, "Also for talking to yourself."

She took three sips of her coffee, which was tepid, bitter, and one cup too many in the first place.

"I'm going to get this over with," she said.

Hands shaking ever so slightly, she dug through a drawer and found a pen for writing checks and a pencil for recording them in the register. She grabbed the offending checkbook off the counter and sat down to pay her bills.

She added in her monthly Social Security check—which should have reached her bank by auto-deposit that morning—to the total of funds. Then she stared at the number. It looked okay. Heartening, almost. But then, it always did. Before. It was after she'd written checks for the rent on this little trailer—not just the space on which it sat but even the trailer itself, which she and Herbert had once owned—the gas and electric, the water and garbage service, the phone bill. That was when the numbers began to look scary.

And this month there had been something more. A minor medical procedure to remove a skin abnormality that could have been cancer but, thank goodness, had revealed itself to be benign. Five months earlier she'd had to drop the Medicare gap insurance to save herself its monthly premium. Now, as she stared at the bill from the dermatologist, she realized the co-pay on this one visit had wiped out those savings almost twice over.

She looked up and out her window to see that awful Lettie Pace walking that awful brown poodle-mixed-with-something-or-other—looked like a dirty string mop if you asked Bea—across Bea's tiny patch of grass. Lettie paused to allow the dog to sniff.

Before Bea could even struggle to her feet, the mop-dog hunkered down and rounded its back into that unmistakable and undignified position, preparing to leave a pile on Bea's grass.

Bea rushed to her front door and threw it wide.

Lettie and the mop were already scurrying on as if nothing had happened.

"Lettie Pace!" Bea shouted.

Lettie was a younger woman—at least, younger than most of the residents of the mobile home park. Late fifties, maybe, which made her a good twenty years younger than Bea, which irked Bea in some indefinable way. Lettie should have been able to hear just fine. But she walked on as if she could not. As if Bea did not exist. And nothing—but nothing—infuriated Bea more than to be treated as if she did not exist.

Bea reached down and grabbed up a piece of white gravel from the decorative border around her defiled patch of grass.

For a flicker of a moment she only stood, staring at it in her hand.

*Bea wound up like a big-league pitcher on a mound in a real televised game. She let the stone fly. It hit the dog squarely on the behind. A yelp cut through the air of the park, and Mrs. Betteson, out trimming her roses, looked up to see what the trouble might be.*

*Lettie Pace turned back to Bea, teeming with rage and indignity, and stomped back to where Bea bravely stood her ground. Her nose came within inches of Bea's nose. Still Bea only stared. She did not waver or retreat.*

*"I can't believe you would hurt an innocent animal," Lettie said.*

*"Yes," Bea said. "I agree. I'm very sorry about that."*

*Lettie's eyes struggled to keep up with the atmospheric changes. "You are?"*

*"Absolutely. I didn't mean to hit that dog in the butt. The butt I was aiming for was yours. I never blame it on the dog. He's a dog. What does he know? You're on the business end of that leash. You're the one who deserved to be stoned."*

*For a moment, nothing. Then a flare of anger filled the scant air between their noses. There would be a fight. And Bea was not afraid. In fact . . .*

The drone of an airplane broke through Bea's reverie. It was coming in low for a landing and this place was in the flight path. It roused her from her waking dream. She looked down at her hand to see the pebble still sitting on her palm. She raised her gaze. Lettie Pace and the brown mop were mere dots in the distance, just rounding the corner into Lane C.

Bea shook her head a few times.

It was one thing to imagine a better ending to a confrontation, but in the past she had mostly been aware, all the way through, of what was real and what was imagination. This time she was surprised—nearly shaken—to see that stone still sitting on her palm.

She dropped it quickly, and looked around at her little patch of grass. That pile would need to be picked up. The idea that someone besides Bea could be forced to do the ugly job—the dog's owner being the obvious example—had just rounded the corner of Lane C.

Mrs. Betteson offered a sympathetic smile.

"If that were me I'd complain to Arthur," she called out.

"I might," Bea said. "I'm about to go bring Arthur my rent check, and I just might."

But in real life, she knew, such acts of courage remained more elusive, harder to pin down.

———

"There," Bea said, and set her pen back in the drawer.

She sat at her desk, her ancient tortoiseshell cat, Phyllis, curled on her lap. Now and then Bea would reach down and run a hand over the dry fur of the cat's back. Phyllis would respond by lazily digging her claws into Bea's thighs through her slacks. It smarted, and Bea said "ouch" every time. But still she felt compelled to pet the cat now and then.

She had written checks for all the bills, sealed them into envelopes, addressed them, and affixed a postage stamp to each one. Now she would be forced by curiosity and dread to turn the calculator back on and do the math in her checkbook. Run the numbers, as Herbert would have said.

She ran the numbers. Twice.

Then she sat staring at the final number.

## $741.12

When Herbert died, he'd left her no insurance or other financial means. It wasn't so much carelessness on his part, just . . . what did he have to leave? But they had struggled to put away a small pot of savings. About $5,000, which had seemed like quite a lot of money at the time. But the Social Security check never covered the month's expenses. No matter how hard Bea tried to economize, no matter how inexpensively she fed herself, there was always a shortfall. So, for lack of a better plan, every month that shortfall came out of her little pot of savings. Which had now dwindled from $5,000 to $741.12.

Bea had never sat down and figured the average monthly shortfall so she could know how long those savings would last. She quite purposely hadn't. Because she had no plan for the day when it ran dry. This was not owing to any irresponsibility on Bea's part. There simply was no plan to be had.

A few months? Probably. Definitely less than a year.

The phone rang.

For a moment, Bea only stared at it. Because it never rang. She used it to make outgoing calls from time to time, but that was all.

Still, the phone was ringing, and it was unlike Bea to ignore such a blatant demand.

She rose—gently moving Phyllis down to the carpet—walked to it, and picked up the receiver.

"Yes?" she asked in place of hello. Already a bit defensive. "What is it?"

"My name is John Porter," a young male voice said. "I'm with the IRS."

His second sentence hit Bea as if she had been stabbed in the gut by a knife fresh out of the freezer. She reached one hand out to the back of a chair to steady herself. Then she sank down, and sat.

"I have no business with the IRS," she said. "I pay my taxes."

"Well, you didn't pay enough for the calendar year 2014."

Her stomach sank under the weight of several more layers of ice, but it was almost hard to notice.

"Twenty fourteen? Well, why did it take you so long to figure that out?"

"Ma'am, we have a right to keep auditing the returns for six years."

Twenty fourteen. The first year she'd had to do taxes on her own, after Herbert died. She'd looked into using H&R Block, but she and her husband had no taxes withheld. Herbert had owned a small, struggling business. A bakery. No withholding meant no return. Which meant she would have had to pay a tax preparer out of pocket. So she'd struggled through the instructions herself. But it had been confusing. Overwhelmingly so. And she hadn't really known much about the bakery's last year of earnings—or any other year for that matter—so she'd had to rely only on what Herbert had left behind. Bank deposit records, boxes of loose receipts.

When she stopped to think about it, what were the chances she would have gotten that exactly right?

*At least it will never happen again,* she thought, and the revelation eased her mind some. All she had now was her Social Security, which was not taxable. She would never have to file a tax return again. But she had filed that one, for 2014. And she still owed.

How much of the $741.12 was that mistake about to claim?

"Ma'am?" the voice on the line asked. "Are you still there?"

"Um. Yes."

"There's a balance due of three hundred dollars. And it has to be paid today. If it's not paid today, a whole series of collection procedures will be put into place. You don't want that. You really don't want that. And once the process has started, there's nothing we can do to stop it again."

*Bea straightened, and dropped her voice into a more authoritative range.*

*"Well, that's just plain unfair," she said, pleased with the strong sound of it. "If it's due today you should have told me weeks ago. There must be some kind of requirement for that. I could have mailed you a check. I'm going to complain to my congressperson and my senator. Why, I'll call the newspapers and the TV news if I have to. This is no way to treat the taxpayers who pay your salary."*

"Ma'am?" the voice asked again. "Are you there?"

"Um. Yes. So I have to drive a check to the office?"

"We're in Sacramento."

*"Sacramento?"* It came out as more of a screech than a word. "That's hours from me! More than seven or eight hours! There's no way I could even get it to you before your office closes!"

Bea felt the panic close in all around her, cutting off her oxygen supply. As if the room had filled up with water from the walls in.

"Ma'am, relax. There's an easy solution."

"Oh. Good." She pulled in a breath, and it was indeed oxygen. "What is it?"

"You just give us a little banking information over the phone. A routing number and your account number, and then the PIN or code you've established with your bank. We can do a direct withdrawal. The whole thing will be cleared up in no time."

"Oh. Good. Thank goodness. Yes. I'll just go get my checkbook."

As she crossed the room to fetch it, the new balance popped into her head. $441.12. She pushed it away again. At least she would have no more trouble with the IRS, and nothing could be more frightening than that.

"Okay," she said, grabbing up the receiver again. "I've got it."

"First," he said, "your name."

"Beatrice Ann Kraczinsky."

Later she would run the moment through her mind dozens of times. Hundreds of times, to be more honest. Each time she would see so clearly what she had not seen at the time: that if the IRS calls you to tell you there's a balance due, they must already know your name. Otherwise how would they know whose balance is owing? How would they even have known which taxpayer to call?

And there would be other things that would occur to her later. That $300 was an awfully neat, round figure, for example. That the IRS was more likely to determine that you owed them $317.26 or some such raggedy number. Nothing quite so convenient as rounding off in whole hundreds.

And that the only other time there had been communication from the IRS to Herbert it had come in the form of a registered letter.

And that they may well have the right to audit returns for a number of years, but they tend to conduct the audits with the taxpayer present.

All these things Bea would see very clearly. Later.

But this was not later. This was not a moment enhanced by the wisdom of hindsight. This was the moment in which Bea gave the man her routing number, her account number, her PIN.

No amount of hindsight would change that.

———

After finishing up the dreadful call, Bea gathered up her bill envelopes. She took a brown paper sack out of the cupboard. Then she grabbed a plastic sandwich bag to cover her hand.

She let herself out the trailer's front door, carefully locking up behind her.

Bea picked up the nasty pile from her grass and dropped it into the paper sack.

Then she placed the bill payments—all except the rent check—in the mailbox and raised the red flag so the postman would know to collect them before stuffing in more bills.

She drove her van down the rows of brightly colored trailers, occasionally waving to a neighbor in a garden, or on a porch, or through their windows. She drove not because she literally could not walk the equivalent of a block or two—though a walk that long would have been a struggle—but because it was already 108 degrees. She kept driving, blasting the air conditioner, until she had reached the mobile home park office. Arthur was not there. She could tell. Because that little "We Will Return in . . ." sign was hanging on the door, its "clock" manually set to 2:00 p.m. She dropped her rent check through the mail slot in the door instead.

On the way back, she purposely took the long way to go by Lettie Pace's trailer. There she left the paper sack and its contents on Lettie's stoop.

Really. In the real world. When she looked back over her shoulder, she was pleased to see it was something she had actually done.

# Chapter Two

*After The End of Everything*

Bea woke with a start, effectively dead. And yet, at the same time, not dead at all.

It happened to her more and more frequently. A couple of times a week these days. She would drift into that twilight of half-asleep, and something would happen that she immediately recognized as The End of Everything. But, curiously, the thing itself was never big or dramatic. A shadow that fell over her in her sleep, or an envelopment in something like smoke. But with a jolt of fear she clearly knew everything ended with the smoke or the shadow, and that she had known this truth all along. And that she had been waiting for it. Then, startled awake, she would lie frozen for a moment, wondering why she was still so . . . *there*. If that had been The End of Everything, why was she still in her bed thinking thoughts in the wake of it?

Eventually her brain would clear enough to understand the moment for what it was: a half-asleep, half-awake dream experience.

It usually took her almost half the night to get back to sleep after such a fright.

Bea lay frozen for a moment, wondering why it was still so hard to breathe. She reached a hand up to her chest and found Phyllis curled on her collarbone.

"Phyllis. Honey. You have to move."

She gently nudged the cat down onto the bed. Phyllis rose, stretched, then slithered under the covers and curled up next to Bea's hip.

Bea breathed deeply a few times and poked at a thought hiding somewhere near the back of her consciousness. She wasn't sure quite what it was yet, but she'd been aware of it several times earlier that day. Each time she had felt a tightening in her belly, but she'd tried her best not to go after the thought that had evoked it.

This time she held still and the thought caught her.

What if that man had not been from the IRS in any way? He hadn't known her name.

She sat up in bed.

What if she had just given away $300 of her $740-something to a non-IRS stranger for no good reason whatsoever? What if she had been duped? You heard of such things these days. Read about them in the paper or were warned against them on the news. And they seemed to like to target older people.

"I can't afford a loss like that," she said out loud to the dark room.

She decided to pick up the phone and call the automated phone line for the bank.

Being an organized woman, Bea had its number in the directory on her phone. And she knew her PIN by heart. It was the last four digits of an older phone number, one she'd kept stored in her memory for years. One from back in the days when she and Herbert had owned a house. She would never forget it as long as she lived, but no one would associate it with her, or guess it. And she had been told to be extremely careful when choosing passwords and PINs.

Another cold grip in her stomach reminded her that it doesn't matter how carefully you choose your PIN if someone can just ask you for it on the phone. And you give it.

The familiar canned voice on the line welcomed her to her bank's automated services line, then began a menu of choices. Bea didn't wait. She punched number three, because she knew it would bring up account balance and information.

"I don't like this new world," she said out loud, to no one. "I don't like it one bit."

Sighing, she punched in her account number and PIN.

"Your balance is . . . zero dollars . . . and . . . zero cents. To hear this information again, press one. To return to the main menu, press two. To end this call, press the pound key, or hang up."

Bea hung up.

She sat with the phone in her hand, in the dark. For how long, she would not have been able to say. She knew she was awake, and yet here it was again. The End of Everything.

And, just like in the waking dreams, Bea was still there. Still thinking. Still wondering how there could be anything on the other side of The End.

Despite being stunned, despite feeling her belly buzz and tingle with electricity, mostly Bea felt a bizarre sense of relief. Finally, it was over. She had gotten it over with. For years she had been watching herself move closer and closer to the edge of this cliff. Now she was off the edge, free-falling. Somehow utter unmitigated disaster felt preferable to the constant, compulsive, nervous anticipation of that disaster.

And in some way or another, she was still here.

What life would look like from this point on, well . . . that was a mystery for now.

She never got back to sleep.

# Chapter Three

## It's All about the Weather

Bea rose first thing in the morning and drove to Palm Desert. The guard at her friend Opal's gated community recognized Bea and her old white van, and waved her right through.

She pulled up to Opal's condo—or rather Opal's son's condo—to see her friend sitting on the front porch swing, in the shade, fanning herself with the genuine Japanese fan her son and his wife had brought home from their last vacation. It was made of silk and silver, and must have been expensive.

Bea couldn't help but notice the condescending look from Opal's across-the-street fussy housewife neighbor as she parked the van.

> "Yes, that's right. Go ahead and stare," Bea shouted. "Imagine, somebody having to drive an older vehicle. Not having money bursting from every orifice like you. How shameful! Really get a good look now."
>
> The woman turned and hurried into her house, chastened and ashamed.

Bea cut her eyes away and silently turned her back to the rude neighbor.

"You don't look good," Opal said as Bea struggled up the steep walk in the gathering morning heat.

"Well, good morning to you, too."

"I didn't mean it as an insult. I just meant you don't look happy. You look like you've been worried and haven't slept."

"Yes," Bea said. "All of the above."

She stood on the porch at last, puffing, sweating. Staring at her friend.

Like Bea, Opal was a physically generous woman—as Bea's mother used to generously phrase a thing like that. Unlike Bea, she had a shock of white hair, thick and glossy, that fell all the way to the middle of her back. The hair made Bea jealous, as her own had been thinning into near nonexistence for years. But she had never said so.

"I've come to ask a series of favors," Bea said. "I'll just put that out up front. If you're in no mood to be asked favors this morning, you'd best tell me to hit the road right now."

"Depends on the favors," Opal said. She had a slow way of talking. Lazy, almost. Like a southern woman sipping a mint julep in a movie, but Bea happened to know Opal was from Duluth. "You can ask whatever you want. If I can, I will. If I can't, I'll say. You know that about me by now."

They held still a moment, regarding each other. As if there were a protocol dictating who would speak next, but neither knew what it was.

Then Opal said, "Start me off with a nice, easy request."

"A cup of coffee."

Opal pulled her great bulk up out of the porch swing. "That's simple enough, yes. But I hardly think it's one of the favors you drove all the way over here to ask me."

Opal held the door open for Bea, who stepped into the glorious air-conditioning with a sigh.

"Actually, though, it is. I really do need a cup of coffee. I'm out of coffee at my house."

She followed Opal into the massive, modern kitchen. It had a chopping-block island, and Italian marble tile counters, and LED lights recessed into the ceiling, and one of those ovens that are always on and cost more than Bea's trailer had when it was brand new. And the kitchen was bigger than Bea's trailer, too. Maybe by half again.

"They sell it at the grocery store, you know," Opal said, taking a foil package of imported coffee from the stainless steel freezer.

"There's a problem with the store, though. They want you to bring money for every little thing you care to buy."

Opal looked up at Bea and narrowed her eyes with concern.

"Uh-oh."

"Yes. Uh-oh."

"It ran out?"

"It ran out."

———

"I'm afraid I know what the other favor is," Opal said. "I feel just terrible about it and I want you to know I would if I could. But honey, I swear, things being what they are between me and my daughter-in-law, I'm never sure from one month to the next if there's always gonna be room in this place for *me*."

"I didn't come here to ask to move in. I know you can't do that."

They sat on a glass-covered porch at the back of the house, overlooking a duck pond with a fountain, and the golf course. At least, it looked like glass to Bea. But she had been told it was some material more resistant to stray golf balls. In any case, it held in the air-conditioning.

"I would if I could, Bea, I swear to that."

"I know. Besides. Nobody wants to live with me, and I know it. And I don't want to live with anybody because I don't like anybody. Oh, don't be too offended. I like you well enough, but I'm sure that would change if we tried to share any kind of space together. I didn't for a minute imagine that anyone would want to put up with me."

"You're not as bad as you make yourself out to be."

"I'm worse. You just don't know because we only visit for a few minutes at a time."

"You're a little disagreeable, I suppose."

"Ha! You have no idea."

"I'll just let you ask in your own good time, then."

"Ask what?"

"Whatever you came here to ask."

"Oh. Right. That. I need to borrow twenty dollars."

"Seems to me you need to borrow more than that. How will you pay the rent on that little place? And keep the utilities on? And feed yourself and the cat?"

"I can't just borrow money to get out of this fix. Because I'll never be able to pay it back. I mean, twenty dollars I can. I can pay that out of my next check. I bought cat food to last the month with what cash I had in my purse. Then I didn't have enough for food for me."

Opal snorted. "Some priorities."

"She relies on me."

"She could eat the cheap stuff. That dry food for pets they feed at the shelters. Costs nearly nothing."

"She can't eat dry food."

"Why can't she?"

"She has no teeth. You know that."

"Oh. Yeah. I guess I did know that. I guess I just forgot. You sure you don't want to borrow more than twenty?"

"Yes. I'm sure. I can't get out of this by borrowing."

"Then I won't loan it to you. What I *will* do is I'll *give* you twenty dollars. And don't be arguing about it with me, either."

"Thank you," Bea said.

They watched in silence as two women smartly dressed in sportswear—their own age but quite a bit more fit—played through on the third hole.

Then Opal said, "I keep wanting to ask what you're gonna do, but I hate to even bring it up."

"I have a plan."

"I'm relieved to hear that."

"I've decided it's all about the weather."

A silence.

"The weather, you say. News to me. Here I thought it was all about the money."

"Well . . . yes. Of course. Everything is. But when you don't have money, it's all about the weather. You see . . . I've been thinking. I can pay my rent. My check covers that. I can even pay my rent and have money left over for food. No problem. But I can't pay rent and then both eat and pay the electric bill. Now if I lived somewhere the weather was mild, never very hot or very cold, my electric bill would be low. Or I could even live without electricity. But here in the valley, if they turn off my power and there's no air-conditioning, the heat'll kill me."

"Got that right," Opal interjected. "You know the public utilities have to offer discounts to low-income folks and seniors, right?"

"They already do. And it's still my biggest expense after rent."

"So let me get this straight. Your plan is to make the Coachella Valley cooler."

"No. Of course not. I was just lying in bed last night, and I thought, 'Imagine if I could pick up my home and move it up into the mountains.' You know. Instead of turning on the air-conditioning."

"Those mountains get cold in the winter."

"Then I could move it back down."

"Honey," Opal began. It was clear from her tone that she had decided Bea's thoughts needed straightening out, and fast. "I know they call that place you live in a mobile home. But in this case it's just a figure of speech. That particular one isn't going anywhere."

"I know that," Bea said. "I'm not talking about my trailer. I'm talking about my van."

A long silence fell. Bea sipped at her coffee. In time she braved a look into Opal's eyes. Their gazes met, and stuck. Because now they both knew exactly what Bea was talking about.

"There must be something else you can do, Bea. Honey, there's got to be something better than that."

"The only other thing I can think of involves sleeping on a park bench and pushing my belongings around in a shopping cart. Look. Opal. People live with less. All over the world people are living with less. I'll have a roof of sorts over my head. I'll have curtains. I'll have my easy chair, and some books. And my cat."

"And a litter box right in the middle of the whole deal."

"That can go on the passenger floor and be out of my way."

"And there's no bathroom for *you*. You can't use a litter box."

"I can park by a gas station. Or by a public restroom."

"And how will you get your monthly check?"

"I won't have to. It'll go straight into my account every month and all I'll have to do is bring my debit card for gas and food."

But a thought struck Bea, quite suddenly. Before the next check landed in her account she'd better stop by the bank and change that compromised PIN. In fact, she might do better to close the account and open a new one, just to be safe. And notify the Social Security Administration of the change. It made her feel vulnerable and ashamed, and less than sharp-minded, that she had just now thought of it. What else was she forgetting?

Oh yes. Get a new debit card for the new account.

"And you'll spend all your savings in gas," she heard Opal say, knocking her back into the moment.

"No. No, I won't. It doesn't have to be that way at all. I don't have to keep moving constantly. I could stay in one place for months if the weather holds. I thought about it a long time. I just need one other thing from you and that's to put a few of my things in your garage. I can only take just so much along. Just what I need to live. I've been thinking a lot about what I really need. About what makes a home a home. I don't care about my couch or my bed. I can sleep in my easy chair. That's all the furniture I need. Without my easy chair, life wouldn't be comfortable enough to bear. But with it . . . I sleep in it all the time, when I have acid reflux, or when my sinuses won't drain. It's just as comfortable as my bed, if not more so. So long as I can draw the curtains and turn on a little battery-powered light and read a book with my cat on my lap, it won't be so bad. I'll be okay."

"You'll be homeless," Opal said.

Bea would have liked to keep that ugly word out of things. But there it was. Sooner or later it was going to be said. By someone. It was inevitable.

"I didn't say it was a great plan. I said it was a plan."

"You've got till the end of the month, right? Everything's paid up for now?"

"Yes. For now."

"Then we have time to think of something better."

"Sure," Bea said. "We'll think of something better."

But she knew it wasn't true. *If there were a nice, easy solution to homelessness,* she thought, *a million homeless people would have found it by now.*

# *Chapter Four*

---

### *The World May Not Owe Me a Living, but It Owes Me $741.12*

Three days later, in what should have been a quiet month of transition, Bea was startled out of sleep by a knock on the trailer door.

This almost never happened.

No one came to Bea's door except Opal once in a blue moon. It was embarrassing to have Opal over, as she lived in such opulence—even though none of the opulence was technically hers. So Bea's sole friend visited seldom. And no one else visited at all.

Bea couldn't help feeling, as she struggled into her robe and combed her hair with her fingers, that this was unlikely to be good news. She glanced at the little clock on the stove as she hurried by the nook of the trailer's kitchen. It was barely seven a.m.

"Who is it at this hour?" she called through the door. "Awfully early to come knocking."

"It's Arthur," Arthur said.

That might not be so bad. Maybe Mrs. Betteson had told him about Lettie Pace's rudeness and he had come around to hear her side of the thing.

Bea swung the door wide, wincing into the morning light.

"We've got a problem," Arthur said.

"What problem is that?" she asked, trying to sound casual. But her heart took to pounding and her stomach turned to concrete.

"It's your rent check."

"What about it?"

"It bounced."

Bea opened her mouth to say that was silly. There was no reason it should have. Then it all came pouring down on her at once.

She closed her mouth.

She took two steps backward to her easy chair and lowered herself down.

That was the something else she'd been forgetting. Another aspect of the situation her brain could not be trusted to grasp. The day she'd gotten that awful call from the scammer pretending to be the IRS, she had just written all her checks for the month. As she'd deducted them from her checkbook, she had considered them paid. In her mind they were paid. But they were not paid. The utility checks had been sitting in the mailbox when her account was raided, and the rent check had been lying on the floor of the mobile home park office, having only recently been slipped through the mail slot.

So the scammer did not get $740 and change. He got the nice, reassuring total she'd seen in her checkbook when she added in that month's Social Security. He'd made off with over $1,600. And all of her monthly checks would now bounce.

"Mrs. Kraczinsky? You okay?"

She looked up at Arthur, backlit by morning in her doorway.

It was an additional problem that she hadn't seen all this coming—that her brain had not made the jump. She knew that now. Anyone with a reasonable mind would know that checks written are not checks cashed. Why, when she'd gone to the bank to close that compromised account and open a new one, they'd even asked her if she had checks outstanding. And she'd said no.

She'd spent the better part of three days fixing her banking problems. Talking the bank into waiving its rules by establishing an account with no opening balance. Changing the direct deposit arrangement with the Social Security Administration to the new account. Getting a new debit card to take on the road. She'd felt such a sense of satisfaction, knowing she'd handled things so well.

Meanwhile all her checks were bouncing.

And the account on which she'd written them had been voluntarily closed.

And she hadn't told anyone about the scammer, because she was ashamed. And because there was no way to catch him anyway, and everybody knew it. And because she didn't want their pity. And now it would appear that she had written checks on a zero balance and then closed the account before they could come in.

"Mrs. Kraczinsky?"

"Yes, Arthur. I'm fine. It's just a mistake. I know what went wrong and I can fix it. I just need a few days. Give me three days, okay?"

Because that's how long she figured it would take to load up the van and clear out.

"Well . . . ," Arthur said. He scratched his very bald head. "I'm not too happy about that, but . . . if you're sure it's only three days."

*"Why, you sanctimonious little rodent," Bea spat.*

*Arthur stumbled back a few steps from the force of her words.*

*"Here I've lived in this ratty little park for almost two decades, and have I ever once paid my rent even one day late? No. Not once. And when Herbert and I had to borrow money using the trailer for collateral, and we got behind, you were more than happy to take it off our hands and rent it back to us. Like you were doing us a big favor, keeping the bank from foreclosing. But it was*

*a favor to yourself and no one else, because you rented it
back for more than it was worth, and even that didn't
stop you from raising the rent twice more in the following years. And then you have the gall to stand here while
my life is falling apart and act like three days is a major
imposition? How dare you? How dare you stand in my
doorway at seven o'clock in the morning and make yourself too important to try to make me feel small? Just who
do you think you are?"*

"Mrs. Kraczinsky?"

"Yes, Arthur. Three days. I promise. I won't let you down."

Bea rose, walked to the door, and closed it, blotting out Arthur's face.

To her surprise, she didn't feel guilty about her lie. At least, not as
guilty as she'd expected. Of course she would let him down, and she
would live with that. After all, other people let her down all the time.

*Let somebody else cope with it for a change.*

She turned on the air-conditioning. Yes, at seven in the morning.
She would bathe herself in cool comfort until it was time to go. The
check to the electric company would bounce, and they would never be
paid for last month, or the power she used in the first few days of this
month while getting ready to leave. And she was doing it anyway. They
had plenty of money, and they got it by taking it from people like her.
They could simply deduct the loss from their taxes, which they didn't
pay nearly enough of anyway. She and Herbert had spent their lives
making up the tax shortfall caused by these big, heartless corporations.

Now she would short them and see how they liked it.

She didn't believe herself one hundred percent. She wasn't comfortable with these ideas so much as she was forcing herself to make her
peace with them, and fast.

One thing she could not deny. The world owed her $741.12, and
it was high time the world paid up. For a change.

# *Chapter Five*

*Van Sweet Van*

Bea's new home was twelve years old and boasted 145,216 miles on the odometer. It had decent tires, and air-conditioning in the dash that still worked.

It had two windows in the back, one in each of the double doors, and no windows on the sides. That was fine with Bea. The less she had to convert the trailer's old drapes to work in her new quarters, the better. The harder it was for passersby to see in, the happier she would be.

Its sides were painted with the words "Sun Country Bakery," with a stylized sun in the bottom curve of the *S*. But over the years the weather had been hard on the lettering, causing the paint to chip and peel at the edges, like Herbert's chaotic and poorly run business near the end. Like her life with him.

It had a sticker on the rear bumper that read, "If I'm driving slowly, I'm delivering a wedding cake." Because, in its day, that's mostly how the vehicle had been used.

Bea worked on its interior for two days. Both days she waited until nightfall to do so, for obvious reasons.

She was inside it now, on the second night, duct-taping the bathroom curtain rods across each of the back windows. She had already done something similar with the living room drapes—affixed the curtain rod from one side of the van to the other, just behind the seats. She could now draw that curtain to separate the back of the vehicle from its cab. Anyone looking through the windshield would see nothing but two empty seats. She could draw the curtains aside while driving, to allow a rear view.

The easy chair sat in its new place in the van, which made it hard to get comfortable inside the trailer now. The previous evening she had knocked on the door of Kyra and John, the only young residents of the mobile home park, and asked their help moving it, claiming she was giving it to a friend. Kyra and John were used to such requests. To be young in a community of old people would always involve a lot of lifting and hauling, and they had learned that well enough.

She'd wanted to put it behind the driver's seat, but John had insisted on placing it at the passenger side.

"If you were in an accident," he'd said, "or had to stop suddenly . . . why, that thing could come flying forward and turn you into a dashboard pancake."

Over the chair, on the van's ceiling, Bea had stuck a self-adhesive battery-powered light she'd picked up at the dollar store. Beside the chair was a box of tissues and a carton of carefully ordered paperback books she had not yet read, or might want to read again.

She'd been able to move the chest of drawers herself, because it was only cardboard. It wasn't her real dresser, just something she'd kept hidden in the closet because it looked cheap. But it would hold two changes of clothes, underwear, bras, socks. Two towels.

She had filled her little travel cosmetics bag—which was a silly thing to own, since she didn't travel—with a hairbrush, toothbrush and toothpaste, ear swabs, and a washcloth. She could carry it into a public restroom without attracting attention.

"I'll be traveling *now*," she said out loud, to no one.

In the corner of the van she had placed a plastic bucket. It embarrassed her to look at it, but she knew she needed it along. Maybe there would be no adjacent restroom on any given night. Or maybe it would be cold out, or she would doubt the safety of the neighborhood in which she had parked. She could always empty it and clean it out in the morning. Maybe she would be lucky and would never·have to use it. But why take chances with a thing like that?

Every blanket she owned was stacked, neatly folded, in the other corner.

She started the van briefly and looked at the gas gauge. About two-thirds of a tank. That was all she had to last for the next three weeks. Her heart pounded again as she attempted to mentally grasp the challenge. Before the gas ran out, she had to find a place that was not life-threateningly hot, but where she would not freeze at night. She had one shot. If she chose wrong, there would be no going back on the choice. Not for more than three weeks.

*It wasn't supposed to be like this,* she thought for the hundredth time.

She was supposed to be able to wait and take off on the third of next month, with a bank account full of money. With that lovely feeling that it was all hers this time. No rent, no bills. Just gas and food, and maybe some loose quarters for a Laundromat or a campground shower.

She wasn't supposed to have to take off with a bank balance of zero, leaving behind half the food she'd bought for the month because she hadn't realized when she'd bought it that she would be giving up her refrigerator so soon.

*Then again,* she thought, *it wasn't supposed to be like any of this. I wasn't supposed to be making plans to live in this old van at all.*

Bea climbed down from the driver's seat of the van and walked back into her trailer.

Three boxes sat in the middle of her living room floor, where the easy chair had once lived. They were carefully taped and labeled with a marking pen in big, bold letters: "OPAL MARTIN C/O ROBERT MARTIN." Those she would drop off on her way out of the valley. Not to Opal personally, because her friend would only try to talk her out of going, and feel guilty that there was not more she could do. No, Bea would leave them with the guard at the gate, and be long out of town before Opal knew she was gone.

Everything else except the cat would stay.

Bea stood in the living room, looked around, and was struck by her first overwhelming wave of panic. Everything in this tiny place, no matter how small and insignificant, was something she wanted to keep. It all had a history. It was all so familiar. It was her life, it was her. She couldn't leave all this behind.

Every lamp had a story as to where she had gotten it. Every kitchen utensil felt weighted with history. The spoon rest from the Santa Barbara pier, bought on their first trip to the coast. The champagne glasses that had been a wedding gift. The mugs brought from Herbert's bakery when it closed its doors. The idea of walking out and abandoning the minutiae that added up to her very existence made Bea dizzy. Literally, physically dizzy.

She sat on the couch for a moment or two, steadying herself.

Then, in one sudden act of mental fortitude, she decided it was time to go. Now. Not tomorrow, now. Arthur might stumble on the evidence of her planning if she waited. And besides, it might be like everything else: The anticipation of the thing might be worse than the thing itself.

She loaded up the three boxes for Opal, and as much perishable food as she felt she could stuff into her face before it spoiled. She had a picnic cooler, so at least it would last two or three days if she used all the ice in her freezer.

She cleaned the litter box and carted it out to the van, placing it on the passenger-side floor.

Then she made her final trip—for Phyllis.

She scooped up the ancient cat, hugging the warm, purring body tightly to her chest, then placed her in a box she'd prepared, with holes for air. Phyllis likely wouldn't be in it long. Just to go from trailer to van. But still, living things need air.

Phyllis—who had never been outside once in her life, and had not lived anywhere but the trailer in the eighteen years since Bea had adopted her as a kitten—yowled. It was a deep, threatened, and threatening sound, emanating from a place low in the cat's throat. It was loud. It carried.

And of course Bea wanted no attention drawn to her nighttime retreat. So she ran like a thief, tossing the key to the trailer over her shoulder and onto the carpet, and leaving the door unlocked.

It was likely for the best, and probably saved Bea from another moment of abject panic. She was too busy racing out of her home of nineteen years to fully absorb what it meant to do so.

At least, in that moment.

Later it would catch Bea, and catch her hard. And she knew it.

But this was not later. And Bea had no intention of hurrying trouble along. So she only gunned the engine and tore away.

# Chapter Six

## Why Do You Have So Much, and Why Do I Have So Little?

Bea parked the van at something like ten a.m., and turned off the engine. She listened to the ticking of metal as it cooled.

She might have been in Ventura, or it might have been Oxnard. Bottom line, she had made it to the Pacific Ocean. And she had found a BuyMart parking lot where she could park under a light and a security camera.

*For three weeks?*

Maybe. BuyMart was vocal about welcoming RVers to park overnight. And wasn't Bea just an RVer but with a smaller rig?

It had been a long drive, and the gas gauge hovered frighteningly under one-quarter. But she felt it had been worth it to get to the coast. It was always cooler by day and warmer by night at the coast.

Her first thought had been the mountains, but she was afraid. Towns were few and far between up there. What if she ran out of gas in exactly nowhere? What if there were no support services? She needed more than just a restroom. She needed access to water, and the safety of other people in case of emergency. She couldn't just park in a wilderness setting. So she had aimed for the comfort of the beach climate, not at all sure the gas would last.

She saw a woman walking through the parking lot between cars, not far away. She powered down the driver's window and called to her.

"Excuse me."

The woman looked around. "Me?"

"Yes, you. Do you live around here?"

The woman's face twisted into a mask of defense and suspicion.

"Why?"

"I just wondered what the weather's been like here. Does it get hot in the day?"

"Midseventies," the woman said, her face and body language relaxing some.

"What about night? Is it cold at night?"

"No. Not cold. Fifties, maybe."

Bea waved her thanks and put the window back up. Removed her key from the ignition. She stepped into the back of the van and pulled the curtain closed behind her. Then she moved to the rear doors and pulled those curtains closed as well.

She lifted the box of cat from her easy chair and sat.

The plan had been to let Phyllis out immediately. And Bea had. But the cat had nearly caused an accident by hunkering down under the brake pedal, then throwing her full weight on the gas when Bea tried to move her with one foot. So she'd gone back in the box until the van was holding still. Until Phyllis could look around and get comfortable without causing trouble.

Bea opened the box, and Phyllis stuck her head out like a soldier daring to rise out of a foxhole on the front lines. As if missiles might whiz between her ears at any second. Then she leapt out of the box all at once and ducked under the curtain, disappearing into the van's cab.

Bea sat back and sighed.

*Well, here I am,* she thought.

What followed qualified as her second moment of abject panic.

Here she was. For weeks. Now what? What was she supposed to *do*?

Bea felt overwhelmed with a sense of claustrophobia. The inside of the van felt close and dank. How could there be no more to her world than this? How was that even possible? What was she supposed to do to make these hours, these days, pass?

*Breathe, Bea,* she thought. *Books. You brought books. And you can have a little something to eat.*

But her stomach felt tight and chancy, and she read page after page without any absorption of the words and their meanings.

———

In time she abandoned the book and pushed her easy chair closer to the rear doors of the van, where she sat, holding one corner of the curtain back. Watching the people go by. Thinking.

She would need money for food. She didn't have enough food to last until next month. She would need money for gas if the BuyMart people asked her to move.

She needed so much money. And these people had so much money.

She couldn't stop staring at them. They had shopping carts full of food and toys, but they looked bored and unhappy. How could a person go to the store, buy everything she needed—and wanted, from the look of some of those carts—and still seem dissatisfied? What more did they need to be happy, then? If all this wouldn't do it?

And there was something else about them. They had these devices in their hands. Bea knew they were phones, but couldn't quite imagine how a person would make a call on such a thing. The more she watched, the more she became obsessed with people's phones.

Bea had seen cell phones. Little phones you flip open, with regular keypads for making a call. But these electronic gadgets in people's hands—they were nothing like a simple flip phone. They were all screen, with no buttons, and people stared at these devices as they walked by, tapping out some kind of communication with both thumbs. Bea watched more than one person nearly run down by a car, so complete was their attention to the screen.

It seemed as though everyone had one of these gizmos with them wherever they went—that no one could so much as go shopping at the BuyMart without keeping their eyes glued to the things.

After an hour or more of staring, Bea needed to use the restroom. She let herself out of the van, careful that Phyllis didn't dart out the open door, and walked stiffly into the store.

She used the ladies' room and washed her hands, then stared at her own face in the mirror. She looked tired. Ragged and unkempt. Lost.

In her third moment of abject panic, it struck Bea that soon people might know she was homeless just by looking at her.

*No.*

It wasn't going to be like that. She could take washcloth baths anytime the bathroom was private—not multistalled. She could wash her hair in the sink, and keep it nicely combed. She had that little kit she'd made up . . . but, she realized, she'd left it in the van.

No matter. She would get better at this as time went by.

She let herself out of the ladies' room. At an angle across the crowded store Bea saw an electronics counter. In its glass case she could see dozens of those computer phones.

They drew her in their direction.

She didn't want one. Not at all. In fact, she found the idea of walking down the street staring at those little devices repugnant. But she wanted to know what they did for their owners. Even more than that, she wanted to know what they cost.

She expected a salesperson to come along and try to talk her into buying one. But there was no one behind the counter. Bea felt invisible. She walked up and down in front of the glass case, eyeing the baffling devices. They were packaged in boxes that sported colorful photos of the phones at work. On their screens Bea saw weather reports, and sports images. She saw them playing videos, like a small TV set hooked up to nothing.

They cost as much as $700!

These people walking back and forth by her van were paying almost as much for these ridiculous little toys as the Social Security Administration expected her to live on every month of her life.

Bea walked back to her van in the bracing ocean breeze, but forgot to enjoy it. Something was changing inside her, and changing fast. Bea would not have been able to quantify the feeling, or wrap words around it. But there was a definite sense that all bets were off now. The line she had so carefully toed all her life was just a smudge in the dirt behind her. Bea did not feel inclined to look back.

Life was new. Not good. Just new.

# Chapter Seven

## *How Do You Wipe This Thing Clean?*

Bea lay on her side on the asphalt of the parking lot, half raised on one arm, waiting for someone to come by. It was dark, but only just barely, and the van was close by if she needed it. She was also close enough to the van that it blocked her view of the BuyMart security camera—and its view of her, which was key.

Her arm was getting a bit tired of holding her up, and still no one had been by. Just her luck to choose a lull in shopper traffic.

To pass the time, she sank more deeply into her role. She had taken a real fall once—well, truth be told, more than once, but she didn't like to admit it—and she summoned back that feeling. The sense of being physically rattled and mentally disoriented. The way everything that came before the fall is suddenly gone.

"Ma'am? Are you okay?"

A man's voice. She levered herself up a bit more and looked feebly over her shoulder.

He was a man in his late thirties with a shopping bag in each arm and a young blonde girl on either side of him holding the belt loops of his jeans for parking lot safety.

"He took my purse," Bea said. "He knocked me over and then before I even knew what was happening I saw him running off with my purse."

She tossed her head in the general direction of the bushes between parking lot and street.

The man jogged to her, his little girls running to keep up.

"Are you okay? Did he hurt you?"

"Yes, I'm all right. I'm not injured. It just surprised me and I hadn't quite managed to get back on my feet yet."

He set his bags on the tarmac and reached his arm out to her, and she took hold of it, and he helped her to her feet.

"I can call the police," he said, fishing one of those maddening devices out of his shirt pocket. "I have a cell phone."

*Of course you have a cell phone,* she thought. *With the exception of me, who doesn't these days?*

"Oh, I don't even know if that will help." She brushed off the seat of her slacks as she spoke. "You know they'll never find him. I didn't get a look at him at all. There's not one thing I can tell them to help them solve the crime. And I'm not injured. I'll have to get a new driver's license is all. And I'll have to cancel that credit card. And . . . Oh. Uh-oh. I just thought. I'm almost out of gas, and I was going to use my card to fill up my tank so I can go home. I live all the way up in Santa Maria and I'm almost out of gas."

The man pointed at a gas station sign that rose up between the BuyMart parking lot and the ocean.

"We'll meet you right over there, okay? And we'll use my card and we'll fill you up."

"That's awfully kind of you. Are you sure you can afford it?"

"Of course I can. Don't even worry about it. You have to get home. Are you sure you're okay?"

"I'm sure. Thank you. A little shaken up is all."

"You can drive over there?"

"Absolutely. I'll see you there in just a few minutes."

———

"You don't have to wash my windshield," she told him. "That seems like too much to ask."

"I don't mind," he said.

He had parked his SUV close, right at the other side of the pump, so he could keep an eye on his two blonde girls in the backseat. He looked over every few seconds. Meanwhile the pump ran without him, filling her tank.

"I hope you don't mind, though," he said. "I did call the police. While I was driving over. They'll meet us back at the spot where it happened. I just thought it was important. You know? What if he does this to somebody else? And maybe somebody gets hurt next time? Besides, maybe you don't need to've seen him. They have security cameras."

"Unfortunately my van was blocking the spot where it happened. I'll bet anything he did that on purpose."

"But maybe one of the other cameras picked it up."

*Oh,* Bea thought. *Right. Maybe so. Maybe one of the other, farther-off cameras had a view of the scene. That could be a problem.*

She looked into his eyes, and he looked back. He seemed curious, as if unsure what he would find there, or what he was looking for. Then he smiled in a way that looked reassuring. Bea felt bad because he was being so kind. But, she reminded herself, it's not like he would suddenly wake up in the middle of the night and know he'd been scammed. He felt good about what he was doing. He was helping an old woman mugging victim—he thought—and that was a good thing for him. And he could afford the gas. He'd said so himself.

Still, Bea made a decision while looking into those eyes. Just in that split second. She would have to think of a different scheme. No more helpless old woman pretending to be hurt, because that only brought out the best in people. And who wants to take someone for money while they're showing you their better nature?

No, she would just have to take people who deserved taking. She didn't figure they would be hard to find.

"I guess I see your point about the police," she said. "But one thing I insist on. You've done enough. You and your girls go home now. I can wait in the parking lot in my van with the doors locked. I'll be fine. I refuse to impose on you for one more thing."

"I guess that would be okay. If you're sure."

"I'm sure," she said.

He topped off her tank and replaced the pump nozzle, and waved. She thanked him, and waved in return. And he drove away. And she drove away.

And Bea kept driving until she got all the way to Santa Barbara.

—

Bea woke in the morning, struggled out of her easy chair, and pulled back the curtains. She was parked on the street at the Santa Barbara waterfront. On her right, waves washed up onto a white sandy beach. Between her van and the ocean ran a strip of narrow park with a bike lane. Now and then joggers or roller skaters breezed by, usually in pairs.

Bea had stopped here because it was a close walk to the pier, and she knew from ancient prior experience that there were public restrooms.

She climbed down from the van and onto the street. As she made her way to the sidewalk, she had to step over a storm drain at the curb.

That was the moment a big idea was born.

Bea stalled there for a minute or two, standing right over the storm drain. Waiting. Waiting for a person to come by with one of those absurdly expensive phones. She couldn't imagine it would take long.

*It's interesting,* she thought. *The same brain that couldn't grasp the concept of outstanding checks just had a clever idea.* She didn't think it out expressly, in words, but the pattern—the fact that her brain grasped what it wanted and dropped what it didn't want—was hard to miss.

While she waited, she noticed how different everything felt. The sun was strong on her shoulders and scalp, and the breeze seemed to blow right through her and leave her feeling clean. She did not feel at the mercy of the world. She did not feel afraid. Or small. Or out of options. She tried to remember if she had ever felt this way before, but nothing came to mind.

Two young mothers came jogging down the bike lane together, pushing strollers. The taller of the two was staring at one of those infernal devices. Not looking where she was going at all.

"Excuse me," Bea called.

They stopped.

"Excuse me. May I ask a favor of you? My van is broken down and I need to call the repair shop. My usual man. You know. He'll come out and give me a tow."

The woman just stood there for a few seconds. Both women just stood.

"It'll only take a second. It's a local call."

The woman with the phone looked down at it. Stared at it almost longingly. As if that were her child in her hand, and the passenger in the stroller only an afterthought. As if it pained her to think of parting with it for a few seconds.

Then she walked closer and held the phone out to Bea.

Bea had no idea how to use such a contraption, of course. But it hardly mattered. She looked down at it, then turned away, shading her eyes, as if to find a direction that would produce less glare on the screen. She slipped the phone into the inside pocket of her jacket. Then she reached down suddenly as if trying to catch a falling object.

"Oh no!" she cried, turning back. "I'm so sorry. I didn't mean to drop it."

She held up her hands to show how empty they were.

"Did it break?" the woman asked, running back to Bea now, her voice shrieky.

"Well, I don't know. I can't even see it. It went down there."

Bea pointed. Down. She and the woman stood a moment, staring into the seemingly endless dark abyss of the storm drain.

"That was a seven-hundred-dollar iPhone 6!" the woman squeaked. "That was almost brand new!"

Bea thanked the woman, silently, in the privacy of her head, for being someone she didn't mind taking.

"I'm so sorry. I feel just awful. I'd pay you for it if I could. But I don't have that kind of money. I don't know what to do."

Bea watched the woman's face in the intervening silence. It was reddening. To an alarming degree. And still nothing was being said. And yes, Bea was afraid. Of course she was. Who wouldn't be? But the fear made her feel exhilarated. It made her feel alive.

All her life Bea had felt fear, especially fear of the lack that seemed to hide around every corner, and all her life she'd been ruled by it. But now she had a new secret weapon: nothing to lose. And that was a freedom the likes of which Bea had never known.

A few seconds later the woman's friend came, took her by the shoulder, and led her back to the bike path, while they shared clipped words together.

"But she—"

"There's nothing you can do, Bev. It was an accident."

"But it was my brand-new—"

"She doesn't have money. She can't pay you for it. Come on. Let's just go."

The aggrieved woman looked over her shoulder once at Bea. As if there might be some remote chance of having her losses restored. Then she turned away.

Bea waited and watched until they were gone.

She began the slow, longish walk to the pier and its public restrooms.

"Excuse me," she said to the attendant of a parking lot as she passed by. "Is there a pawnshop in this town?"

"There are a couple," he called back. "How well do you know the city?"

It was ironic, when Bea thought about it. Based on what she'd seen in the BuyMart display case, the phone in her pocket could probably have located a pawnshop for her. If only Bea knew how to use it, or even cared enough to learn.

———

"It was a present from my granddaughter," Bea told the man behind the counter. "It's really important that I not hurt her feelings. She can't know I'm selling it. But I'll never use it. So I just need you to tell me how to make sure she won't find out. She'd be crushed."

Bea honestly didn't know if these gadgets stored identifying information. But she knew she'd had a log of numbers and a call history on her home phone, and that it would be best if the new owner of this device received no calls intended for the jogger.

"Oh, that's easy. Assuming it's not locked, or if you have the password, we can erase everything in one go," the man said. He had big muttonchop sideburns, which Bea thought had gone out of style years ago, and wore a denim vest over a short-sleeved T-shirt. "Just go to 'Settings' . . ."

"I have no idea how to go to 'Settings.' I never got the hang of the thing at all."

"Here. Want me to?"

"Please."

She handed it to him, and took her own emotional temperature. She couldn't help it. It was such a daring thing to do. She knew she should be afraid. But, oddly . . . not so much. She was just a little old lady, after all. Who would suspect her? And the phone had not been reported stolen. It would never be reported stolen.

Bea felt . . . well, it was a hard thing to admit, even inwardly, but she felt proud of herself for figuring out how to steal a phone in such a way that no one would ever report it stolen.

"You sure you want everything deleted?"

"Yes, everything."

"Okay."

While she waited, Bea looked around. She saw a saxophone in a glass display case. Two rifles hanging on the wall behind the counter. Several amplifiers on the floor, the kind musicians use. An electric guitar.

She thought about her lamps and kitchen utensils at home and wondered if the people who pawned these items had felt the same panicky sense of loss—the kind that almost feels like an erasure of one's identity—and whether any of them would see their precious belongings again.

"Okay," the man said. "Done."

"That was fast. What will you give me for it? Maybe I should have asked that first."

"Depends on whether you want to pawn it or sell it outright."

"Oh, sell it outright. I'll never want it back."

"Did you bring the power cord to recharge it?"

"No, I didn't think of it. Is that a problem?"

"I could offer more if you had it. But this is a nice new model. I can go seventy-five."

"I'll take it."

He counted the cash into her hand.

She walked out into the street and blinked in the bright sunlight. The air was temperate and warm, the breeze cool. She had a full tank of gas. She had enough money in her pocket for another tank of gas when that one was gone. She could even stop for a hamburger if she wanted, at that fast-food grill she could see from here.

But she wouldn't stay in Santa Barbara long. She decided that almost instantly. Because she didn't need to. She would cruise on up the coast. Sitting in one place is for people who can't afford gas money.

When she returned to her van, she found Phyllis sunning on the dashboard.

*We're both getting used to things,* Bea thought.

Imagine thinking this new life would be boring, with endless hours to kill and nothing to do. The world was full of places she'd never seen, and people and cell phones to get her there.

"Where to next?" she asked the cat.

Then she started the engine. Phyllis half jumped, half fell into the litter box below, then scrambled under the passenger seat to hide.

It should have been an omen to Bea. A warning not to get too confident. But in that moment she was too busy feeling good for a change.

———

That night, with Phyllis snoring on her lap, Bea lay awake in her easy chair for a long time, wishing she had that phone back.

If she still had it, she'd figure out how to use the darn thing. Then she'd call Opal. Even though she really wouldn't have, not at that hour, because it wasn't Opal's house and she wouldn't want to make trouble by calling late. But an ache inside her wanted to hear a familiar voice.

She had to settle for Phyllis's snoring.

# PART TWO

ALLIE

# Chapter Eight

## Carmen Miranda's Outlaw Sister

For Allie, it began like this: She knew and she didn't know. She watched her parents and knew something was wrong. Anybody can do that. Any idiot knows when something is wrong. *What kind* of something—that's a brass-ring prize, and Allie had not managed to reach out and grab it.

For weeks she'd walked into the professionally decorated rooms of their Pacific Palisades home and noted how quickly her parents went silent. How their whispering heads jerked farther apart.

Allie guessed maybe her father was having an affair. That her parents were about to announce a divorce.

She did not guess that she would walk downstairs one evening to see her aggressively upper-middle-class father—who had never been in trouble with the law as far as Allie knew—led out of the house in handcuffs as her mother was Mirandized.

So when that very thing happened, in the hazy shock of it all, Allie let herself off the hook for being a bad guesser. Not in a glib way, as it might sound, but in that jumble of disconnected thoughts that accompany sudden panic. When her mind should have jumped to what was happening, and why, and what it would mean to her future, it instead hung up on that minor point like a pant leg on a protruding nail. It made sense that she hadn't managed to guess this one, because it was just too far outside the probable.

She never did see her father's face that night. He never looked back. He must not have known she had come down the stairs. She saw his back going out the door, and that was all. A man in a suit was walking him out by one elbow. Neither of the strangers wore a uniform, which could have made the situation initially hard to decipher. But some things are simple enough on their face, and can be understood by observation.

When a man in a suit and tie is handcuffing your mother and telling her she has the right to an attorney—and that if she can't afford an attorney one will be provided for her—and asking her if she understands these rights, you know your mother is under arrest.

When she nods her head to indicate that she does understand those rights, and asks no questions, you know your mother is less surprised by her arrest than you are.

What you don't know is why.

Allie had her feet all the way down on the hall floor now. She watched her mother being led away. Just as she was thinking, *Wait. What about me? That's both my parents you're taking,* her mother looked around and saw Allie standing near. She said nothing in actual words, but her eyes spoke volumes. Her eyes said she was sorry, and ashamed, and that the greatest part of her had never once planned to end up this way, even though she was clearly not surprised.

Then, because she had looked around, the man leading her out of the house looked around, too. He stopped. Her mother stopped. Her mother looked away from Allie, probably worn out from everything her eyes had just been forced to say.

"Alberta Keyes?" the man asked.

As though Allie could be any number of different people. As if the house could be a veritable clown car of potential inhabitants.

"Yes," she said, but her voice sounded strange. Her tongue felt too thick, the way it might after awakening from a deep sleep.

Meanwhile all she could think was *Reverse. Reverse.*

A few seconds earlier everything had been normal. There had to be a way to get back to that. This strange new disaster was only seconds old. Maybe it didn't have to stick. Maybe it was too fresh to be necessarily permanent. Maybe she could still jump the gap back to normal from here.

"We have an officer coming to stay with you until—"

"He's here, Frank." A voice from her front porch. Not a familiar voice. She guessed it must have belonged to the man who had handcuffed her father and taken him away.

"Oh, good," the man still in the house said.

He raised his eyes and looked right into Allie's. For a split second she allowed it out of sheer surprise. Then she looked away, waves of shock radiating from her gut and up through her chest.

*It's very bad, what's happening to you.*

She had seen that in his eyes.

She looked up again to see a blue-uniformed policeman standing in her foyer. Everybody else was gone.

—

"We might as well get comfortable," he said to Allie a few seconds later, when not talking had already become a strain.

He was young. Not young like Allie, of course. He was a grown man with a job. He looked about twenty. But Allie wasn't sure if you got to be a policeman when you were only twenty, so she figured maybe he was deeper into his twenties but looked younger. His face was shiny and clean shaven. He took off his policeman's cap and held it in his hands. His dark hair was slicked back with some sort of product that made it look wet and preserved the comb marks.

"What are we waiting for?" Allie asked.

It felt bizarre, she realized, to have paused even a few seconds before asking. It was such an obvious question. It filled the room so completely that it displaced all the oxygen. Allie could barely breathe.

She felt her heart beating—pounding—but it seemed to beat in her ears rather than in her chest.

"I have to stay here with you until CPS arrives on the scene. Come on. Let's sit down."

He reached out to take her elbow but she jerked it away. The image in her mind was too fresh: her parents being led out by their elbows. Forced to leave their own home. To leave her.

"I'll go," she said to break the tension. "You don't have to lead me."

She walked with him into the living room. He sat on the couch. She sat on the opposite side of the room in her father's recliner, but upright. Perched on the edge. The TV was blaring. Some kind of cop show her father must have been watching before that black hole opened up and swallowed their lives.

Allie reached for the remote and muted it.

"Thank you," the cop said. "Couldn't hear myself think."

"What were you trying to think?"

"I guess how to let you know I'm not the bad guy."

"I never said you were."

"No. I guess you didn't."

Silence echoed. Allie would have sworn she could poke a stick into all that silence. Follow its waves throughout the room. Meanwhile she could still see the blue-uniformed cops on TV. They were chasing a perp through the streets of some big city. And then there was the cop sitting on her couch.

"Officer Macklin," he said. "But Johnnie is okay."

More echoing silence.

"This's the part where you say your name," he added.

"You don't know my name?"

"No. Why would I? I just got here."

"The other guy knew my name."

"The other guy is part of this case."

"And you guys don't talk to each other?"

"Within the department we might. But those guys are not my department. To put it mildly. Those were the *Federales*, right there."

He put an ominous emphasis on the word, and pronounced it the way a Spanish-speaking villain might in a western movie.

"I don't know what that means," she said.

"The Feds. Federal agents."

"So my parents were just arrested for a federal crime."

"Apparently so."

"But you don't know what crime."

"I'm afraid I don't."

*This is not my life. This can't possibly be my life. Someone misfiled my karma card. How do I apply for a correction?*

"What *do* you know?"

"I know I was headed back to the station when I got a call that a minor needed supervision pending the outcome of a CPS call."

"CPS?"

"Child Protective Services."

"Oh."

A good four minutes ticked by in utter silence. Literally. Ticked. The clock over the fireplace was an old-fashioned windup, like a miniature grandfather clock. It ticked loudly.

"I can stay alone, you know," she said at last. Her voice felt cutting. Shocking. Like a knife violently splitting all that silence. "I'm not a child. I'm fifteen."

"Maybe you can," he said. "But there's a difference between can and may. You may not. You're a minor, and till you're checked into the system at CPS, somebody needs to be with you."

"What's going to happen to me?"

The question bent her mouth around. Made her lower lip quiver. She couldn't keep everything lined up anymore. No tears fell—yet. But her mouth gave her away.

He noticed.

"I have no idea," he said. "I'm sorry."

Back to the ticking silence.

—

"You know," she said, and he jumped. "When I was a kid . . . this is weird . . . when I was a kid and I learned about the Miranda thing? How they have to read people their Miranda rights? I thought it had something to do with Carmen Miranda. Remember her?"

She paused, but he didn't say if he did.

"That dancer who used to wear those big hats with all the fruit on them? I thought she'd gotten arrested or something, and that when they came up with the law about the reading of rights they named it for her case. But then my teacher said it had nothing to do with her. But somehow I still got it in the back of my head that it was about someone in her family. Like maybe she had a big, bad sister who got in trouble with the law."

Allie stopped talking. A voice in her head expressed relief about that. It said, *Wow. What the hell was all that just now?*

The room had fallen silent again. So she figured Johnnie Macklin must have been wondering, too.

"I guess that's a weird thing to be talking about at a time like this."

Still nothing.

"I mean . . . is it?"

He looked up into her face. And there it was again. Just like the last lawman to look into her eyes.

*This is very bad, what's happening to you.*

Not that she didn't know it. But her brain was taking time to catch up. Meanwhile other people's brains had already arrived.

He spoke, startling her for no apparent reason.

"You're asking me what I think?"

"I guess."

"I think this sucks, what you're going through right now. I think I wish there was more I could do to help you. But I can't think what that might be. So I figure, you just handle this whatever way works for you. I'm not inclined to judge."

That was the moment Allie's brain caught up to everybody else's. And she cried. Mouth and eyes, both. She just let it go.

# Chapter Nine

## *Controversial Suitcases*

The woman from CPS made Allie wish for Johnnie Macklin back, with his blue uniform and all. Allie had at least felt she and the cop shared some sort of familiar humanity. Allie figured this new person, whose name she had already forgotten—or blocked—had been sent because Allie was supposed to feel more comfortable with a woman.

It wasn't working.

In her fifties, she was one of those women who wore nylon stockings under her polyester slacks. Knee-high or actual panty hose, Allie didn't know. And didn't care to know. But Allie could clearly see them at her ankles, because her slacks were too short. And Allie simply had no way to relate to any of her. Plus, she'd introduced herself to Allie as her social worker. There was really no way to wrap her head around that.

"You should be gathering your things," the woman said.

She'd given Allie a sheet of paper with a list of things to pack. A handout of sorts, but for life instead of classwork. It sat on the bed beside Allie's hip, as untouched as humanly possible.

Meanwhile, the social worker was filling out a form, or just making notes. She didn't have a clipboard, only a file folder that kept bending as she pressed her pen down. Allie couldn't help focusing on the small ironies and weirdnesses of her situation. Rather than looking the big picture right in the eye.

Allie didn't make any moves toward packing her things. She wasn't trying to be difficult. Her body just seemed fresh out of locomotive abilities. She remembered a similar feeling when she'd had the flu the previous year, and then after a week or so she'd tried to get up and go back to school—with astonishingly poor results. Her body felt like a giant bag of lack. Lack of motivation. Lack of strength. Lack of rigidity. Lack of caring.

Nothing seemed to be in working order.

"How many of your grandparents, if any, are living?"

"Two."

"Good. That's good. We'll contact them and see if they're willing to take temporary custody."

"I don't think so," Allie said.

"It pays to ask."

"They both live in nursing homes."

"Oh."

The woman had been using an artificially upbeat voice. But on the word "Oh" its facade cracked. Because, really, there was nothing to be upbeat about, not anywhere on the premises, and they both knew it.

"What about aunts and uncles?"

"No. Neither. My mom was an only child. My dad had one brother but he was much older, and he . . . passed away."

Social Worker Lady made notes on her wobbly file in silence.

"Friends whose parents might let you stay in the very short range?"

Allie sighed and closed her eyes. She missed Angie. Angie might have gotten her out of this.

"I really only have three friends. Most people don't like me much. My best friend Angie just moved to Michigan with her family. And I mean *just*. They're probably still driving. They haven't even moved into a new house yet. And then my other friends . . . well, maybe I was wrong.

Maybe there are only two. One of the girls I was thinking of, Paula . . . yeah, she's my friend all right. But she's scared to death of her dad and so am I. She could never ask him a thing like that. And I wouldn't go near her house on a dare. And the other one . . . I don't know. I don't think she really likes me. Sometimes even the people I think of as my friends . . . I wonder if they really like me."

Then Allie closed her mouth, humiliated at most of what had just spilled from it.

"Okay," Polyester Lady said. "Not hearing much there."

"So what happens to me?"

"I'll figure that out. It's what I get paid to do. I'll need to find you a placement."

"What kind of 'placement'? I don't even really know what that word means. I mean . . . I know what it means in general. But I'm not sure what a placement would look like in a situation like this."

"We always strive for a foster home placement. That's most like the family setting we know children are used to. I'm sorry to say right at the moment there's not one available. Not even an emergency foster home. I just couldn't get one."

A pang of fear constricted Allie's chest, making it hard to draw a full breath. Of course she had been afraid before. Many times. Including every minute of that evening. But this feeling was distinctly new.

"What do we do, then?"

"Well, I have to find you one."

"Where will I be while I'm waiting?"

"Sometimes, just in a real emergency, we might take a teen to juvenile detention. Short-term, of course."

In the silence that followed, Allie noticed her mouth hanging open, but couldn't focus on how to fix it. There were too many other things standing in line waiting to be figured out.

"That's jail."

"In this case it would simply be—"

"I didn't do anything wrong!" Allie shouted, her voice an embarrassing screech.

"I understand that, dear, but I'm just temporarily short on options. We have an opening in a group home, but it's not exactly procedure to use them as an emergency placement. Or to drop a teen off there late at night."

"Please don't take me to juvenile . . . jail. Please. Anything is better than that."

"I don't know. It's not proper procedure otherwise." A long, dread-filled silence. "Really, though," the woman said, "you need to gather your things."

Allie pulled a deep breath and stood. It seemed to work. Her body apparently remembered how to stand. She took a few steps toward her open bedroom doorway.

"Where are you going?" the social worker asked.

"To get suitcases."

"We'd like you to put your things in the bags I brought."

She didn't say exactly who comprised "we." Was she speaking for the entire county of Los Angeles? Nothing seemed out of the question.

With a flip of her chin, she indicated two folded plastic garbage bags that had been sitting on the bedroom rug. Allie had noticed them, but could not imagine their relevance to her life. Not even her horrible new one.

"But I have suitcases."

"This is standard procedure."

"But it doesn't make any sense. Fine. Bring trash bags with you to a kid's house. I get that. If the kid doesn't have any suitcases he can use the bags. But I do. So why can't I use them?"

"Not all the girls you're about to meet are as fortunate."

"So I'm supposed to pretend I'm too poor to have suitcases so nobody else will feel bad? My stuff is not garbage. I don't want to carry my stuff in garbage bags."

Allie paused. She ran her comments on a quick instant replay and decided she didn't like the sound of them. She wasn't snotty or insensitive to others. At least, not as a rule. Not under normal circumstances. But since normal circumstances had never evaporated on her before, everything would be a surprise now, including her own character. Including the person she would prove herself to be.

She set off in a different direction, with more of an effort to be clear.

"Look. I'm having the worst night of my life. My parents were both arrested. I have no idea why. I have no idea when they're coming back. You can't even tell me when I'll be able to talk to them on the phone. I'm on my way to live in a totally strange place with total strangers. And I don't blame any of that on you. Everything bad that's happened to me so far tonight . . . there's nothing you could've done about any of it. But this last bit about the garbage bags is too much. It's too awful. And this is the one part of the horribleness of this night that you can do something about. So give me a break here, all right? It'll be the only break for me in this whole lousy . . ."

Then she realized she didn't have a word for what was happening to her. For what it all added up to. Besides, it hadn't all added up yet. That was the scariest part.

She looked up to see Polyester Lady staring right into her eyes with a look that suggested she cared, except to the extent that she was exhausted from caring. For her these disasters were anything but breaking news.

"It's not the only break you're getting tonight. I'm also going to bend the rules and take you to that group home instead of juvenile detention. I hope I don't lose my job for it. But . . . well, okay. Very well. Go get a couple of suitcases, and then I'll help you pack your things."

# Chapter Ten

*Getting to Know Fear. Getting to Know All about Fear.*

Allie sat in the kitchen of the group home with the tiny elf of a woman who supervised the place. It was late, possibly after midnight, and Allie and her social worker had rousted the woman out of bed.

Allie heard the click of the front door closing and knew it was her social worker letting herself out. Surprisingly, it brought back that breath-killing chest constriction of fear. Who would have imagined that by the end of this horrible night Polyester Lady would be her closest tie with familiarity? That it would scare Allie to hear her go?

Allie felt a pang of longing deep in her belly. She wanted her mother.

The kitchen was illuminated only by a soft light over the stove. Everything else in the house was dark. Unseen. Unknowable. A cocoon of potential surprises.

"Where are we?" Allie asked.

"We're at New Beginnings for girls."

"Yeah, I know that part. But where? It was dark and the neighborhoods kept getting less and less familiar. But it felt like we were going downtown."

"Pretty much. We're right outside downtown L.A. Where did you come from?"

"Pacific Palisades."

"Oh. I see. You *are* a long way from home, aren't you?"

It was a statement that worked on a couple of levels. Nearly poetic. Certainly symbolic. Definitely more than geographic.

Allie didn't answer.

"So," the woman said, and then paused. As with the social worker, Allie had already forgotten her name. "There's a lot you need to know about this place, and living here. There are rules, and they're important. I ask the girls to sign a paper stating that they understand the rules and agree to abide by them."

"What if I'm only here for a day or two, though?"

Allie watched The Elf blink in the soft light. She had curly hair bordering on frizzy. Carrot red. It reminded Allie of a wig a circus clown might wear.

"That would be unusual. Why would you think you'd only be here a day or two?"

"In the morning they'll have to bring my parents in front of a judge. Right? And the judge will probably set bail. And they can afford bail."

The Elf turned her eyes away. Looked over at the light on the stove. As if something significant were happening in that direction.

"Even so . . . ," The Elf said. Then she faded for a time. "Even if your parents came home on bail tomorrow . . . once you're in the system . . . they'd have to do more than just come pick you up. They'd have to file to have you placed back in the home again. There'd be factors to consider. When they go to trial. The charges. Whether their . . . activities . . . ever endangered you."

Allie felt no emotion in response to the news, because the only emotion available to be felt was crushing disappointment, and Allie refused it.

"When can I talk to them?"

"Well, I don't know. That's something your social worker will tell you."

Allie had asked. Of course she had. Multiple times. But Polyester Lady hadn't known yet. Allie realized she had been foolish to think The Elf would somehow know more.

"I know you must be tired," The Elf said. "I know this was a hard day for you. So let's just get you to bed and we can worry about the rules and the orientation after breakfast tomorrow."

"Breakfast," Allie said.

Most of the rest of this new world fell down around her ears. Just all at once like that. A ceiling that had been crumbling and shedding plaster and then let go.

"How am I going to eat here?" she asked, not sure if she was addressing The Elf or talking to herself.

"I'm not sure I understand the question."

"I'm vegan and there are a lot of things I don't eat. Like sugar. And refined carbs. Or anything with soy or hydrogenated oils or high-fructose corn syrup. Which is everything processed. Once I'm outside my house it's really hard to get something to eat. The things other people think of as food are not things I would eat at all."

"We do have vegetarian dinners twice a week. Usually macaroni and cheese."

Allie peered into The Elf's face in the mostly dark to see if she was kidding or not.

"Macaroni and cheese is not vegan. It's a bunch of refined white flour with butter and milk and cheese on it."

"Oh. Well. We'll figure something out. I can always separate out some macaroni before I put the cheese sauce on. And we usually have salad and bread and butter. Oh. Butter. Right. Well, there'll be bread. And I can do the same thing with potatoes. Separate some out before I put on the butter and cheese. And we always have oatmeal with breakfast."

Allie didn't answer. Couldn't answer.

*Say goodbye to protein.* That was all she could think. *And speaking of thinking, do lots of that while you can. Because when food is nothing but pasta and potatoes and bread and oatmeal, you won't be doing much clear thinking.*

Too many carbs and not enough protein always made her brain foggy and thick, as though she'd slept too long and couldn't quite wake up.

"Maybe you'll decide to relax the meat thing a little while you're here."

Again, Allie looked into The Elf's face as best she could in the dim light. As if she could physically see whether this was the little woman's clearest thinking.

"I can't just 'relax' it."

"Why can't you?"

"I've been a vegan since I was nine years old. My digestion wouldn't be able to handle meat anymore. It would make me incredibly sick. And that's if I would consider eating it. But I won't. Because I won't be any part of that cruelty. I just couldn't."

Allie waited, in case the woman wanted to answer. But she wasn't honestly expecting a response.

"I'll show you to your room," The Elf said. "But we'll have to be quiet so we don't wake up your roommate. I'll get your things."

The Elf rose and made her way down the dark hallway to the front door. Allie did not follow. That feeling of dread had locked up her chest again. She wouldn't have even the tiniest space that was private. Nothing that was hers alone. Somehow she had not seen that indignity coming.

"Oh," she heard The Elf say from the hall. "Suitcases."

Allie rose and met her halfway.

"Here, I can carry those," she said.

"We don't usually get girls with suitcases."

"So I hear."

Allie reached out and took her bags from The Elf's hands.

"Sometimes we get girls with those backpacks people make up and contribute to social services. But we don't see a lot of soft-side suitcases come through the house. This might be a first."

"I don't know why everyone is so down on suitcases," Allie said, hauling them up the stairs in the dark.

"You might when you see how little space each girl gets to store her things."

"Oh."

They tiptoed along an upstairs hall together. The house was huge, with lots of bedrooms. An old-fashioned house from L.A.'s earlier days. Probably classy in its time. Maybe even a multifamily home way back when. Allie guessed that when the sun came up she would find it was the only one in the neighborhood that hadn't been converted to apartments.

"Couldn't I just store them under the bed?"

"Oh. I suppose so."

They passed three closed doors, then The Elf opened a door on the right side of the hall.

"Your roommate's name is Lisa Brickell," The Elf whispered, her lips close to Allie's ear. "The bathroom is that way down the hall. And breakfast is at seven."

Then she disappeared into the darkness.

Allie climbed into bed without bathing or brushing her teeth. She lay in the dark imagining her mother's face. Imagining herself wrapped in her mother's arms. Likely she wouldn't be, anyway, even if her mother were there. She wasn't much the cuddly sort, Allie's mom. But it was a nice thing to imagine all the same.

—

Allie woke, blinking too much. The room felt bizarrely light. Offensively so, and she couldn't understand why. She sat up and looked around.

Lisa Brickell was already fully dressed for the morning, in jeans with purposeful-looking holes in the knees and a patched denim shirt. It felt strange to face off in only pajamas. It seemed to put Allie at an embarrassing disadvantage.

"Hey!" she said again, because her first "hey" had gotten no response. "You can't do that."

Lisa Brickell pulled the second heavenly sock into place.

*When I get them back from her I'll have to wash them,* Allie thought.

"You might be wrong about that. I mean . . . I just did. So it's a little weird to tell me I can't do something. You know. When I've already done it. Kind of makes you seem like you don't know what you're talking about."

"Give them back."

"Or . . . ?"

"They're mine."

"They were. But I don't think they are now."

"Give them back."

"Or you'll do what?"

"Or I'll tell . . ." Allie realized she didn't even remember the name of the woman who ran the place.

A movement caught Allie's eye. The door to the bedroom was standing open, and another girl was walking by on her way to the bathroom, a towel clutched to her chest, a toothbrush in one hand. She was lanky and tall. Pretty, with butt-length brown hair. There was a gentleness to her. Allie had been searching for gentleness since leaving home. She just hadn't realized it yet.

"You'll *tell?*" Allie's roommate was on her expensively socked feet now, moving in Allie's direction. Her face had hardened further—if such a thing were possible—her icy eyes drilling into Allie's brain. "You'll *tell?*"

Allie looked past her to the girl in the hall, hoping for some help. The dark-haired girl shook her head carefully, and Allie could tell how she meant it. She was suggesting an answer to Lisa's question. She was clearly feeding Allie the right line.

"Well, no," Allie said. "I won't tell."

The girl in the hall nodded. Breathed visibly.

"Glad to hear that. For a minute there I thought you were so new and so spoiled and so stupid that you honestly don't know what happens to girls who tell."

"No," Allie said. "But I want my socks back."

"I want a lot of things. A Ferrari. A house by the beach. But I don't expect to get any of them from you. And you shouldn't be looking to me for socks."

"But they're my socks."

"They were."

Finally, finally, the icy eyes cut away. Lisa Brickell turned and walked out of the room.

Allie looked up at the girl in the hall.

"Hey," the girl said.

"Hey."

Allie envied the girl the silky straightness of her hair. Allie's hair, a sort of long, thick, wild bird's nest of curls—quick to turn into frizz at the slightest hint of humidity—had always felt like quite a burden to bear.

"You're new."

"Yeah."

"I'm Jasmine."

"Allie."

"Be careful of Brick. I mean, really careful. She can be crazy, and I don't just mean it the way people usually say 'crazy.' I mean seriously. She can be dangerous."

Allie tried to breathe around the chest girdle of fear. She only barely succeeded.

"Just my luck to get her as a roommate," she said, trying to keep her voice artificially light.

"Oh, there's no luck about it. So long as there's any space in any room, no girl's gonna room with Brick. Has to be a thing where the last girl in the last space gets her because there's no other choice."

They stood a moment, awkwardly. Saying nothing.

Then Allie asked, "How do I get my socks back?"

"Depends on whether they're worth risking your life for." Another awkward silence fell. "I better get in line for the bathroom. You know. While the hot water holds."

———

Allie sat at the breakfast table looking at the nine other girls' faces. Preferably when they weren't looking back. She wanted to memorize the residents. Size them up in some way that might be useful. But she wasn't entirely sure what *useful* would mean in this context.

The table was clearly built to accommodate six comfortably, eight at the reasonable max. The other girls seemed to have perfected the tucking of elbows. Allie was learning the talent the hard way.

She poked her spoon into her plain oatmeal. Her choices of toppings had been butter, milk, sugar, or syrup. Pass, pass, pass, pass. If this had been Allie's home, there would have been almond milk. Golden raisins. Dried dates. Toasted pecans.

*In case I needed a reminder that this is not home,* she thought.

The Elf wandered off into the living room, and Allie stared directly at Brick, who was seated diagonally across the table.

"What?" Brick asked. Playacting extreme innocence.

"I want my socks back."

Suddenly every other girl at the table found a new place to look. All at once. Under better circumstances it might have been comical. One began inspecting the ceiling plaster, another the back of her hand. A heavy girl with thin, stringy hair pulled a cereal box close and began reading its ingredient list in fascination.

"I have no idea what you're talking about," Brick said.

Allie set down her spoon. Her heart pounded, and she was afraid the fear would leak out into her voice. But sometimes you can't back up. It's the principle of the thing.

"So you're just going to go through the world like this? Your whole life? Just bullying people out of anything you want and threatening them with violence if they mind? This is your contribution to society? Seriously? You've thought it over, and this is the best plan for living you could think of?"

Brick changed her grip on her knife. Held it more the way you'd hold a knife going into a fight. It was only a dull butter knife but the message came through.

"Yeah. It's working out fine. Thanks for asking. For example, my feet are *really comfy.*"

"I'm not just letting this go. I don't care what happens to me." She did care. Actually. It would have been more accurate to say that all her caring about what would happen to her—which was quite a lot of caring—was unable to slow her forward progress. Allie felt like a person trying to stop a speeding freight train by dragging her foot. "Because wrong is just wrong. What you're doing is wrong. And if I shut up and walk away because you're the threatening type, then I'm just part of that terrible system. And it's all just wrong."

Allie could see Jasmine desperately trying to catch her eye. Finally Jasmine's efforts burst out into words. Well . . . word.

"Allie!"

"I don't care, Jasmine. It's just not right. It's the principle of the thing."

Brick laughed a snorting, sneezing laugh. Then she got up and walked away from the table.

"So, new person," the big girl with the cereal box said. "*Your* days are numbered."

Allie tried to pick up her spoon again, but her hands were shaking, and she didn't want the other girls to see. It wasn't because of the comment about her numbered days. That had been a tossed-off sort of thing, whether there was any truth behind it or not. The deep upset was more about the courage it had taken to directly confront someone. Allie had marginally held it together while it was happening but, now that it was over, the stitching was disintegrating at all of her seams.

She looked up to see Polyester Lady standing in the kitchen doorway.

"Alberta?"

Which seemed strange. Because she was looking right at Allie. So what was the point that needed clarifying?

"Um. Yes."

"You ready?"

"For what?"

"We have to get you registered for school. And then I'm going to try to arrange a phone call with one of your parents."

# Chapter Eleven

## *Define Okay*

Polyester Lady's desk had a ring-shaped coffee stain. Allie couldn't stop staring at it.

First of all, it was a spectacular desk. Because this was a government office at the Department of Social Services, Allie figured the desk was just old and had been sitting in the room for generations. Probably no one had noticed it turning into a valuable antique. But it had, and it was worth caring for.

Second, the stain was right in front of Allie's chair, on the non-owner side of the desk. Which meant some visitor had carelessly left it.

If this had been Allie's desk, she could not have forced herself to cede her irritation over that thoughtlessness. She already couldn't, and she might never sit in this office again.

All of these thoughts provided an effective distraction from the more crucial thoughts. Thoughts like *Please let this be Mom I talk to. Not Dad. I'm too mad at Dad and we never talk to each other in a way that means anything anyway.*

And, *What is she going through where she is?*

And, *When will I see her again?*

"I'll give you a signal," Polyester Lady said, holding up three fingers. "I'll signal you at three minutes left, two minutes left, one minute left. I don't mean to sound callous, but inmates can only call collect, and somebody has to be picking up the tab here."

*Why don't I have money?* Allie wondered. *I always did before. Why wasn't that on the printed list of things I was supposed to pack before leaving the house?*

The phone rang. Allie crystallized into a solid block of fear. She wasn't sure exactly why. Once upon a time she had talked to her parents every time she turned around. The most recent example of once upon a time had been yesterday.

*This should be easy,* she thought.

It didn't make it any easier to think so.

"Yes, I'll accept the charges," Polyester Lady said.

She extended the dangerous phone in Allie's direction.

Allie stared at it for a couple of beats too long. Then she reached out and took it. Swallowing with difficulty, her eyes glued to that maddening coffee stain, she held the phone carefully to her ear.

"Allie?" Her mom. "Honey? Are you there?"

"Yeah."

"Are you okay?"

It struck Allie as a ridiculous question and left her literally speechless. Like something from the theater of the absurd. Still, that ring of coffee taunted her. *Just use a coaster, you know?*

"Honey? Are you there?"

She was. But she had been lost for a moment, drowning in the emotion of a reaction to her mother's familiar voice.

"Yeah. I'm here."

"Are you okay? Where do they have you?"

"In a sort of a . . . group home . . . type thing."

"Is it okay there?"

"Depends on your definition of *okay*, I guess."

Much to Allie's alarm, she could hear her mother dissolve into sobs.

"Honey, I'm so sorry," her mom said.

But Allie didn't want to hear that her mom was sorry. She wanted to hear the parts of the situation that didn't seem to go without saying. Why. How long. The meaty stuff like that.

"I need to know what happened," she said.

"It was . . . your father and I . . . Well. You know how things were really good with your dad's business in the last few years . . ."

"Mom. I'm sitting in the office of a social worker who's going to give me finger signals when I'm running out of phone time. Because a collect call is not within my budget these days. I need the short version. You and Dad were arrested and charged with . . ."

"Tax fraud."

Allie stared at the ring of stain in silence for a moment and watched it move—float—in a way it should not have. Maybe she was just staring too hard. Or maybe not.

"So . . . ," Allie said. Then she paused, waiting to see if this was something she could bring herself to say or not. "So . . . when you had the pool installed in the backyard . . . and when Dad bought the boat, you could have just given the money to the IRS instead, and we'd all be at home now, and none of this would be happening?"

Silence on the line, not counting a sob or two.

"Hindsight is twenty-twenty, Allie. It's easy to go back and see how to do things—"

"No. No, Mom. Don't *even*. It's always easy. When you owe taxes, you pay them. And everybody knows it. Why didn't you tell me this was about to happen? Give me a chance to be halfway prepared."

"We didn't know we'd be arrested, honey."

"Yes you did! I saw you guys whispering to each other and then shutting up when you saw me coming."

"We suspected, but we didn't know for sure."

"Why didn't you tell me?"

"Because you're so . . . well . . . you know how you are."

"No. How am I?"

"You have these . . . rigid ideas about what people should do."

Again the coffee stain spun slightly. Allie raised her eyes to Polyester Lady to see if she had any polyester fingers raised. Not yet.

"You're seriously insulting me for being honest?"

"Of course not. Not at all, honey. I'm just trying to tell you why we were afraid to get into it with you."

A movement caught Allie's eye. She saw three fingers go up.

"Look, we can talk about this later, Mom. Right now I need to know if you're getting out on bail."

A pause. Then, "No."

"The judge didn't give you bail? You're not murderers."

"No, he did. He set bail. It was kind of high because I guess they thought maybe we were a flight risk. But we got a bail amount. But . . . Oh. How do I put this? When the IRS finds out you owe them a lot of money . . . but they don't know how much yet . . . they have to do a big investigation to find out what income was hidden. Until they do, they pretty much slap a lock on everything you own. Literally or figuratively. Or both. The house. The boat. The bank account. Not technically ours at this point. None of it. None of it is anything we can access right now."

Allie said nothing. Because she had no idea what to say. She wanted to know if they would lose the house she'd lived in since birth. But if she asked, she might find out.

Polyester Lady folded down one of the three fingers.

"Most people have relatives," her mom said. "To go to a bail bondsman and put something up for them. But all we have is Nanna and Pop-Pop, and their nest egg is just barely covering their nursing home, and it's disappearing fast. They can't go anywhere anyway . . ."

"Right. I'm clear on our lack of relatives. Right now especially. Aren't you worried these phone calls from the jail get monitored or

taped or something? Or overheard by somebody? And here you are
more or less admitting to me that you guys are guilty of tax fraud . . ."

"We have no intention of trying to claim innocence, honey. We're
just going to throw ourselves on the mercy of a judge and hope he
goes easy."

"So we're talking years. I'm out here on my own for years. In two
and a half years I'll just be grown and I'll turn eighteen and walk out of
the system on my own? That's what I'm being told here?"

Allie looked up to see only one polyester finger.

"Not years. I mean, maybe not. Maybe we'll get lucky. A year or
two maybe."

"Two years qualifies as years."

The one finger began to wave.

"Look, Mom. I've got to go."

"Honey, I just can't tell you how—"

But Polyester Lady was signaling Allie to set the receiver back on
its base. So she did.

She sat a moment staring at that coffee ring.

"Doesn't that drive you crazy?" Allie asked.

"Doesn't what drive me crazy?"

"That stain."

"No, why would it? Desk still works fine."

"It would drive me crazy because I'd keep thinking about the person who was so careless with their mug."

"I never pay any attention to it. Mind if I ask you a question? Why
did they charge your mom, too? Wasn't it your dad's business income?
I'm not trying to be nosy, I swear. It's just hard to see a young girl lose
both parents to jail at once. So I just wondered . . ."

"She's his CPA."

"Got it," Polyester Lady said.

———

Allie sat in the Polyester Lady's car, staring at her hands. Until the car pulled over to the curb and stopped. When she looked up, Allie was surprised to see they were back at New Beginnings.

"I thought I had to go to school."

"I told them your first day would be tomorrow. I wasn't sure how long it would take to get you a call from one of your parents. And I knew how important that was to you. So just take the day. Rest. Take a nap or something."

"Thanks."

Allie climbed out of the car. It wasn't as easy as it should have been. She felt limp and wrung out. For a moment it occurred to her to ask her social worker's name again, but she never found the energy.

She slammed the car door and walked up the concrete path.

The door to the home was locked, so Allie had to ring the bell.

The Elf answered after a time, pulling back a curtain behind the glass insets of the door. Frowning. She opened the door a few inches but didn't seem inclined to let Allie by.

"You're supposed to be in school."

"My social worker says I can start tomorrow."

"Why would she say that?"

"Because after she signed me up we had to go to her office. So I could talk to one of my parents. And she didn't know how long that would take . . ."

The Elf's eyes narrowed.

It dawned on Allie that her new living situation was not only over-crowded and potentially dangerous, but also highly conditional. Maybe if she didn't have the right answers at the door she wouldn't be allowed in at all. Clearly there were a lot of things that could go wrong here. Too bad Allie didn't know what any of them were.

"You realize I'll have to call your social worker and verify your story."

"Whatever," Allie said, suddenly twice as exhausted.

The Elf stepped aside and allowed her in.

"I'm going to take a nap," Allie said. "My social worker's suggestion. And you can check that story with her."

She waved weakly as she trudged up the stairs.

—

Allie lay on "her" bed for a few minutes, but a nap seemed out of the question. The mattress was horrible. Lumpy and ancient and thin. And her carbs-only breakfast had long since abandoned her, which was never a good recipe for sleep. Nothing like low blood sugar to keep you staring at the ceiling.

Instead Allie stared at her socks for a second or two, then sat up sharply. The sudden movement made her head spin.

She leaned over the edge of the bed and pulled out one of her two suitcases. She hadn't had time to unpack them, and she didn't plan to spend this free moment on organization. She just wanted to check on her socks.

There were no socks. Then again, her crazy roommate had pulled all of her belongings out onto the floor, and Allie had hastily gathered it all up again. Maybe the socks had landed in the other bag. She pulled out the second suitcase and flipped it open. Right in the middle, right on top of everything, lay four pairs of socks. White. Floppy. No elastic. Holes.

Allie jumped to her feet, fighting off another round of dizziness. She crossed the room to the dresser on Brick's side and opened the top drawer. In it were four of her six pairs of fabulous socks. The pairs that were not currently on Allie's—or her roommate's—feet.

She took them back and tucked them under her mattress, gathered up the four pairs of white socks, put them in Brick's dresser drawer where they belonged, and pushed the suitcases back under the bed.

She lay awake for a long time, sure she would never nap. But even so, it felt like a little bit of heaven. Just to lie there. In the quiet. With no one around to challenge her in any way.

It felt like a moment that belonged to Allie, a luxury she'd been unsure she would ever enjoy again.

In time she did manage to drift off to sleep.

—

Allie woke with a start, in pain. Someone's knees had landed on her back and one of her arms was being twisted up to meet her shoulder blade.

"Hey!" she yelled, hoping it would be loud enough to bring The Elf running.

"You went in my drawers?" The voice was a throaty hiss near her ear. She could feel the breath of it. "You could die for less than going in my drawers. That dresser is mine. You don't even touch it! You don't even brush against it! You have no idea what I would do!"

Allie gathered up all her strength and rolled over fast, throwing Brick onto the hardwood floor.

Allie jumped to her feet. Ready. But, oddly, Brick stayed down. She did not attack again.

"The dresser is yours," Allie said. "I hear that. I get it." Her voice trembled but she tried to ignore it. "But the socks are mine. You never again take anything of mine and put it in your dresser, and I absolutely promise I won't touch your things. You don't steal my things and put them in with your things again. I don't touch anything of yours ever. Deal?"

Brick opened her mouth. But before she could speak, they both looked up to see The Elf standing in the bedroom doorway.

"What on earth is going on up here?"

Brick looked to Allie. Challenging her. Daring her to answer.

"Nothing," Allie said. "She just tripped. We're okay. For a minute I thought we had a problem, but I think it's all worked out now."

And, with the absolute overconfidence of youth, Allie believed that what she had just said was true. That the way she had summarized it was the way it would be.

# Chapter Twelve

## Weed Oasis

It was Allie's first Saturday at New Beginnings, about four days later, when she walked into her shared bedroom to find Brick lying on her back on the bed counting money. More money than it looked like a girl in this place should be able to have. Twenties. Allie couldn't see exactly how many. At least five or six.

Brick looked up into Allie's face and smiled an unsettling smile. Allie said nothing. Brick began to hum a vaguely familiar tune. Some ancient song from long before the turn of a couple of centuries. One of those tunes everybody more or less knows whether they were alive back then or not.

Allie sat briefly on her bed, hoping the humming would end soon. She hated any kind of distraction like that. Humming, singing. Foot tapping. She couldn't remain in her own head, her own thoughts, and block out other stimuli.

A twitchy moment or two later she got up and left the room to shake the annoyance. Just as she was moving down the hall she realized what the tune was. That old song about being in the money again, after the Great Depression.

Allie trotted downstairs, thinking it would be nice to sit out in the sun in the backyard.

It was a sprawling, messy patch of yard, a mix of concrete and chin-high weeds. Allie whacked through the weeds with the backs of her hands, looking for a suitable spot to sit. When she found a small clearing, it was already occupied. Jasmine was there, hugging her drawn-up knees and smoking a cigarette. The tips of her long, straight hair touched the dirt.

"Shh," Jasmine said, drawing out the sound. She held one finger to her lips. "Don't tell on me."

Smoking was one of the transgressions that could get a girl ejected from New Beginnings. One of many.

"I won't," Allie said.

Without even asking first, she sat cross-legged in Jasmine's tiny clearing. Because if she had asked permission she might not have gotten it. Allie missed having friends, such as they were. Having anyone. Not being the only person on her lonely, solitary planet. She wished she could call Angie. But she had no money and no phone. Besides, Angie's cell phone number was on Allie's phone, at home. She didn't know it by heart.

Jasmine did not seem to object.

"I'm really not a person who tells on other people," Allie said. "I mean, especially if it's none of my business like this. I only said that because . . . well, I didn't know what to say. Somebody takes your things like that and asks what you're going to do about it. And there's not a damn thing you can do, but you don't want to say that . . ."

"The less you say to Brick the better."

"Other than you, she's the only one here who even talks to me."

"Don't take it personally. It's just that they don't want to get on the wrong side of *her*. They're mostly okay, the girls here. With maybe one or two exceptions. But nobody wants trouble, you know? So they just keep their heads down. They don't want to seem like they're taking sides."

"I guess." Allie wondered what she would do in their situation. Would she stand up for the embattled girl? She hoped so. "*You* didn't just keep your head down."

"Ah," Jasmine said, and flicked her ashes off into the weeds. "I won't be here much longer. I'm about to take off again."

"You mean . . ."

"Do I mean what?"

"Never mind. None of my business."

"Yes. The answer is yes. I mean take off. As in, without official permission."

"And go where?"

"I have a boyfriend."

"Then why even be here to begin with?"

"Well, you know. I'm sixteen. I'm not supposed to be living with him. If I get in trouble I'm back on the radar and then I end up here. If I can lay low I can be there. Just depends on how things go."

Allie listened to the silence for a moment and nursed her disappointment.

"Too bad," she said. "One girl in the whole place who talks to me . . . and isn't crazy . . . and you're leaving."

"Come with me."

It was a statement so out of place that Allie actually backed up some. As much as possible while sitting cross-legged. Her upper body leaned back, in any case.

"You don't even know me."

"You seem okay."

"I'm sure your boyfriend would be thrilled if you brought a stranger back with you."

"He'd be totally fine with it. But it's okay. I get it. You think you have a better chance here. I used to be like you. Just be careful. This feud you have going with Brick could cost you."

"It's not a feud. I think we found a way to keep out of each other's faces."

"So you're not pissed that she sold your suitcases?"

Allie opened her mouth. Nothing came out but an embarrassing sputter.

———

Allie pushed open the door to her shared room and found it unoccupied. No Brick. She stood a few moments, breathing deeply. Breathing out more fear than she'd known she was holding.

She crossed over to her bed, dropped to her knees, and looked underneath. She was not surprised to see nothing there.

———

She found The Elf in her office. An office of sorts, anyway. At one time it had apparently been a small den, but now housed a huge, cheap-looking desk overflowing with papers and files.

*Utter chaos,* Allie thought. *How can people work in such chaos?*

The Elf was staring at an old computer monitor. Close up, as though her eyes were bad.

*No wonder she misses so much of what goes on around here.*

"What can I do for you, Alberta?" The Elf asked, the first sign that she had noticed the presence of someone in the room.

"I have a problem."

"Take a seat, then."

Allie did. And waited. For a bizarre length of time. Long enough that she began to wonder what she was waiting for. Still The Elf stared at her monitor, her eyes just inches from the screen.

Allie was finding it hard to sit still. Her mood felt like electricity firing off little charges in her muscles. She wanted The Elf to do something. To help her not feel this way anymore. But she knew it was highly unlikely The Elf had anything nearly so useful up her sleeve. Nothing was going to make this all better.

Finally The Elf broke off her attention and turned to face Allie.

"Talk to me."

"I'm having trouble with my roommate."

The Elf sighed. "What sort of trouble?"

"She stole my suitcases and sold them."

For a moment, nothing. No reaction.

Then, "See, this is why sometimes it's better not to bring things of value into a home like this."

"You're seriously blaming her stealing my suitcases on the fact that I have suitcases?"

"No. I guess not." Another big sigh. Another long wait. "It's a serious allegation. How do you know it was her?"

"Because she told . . . everybody . . . what she did."

Allie had no idea how many of the girls Brick had told. She knew only that she didn't want to bring Jasmine into this mess. She didn't even want to mention her name.

"What would you like me to do? Do you want me to talk to Lisa?"

"She's not going to change her ways just because you talk to her. And even if she did, that isn't going to get my suitcases back."

"We could discuss it with the social worker who oversees this home."

"I didn't know one did. I haven't even met that person yet."

"Well, you're new. Do you want to report this to the police?"

Allie opened her mouth, then closed it again. She knew the next words to come out of her would carry a lot of weight. They would determine her immediate future. And still she didn't know the right thing to say. Getting her roommate arrested was big. A radical, dangerous act. Maybe better to do nothing at all. Except . . . until she stood up for herself, this would never end. Brick would push her. And push her. And push her. It was a game now. One Allie didn't want to play, but she was mired up in it all the same. It would go on until Allie owned nothing at all. And she already owned so little. So close to nothing. How much more could she afford to lose?

Allie's whole body felt strangely awake and alive. It was that feeling only danger can produce. She felt herself poised at the edge of a high cliff, her toes lapping over the edge. And no real option for backing up.

She took a deep breath and jumped.

"Yes. I want to report it to the police."

Then, just like that, the glorious split second in which she assumed she had awakened in her own room, her own life, ended. The vanishing illusion abandoned her at New Beginnings for girls.

In the middle of the scuffed hardwood floor sat a girl Allie could only assume to be her new roommate, Lisa Brickell. For some odd reason that one name had stuck in Allie's head. Lisa was skinny and insubstantial, with sun-bleached blonde hair in dreadlocks. Her skin was tanned to the point of damage, which made Allie feel weirdly pale. Which she was. The girl had Allie's leather suitcases out in the middle of the floor and was carefully combing through Allie's belongings. Or what was left of them.

"Excuse me," Allie said.

No response. Not even a tilt of the head. No sign that this strange girl had heard.

"Excuse me," Allie said again. Louder this time.

Lisa Brickell lifted her eyes to Allie. They were a light blue, so light as to be nearly gray. In fact, they seemed to border on no color at all. And in them, Allie saw . . . nothing. No caring. No personality. Just the coldness of an empty space.

"You're excused," Lisa Brickell said. Her voice sounded raspy and deep, like an aging smoker. "Just don't ever let it happen again."

She returned to sifting through Allie's clothing, where she zeroed in on the socks.

Allie's socks meant a lot to her. They cost more than thirty dollars a pair, and were guaranteed for life and made with serious backpackers in mind. But Allie wore them every day, because they made her feet feel pampered.

Lisa Brickell pulled off her own socks, thin and white and floppily non-elastic, with holes worn through at the heels. She tossed them onto the pile of Allie's clothes and began to pull on the backpacker socks.

"Hey!" Allie said, and jumped to her feet.

# Chapter Thirteen

## Lights-Out, in More Ways than One

"I can't believe you did that," Jasmine said.

They stood at the living room window together, Jasmine holding one side of the curtain back. They watched the two uniformed policemen walk away. Walk back toward their patrol car.

"I know," Allie said. "It's weird. It's big. Or it feels big anyway. But I had to do it. Thank you for telling the police what she told you."

"Yeah. Whatever. But . . ."

Allie followed Jasmine's eyes to see why her sentence had stalled. Brick was coming home. Walking down the street toward New Beginnings. She was looking down, tapping on a smartphone she held in one hand.

"Did she always have a phone?" Allie asked.

"Not that I know of. Maybe that's what she bought with your suitcase money."

"Damn. I should have sold those suitcases and bought a phone. I didn't get to bring mine. And I still don't know why not."

Allie silently noted, as she heard herself speak, that she sounded outwardly calm. It didn't even feel like something she was doing on purpose. There was a ball of fear inside, one she had not yet tapped into. It felt as though there was no door into it. No access. Not that she wanted to access it.

"Because there's nobody on the other end paying the bill anymore. Think she even sees the cops yet?"

"Apparently not."

But the cops saw her. Allie could tell. They had stopped on the sidewalk by their patrol car and seemed to be waiting to talk to her. After all, they had her description, and it was a good one. None of that "average height, brown hair, brown eyes" muddle. Blonde dreadlocks. How often do you see a teenage girl with blonde dreadlocks?

A mere ten steps from the cops, Brick seemed to notice something in her peripheral vision, above the small screen in her hand. A flash of blue, maybe.

She stopped cold. Looked up at the cops. The cops looked back.

"She sees them now," Jasmine said.

For one strange, frozen moment, nobody and nothing moved. Not inside the window. Not on the street out front.

Then Lisa Brickell broke in the opposite direction and ran like a thief.

*Fitting,* Allie thought.

It took the younger of the two cops only ten or twelve running steps to catch her. He dragged her back by one upper arm and loaded her into the rear of the patrol car. Just the way you see on TV, with one hand on top of her head.

Just before the cops closed the door on her, Brick looked up to the house and saw Allie and Jasmine standing at the window watching. Jasmine dropped the curtain, but not nearly fast enough.

"At least she helped your case by running," Jasmine said.

"I just hope they don't bring her back here tonight. Or, you know . . . ever. But the way the cops talked about it . . . What did they mean about 'citing her out'? I was embarrassed to ask because I figured it was one of those things everybody knows but me."

"It means they write her something like a ticket. And she has to pay a fine. If she can't pay the fine she might have to do a few days in jail or juvie, but she has time to come up with some money to pay it. So for the next month at least she'll still live here. And she's going to kill you."

Allie laughed. Or tried to, anyway. A sound came out, but not the sound she had intended.

"Not literally, though." A silence. Too long a silence. "Right?"

Jasmine flipped her head toward the back of the house. Allie followed her out into the yard. The sun felt strong, the air surprisingly clear for downtown. A warm breeze was holding the smog at bay. It felt wrong. It felt as though the world was going on with its business, painfully unaware of the disaster that was Allie's life. That didn't seem fair.

They sat in Jasmine's weed clearing, their knees close.

Allie had to wait for Jasmine to light a cigarette. Wait to hear what her only friend had to say. How bad Allie's future might truly be.

"Maybe literally," Jasmine said. "Or maybe not literally *kill you* kill you, but then you have to think whether killing you is the only thing she can do that would scare you."

"I outweigh her at least."

"You don't outweigh her boyfriend."

A cold tingle in Allie's gut. She spoke around it as best she could.

"She has a boyfriend?"

"Oh yeah. He was in jail just a few months ago. Not sure the whole story of why, but it was bigger than stealing somebody's suitcases. He was inside for years. He drives a motorcycle. Big guy. Last time a girl made trouble for Brick, she had her boyfriend hold the girl for her. She didn't kill her. But the girl wound up in the hospital with, like, two hundred stitches. The girl didn't dare rat, so Brick never got in trouble for it. She just walked away."

A cold, clammy feeling gripped Allie's stomach. Wet. Liquid fear. A sensation Allie couldn't imagine living with for long. At the same time she knew it would not be going on its way anytime soon.

She never answered, but Jasmine must have seen the fear in her eyes.

"I tried to tell you, Allie. I tried to warn you. I said this thing was for real. Seriously dangerous. That she was really crazy, not just the way people usually mean it when they say that word."

"Yeah, I know. You did."

Allie's head spun with possible retreat plans. She could go to The Elf. Get herself placed somewhere different. Hell, if she had to she could even do something to get arrested. At least in police custody she would be safe from Brick. She tried not to picture where on her body that poor girl had needed all those stitches.

*Not her face. Please don't let it have been her face.*

"I just . . . ," Allie began. Then her thoughts ran dry.

"I know. Where you come from, nothing was ever so dangerous."

"Right!"

It was a small comfort, to be understood.

"Welcome to the real world, Allie. Safe is not a guarantee."

They sat for a long time, Allie twisting her body slightly to get more upwind of the smoke. She hated breathing anybody's smoke.

"So," Allie said, continuing to nurse that liquid fear. "That offer to go with you still hold?" She was half kidding. Or maybe one-quarter kidding.

"Yeah. Absolutely. I'll probably go tonight or tomorrow. Just in case she found out I talked to the cops, too."

—

"I'm not sure it has to be anything so radical as running away," Allie said. She was lying on her back on Jasmine's roommate's bed—after a dinner that Allie had not so much as nibbled—waiting to see if Brick was coming back. And thinking about her mother. Picturing her face. Wishing they were home together. "I could ask them to put me in a different home."

"They don't usually have openings. You were lucky to hit an opening here."

"This is lucky? Where would I have gone if I was unlucky?"

"Probably that big juvenile detention place downtown. You think this place is bad? You don't want to go there. That place is hell compared to this."

"Oh," Allie said.

Then she let a long silence fall for lack of anything helpful—or even coherent—to say.

———

"I just couldn't stand her taking my stuff," Allie said. Probably a good hour of silence later. "About a week ago I had all this stuff. I never even thought about it. I just sort of took it for granted. I'd always had enough stuff. You know. Everything you need and most of what you want to be happy. Then the social worker showed up and made me leave most of it behind. What I had to leave behind . . . it feels like me. I'm not even sure who I am without it. I always swore I wouldn't be one of those people who's all about their stuff. But now I just have these two bags' worth. Then Brick starts going through it and taking the best of it for herself. And she wasn't going to stop. You know that as well as I do. She would have taken everything I had if I hadn't stood up to her. I mean, really." She propped herself up on her elbows and looked at Jasmine, who looked back. Right into each other's eyes. "What was I supposed to do?"

"I don't know, Allie. I really don't. That's a tough one. I figure the minute you got thrown into a room with her, your life was more or less over."

———

Jasmine's roommate showed up about an hour later. A plump, round-faced girl with big hair and a knowing face. She looked at Allie trespassing on her bed and said nothing for a time. Just hung in the doorway as if trying to figure out where things would go from there.

"Hey," Jasmine said to her. "Is there anything . . . and I mean anything . . . I could say or do to convince you to room with Brick just for a little while? I mean, if she even comes back. If she doesn't, you get your own room."

"Nothing. Nuh uh. No way. Not one single thing. Up to and including 'That hard thing I'm holding to the back of your head is a loaded gun. Very high caliber.' Nope, not doing that. Sorry your new friend here is gonna die. We're not wishing it on you, girl." She said that last sentence in Allie's direction.

"Hmm," Jasmine said.

Allie took heart at that simple sound. Maybe Jasmine had another idea up her sleeve. Maybe she really was serious about offering Allie some kind of protection. Or assistance, at least. Or, failing that, friendship. Someone who was on her side.

"Anything I can do to convince you to slip downstairs after lights-out and sleep on the couch?" Jasmine asked her roommate.

The girl—Bella might have been her name, but Allie didn't trust her memory—mulled that over for a few seconds. She seemed to be chewing on the idea, almost literally.

"Yeah, okay. I guess that much wouldn't kill me." She looked over her shoulder at Allie before walking away. "Good luck," she said.

Allie waited, wincing slightly, sure the girl would add some comment about how much luck Allie would need.

She never did.

Then again, she didn't need to. It was a thing that went without saying.

———

Half an hour before lights-out The Elf came knocking on Jasmine's bedroom door. Then, immediately after knocking, she tried to let herself in. It didn't work. Jasmine had wedged the back of a wooden chair underneath the knob.

"Jasmine? Bella? How is this door locked? Did you put a lock on this door? That's strictly against the rules."

"No, ma'am," Jasmine called. "No lock. There's just something up against the door."

"Do you know where Alberta is?"

Jasmine looked at Allie, an obvious question in her eyes.

*So this is how the new life goes,* Allie thought. This is how seriously these girls take the concept of not telling on someone. Jasmine was not going to answer the question without Allie's permission. There was a whole set of rules, a complex code. And everybody in the world apparently knew it except Allie.

"I'm here," Allie said.

"Okay. I see. Well . . . I'm going to get Lisa and bring her back. I can understand your being a little nervous, but rest assured—I'll have a talk with her on the way home and make it clear I won't tolerate any kind of revenge."

"Um . . . ," Allie said. Then she didn't know where to go from there.

Jasmine rolled her eyes at Allie and Allie rolled hers in return. It felt good to make light of something for a change.

"You can spend one night outside your room if you really feel it's necessary, Alberta, but tomorrow morning we're going to sit down and talk, the three of us, and settle this once and for all."

"Okay," Allie said. "Thank you."

Tiny elf footsteps disappeared down the hall.

"Oh, she's going to *talk* to her," Jasmine said, stressing the absurdity of the word. "That should turn her into a normal person again. You've got nothing to worry about anymore."

"Yeah," Allie said. "I feel so much better now. What's *with* that lady, anyway? Does she not get how awful Brick is? Or does she just sort of figure we deserve her?"

"I don't think she knows. Brick's quite the actress. And besides, the only person who ever thought it was a good idea to tell on her was you."

———

Less than an hour later they heard the front door of the house open and close. Allie lay awake in the dark, her eyes open wide. She couldn't see Jasmine well in the dim light, but she found it hard to imagine her friend was asleep.

"You awake?" she whispered.

"Yeah."

Allie waited, desperately trying to breathe, her panic lodged in her chest. Not like an obstacle she couldn't breathe around. More like a paralyzing agent that prevented her diaphragm from functioning, creating even more panic.

She heard Brick's footsteps fall along the hall. Past the barricaded bedroom door. She waited for that moment when Brick opened the door to her—and Allie's—room and saw that Allie was gone.

Nothing happened.

The door opened. Then it closed.

Somehow life went on.

Allie breathed as deeply as possible until her chest eased some.

Had all that buildup been for nothing? Somehow it felt logical to assume that it had. Girls cutting each other in group homes in "the system"? That was the stuff of TV movies. Everybody was being too dramatic.

It made so much more sense to think so, and felt more like the world Allie had always known.

She lay awake for a time, revising her own predicament in her head. Settling. In time she even slept some.

—

"Allie," Jasmine hissed.

Allie sat up fast, almost head-butting her friend, who was leaning over her on the bed.

"What?"

"Brick just went downstairs and let herself outside."

Allie tried to clear her brain. To come fully awake. She even tried physically shaking the sleep away. But still she had no idea what to make of this news.

"So . . . what does that mean?"

"I don't know yet. But I thought we better be awake and watching until we figure it out."

Allie got up and moved to the window. She'd been sleeping in her clothes. They both had. In case any fast moves were required.

"See?"

Jasmine pointed to a slim, ethereal figure standing on the house's walkway, three-quarters of the way to the street. Just standing there in the faint moonlight, as if waiting for something.

"Maybe she called her boyfriend," Jasmine said.

And on that note—exactly on the word "boyfriend," as if scripted—they heard the roar of the motorcycle.

"Come on," Jasmine said. "We need to go."

"Wait!"

"For what?"

"What if it's not him? What if it's some random motorcycle and it goes right by?"

"What if by the time it stops it's too late?"

They froze for a matter of seconds. Maybe the count of three. The motorcycle stopped a few doors short of the house. Before it even cut its engine, Brick walked in that direction to meet it.

"That's it," Jasmine said. "You believe me now?"

They looked at each other, then bolted for the bedroom door. They got there at exactly the same time. So much so that their shoulders and hips slammed together, and they bounced apart again. Allie ended up on her back on the floor.

By the time she'd made it to her feet again, Jasmine had the chair moved and the door open. They tiptoed fast down the hall together. Allie gave one sorrowful thought to the rest of her belongings, but there was nothing to be done about that now. She had more important things to worry about, like whether the four of them were about to meet at the front door.

"Come on," Jasmine whispered. "We'll go out the back."

Just as they slithered out the kitchen door, Allie heard the front door creak open.

She ran through the dark yard behind her friend. They made it to the gate in seconds, but it was locked with a padlock. The board fence was six feet high, with no real way to climb it. At least, no way Allie could see.

"I got this," Jasmine said.

They were the three most beautiful words Allie could imagine. Every one of her internal organs filled with gratitude and appreciation for Jasmine, who knew what to do. Without Jasmine she could be dead right now. She could have some big guy holding her while Brick . . . She forced the thought away again.

Jasmine dug around in the weeds near a corner shed. Suddenly there was a ladder. Jasmine pulled it upright, as if out of nowhere. Like magic. Or, in any case, the magic of knowing where to find what you need.

Jasmine leaned it against the fence and trotted to the top step. From there she stepped onto the top of the fence boards. She teetered there a moment, all attention to balance. Then she jumped, and disappeared.

Allie tried her hand with the ladder, but she didn't feel nearly as confident as Jasmine had looked. The higher she got, the less secure she felt. She stalled, convinced she could not negotiate that last step onto the fence without falling back into the yard. But this was life or death. So . . .

She reached high and fast, grabbed the top of the fence, and pulled herself up. She swung a leg over, straddling the ends of the boards. Then she slipped over onto the other side, hung from her arms for a split second, and dropped down.

Her heart pounding in her ears, she ran after Jasmine down the dark alley between fences. For the first few seconds she felt a sense of terror mixed with elation. They had done it. They were out. They had survived.

Before they even reached the end of the block the elation evaporated, leaving only terror.

They were two teenage girls alone in the inner city late at night. And going . . . where?

# Chapter Fourteen

*To the Victor Goes . . .*

By the time they burst out onto a major thoroughfare, a street where she could actually see passing cars instead of just hearing them, Allie felt as though her chest would explode.

They stopped for the first time since jumping the fence, and Allie leaned on her own knees and panted.

When she straightened up she saw Jasmine holding one thumb out to traffic. Hitching a ride. It seemed alarming to Allie. It was late on a Saturday night in downtown L.A. They were two young girls. Didn't Jasmine have internal warning bells and red flags to tell her what not to attempt?

Even more alarmingly, they already had a ride.

A driver was pulling over and stopping. A big one-ton pickup truck. One single guy. Looked like he might be fifty.

"See?" Jasmine said. "Easy."

"You're kidding, right?"

"No, why would I be kidding? We're out of here."

"You don't think this is a little . . ."

"Trust me. I'm a really good judge of people. I can handle myself."

*Maybe,* Allie thought. *Maybe you can handle yourself, Jasmine. But now it's not just you you're affecting with these decisions. Now it's also me.*

But Jasmine had already climbed into the front seat. She was holding the door open for Allie. Allie didn't want to be left out on the street alone. To put it mildly. For a brief second she closed her eyes and allowed herself to be overwhelmed with that unlikely image again— being wrapped in the safety of her mother's arms. When she opened her eyes, she was still out in the world with no one but Jasmine. So she climbed in, glad to have a whole person between herself and the stranger.

She slammed the door and the truck surged forward with a frightening roar of its engine. As if the guy needed to show off. Show that his truck had horsepower, and he wasn't afraid to gun it.

"Where you lovely ladies headed tonight?" he asked. Definitely on the flirty side.

*Handle it, Jasmine.*

"Well," Jasmine said. She drew it out long. Just kept saying it. There was no mistaking it, no missing it—she was being flirty right back.

Jasmine was flirting with a fifty-year-old stranger. Jasmine had just turned into someone else entirely. Someone Allie had never guessed she could be.

*I want to go home,* Allie thought. She squeezed her eyes closed. But of course when she opened them she was still in some stranger's truck in the middle of the night. Or maybe she was in the company of two strangers.

"If you'll do me a big favor," Jasmine continued, "it would make it easier for me to figure that out. I have to call my boyfriend and find out where he wants us to meet him. So if I could just use that phone . . ."

The phone was sitting in a cup holder on the dashboard, and Jasmine reached for it and took it into her hands. As if there were no possibility that her request could be denied.

"Knock yourself out. I'm just disappointed you have a boyfriend. If I'm being completely honest."

Jasmine flashed a set of dazzling white teeth. Allie had never seen Jasmine's teeth before. Jasmine had never showed them off at New Beginnings.

"Well, don't be *too* let down. Victor and I have a good understanding."

*Where am I and what's happening to me? And how do I get it to stop?*

"Victor," Jasmine said into the phone.

A pause while Victor talked. Allie couldn't hear his end.

"Yeah, I'm out. Where do you want to meet up?"

Pause.

"Yeah, I think I know that place. We ate there once. Just tell me the street again."

Pause.

"Okay. Whenever. We'll eat something while we're waiting. I'm bringing another girl."

A longer pause fell. It hurt Allie's stomach. What a ridiculous idea, to think he wouldn't mind. Allie had known in her heart such a thing wasn't possible. Known it all along. It didn't make any sense. Plus, on a larger scale . . . what if Jasmine was simply . . . unreliable? What if her understanding of the world was not something on which Allie should try to depend?

"I think so," Jasmine told Victor. "We'll see."

She clicked off the call and dropped the phone back into the cup holder.

"We're gonna meet at Auggie's. The restaurant. You know where that is?" Jasmine asked the driver.

"I might."

"You make a right at that next light. Unless you want to drop us off at the corner and we'll walk."

"Let me take you to the door. Two young girls in the city at night. It's safer."

A silence fell.

Allie broke it.

"What will you see about me?"

"Oh. What I said to Victor? Did you think that last part was about you? No, change of subject. We were on to something else by then."

"But what did he think about me coming too?"

"He's totally fine with it. I told you he would be."

———

She followed Jasmine and a hostess to a table at Auggie's, still too stunned to voice her apprehension. It was a fairly nice restaurant. Not dress-code fancy, but not fast food or a dive, either. A real dining establishment.

The hostess handed her a menu, which she took, because that's what you do in a restaurant, especially when you don't want to explain that you have not one cent to your name.

Then it was just Allie and her new . . . what? Was Jasmine her friend? Should she be? Did Allie dare be friends with this new person, this strange, bold, flirty girl only just now coming out of hiding?

"He's coming from Sherman Oaks," Jasmine said. "So Saturday night traffic and all, we have probably forty-five minutes at least. Maybe an hour. That's why we're sitting down and we're gonna eat."

Allie leaned closer and spoke quietly near Jasmine's ear.

"We can't order food."

"Sure we can." Jasmine resumed scanning her menu.

"I have no money. Do you have money?"

"Victor will pay the check when he gets here."

"How do you know? Did he say that on the phone? Did he definitely say that in words? In those words?"

Jasmine set her menu down. Looked directly into Allie's face.

"I know because I know him. Because all this's happened before, just like it's happening now. Look. Allie. You need to take a deep breath and calm down. We're fine. You're letting yourself get all in a panic over nothing. You didn't eat any dinner and that's probably not helping. Order something nice. After you eat you might feel better."

"Oh," Allie said, and picked up her menu. "That's a good point, actually. Not only did I skip dinner, but all I've eaten for the last . . . I don't even remember how many days is bread and salad and pasta and oatmeal. All those carbs and no protein. Makes me feel kind of scattered. Makes it hard to calm down."

Was it possible that all this was okay and Allie just wasn't able to see that yet?

"Have a good meal. It's on Victor."

Allie ran her eyes down the menu. Auggie's had a whole section of vegetarian dishes, most with a vegan option. It wasn't just pasta, either. There was a stuffed portobello mushroom, and a black bean and barley veggie burger. There was even a dish called Beans & Greens, with a tahini sauce topping.

"I can't believe this," Allie said. "This is amazing. There are three or four things here I can actually *eat*."

—

"Feeling better?" Jasmine asked over dessert.

Jasmine had ordered tiramisu. Allie, who didn't want to mess up her newly found tranquility by eating sugar, had asked for a bowl of fresh berries.

"I really am. I have to say. It's kind of amazing how a full belly calmed me down. I couldn't eat at New Beginnings. Not right, anyway. I'm sorry if I was being weird."

"No problem."

"I mean, I still have things I'm kind of worried about. Like, for example, I have absolutely nothing except the clothes on my back. I don't even own a toothbrush. But I'm not totally freaking out about it like I was a few minutes ago."

"Good. You'll get what you need again."

A silence. A few spoonfuls of raspberries, which were amazingly good. Blindingly good. They forced Allie to realize that she had been shut down to the simple experience of being alive. Those berries woke her up again.

Still, a few details played on a loop in her mind.

"How?" she asked Jasmine.

But it had been too long since the original statement.

"How what?" Jasmine asked around a mouthful of tiramisu.

"How will I end up with everything I need? What do you do out here? How do you buy things? Am I supposed to work some kind of job now? I would. I don't mind. I'm not lazy. But I'm . . . you know. Fifteen. I'd have to have working papers. Which I don't have and can't possibly get."

"You're getting all amped up again."

"Not really. I just wondered."

"There's plenty of stuff to do where nobody asks for working papers."

A shadow fell across their table. Both girls looked up.

A man was standing over them. Looking down and smiling a broad smile. The smile was . . . Allie couldn't quite decide. Reassuring? Oily? A little of both? And he wasn't moving along. Just standing there.

He was at least in his late thirties. Maybe even forty. He had pale hair that could have been blond or it could have been gray. Or it might have been transitioning from one to the other. It was long and sparse, combed along his head so its length mostly showed where it touched his collar in the back. His skin was tan and divided with smile and frown lines. He wore an expensive-looking black leather jacket despite the warm night.

"Well, here are a couple of lovely ladies," he said.

*Please don't let Jasmine start flirting back with him,* Allie thought.

Jasmine leapt to her feet and threw her arms around his neck. They kissed. On the mouth. Not briefly, either. Long enough that Allie would have squirmed uncomfortably no matter who these two people were.

When they finally, finally broke off the kiss, Jasmine turned to Allie, her arms still around this nearly middle-aged man's neck.

"Allie, this is Victor. Victor, Allie."

# Chapter Fifteen

*Knowing for What, Exactly, You're Not the Type*

Allie woke suddenly, jolted out of a dream she could not remember. It took a minute to orient herself—to know not only where she was but where she expected to be. Neither half of that equation was a given anymore.

She sat up, wincing into the light.

She had been sleeping on the backseat of a vaguely familiar car. She looked out the window at her surroundings. The car was parked in the fenced-in front yard of a neighborhood Allie assumed to be Sherman Oaks. Because that's where Jasmine had said Victor lived. The house was a two-story stucco, a sort of faded salmon color, and huge. Not well cared for. The vegetation was ridiculously overgrown and the house hadn't seen a decent coat of paint in decades. But still, it was not a cheap property nor a bad neighborhood.

Allie rubbed her eyes and tried to pull together what she could recall.

Victor had ordered three glasses of wine, winkingly swearing to the server that all three were for him. The server had delivered them, though he must have known better. Allie had been encouraged to drink one, and she had. Normally she would not have, but her nerves had been jangly and raw, and she had felt stuck in a nightmare with no exit. And as most any adult will tell you—or at least betray by their actions—alcohol is the exit in a fully closed and locked room.

There had been another glass of wine, and the drive here. Allie had sat in the backseat to stay away from the energy of them, and to give them something like privacy. Jasmine had ridden with her arms around Victor's neck. Every few minutes Victor had turned to kiss her with an intimacy and focus that not only embarrassed Allie but made her want to shout, "Watch the road!"

Then it had all caught up to Allie. The fear. The stress. The lack of sleep. The near starvation, at least of protein, followed by the groggy solidity of her first decent meal in days. The wine. She must have fallen asleep before they arrived home.

Still, it seemed strange. They couldn't have wakened her and asked her to come inside?

She opened the door of the car and stepped out into the green jungle of yard. The morning was dense, the air close. It was already warm.

She walked to the front door as if it were a bomb she had just been ordered to defuse. If she'd had any other place to be, she would have run from this house in that moment. But life had been stripping Allie's options. There was nowhere else to go that she could think of.

She tapped lightly on the door.

She had no way of knowing what time it was, and didn't want to wake anyone. Her senses told her it was early.

A split second before she gave up and collapsed onto the stoop, probably in tears, Allie heard footsteps on the other side of the door.

It clicked open, and a girl stared out at her, blinking into the light. A girl Allie had never seen before. She was older. Maybe nineteen or twenty. She had blonde hair done up in a style that might have been fancy the night before, but had devolved. Her dress was turquoise, tight, and surprisingly short. She wore a lot of makeup, and under her eyes it had smudged.

"I think I have the wrong house," Allie said.

She meant it in that moment, but it made no sense. Because it would mean Victor had parked his car in somebody else's yard.

"Who were you looking for?"

"Jasmine."

The girl's face fell slightly, as if she'd just heard sad news.

"Oh, sorry. Jasmine's gone. She got popped and had to spend five months in juvie, and then the county sent her to live in one of those group homes."

"No, she's out. She got out of the group home last night."

"Really? Oh. Okay. Maybe she's here, then. I just got back. Come on in."

Allie stepped inside.

She followed this strangely calm girl into the kitchen as if walking through a dream. Which might have been wishful thinking on Allie's part.

"I'm Desiree," the older girl said.

"Allie."

"Want some orange juice, Allie? I was just about to have some."

"Um. Sure. Thanks."

Allie sat on a high stool at something like a breakfast bar. Her feet didn't touch the floor, which made her feel small and young, which made her feel helpless. She looked around. The inside of the house appeared lived in and then some. Maybe lived in by an army. Clothes and purses lay strewn over furniture and on the orangey-colored shag carpet. The counters and sinks were mounded with used dishes nobody apparently had the time or inclination to wash. It made Allie's skin crawl.

"I live on this stuff," Desiree said.

She set a huge glass of orange juice on the bar in front of Allie. It looked like an iced tea glass. Probably held twenty ounces or more. Allie sipped at it. The acid made her stomach flinch.

"When you work with the public like I do," Desiree continued, "it kinda saves your ass. I used to get sick all the time. Now not so much." She paused in her own gulping. Stared deeply into Allie's eyes. Or tried to, anyway. Allie looked away. "You just here to visit Jasmine? Or are you new?"

"New?"

"Are you, like . . . *here* here?"

"I don't know," Allie said. "There's a lot I haven't figured out yet."

Desiree cut her gaze away and bustled off to the refrigerator. Apparently her appraisal of Allie was done. She seemed satisfied.

"Happens to all of us. Don't feel bad. We all have those crossroads in life." She pulled a carton of eggs out of the fridge. Turned and considered Allie again for a squirming, uncomfortable length of time. "I gotta say, though, you really don't strike me as the type."

"The type?" Allie waited, but nothing happened. No answer. She sipped at the juice again, but her stomach rebelled more forcefully. "The type for what?"

"Got it," Desiree said. "There *is* a lot you haven't figured out."

Allie waited, watched the girl scramble eggs, and thought Desiree would say more. She never did.

Allie felt relieved by that.

A few minutes later the front door opened and another girl came in. She was round and full figured, with a leather skirt and a tube top that showed off her midriff in an unflattering way. Her makeup seemed almost clownish to Allie.

This new girl moved into the kitchen without a word, her face sour. She never so much as looked at Allie. She stared into the pan of scrambled eggs. She and Desiree grunted a greeting to each other.

"Bad night?" Desiree asked.

"Aren't they all?"

"Want food?"

"No. Hell no." Her face twisted with revulsion. "I'm just going straight to bed."

And she did.

———

Allie felt a hand on her shoulder. Her eyes sprang open.

Victor was sitting by her hip on the edge of the couch, leaning over her. Somehow Allie must have fallen asleep again, though the plan had been to avoid it.

He smiled down at her in a way that made her stomach feel as if it were rolling over in place. He still had not moved his hand off her shoulder.

"Allie, right?"

"Right."

"Come on. We're going for a ride. Just you and me."

He stood. Held a hand out to her, as if to help her up. Allie lay still, staring at the hand. A cold map of fear spread through her midsection, identifying lands she had never known existed.

"Where, though?"

His smile changed. Morphed into something more like a smirk.

"Yeah. Jasmine told me you were the cautious type."

"Jasmine." *Right. Jasmine. My lifeline.* "Where *is* Jasmine?"

"She had some work. Come on. I won't bite you."

Allie sat up. "Just . . . where are we going, though?"

"I'm going to buy you a really good meal. Jasmine told me it's hard for you to get something to eat. So we're going to go somewhere you can get the best meal of your life. And I'm going to take you shopping. You know. For clothes."

Allie sat blinking a moment, unsure what to think.

"That's so nice of you," she said.

She didn't know how to ask if he was simply a nice guy or if there was more going on that she did not understand. She braved a look into his eyes but found no answers there. Just a good poker face.

"But . . ."

"For once in your life, kid, skip the buts."

"I can't. I'm just not a person who lets those things go. How will I ever pay you back?"

"When you're working, you can pay me back. Easy."

"Oh," Allie said. "Right."

It did sound easy. And it made sense. Allie had been waiting for something—anything—with those familiar qualities to come along. The strain of attempting to assess this situation had begun to wear her down, causing her to want desperately to think Victor was okay. So she jumped at a chance to believe it.

"Okay, then," she said. "Let's go."

———

Victor had a habit—a nervous one, perhaps—of running his hand along his hair, as if to smooth it back, his palm pressing it into place. But it had never been out of place to begin with. It didn't need smoothing.

He looked over at her several times as he drove, taking his eyes off the road for too long. He wore expensive-looking sunglasses that did not hide the crow's feet at the corners of his eyes. But it did hide his eyes. So it was hard to tell in what way she was being assessed. Still, something about his attention was making her uneasy. Well, *more* uneasy. She'd been uneasy ever since she had walked down the stairs to witness the handcuffing of her parents. Her life seemed to get worse at every juncture. Every intersection involved sudden turns into more and more dangerous neighborhoods.

"This is none of my business," she said, mostly out of desperation to fill the car with words, "so don't answer if you don't want. I just wondered. Who are those other girls?"

"Well," he said. And paused. And smoothed his hair back. "They're . . . girls. They're the girls."

"They all live with you?"

"Yes."

"But you're Jasmine's boyfriend, right?"

"It's a little more complicated than that."

"Never mind," she said quickly. "Never mind. It's none of my business. I don't need to know."

They drove in silence for a time. A mile, maybe, with traffic lights at every corner, none of which Victor managed to catch on the green.

Sitting at a red light, he turned to stare at her again for an uncomfortable length of time. Allie stared out the window, her face angled away.

"You have a nice look," he said. He waited to see if she would reply. She didn't. This was not a body of water into which she intended to wade. "I'm not saying you're the most gorgeous girl who ever lived or anything like that. But you have a nice face. And you've got a way about you. Innocent. A lot of guys really like that innocent look. It's kind of . . . almost a virgin thing. Are you a virgin?"

Inside a head that had begun spinning, Allie began to grasp at options. She could run away in reverse—ditch this place and run back to the group home. Oh, right. No she couldn't. She might end up with two hundred stitches. She could run away from Victor and find a police station. Throw herself on their mercy.

Not a great set of options.

Maybe she could simply be more direct with him. Tell him what she did and did not want in the way of attention. It felt worth trying.

"Can we talk about something else?"

The light turned green, and Victor stepped on the gas, causing the car to surge forward too suddenly.

"Of course. I'm sorry if I made you uncomfortable."

Allie breathed deeply for what felt like the first time in ages. In as long as she could remember.

———

As they stepped out of their fifth clothing store at the Sherman Oaks Galleria, all four of their arms laden with bags of purchases, Victor stopped and regarded her again. A sea of humanity flowed around them like a river, turning them into an island of two.

It was helpful to Allie to be in this place. Upscale malls she understood. It was a relief to have part of her old world handed back.

"What else do you need to be happy?" Victor asked.

Allie's chest filled with a warm sensation. Had she been misjudging him? Did he really want her to be happy?

"I think this is enough for clothes."

"That wasn't the question. I didn't ask if you had enough clothes. I asked what more you needed to be happy."

"Oh. Well . . ."

At first her mind only felt blank. She knew she missed money. Just the normal feeling of having money in your pocket to do what you needed to do. There was a safety about it. You could take a cab. Make a phone call.

*A phone call.*

It hit Allie, just that suddenly, what she missed most among her many abandoned belongings.

"It would be nice to have a phone."

She said it hesitantly, then almost wished she could grab the words back again. A phone was expensive. Then again, so were all these clothes.

"Of course. Of course you need a phone. On to the Apple Store."

It was just that easy. *Ask, and it appears.*
*Almost like having parents.*
*Who are not in jail.*

———

They sat outside, dining alfresco at a small bistro on Ventura Boulevard. The air was hot and thick. A printed red-and-white umbrella threw much-needed shade across their table.

Allie looked down at her amazing lunch. Or was it dinner? She didn't know what time it was.

She had ordered a mushroom and quinoa veggie burger on a whole-grain bun with sliced avocado, sprouts, and aioli mayonnaise—sweet potato fries on the side. It tasted like heaven, like being saved. Victor had made good on his promise to buy Allie the best meal of her life.

Their two unused chairs sat heaped high with bags of clothing, and Allie now and then glanced down at the iPhone sitting beside her plate. Not for any special reason. It had none of her information on it yet, and no one had called or texted her. She looked at it because it was hers.

"We should have left all these clothes in the trunk," she said.

"Nonsense. They should be piled all around you. It makes you feel . . . rich. You deserve a sense of plenty."

"Why are you being so nice to me?" she asked suddenly.

The euphoric mood of the meal broke like a fever. Suddenly Allie's stomach couldn't decide if it wanted the amazing food or not. She took another bite of her mushroom burger but it seemed to have lost its flavor.

She glanced up at Victor, whose face had gone blank.

"I can be nice," he said, sounding strangely hurt, like a child.

"I'm sorry. I didn't mean it like that. I didn't mean you couldn't. Of course you can be nice. I think I'm just worried because . . . you spent so much today. I guess I'm worried about how I'm going to pay you back for all this."

"It's not a problem. I told you. You start to work, I call it even."

Allie felt her forehead wrinkle. Something wasn't adding up.

"I thought . . ." But she never finished the sentence.

"You thought what?"

"I thought I would get a job and actually pay you back the money. You're saying we'd be even just because I was working? So it's like I'd be working for you?"

Allie dropped her burger. Literally dropped it. It hit the plate, but the top of its bun rolled off the table and landed on the concrete patio, causing a flap of wings as pigeons rushed to claim it.

"Oh crap," she said.

She hadn't meant to say it out loud.

It all came together in her brain, just in that moment. The multiple young girls all living with the same much older man. The girls having been out working at night, in skimpy clothes, just coming back in the morning. The makeup. Jasmine getting "popped" and having to spend time in "juvie."

Suddenly it was all so clear.

Allie felt like the perfect fool for not seeing it all along.

"I can't," she said. "I won't."

"What won't you?" Victor asked, his voice cool.

"I won't do anything that's . . . you know. Illegal. And not . . . something I would do. I'm fifteen. I haven't even gone all the way with a boyfriend yet, not even somebody I loved. I can't be part of anything like this. I'll just go."

Silence. A long, dangerous one. Allie did not dare look up into Victor's face. Instead she watched the pigeons fighting over her bun. Pecking at it. Pecking at each other. Forcing each other to drop it.

Finally she braved a glance up at his face. It seemed to be carved from cool marble.

"After I spent almost two thousand dollars on you. You'll just go."

"I'm sorry. We can take it all back. We have the receipts."

"That would take all afternoon," he said. "I was just getting ready to call it a day."

"I'm sorry. I don't know what to say. *I'll* take the stuff back. And then I'll walk to your house or take the bus and bring you back the money. I'll do whatever it takes to make it right. Anything except . . . you know. That."

Another long and potentially dangerous silence.

"Well," Victor said. His voice sounded tight. "I'll have to have a talk with Jasmine for putting me in this position. She's supposed to be judging anybody she brings home better than that." Then he sighed, and the tightness seemed to leave him. To drain out, audibly, with the air of his breath. "Okay. Whatever. I guess these things happen. Let's just go home. You can stay tonight and then in the morning we'll figure out what to do."

They rose and left the bistro together, Allie leaving the best meal of her life abandoned on her plate. She looked back at it, regretfully. At least, in theoretical regret. She no longer had the appetite for it, but she hated to let it go. She watched the pigeons set upon it, eager to tear it apart.

# Chapter Sixteen

## The Question "What's Worse than Juvie?" Answered

Allie sat in Victor's living room in the dark, alone. On the couch, with her knees tightly drawn up to her chest. It was late, probably very late. Of course she was not sleeping. It felt like a blessing to be alone, given the company she had at her disposal. Then again, it felt like a sea of isolation. Allie had, for all practical purposes, no one. It was hard to believe she couldn't just call her mother to come get her. All her life that comfort had been there for her. It felt beyond frightening to reach for that familiar presence and feel nothing. A void.

She thought of her few friends at her old school in Pacific Palisades. Maybe whether or not they truly liked her was not the issue at a time like this. Still, they weren't like adult friends who had their own place and would let you crash on their couch. Allie was a runaway now, and needed to avoid parents. Anybody's parents.

But maybe one of them could just wire some money or something . . .

Allie quietly searched the house for a phone. But as best she could tell in the dark, there was no landline. And if Victor had a phone, it was in the bedroom with Victor. And she had no money for a pay phone.

She heard a soft sound, and spun to look.

Jasmine was walking out of one of the downstairs bedrooms. Allie hadn't known Jasmine was in the house. She'd thought only Victor was home, brooding in some distant room. Disappointed with Allie, or angry with her. Or both.

Jasmine turned on a soft light beside the couch and sat close to Allie's hip.

"I'm not your biggest fan right now," Allie said, avoiding Jasmine's eyes.

"Look. Allie. We could go on all night about whatever issues you have with me. But that's not your big problem at this point. There was a lot I wanted to tell you about Victor before you spent any time alone with him. You don't say no to him. You just don't."

"I already did."

With those words, Allie raised her eyes to Jasmine's face. Jasmine's right eye was swollen half shut, a jagged purple bruise forming. Allie's shock must have registered on her face.

"It's nothing," Jasmine said, lowering her face and letting her hair fall over the problem. "I just ran into something."

*Victor's fist?* Allie thought. She wisely did not say it out loud.

"I told him no and he seemed to take it okay," she said instead.

"*Seemed to.* Look, Allie, you're really, really super naïve. I sort of knew that but I guess I didn't see how much. You need to get out of here. Like, now."

"Now?" It came out as a screech, and Jasmine shushed her, glancing over her shoulder toward the bedroom. Alarm buzzed in Allie's stomach, a sickeningly familiar feeling. Her constant companion. "I can't go now. It's night. I can't go out there all alone at night! Where will I go? How am I supposed to take care of myself out there?"

"I think if I were you, I'd take my chances."

"I could go back to New Beginnings, I guess. I couldn't live there, though. Brick would kill me. But I could go back into the system and get them to put me someplace else. Anyplace else. Couldn't I?"

"Yeah. You should. That's what I would do. I mean, they'll put you in juvie, but—"

"They'll *what?* Why? Why would they put me in juvie?"

"Because you ran away. That's what they do with runaways from the system. Trust me. I know."

Allie took a moment to breathe. To stabilize the room as it appeared inside her tilting head.

"I'll only stay till morning and then I'll figure something out. I can't leave now." Silence. "What could happen to me if I don't leave now?"

More silence.

"Victor only helps girls who play the game," Jasmine said. "The ones who stay with him on purpose. That's just how he operates. But some guys're not like that."

Allie gripped her own knees more tightly and waited for Jasmine to go on. She never did. Allie was left with no real understanding of Jasmine's words. No way to apply them to her own situation.

Those other guys were not here, right? So why had they even come up in conversation? It sounded like Jasmine was saying Victor was better than most, but that hardly answered the question of why she had to clear out tonight.

Several minutes ticked by in an electrical silence. At least it felt electrical to Allie, whose nerves had reverted to their new normal: paranoid high alert.

"Why do you live like this?" she asked Jasmine after a time. "Why not stay at the group home?"

"Let's not make this about me, okay? I came out here to tell you I'd leave tonight if it was me. Don't tell Victor you're going. Don't get caught leaving. Leave everything he gave you and get as far away as you can as fast as you can. Now that I've said that, it's up to you. I warned you. I did all I could."

With that Jasmine rose and disappeared into the bedroom again, leaving Allie even more alone. If such a thing were possible.

—

Over the next three or four hours, Allie rose from the couch and headed for the door more than half a dozen times.

Once she even opened it.

The blackness of the city night forced her back again.

Which was worse? To walk out to Ventura Boulevard alone? Hitchhike somewhere? Or wait for a bus? To where? And did they even run at this hour? Allie had never taken a bus, and had no way to know. Then she realized she had no money for a bus, so it didn't matter.

Or she could walk. With cars buzzing by, which they would, even in the middle of the night. What if one of them saw her all alone and stopped?

Allie took a step back inside and shut the door.

No one was even awake now. Maybe nothing would happen until morning. But by then she feared she might fall asleep. So something could happen before she even knew Victor was awake.

*You don't say no to him. You just don't.*

Allie sat on the couch again, her mind a frightening blank. A moment later it filled with an option. Her only one, really. She just hadn't seen it before. She didn't even feel as though she had reached out for it. It had just let itself in.

She would go out into this dark world, once again, with nothing but the clothes on her back. And she would find a place to hide. Someplace not far away. Maybe right in this neighborhood. She would crouch down behind someone's hedge, or find a gardening shed. Or maybe there would be an all-night restaurant on the boulevard, and she could sit there in the company of someone—anyone—until dawn.

Yes. That was it.

She would clear this place, just barely, then secure a position until the dangerous night had moved on. And then . . . Allie had no idea. She had no plan for the morning, other than to turn herself in. Which she probably would. But she had to survive until that moment arrived.

Allie launched herself off the couch and tiptoed to the front door. She opened it carefully, silently, then stepped out into the overgrown yard. She heard a car door slam. It seemed to be parked between the spot where Allie stood and the gate she needed to reach. Maybe one of "the girls" coming home from "work"?

Would they tell Victor if they saw her leaving?

Allie dropped her head and bolted for the gate, all surging adrenaline and not much solid thinking. A second or two later a hand grabbed her wrist and wrenched her to a halt. A big hand.

Allie looked up. Her eyes had not adjusted to the darkness, and there was only just so much detail she could make out. But this was not one of the girls. This was a mountain of a man. The kind of man you see playing defensive football, or working as a bouncer in a club. And he had Allie in his grasp.

He twisted her arm around behind her back, turned her toward the house again, and marched her to the front door. He knocked loudly. Pounded, really. With the flat side of his fist.

Allie lost her ability to breathe. Her heart couldn't decide whether to beat too much or too little. It hammered in her chest so hard she feared it might break, explode. Then it missed a beat or even two, leaving a sickening void in the middle of her body that felt like dying.

A terrifying pause. Then a light came on inside the house.

Victor opened the door, his face muddied by sleep. His hair looked disheveled, not perfectly slicked back, and he wore a haze of light beard. The light in the living room haloed him from behind. Allie couldn't see the look in his eyes, but just his gaze in her direction made her heart skip beats again.

The big man who held Allie spoke in a deep bass.

"This the one you called about?"

"The very one," Victor said. "Where'd you find her?"

"On her way out."

Victor made tsk noises with his tongue. Three of them. It made Allie feel like a trapped animal. Like the prey of a wild cat who likes to play with his terrified catch before . . . Allie didn't want to carry the analogy any further than that.

"You'll have your hands full with this one," Victor said.

"Makes no difference to my situation. I drive her up there, I hand her over. I don't care. She won't get away from *me*."

He reached out a hand to Victor. The hand that was not holding Allie's arm wrenched behind her back. In that big hand, in the spill of light from the living room, Allie saw a small manila envelope. Thick with something.

"You can count it," the giant said. "I won't take offense."

"That's okay. You work for Lassen; I trust you."

Victor grabbed the envelope from the giant hand and swung the door shut. Hard. The slam made Allie jump.

She felt herself turned again, and marched toward the giant's car. The pain caught up with her in that moment. It hurt. The position of her arm was painful. Apparently she had been too preoccupied with fear to notice.

The giant opened the back door of his dark sedan and pushed hard. Allie fell across the backseat, hitting her head on the opposite window. She sat up just as the door was slammed shut behind her. As the giant began to walk around to the driver's side front, Allie seized the brief opportunity.

She tried the door. It was locked. She tried to lift the lock. Fast, desperate. Over and over. It wouldn't budge.

The dome light came on, causing Allie to wince. The big man was in the driver's seat now, looking back over his shoulder at her. As her eyes adjusted to the sudden, almost violent light, she was able to see his features clearly. His hair was buzzed so short it practically did not exist, his nose wide and misshapen. His thick, short neck was hardly a neck at all. More of a slope to broad shoulders. He smiled at her, exposing a row of white but crooked teeth.

"Child safety locks," he said in that cartoonishly deep bass. "Wouldn't want your child getting away."

Then he started the engine, shifted the car into gear, and drove.

A thought flashed through Allie's head, a sort of wordless emotional version of "I want my mommy." But it was too late for all that now.

———

"Can you at least tell me where you're taking me?"

Allie's voice sounded breathy to her own ears. She had been struggling for the better part of an hour to catch her breath, but the grinding fear kept snatching it away again.

For a time he didn't answer.

They had driven well out of the San Fernando Valley. Allie could see the ocean in the dark, a faint crescent of moon setting at the black horizon. It was beautiful, except to the extent that nothing was beautiful, because nothing possibly could be. Not at a time like this.

They might have been driving through Camarillo or Oxnard, or it might have been Ventura. In the darkness and panic, it was hard to tell.

He met her eyes in the rearview mirror, his face revealed in the faint glow of the dashboard lights.

"San Francisco," he said.

Which didn't answer the question. Not really. Allie hadn't meant to ask *where*, exactly. Not geographically where. "To what?" would have been more relevant, but Allie didn't ask that question. She wasn't ready to know.

She watched the moon set over the Pacific and thought about a teacher—Mr. Callahan, her English and creative writing teacher—who taught her the Mark Twain quote "I've had a lot of worries in my life, most of which never happened." They'd had a class discussion about problems, about how they're mostly *perceived* problems. Borrowed trouble. Usually the brain wandered into the future until it identified a potential problem and seized on it. By the time that future came to pass, though, circumstances would change and the problem would never materialize. Mr. Callahan had said it was rare for most people to have a genuine problem in the moment—literally, unavoidably happening.

She would have to tell him about this. If she survived.

The adrenaline had been with her too long. She felt exhausted, her nerves jangled nearly to the point of collapse.

A thought came into her mind. Suddenly. Almost as if from outside her. *Don't just sit there. Try. Try to save yourself. Try anything.*

"Do you have kids?" she asked him.

He met her eyes again in the mirror. Narrowed his own, his eyebrows squeezing downward.

"No."

Allie waited, but he said no more.

"Don't you ever feel . . . sympathy for girls like me?"

"Sympathy?"

Almost as though he didn't understand the word.

"Don't you feel sorry for the girls you take up to San Francisco? I mean, I've never been so scared in my life. This is absolutely the worst thing that's ever happened to me, and I've had some pretty terrible things happen lately. Doesn't that make you feel anything at all? How can you not feel sorry for someone who didn't do anything wrong and who's so terrified? And you have the power to change it."

A long silence. She could see part of his face, including his eyes, in the mirror. But he wasn't looking at her. He was watching the road. She tried to see something in those eyes, some evidence that he was thinking about what she'd asked. Or, better yet, feeling. But his face looked slack and blank.

"You talk too much," he said.

"Sorry."

"Don't do it anymore."

"Okay. Sorry."

They drove on. Allie watched the slightest hint of dawn form over the hills to the east. The sky turned a lighter color, fading the stars. Morning was coming. The same morning Allie had thought would bring safety.

It was far too late for such an extravagant hope.

———

"I need to go to the bathroom," Allie said.

They had just passed the ridiculously ornate Madonna Inn, and a freeway sign a few miles back had announced that the next few exits would be San Luis Obispo. Allie did have to go to the bathroom, but she could have held it. But still she had a mind to save herself. She was not yet beyond trying.

"I wasn't born yesterday," he said.

Allie didn't speak for a time.

"I don't know what I'm supposed to do if you won't stop."

"Hold it."

"I can't hold it all the way to San Francisco. That's hours from here."

"Try. We don't stop."

"Okay. But I just want you to know, I won't be able to hold it much longer. I'm really thinking of *you*. And your car. This car has these really nice leather seats. And what a mess it would be to clean that up. It'll go all down behind the seats. And the smell! But it's your car. I was just trying to save you all that trouble."

"I told you not to talk so much."

Allie shut her mouth, firmly. Suddenly. She decided her best bet might be to keep it shut. The last thing she wanted was to make him angry.

Less than a minute later he swerved suddenly onto an off-ramp, as if it had been a spontaneous last-minute decision. He made a right onto a city street that was signed Route 1, and drove for a few blocks until several gas stations came into view in the early morning light.

"Here's how it's gonna be," he said. "We're gonna find a place with the bathrooms on the outside. Not in the store. I'm gonna park close to 'em. Real close. Blocking it right off. We're gonna wait till there's nobody around for you to run to. If you try to run inside the store, or out into the street, I'll be on you in a heartbeat. If somebody sees me put you back in the car, so be it. I'm a good actor. I'll tell 'em you're my kid, and you're a runaway, and I'd do anything to get you home safe this time. If you try something, you'll lose. And after you lose, you'll be one sorry little girl. Sorrier than you've ever been in your very short life so far. Got that?"

It was the first direct threat from him, and it caused Allie's heart to beat erratically again. Too strong, then skipping beats.

"Got it."

He pulled into a deserted station. Drove as close as he could get to the ladies' room door without jumping a wheel up onto a curb. Unfortunately, the restrooms were located around the back of the place. Utterly out of view of the street. That was a bad break, and Allie knew it.

She felt her hopes sickeningly contract. Wither. All but die.

He cut the engine. Got out. Came to the back door of the car and unlocked it with his key. Swung it wide.

Allie felt the fresh air hit her face. The freedom of the real world. Life was going on all around her. Other people were having average mornings.

He took hold of her arm and dragged her three steps from the car to the ladies' room door, which he held open. He peered inside, as if to assure himself there was no window. No other exit. He stopped her before she stepped inside, his voice a deep growl in her ear.

"I'll be inches from this door. *Inches.* And don't lock it."

He gave her a strong push and closed the ladies' room door behind her.

With shaking hands, Allie used the toilet and washed up at the sink. She really did need to, especially now, when a flurry of activity was about to happen. For better or for worse, even if it resulted in the beating of a lifetime. Even if she didn't survive. She had to try. She couldn't just step back into the car and let him drive her to a life of utter, demoralizing slavery.

This might be her last chance.

She heard a bumping on the door, and jumped.

"Just a reminder," he said. "That I'm . . . Right. Here."

Allie walked to the door and touched it. It was encased in sheet metal. Heavy and huge. Probably because it opened onto the outside, and the gas station people didn't want anyone breaking into it to sleep at night. Homeless people slept in gas station bathrooms, if they could. Allie had heard this somewhere. She couldn't remember where. But she understood now. It made sense, suddenly, that so little shelter and comfort could seem appealing.

Maybe she should stay in here. Lock the door in spite of his directions. Wait it out.

No. He was a good actor. He'd tell the gas station mini-mart clerk that his runaway daughter was locked in the bathroom. Get the guy to open the door.

Allie felt the walls of her life close in around her.

She was going to try something. She had to try.

She heard his fingers tapping a rhythm on the other side of the door.

"Right. Here," he said.

Good. He was right there. Right in the trajectory of this heavy, metal-encased door. Allie pulled back a step, holding the door handle, and threw all her weight, every ounce of her energy, into sending the door flying open. She felt it hit him. Heard an oof sound come from him. Then the door swung freely again, until it hit his legs where they lay on the concrete.

She burst out through the open space, her breath coming in ragged gasps. He was down. Down on his back, blood streaming from his nose. She had hit him cleanly in the face with that heavy door. Maybe even broken his nose. And there was a split on his forehead that was bleeding heavily, so he hopefully had a concussion.

*Good.*

She jumped over him.

She winced, expecting him to grab for her ankle. He didn't. Or he missed. She didn't know which one. Only that she was across him, and free.

She ran.

She sprinted around the station to the street, desperately looking back over her shoulder. Expecting him to be up, on his feet. Right there, gaining ground. Ready to grab her.

He wasn't there. Not yet. Somehow he must still have been down.

She ran past the mini-mart door, craning her neck to look inside. But she could see no one behind the counter. She couldn't take a chance on that.

She looked behind her again. Still no giant.

She bolted for the street.

Traffic was light to nonexistent as Allie ran out into the middle of this business route section of Highway 1, desperately holding out her thumb.

The only car she could see coming was a shabby older white van with some kind of writing on the side. As it pulled closer, Allie could see an old woman behind the wheel, and, on the dashboard, a curled and sleeping cat.

This odd pair of travelers was looking like her one and only chance.

# PART THREE

## BEA

# Chapter Seventeen

*Kids Today—All Phone Scammers and Carjackers*

"No!" Bea said out loud to the inside of the empty van. "No, no, no. I don't pick up hitchhikers. I don't know you, and it's not safe."

The girl was a good half block down, standing in the middle of the traffic lane. Bea was speaking in a normal tone of voice with the windows rolled up tight. So it was a set of comments made to herself, not so much to the hitchhiker in question. Which might explain why it had that nice forceful tone, like something she'd say in one of her imaginary confrontations. Bea hadn't experienced one of those flights of fancy since leaving home. Life was changing. She was braver on the outside these days.

The girl looked impossibly young to be standing out in the road by herself. Like a child. A little girl. Which probably meant she was halfway through high school. The older Bea got the younger these kids appeared.

This one . . . there was something wrong with her. She couldn't hold still. The closer Bea drove to her, the more she could see the child's unnatural agitation. The girl was jumping around. Looking over her shoulder. Waving the arm that held out the offending thumb—the one that presumed Bea's precious van could be hailed like a taxicab. Waving it wildly, as though Bea would somehow not notice it without all the theatrics.

*Drugs,* Bea thought. *She must be on drugs. So many of the kids are these days. Not like when I was a girl and we were busy working part-time jobs and getting good grades. We had no time to engage in such dangerous foolishness.*

As she pulled close enough to see the girl's face, Bea could only assume the girl could see Bea's face as well. She knitted her brow down until she could feel the wrinkling of it. She shook her head firmly and steered into the left lane.

The girl did exactly the opposite of what Bea expected. She jumped right into the path of the moving van.

Bea slammed on the brakes to keep from hitting her. Phyllis rolled forward a few inches and bumped the windshield. She struggled to right herself, shot Bea a resentful look, and jumped down into the litter box, slithering under the passenger seat.

Bea looked up to see the girl leaning over the short, compact hood of the van, pounding on the windshield.

Bea powered the passenger window down to better express her rage.

"What on earth are you doing? You could have been killed!"

Much to Bea's surprise, the girl reached through the open window and pulled up the lock button. She opened the passenger door and jumped in.

*Oh, good God,* Bea thought, *I'm being carjacked!*

"What are you doing? Get out of my van!"

"Ah!" the girl cried. "Why am I stepping in kitty litter?"

"Because you're someplace you have no right to be! Get out of my van!"

The girl didn't get out of the van. She slammed the door behind her, then threw herself between the seats and landed on the metal floor of the vehicle, inches from Bea's recliner. She scooted along on her belly to the back window.

*"Drive!"* the girl shouted. Shouted! It was alarming. "Please, please, please, I'm begging you! It's life or death. *Drive!"*

Bea perhaps heard all of the girl's words—after all, they were uttered close by, and quite loudly—but did not receive each with the same weight. After the first word, which came off as a barked order, Bea was seized with the idea that this intruder might have a weapon. What if she had a gun? Even the young ones often did these days.

Bea floored the gas pedal, and the van leapt forward. She could hear and feel the blood roar in her ears as her heart pumped faster. Could her heart survive a violent carjacking? Would the old organ hold?

She watched in her rearview mirror as the girl inched along the floor on her belly. When she reached the back window, she lifted her head cautiously, as if it might draw fire. The curtains were open, but they covered a sliver of the window at both outside edges, and the girl made a tiny space between the bunched curtain and the edge of the window. A space no wider than an eye. She pressed her face to it.

Bea could hear the air rush out of the child, even from the driver's seat.

Then they rounded a bend in the street, and the girl stood—as much as the low roof allowed—and walked to the front of the van.

"Don't come near me!" Bea cried. "I'll crash this thing! Don't think I won't do it!"

The girl stood frozen a moment, just a foot or two behind Bea's shoulder. They each watched the other, their gazes locked in the rear-view mirror, but neither said a word.

Bea glanced in both side mirrors to be sure there were no other cars to hit. Then she swerved the van sharply, first to the left and then to the right, tires squealing. The girl went flying, hitting her head on the side of the van and sliding to the floor.

"Ow," the child said. It sounded strangely mournful and weak to Bea's ears.

"I mean it. You lay a hand on me, I'll send us both into a crash. I have less life ahead of me than you do, so I have less to lose. I'd end it all right now for both of us before I'd let you hurt me."

Silence. For several seconds.

Then the girl sat up—gingerly—and plunked into the passenger seat, her feet stretched into the center of the cab to avoid the litter box.

"Why would I try to hurt you?"

Bea glanced over at the girl's face, and her heart calmed slightly. The child no longer appeared to be on drugs. She was breathing deeply in and noisily out, as though shaking off fear. Her face looked lost. Young. Scared. She looked more scared than Bea felt.

"Well, I don't know," Bea said sharply, still dealing with the dregs of adrenaline. "Why would you throw yourself in front of my van? And then jump in against my will? It's all very strange behavior if you ask me. I thought you were on drugs. I thought I was being carjacked."

"Carjacked?"

"Yes. Surely you've heard of it."

"With *what*?" The girl lifted her arms, showing her empty hands. Her clothes did not appear baggy enough to hide anything like a weapon.

"Well, I don't know," Bea said again. "How was I to know what you do and don't have to hurt me with?"

Bea pulled off onto a side street and over to a curb. Even though it was a red curb. She would take her chances with that. She shifted the van into "Park" and set her forehead against the steering wheel.

"You scared the bejesus out of me," she said.

"I'm sorry. I said it was life or death. I said please."

"You did?"

"Yes. I did."

"I must have been too scared to notice."

"I was in a lot of trouble. You were my last chance. Or I thought you were, anyway. I thought if I didn't get into the first car that came by, he might come running out and catch me. But then I looked out the back window, and he never came out. He must still have been down."

"I have no idea what you're babbling on about," Bea said.

"I was being kidnapped. I was about to be . . . well . . . kind of . . . sold. Or maybe I already had been sold. I'm not sure."

"You can't sell a *person*," Bea said. "This is the United States of America."

"You shouldn't be able to," the girl said. "But it seems people still do."

Bea raised her forehead from the steering wheel. Shook her head as if to toss all this foolishness away.

"Jump out now," she said, still jangling in her fear. Needing her quiet world back again. Needing to feel safe herself.

But then, after a moment of stunned silence, Bea braved a glance at the girl's face. Whatever had gone on, the poor kid was genuinely scared. That much this intruder was not fabricating.

"No, please. He might still be out looking for me. Please. Just take me up to the next town. Just far enough away that I know he can't find me. And then if you still want me out, I'll go."

"Oh, I'll still want you out."

Bea shifted the van into "Drive" and made an awkward three-point turn on the side street, then a right on the main drag—the Route 1 stretch of town, going north.

This piece of travel coming up would be her first chance in a long while to drive along the water. For most of the drive north to San Luis Obispo, Highway 1 and Highway 101 had run inland, and often together. Bea had been looking forward to the roads splitting again—to driving along the coast with the ocean on her left. It had been a luxury worth anticipating. And now, instead of enjoying it, she had this mess to deal with.

The business district faded away as she drove, morphing into more of a highway setting, amber pastureland on either side, two lanes in each direction. Plenty of cars. Where had all these cars been when this girl was needing a ride?

"Tell you what I'll do," Bea said. "Next little town up is Morro Bay. We'll stop there and find you a police station. I'll let you off at the station and you can tell them that crazy story you just told me, and maybe they can make sense of it."

The girl said nothing in reply.

In time, Bea looked over at her face. The bulk of the immediate fear had drained away now, leaving this young thing looking heartbroken and lost.

"Damn," Bea uttered under her breath. Now she would have to feel sorry for the kid.

"I can't go to the police."

"Why can't you? If it was as bad as you say? Kidnapping is a serious crime."

"But I don't know anything that would help them catch the guy. I didn't get his license number. I don't know who he was."

Bea felt her brain flash back to that moment in the BuyMart parking lot, lying on the pavement. The way she had told that nice young man how it wasn't worth calling the police because she hadn't gotten a look at her mugger.

"Takes a scammer to know a scammer," she said, still whispering.

"What did you say?"

"Nothing. That's not a 'can't,' what you just said. You don't really say, 'I can't go to the police' because you might not have all the info they'll need. That's more of an 'I'm not sure how much good it will do.' But you said you *can't*. Why can't you?"

A long silence. Bea did not look over at the girl, because she didn't want to feel sorry for her again. Once you get involved in all that empathy, life just gets so darned complicated.

"Because I'm a runaway. I ran away from the system. So they'd put me in juvenile detention. You know, like jail, but for kids. Even though

I didn't do anything wrong. Except run away. But I had to. This girl was going to kill me. Or at least hurt me really bad. I didn't do anything wrong."

"My, my," Bea said. "The world is just full of people who want a piece of your hide, isn't it?"

She heard a gentle sigh from the passenger seat. Then silence.

Then, "Oh! A kitty. Hello, kitty!"

Bea glanced over to see Phyllis craning her neck out from underneath the seat and looking up at this girl. This child full of unlikely stories. It surprised Bea that Phyllis didn't stay hidden, because normally the cat was an excellent judge of character.

"I saw the kitty sleeping on your dashboard when you drove up. But everything was so panicky and weird, and it's like I forgot about the cat or like it didn't exist at all. Like I dreamed that part. Because, really, that's not such a common thing. Most people don't drive around with their cats. Dog, maybe. But not cats. I guess because—"

Bea interrupted the girl's breathy nonsense.

"Wait. If you'd done nothing wrong, you wouldn't have been in the system to begin with."

"No, not that kind of system. I was never in the prison system. It was the child protective system I had to run away from."

Bea watched the little girl scratch the cat's head, especially behind the ears. She heard Phyllis begin to utter that familiar, hoarse, uneven purr.

"I guess I don't blame you for not believing me," the girl said.

"It doesn't matter what I do or don't believe. I'm just taking you to the next town. I don't have to hear your life story. I don't have to judge what is or isn't true. I'm just dropping you off, and we can leave it at that."

They drove in silence for several minutes. Bea was grateful for the break.

In time she saw Morro Rock in the distance, and the three smoke-stacks that sat at the edge of the bay. She and Herbert had come here once for an anniversary. To get away from the heat, and enjoy the ocean.

"I'll say one thing for you," the girl said, startling Bea. "If you ever do get carjacked, I feel sorry for the guy who tries it. You were really fierce. Threatening to crash the van and kill us both. Wow. Brave."

Bea squirmed within the observation for a moment, feeling her face redden.

"I can be tough when I need to be," she said, knowing even as she said it that it had not been true in the past. Not even the fairly recent past.

———

Bea pulled into one of several gas stations on Morro Bay Boulevard, just off the highway. She didn't need gas. More like directions. But she didn't want to get out of the van and leave this strange intruder alone with everything she owned.

Instead she powered down her window and waited for someone to step out of the mini-mart.

"What are we doing?" the girl asked.

"Trying to find someone who can tell us where the police station is."

"I told you. I can't go to the police."

"That's none of my concern. I said I'd take you to one, and that's what I'm going to do. I won't stay around to see if you go inside or walk the other way, because it's not my business anyway. We're strangers to each other, in case you need reminding. We're about to part ways, and then what you do has no bearing on my life after that."

They fell into awkward silence.

A woman in her forties stepped out of the store and crossed in front of Bea's van.

"Excuse me," Bea called. The woman stopped and looked around. "Do you happen to know if there's a police station around here?"

"It's just the next block that way," the woman said, pointing away from the highway. "Right here on Morro Bay Boulevard."

"Thank you," Bea said, and powered up the window. "You can walk from here," she told the girl.

They sat in silence for a time. Too long a time. The girl had her head bowed, looking down at her own lap. Bea wanted this cord cut now. Not a moment later. The girl was a stranger, and Bea intended to keep it that way. Worse yet, she felt herself dangerously close to the line of having to care.

"Go," Bea said.

The girl sighed and opened the passenger door. Stepped down. She looked back at Bea, her eyes wet with emotion.

"Hurry and close the door before the cat gets out," Bea said.

The girl did as she'd been told.

Bea pulled out onto the boulevard and headed back toward the highway. Between it and her was a traffic roundabout, and Bea swung around it to the right, planning to pick up Highway 1 north, toward Cambria and Big Sur. Now *that* was a pretty stretch of coastline.

She glanced at the girl in her rearview mirror. She was walking along with her head down, clearly not in a hurry to get anywhere. Not surprisingly, she was headed in the opposite direction from the police station.

Bea missed the turn for her highway on-ramp while she was watching, and had to take another full loop around the traffic circle. She saw the girl make a right onto a street called Quintana, because there was nothing directly ahead of her but highway. Nothing suitable to pedestrians.

Bea sighed. She swung a right, then pulled up beside the child. She powered the passenger window down.

"Have you eaten?" she asked.

The girl shook her head.

"Do you have money for something to eat?"

"Nothing. Not a penny."

"What will you do, then?"

To Bea's alarm, the girl dissolved into tears.

"I have no idea," she sobbed.

For an extended moment, they only considered each other. The girl raised one arm as if to wipe her runny nose on her sleeve. To Bea's relief, she thought better of it and just sniffed instead.

"All right, all right. We'll go get some breakfast. I'll pick up the check. But after that you're on your own."

# Chapter Eighteen

*More Fortified Refined Carbohydrates, Please*

While the girl stared at her menu, reading about each and every dish as though she hadn't yet found anything resembling food, Bea stared out the window at her van. She could see just a few inches of the rear bumper from the window of this nondescript coffee shop, or diner, or whatever one wanted to call the place.

She could still feel a jangle of nerves from her morning fright, and somehow she couldn't bring herself to take her eyes off the vehicle.

It had never occurred to Bea before this stranger jumped into her van—which was now also her home—what it would mean to lose it. It's one thing when somebody steals your car. You get a ride home and you figure it out. But if someone stole Bea's van they would get her vehicle, her home, her cat, and everything she owned in the world. Except those cartons she had stored at Opal's. Still, those boxes were full of belongings that held sentimental value but were not especially useful. That's why she'd left them behind.

"Something interesting going on out there?" the girl asked.

Bea had been lost in thought, and the words startled her. She looked around to see the girl craning her neck to discover what Bea was watching.

"No. Not at all. I was just thinking." She turned her full attention to the girl. Pulled her thoughts back into the diner. "I can still feel my nerves from that big scare."

The girl laughed. A rueful sort of laugh.

"What's so funny?" Bea asked.

"I know all about nerves. If you could have seen the trouble I was in right before I met you . . ."

"Why don't you try telling me about that, except slowly this time so I can understand?"

So for the next five minutes or so, while they bided their time until the busy waitress could arrive, the girl held court and told her unlikely story. It was like something straight out of a movie. Or maybe there was no "like" about it. Maybe the girl was borrowing from fiction and calling it her life. There were parents who seemed so honest and normal until the moment they were put in handcuffs. There were hardened delinquent girls in group homes who might come after her with knives for no logical reason. Ladies of the night who tried to lure an innocent young girl, and then, when she proved too virtuous, men who kidnapped her against her will.

And of course the crowning touch was that absolutely none of this was the young girl's fault. All she'd been doing was trying to live a right life.

Bea wasn't buying a word of it.

*You can't scam a scammer,* she thought. As a brand new entry to the world of scammers, she felt like something of an authority.

She almost said it out loud, but just then the harried waitress arrived to take their orders.

Bea ordered fried eggs with bacon, pancakes, and hash browns. The girl only asked for a fruit cup and plain oatmeal.

"No butter, no sugar, no milk," she said, sounding very much her young age. Unlike someone who had lived through the dangerous hell she claimed. "But if you have raisins I'll take some."

The waitress nodded, still jotting on her order pad. Then she peeled away.

"I have to say I'm a bit surprised," Bea said.

"About what?"

"When I said I'd buy you breakfast, frankly I thought you'd order everything on the menu."

"This is all they had that I could eat."

"What on earth are you talking about? They have everything here."

The girl only grunted.

Bea almost asked her name, but stopped herself. *It's like a stray cat,* she thought. *Never name them if you don't intend to keep them.*

Bea's plan had been to let the strange comment about food drop. But she was feeling out of sorts after her upsetting morning, all agitated and restless. So she worried at it out loud, like a dog who can't bring himself to stop tugging on your pant leg.

"What do you eat and what don't you eat that you can look at a menu like that and not be able to choose a dozen things?"

"I don't eat anything that comes from animals," she said, torturing her paper napkin into tight twists. "So breakfast is hard. Because everybody eats eggs and meat for breakfast."

"You're a vegetarian?"

"Vegan."

"I don't know what the difference is."

"You don't need to," the girl said with a sigh. "It doesn't matter. If we were about to keep knowing each other . . . if I was riding somewhere with you, I'd tell you. But you're going to dump me right after breakfast. You already said so. And I know it's true. Know how I know? Because you haven't even asked me my name."

They fell into an awkward silence. Bea felt as though she'd been caught in some kind of wrongdoing, but she shook the feeling away again because she didn't like it and didn't feel she deserved it.

"And you haven't told me yours," the girl continued.

"You could have done the same. You could have introduced yourself and asked my name. That would have been a polite thing to do after a carjacking like the one you just put me through."

The girl opened her mouth to speak, but in that moment the waitress hurried up to their table with a pot of coffee. They fell into silence while she turned Bea's mug upright and poured.

"My name is Allie," the girl said as she watched the waitress retreat. "What's yours?"

"Bea. What's the difference between vegetarian and vegan?"

"A vegan doesn't eat any animal products. No eggs, no dairy. A lot of vegans don't even eat honey. You know. Because of the bees that have to make it. They keep them captive, you know. The bees. To make that honey."

Bea paused from her current activity of stirring a great deal of half-and-half and three sugars into her coffee. "My goodness. Why on earth would anybody want to be *that*?"

The girl—Allie—leveled Bea with a look that seemed surprisingly mature and thoughtful for her age. "You sure you want me to get started on that right before she brings your breakfast?"

"Good point. I guess I don't. But here's what I don't understand, Allie. There are tons of things you can eat for breakfast that aren't from an animal. Waffles, pancakes. French toast. Regular toast."

"Waffles and French toast have eggs in them. And besides, that's all just refined white flour."

"And you don't eat flour because . . ."

"Well, I *could*. But why would I? I ordered fruit and oatmeal. That's food. Why should I have a bunch of bleached white flour instead? There's no nutrition in it. They take out all the nutrients when they refine it. And then they fortify it with vitamins, but it's just like taking a vitamin pill. You might as well pop a daily vitamin and skip all the refined carbs, because they only make you hyper and crash your blood sugar and make you irritable. They don't do your body any good. And the only way they taste like anything is after you slather them with butter and syrup, and butter is from animals and syrup is just pure sugar, and sugar's like the worst thing we could possibly be eating . . ."

The waitress came with their breakfasts just then. Bea looked at her four strips of bacon and her three greasy fried eggs, and the mountain of crispy golden-brown potatoes. And the four pancakes on a separate plate.

"My goodness, that looks *absolutely delicious*," she said to the waitress. But it was really more for the benefit of the girl. "Extra butter and syrup, please."

When she left, Bea offered a dismissive look in the direction of the fruit plate.

"Sorry," Allie said. "But you asked."

———

"If you could think of a place to go . . . ," Bea said, her stomach almost uncomfortably full, ". . . you know . . . someplace where you'd be safe, and they'd take you in . . . I might consider driving you there."

Allie looked up from her fruit cup. She had been meticulously sticking a fork into each piece of cantaloupe and honeydew melon and using her knife to carve away the slightest bit of white or green from the rind edge. Bea had been watching and wondering, but choosing not to comment.

"That's pretty generous of you. Especially since you have no idea where I would say I needed to go. What if it was in the exact opposite direction from where you're going?"

"I can go in any direction I choose."

"Where do you live?"

"That's a bit of a personal question."

"How can it be too personal to ask where you live? People ask each other that all the time."

"You don't tell a stranger where you live. It's like writing your address on your house key and then giving your keys to some stranger who parks cars. It's just not the right way to stay safe in this world. Which, let me tell you, is plenty different from the world I was born into."

Allie performed another minor surgery on a chunk of watermelon and then chewed it thoughtfully. "I didn't ask for your address. I just meant the city. What city do you live in?"

Bea said nothing for a time. Just sat and stared out the window and felt her face redden. The last thing she wanted was to be pressured into telling a relative stranger that she was homeless.

"Okay, fine," Allie said. "Never mind. Nothing is any of my business."

"For decades I lived in the Coachella Valley. Near Indio."

"When did you move?"

"I left about a week ago. Maybe a little more. I think I've lost track of the days by now."

"But you're not headed back there?"

"No. Dear me, no. Too hot."

"Why live there all those years if it's too hot?"

"I had air-conditioning back in those days."

Allie pushed her empty bowl away, took her shredded napkin off her lap, and wiped her mouth politely. At least she had table manners. "Okay, I know where I want to go."

"Good. Where?"

"*Your* house."

"Very funny."

"I'm not kidding. I've got no place."

"Well, my house won't do. I was not inviting you to move in."

"You still haven't told me where you live now."

Bea felt the heat in her face grow and deepen. Her gaze instinctively flickered out the window to the van in the parking lot.

"Oh, I get it," Allie said.

"What do you get?"

"You live in your van. That explains a lot. Like why you have a recliner in there. And a cardboard dresser. And blankets. And your cat and his litter box."

*"Her."*

"Her what?"

"My cat is a she. *Her* litter box."

"Fine. Whatever. She. Wow, we have a lot in common. A week ago you had a regular place to live and now you're out in the world alone. Just like me."

"I think that's where our similarity ends."

"Still seems like a lot for two people to have in common."

The check arrived, and Bea laid a twenty on it, which covered both meals and a small tip. She made no effort to continue the conversation.

"So where were you going before I came along?" Allie asked.

"I thought I'd go north along the coast."

"Fine."

"What's fine?"

"You asked me where I wanted to go. I want to go north along the coast. With you."

"I meant someplace you could jump off."

"Well, give me a chance to find someplace. If you let me come with you for a few days, maybe I could find someplace to be. Maybe I could find some work, or make a friend who would take me in. If you get sick of me, you can put me out anytime."

"Well, I definitely agree to that last part," Bea said.

———

As they walked across the parking lot together, something that had been roiling in Bea's mind found its way to the surface.

"You certainly have an optimistic view of the world for someone who's just been through what you claim."

Allie stopped walking. It took Bea a moment to notice. A few steps later she turned around to see where the child had gone.

"You still don't believe me," Allie said.

"It's quite a story."

"You're not a very trusting type, are you?"

"No. Why should I be?"

"Because lots of people are good. Or that's what I believe anyway."

"Well, I haven't met anyone matching that description recently."

The man with the two blonde girls forced his way into her head, but she pushed him out again. She refused to dwell on the tank of gas he had bought her, because it only complicated her thinking.

"Yes, you have," Allie said. "You've met *me*."

Bea stood a moment, feeling the sun bake down on her scalp at the part of her thin hair. It was making her uncomfortable. Everything was.

"Says you. Are you coming or not? Because, with you or without you, your ride's leaving."

———

Within minutes of driving, the big breakfast and the big ordeal seemed to gang up on the girl and put her to sleep. Her head lolled until it touched the window, then stalled and did not move again.

Bea yawned, suddenly feeling too full-bellied and mentally muddy to drive.

She pulled off into a dirt parking area on the ocean side of Highway 1, just north of a little beach town called Cayucos. There she drew the curtains and settled into her easy chair.

"Why did we stop?" she heard the girl say just as her eyes were closing.

"So you could sleep."

"But you can still drive if you want."

"Your sleepiness was contagious."

"Oh. Sorry."

In time Bea heard her undo her seat belt. She wandered into the open area in the back of the van.

"Mind if I take a couple of those blankets? That metal floor looks hard."

"Whatever you think you need."

Not a minute later the girl was fast asleep again, snoring like a buzz saw. Which kept Bea awake all day. Well, that or the fact that she had already slept all night. Or some combination of the two.

Bea lay awake listening to the snoring, Phyllis on her lap, and formed an interesting idea. Maybe she should keep this pesky kid around. Snoring and weird ideas about food aside, a young girl might prove useful. The only thing better than being an older person in need of assistance was being a minor child in need. And yet strangers would perceive her as traveling with her grandmother and so would not literally take her away and try to reunite her with family.

*Yes, let's move into an era where the girl does all the scamming,* Bea thought. *It's the least she can do in return for the ride and the shelter.*

It felt like a relief. It felt good to watch that awful job lift off her shoulders.

"We'll have the little girl do the icky stuff," she said out loud to Phyllis.

The cat raised her head, yawned, and dug her claws deeply into Bea's thighs. Then she stretched and jumped down off Bea's lap. She sauntered over to the sleeping girl and made herself comfortable on the rising and falling landscape of Allie's belly.

Bea took more than a little umbrage at that. But it doesn't pay to argue with a cat.

# Chapter Nineteen

### It's Called Work. Have You Heard of It?

"What is this little town?" Allie asked as they pulled off the two-lane highway.

The girl was still rubbing her hip, which—she had several times said—hurt from sleeping on hard corrugated metal. Bea thought it was a bit overdramatic of her.

*Try sleeping on the side of the road on rocks and dirt, out in the weather. Show a little gratefulness. And it's your own fault for rolling over onto your side. The cat wasn't very happy about it, either.*

"This is Cambria," Bea said.

She turned onto the Main Street of the little town. There was a gas station. Bea had seen it from the highway. But as she pulled closer she was shocked by the prices she saw on its sign.

"Holy moly," she breathed out loud. "I should have filled up farther back down the coast."

"Yeah, you should have," the girl said, in a flat tone that sounded too authoritative and struck Bea as unwelcome. "And when you get up the coast around Big Sur, it's only going to get worse."

"I thought you didn't know this area very well."

"I know it's remote. I know more remote means more expensive."

Bea said nothing in reply. Just cruised a bit farther down the street, past quaint diners, a little live theater, and more antique stores and real estate offices than she could have counted. She saw another gas station on the right, much smaller. A little store with one line of pumps out front. The prices were not great, but they were a few cents better.

Bea pulled up to the pumps.

"What time is it?" the girl asked.

Bea peered closely at her watch. She had been keeping her reading glasses in her pocket at all times, but she didn't bother to reach for them. If she ever lost them she would need a watch with a bigger face. No more giant clock over the stove as she'd had at . . .

She couldn't bring herself to think the word *home*. Couldn't even form it in her head. It stung.

"Nearly seven in the evening."

"I thought it looked like the sun was almost getting ready to go down. Boy, that day went fast, huh?"

Bea opened her mouth to say "Yes, they always do when you sleep them away."

Before she could, Allie jumped out and slammed the door, without the courtesy of saying why. Bea watched her walk into the store, thinking it would have been nice if Allie had offered to pump the gas.

Maybe the girl was off in search of a restroom.

Bea found herself wondering if she would get stuck providing another meal for them both. Probably. What else could she do? She couldn't just eat in front of the child while the little girl starved. Still, just what she didn't need was another mouth to feed.

"If I'd ever wanted children, I would have had some," she grumbled out loud as she stepped down from the van and began to pump her own gas.

—

A good ten minutes passed. Still Allie had not come out.

Bea had grown tired of waiting, and the aggravation was making her feel surly.

She stepped out of the van again and stuck her head into the store. Nothing.

No Allie. Nobody behind the counter. Just a few rows of grocery items, with a mountain of sealed cartons in between, as if a big delivery had just arrived. And there was a deli case with fried chicken and a few other treats. It actually smelled quite good, but Bea decided not to stay and have any. Because the prospect of free gas was far more enticing.

She pulled her head back out, hopped into the van—suddenly spry for her age—and started it up. She drove down a couple of doors and parked in the parking lot of an empty building with a sign that offered it for sale.

She walked back to the store and looked in again.

This time she saw Allie. She was with a woman who must have been a clerk at the little store, or owned it. They appeared to be working. Picking up the cartons one by one and moving them into a back room, maybe a storeroom of sorts, where they stayed away for a surprising length of time.

When they appeared again, Bea made a hissing sound in the girl's direction. Both Allie and the store woman looked her way.

She was an older woman, maybe ten years younger than Bea, or maybe closer in age than that, but tanned and sturdy. It always irritated Bea when women of a similar age to her own were fit and able.

"Bunch of showoffs," is what she and Opal had used to say.

"Go see what your grandma wants," the woman said to Allie.

Allie set down the carton she was holding and walked down the aisle toward Bea.

Bea almost said "I'm no relation to this little beggar." It almost slipped from her mouth before she could think the thing through.

"What are you doing?" she asked the girl in a terse whisper.

"Working."

"Working? What on earth for?"

"It's what people do when they need money."

"She offered you money?"

"Well. Sort of. After she let me use her bathroom I offered to help because she said her afternoon girl called in sick. I just offered to be nice, you know? But then she said if I was really willing to do the whole thing with her she'd pay me."

"How much?"

"She didn't say."

"Rookie mistake. Always find out how much up front."

"Who cares? It'll be more than I had to begin with. It'll be more than I've had since I got dragged out of my house. And then we can go eat and you won't have to spend your money on me."

"Well, I like the sound of *that*. Bring some of that fried chicken. It smells good."

"Ick," Allie said, and wrinkled her lightly freckled nose.

"I didn't say you had to eat it. I said bring some so *I* can eat it."

"Fine. Whatever. Will you just be patient a little longer while I finish? And not drive off without me?"

"You're lucky I have my mouth all set for that chicken now. I'll wait for *that*."

The girl sighed and turned away.

———

Bea found a spot on a corner, about two blocks from her van, with a suitable storm drain. There she waited for a target. Someone not only with an expensive cell phone, but clearly enough wealth to purchase another.

It didn't take long.

A family of three strolled by, a mother and father with a little girl who looked no older than ten or eleven. Granted, Bea was finding it harder to judge, and thought they all looked younger than they probably were.

And *the little girl* was staring at one of those modern phones as she walked, unheeding of what she might plow into.

Now why on earth would a girl that age need such a fancy phone? Bea could almost imagine that grown-ups and their phones had some larger purpose. Keeping in touch with work or not missing a call from the nanny. But a *child*?

"Excuse me," she called.

The family stopped immediately and stared at Bea.

"I'm sorry to bother you, but my granddaughter and I . . . my granddaughter just went into that little store down the street to use the restroom . . . we were supposed to meet her mother here, and it's getting late, and we have no idea where she is. I wanted to try calling her cell phone, but, well . . . you can never find a pay phone anymore. Used to be there was a pay phone on every corner, but the world is changing so fast . . ."

"Right," the mother said. "Everybody has a cell phone now."

Before Bea could say more, the little girl moved in Bea's direction, the phone extended in her hand.

"You can call her on my phone."

"That's very sweet of you, honey," Bea said in her best grandmotherly tone.

Meanwhile she was thinking, *Damn you for being nice. I hate it when the people I'm about to scam turn out to be nice.*

Bea almost aborted the plan. But the little girl had handed her the phone. And Bea had no idea how to fake a phone call. She didn't even know enough about using the phone to pretend. If she let on that she knew nothing, some member of the little family would take it from her and ask for the number she wanted to call, and then what? Bea could make a number up, but a real person might answer.

No, she felt she had no choice but to move forward.

She turned away from the family and slid the phone into the inside pocket of her big, loose jacket. There she had stashed her reading glasses, which she pulled out and placed on her face, as if to peer at the phone. But it was only her bare hand at which she was staring.

That was the trick, Bea had found. Probably the hand-in-the-pocket motion could be seen from behind—though she'd gotten away with it that first time—so Bea was careful to come out of her pocket with reading glasses to explain the motion. Also she was careful to hold her hand as though the phone was still in it.

She pantomimed the drop.

Just as she was reaching down desperately for the invisible phone, she looked up to see Allie standing not five feet in front of her, holding a brown paper bag and looking suspicious and notably unhappy.

There was no time to be distracted, but Bea did feel her face redden with something like shame.

"Oh no!" Bea cried, and turned back to face the family. "I'm so sorry! I dropped it. I didn't mean to drop it. I feel just terrible."

For good measure, Bea sank to her sore and creaky knees on the grate of the drain and placed her hands, fingers spread wide, on its iron surface. She stared down at close range, as if anxious to somehow undo her error.

A moment later she felt a small presence by her side. It was the owner of the phone. The little girl. She placed a hand on Bea's shoulder as if to comfort her.

"I can't tell you how bad I feel," Bea said, her voice just a soft breath of air.

"It's okay. My parents will buy me a new one."

*Right,* Bea thought with a sigh of relief. *If it's not that they're awful people I'm stealing from, it's the fact that they can well afford the loss. I remember now how I make this work.*

"I still feel just awful. I'd pay for it if I could, but I don't have very much money."

"Don't worry," the girl said. "We always get that insurance thing with a new phone."

"You can get insurance on a phone?"

"Oh yeah. I lose them a lot, so my folks always get that. Then if you lose the phone, or break it, or somebody steals it, you get another one pretty cheap."

"Well, that's good to know, but I still feel terrible."

Bea raised her gaze, careful to avoid the eyes of Allie, who still stood close by holding what Bea hoped was her fried chicken dinner. She turned to face the parents, who hovered closer now, looking more than a little distressed.

"I feel awful about this," Bea said. "If I could afford it I would pay you for it."

The mother eked out a smile, but it looked forced. "We're used to it. She loses two or three a year. But now how will you make your phone call?"

"Oh, don't worry about me. I'll walk down to that little market and ask the clerk if I can borrow their phone. Seems the only ones I can be trusted with are the ones attached by a cord to a wall."

"No phones are attached to the wall with a cord," the little girl said. "Well, maybe the base, but not the part you'll be holding."

Bea started to say her phone at home was. But she felt ashamed to admit that she could not follow the changes outside her own tiny world. And besides, it hurt to think about the trailer, with its understandable telephone, and its bathroom and refrigerator and electric lights. And anyway the family was walking away down the street.

The little girl looked back over her shoulder and waved at Bea. Bea waved in return.

Then Bea did what she had been dreading. She turned around and faced Allie, who at least had been smart enough to keep her mouth shut while that little endeavor played out.

"Thank you," Bea said.

Allie held the bag out in Bea's direction. It smelled wonderfully of greasy fried chicken. Once Bea had taken it from her, Allie turned and marched toward the van without a word spoken.

———

They stopped at a little restaurant that served salads and smoothies, and ate outside, Bea with her fried chicken, Allie with her bird food. All fruits and vegetables.

Still Allie never said a word.

———

Bea made a right onto Highway 1, the coastal route, going north.

She felt self-conscious and uncomfortable because Allie still had not spoken to her.

"How much did that woman pay you?" she asked.

At first, nothing. In her mind, Bea rolled around the idea that Allie might be so upset as to never speak to her again. Which meant her anticipated retirement would never come to be.

"Ten dollars," Allie said after a time. Still she stared out the window as she spoke, her head turned to the right, away from Bea.

"That doesn't seem like very much."

"It was like twenty-five minutes' worth of work. That's more than twenty dollars an hour. That's good."

"Well, I suppose if you want to look at it that way."

"And she threw in the fried chicken for free. I told her it was for my grandmother."

"Just so long as you know I'm not really related to you and you don't forget it."

"Oh, don't worry about that. You're not so much the grandmother type. Oh my gosh! Zebras!"

"What on earth are you babbling about?" Bea asked, not attempting to hide her irritation.

She looked in the direction the girl was pointing. On the right side of the highway—the non-ocean side—behind barbed wire fencing, cattle grazed in the fields of tan grasses. Among them Bea saw a dozen zebras grazing in the orangey light of the sunset.

Bea would have assumed her eyes were playing tricks on her if Allie hadn't just called the animals out by name. Besides, there were three cars stopped, their occupants walking to the fence or leaning on fence posts, snapping pictures and staring.

She pulled the van over into the dirt and parked near the other cars.

Allie jumped out and jogged to the fence.

Bea sat in the driver's seat, her knuckles white on the steering wheel. She could just put the van back into "Drive" and pull away. Maybe she should. The girl was talking to a couple of families. Bea wouldn't be abandoning her. Well, not exactly. Well, yes, she'd be abandoning her, of course she would, but at least she'd be dumping her in a spot where someone else could give her a ride.

*Let her be somebody else's problem now,* Bea thought. *The last thing I need is someone looking over my shoulder and judging.*

She reached her hand up to the gearshift, then dropped it again. If she left, she would never learn why there were zebras grazing in a field with the cattle. And now she felt quite curious about that.

A moment later Allie jogged back to the van and jumped in, and Bea shifted into "Drive" and pulled back out onto the highway. She vaguely recalled the highway north of San Simeon. The Big Sur coast. It was winding and narrow and full of tight hairpin turns, rising hundreds of feet above the ocean, with few guardrails. She felt a surge of fear at the mental image of driving it after dark.

"So what was the story with the zebras?" she asked the girl. "Were you able to find out?"

"Yeah, I did. All those people were tourists like us, but one family was just on a Hearst Castle tour today. The tour guide told them about it. William Randolph Hearst used to own all this property, and he had this big castle up high on a hill, and he had famous guests there, and he was really rich. This was like in the nineteen twenties and nineteen thirties. He had this private zoo. Most of the animals are gone now, but the zebras survived all this time and bred and lived with the cows like they belonged here. They're leftovers from the Hearst zoo."

"I see," Bea said.

"You know who he was? I studied him in school."

"Yes, I'm familiar."

"See? There's the castle right up there."

Allie pointed up to a distant hilltop on their right. The castle was a cluster of white buildings, with turrets like bell towers on the big main structure, and palm trees all around.

"Oh my, yes. I can see it. I think I've seen pictures of it in books. Or maybe there was something about it on TV."

They drove in silence for a moment or two.

"What will you do with the phone?" Allie asked.

Bea was startled by the change in conversational direction. It took her a moment to pull herself together to answer. Also to decide how much information to share with her new passenger.

"I took the first one to a pawnshop. But I think that last town was too small to have one. So I'll try when we get to Monterey. If there's nothing there, San Francisco for sure."

A long silence.

"Pull over here," Allie said.

"More zebras?"

Bea craned her neck to the right and pulled off onto the scant shoulder in the fading light. She saw no zebras.

Allie jumped out.

"What are you doing?" Bea asked.

"Leaving. Walking back to Cambria. I think I might be better off with the lady in the store."

"That's ridiculous. Get back in here right now. You're out in the middle of nowhere. There's nothing ahead of you for dozens of miles and it's a couple of miles at least back to Cambria."

"I'm not in the middle of nowhere. I'm a couple of miles north of Cambria. I can walk a couple of miles. I've done it before."

"It's getting dark."

"I don't care. It's not that far."

"Where will you sleep?"

"I'll ask that nice lady at the store if I can stay with her. Besides. What do you care? I'm not your problem. Remember?"

*That's true,* Bea thought. It came as a relief to shake this new set of troubles off her shoulders.

"Close the door," Bea said. "Before you let the cat out."

The resulting slam made her wince.

Bea pulled back into the northbound lane and continued her drive up the coast. She did not look back.

# Chapter Twenty

## Too Many Comments from the Cat

"It's beautiful here, isn't it?" Bea asked Phyllis.

The cat looked up from her plate of canned food. Looked right into Bea's eyes. Bea could swear she saw some kind of feedback there—a slightly critical assessment.

It was the third time Bea had told the cat that their current location was beautiful. This was what Bea's father had used to call whistling past the graveyard, because actually she found the place a bit spooky. Still, it was rude of the cat to point that out.

"Well, it *is* beautiful."

Phyllis returned her attention to her dinner.

Bea stepped out of the van and walked around to the passenger door, where she removed the litter box from the floor. She reached under the seat and felt around until she found the scoop. Then she walked the box over to the trash can that sat in a corner of the dirt parking lot overlooking the ocean. As best she could figure she was somewhere between San Simeon and the Big Sur coast.

As she scooped, she looked north up the coastline. It was almost completely dark now, and the place had a deserted feel. She could see the mountains of Big Sur—the place where the highway rose to hang terrifyingly at the edges of cliffs hundreds of feet above the sea. Yes, there were cars going by at fairly regular intervals. But nobody seemed to want to stop anywhere along this stretch of road except Bea. Perhaps they knew something she didn't?

A horrible sound caused her to drop the litter box, scattering nearly half the mostly clean litter. It was a sound Bea never could have described. Like the roar or snort of some kind of wild animal, but with a strange echoing resonance. It was unlike anything she had ever heard before and seemed to defy classification.

She picked up the litter box again and ran—as best Bea could run at her age—back to the van. There she fairly threw the box and scoop in ahead of her, then locked herself inside with shaking hands.

The sound seemed to be coming from the ocean, which was a good twenty feet down from the bluff. In time she saw the shape of something like a huge seal—or walrus, or some such thing—in a thin stream of moonlight. Well, it had no tusks, so of course it was not a walrus, but it seemed altogether different from a seal. It tipped its head back and released another strange echoing snort. It sported a bizarre profile to its head, like its nose was ten times too bulbous and large.

Bea reached for the key to start up the van, then dropped her hand again. She didn't want to go back to Cambria, because the girl was there. Or anyway, she likely would be there by now. Bea didn't want to seem to be checking up on the kid. Even more to the point, she didn't want to leave herself open to any more criticism from the little know-it-all. Besides, wasn't it hard enough just to take care of herself? What did she have left over to offer to anyone?

She didn't want to go north, because she was terrified of that next piece of highway.

It was an interesting phenomenon, her sudden terror of that road. When she and that girl had begun driving north from the zebra sighting, Bea had been only uncomfortable at the thought of driving that narrow, winding stretch of dangerous highway. A minute later it had paralyzed her to the point of forcing her to stop the van.

She looked at Phyllis, who looked back. The cat's ears were laid back, listening to the strange sea monster noises.

"It's in the ocean," Bea said. "It can't get to us up here."

And with that, Bea felt a little more comfortable herself.

She looked into the cat's perturbed face and wondered something. Was it possible that the highway ahead of her had grown scarier the moment that girl stepped out of her van? Because now Bea would be driving it alone?

"That's ridiculous," she said to the cat, who cautiously returned to eating.

———

Bea startled awake in her easy chair, unaware that she had ever fallen asleep. She winced into a bright light. Someone was shining their headlights into her van. And she was all alone out here with no way to defend herself.

She fumbled her keys out of the pocket of her slacks and ducked under the curtain to the driver's seat, where she attempted to find the ignition. Suddenly there was light in her eyes. She turned to see a male figure standing just outside her window. He was shining a flashlight in her face. Bea's heart stopped, though thankfully only for a beat or two. Then it hammered its way back into the living.

The man reached up with one hand—the one that was not training a flashlight on her—and rapped on her window with the backs of his knuckles.

"Highway Patrol, ma'am."

Bea gasped air and tried to calm herself. With absurdly trembling hands she placed the key in the ignition, turned it to accessory power, and lowered the window.

"You startled me."

"Sorry, ma'am. Didn't mean to do that." He angled the flashlight so that Bea did not have to blink into it like a terrified deer crossing the highway. "But there's no camping or overnight parking anywhere along this stretch of road."

"Oh, I wasn't camping." Bea could hear her voice shake, and wondered if the officer could hear it, too. "I was headed north and I was a bit tired. And it's such a . . . well, it's a dicey piece of road ahead of me. I just thought I should stop and take a little break."

"Okay, I understand. But in about fifteen minutes you'll be within the hours that are considered overnight camping. There's a fine for violations. So you'll need to be somewhere else now. If you're tired, it might be best not to drive the road north of here at night. I'm not saying people don't do it. Plenty do. There's no law against it. But mostly it's the folks who know that road well and feel pretty confident on it. If you're at all sleepy and you have any reservations about the drive, I'd stay somewhere tonight and tackle it in the light of morning."

They fell silent for a moment. Bea was aware of that strange animal sound again. That rolling, echoing snort.

"What on earth is that beast I keep hearing?" Bea asked the officer.

"Elephant seal. This is their territory, right along this stretch of coast."

"I see. So I should go back to Cambria, then."

"Might be a good idea. They have lots of nice little motels and inns, and you could get a good night's sleep and be safer on that road in broad daylight."

"Thank you, Officer," she said, and started up the van.

*Especially thank you for telling me before I got stuck with a citation,* she thought. *Because right now just affording food and gas is plenty challenging enough.*

———

"I have to at least check," Bea said out loud as she drove along the dark and deserted Main Street of Cambria. Ostensibly she was speaking to the cat, but the cat was nowhere to be seen, so it fell along the borderline of talking to herself.

She drew close to the little market with the gas pumps out front. She would just shine her headlights in the direction of the door. If the girl was not there, then she must have found lodging with someone. And so that would be that. Bea could wash her hands of the situation once and for all.

She swung the van to the right to aim her headlights at the door.

In the beams of illumination, a limp and bedraggled Allie sat with her back up against the door of the closed shop. She winced into the light and threw a hand up to protect her eyes.

Bea yanked the steering wheel left and drew parallel to the door where the girl sat. She pulled just beyond the first gas pump and powered down the passenger window. Allie blinked at her in the soft light of a streetlamp.

"She wouldn't take you in, huh?" Bea called.

"She'd already closed up the store and gone home by the time I got back here."

"Yes, it was a longer walk than we thought, wasn't it? I noted that on the drive back."

"You're telling *me*. I just walked it." She sounded as though she had been crying.

*Damn,* Bea thought. *Now I have to feel bad for her again.*

"Well," Bea said, her voice hardening over with self-protection, "you see that little parking lot two doors down? The one in front of the building that's for sale?"

"Where you were parked before."

"Right. That's where Phyllis and I will be tonight."

Allie blinked at her in silence for a beat or two.

"Who's Phyllis?"

"My cat. Who else could it be?"

"You named your cat Phyllis? Why did you name your cat Phyllis?"

"I think we're getting off on a tangent," Bea said, her voice rising with irritation. "All I'm trying to say is where we'll be. You know. If you get cold or scared or something."

A long silence.

Then Allie said, "Thank you."

Bea powered up the window and drove on.

———

Bea had no idea how much time had elapsed before the girl came around and knocked her tiny knock. She had been blissfully asleep.

She stumbled up and opened the back doors. They stood a moment, considering each other as best they could in the dark.

"Cold?" Bea asked with the slightest prickle in her tone. "Or lonely?"

"Both," Allie said in a pathetically small voice.

Bea stepped back, and the girl came in without further comment. She walked straight to the blankets that sat folded in the rear corner of the van and laid them out on the hard corrugated metal of the van floor. She settled herself, still without speaking.

Bea lay awake in silence for a time, unsure of whether she felt the need to explain herself or not.

"This is all because of my getting robbed," Bea said. "Before that I never took from anyone, not in my whole life. Then somebody stole all the money in my bank account and I was homeless. What was I supposed to do? I need to eat. I need gas. Everybody has to live, and so what was I supposed to do?"

A long silence. Long enough that Bea began to think Allie would never answer. Or maybe the girl had already fallen asleep.

"Some people hold up a sign that says they need gas or food. You know. They ask for money instead of just taking from people."

"You must be joking! I would never! How absolutely humiliating!"

Another long, freighted silence.

"So what you're saying is . . . it's all about your pride? You'd rather steal a phone from a little girl than be embarrassed?"

Bea felt her face redden. She felt flummoxed, almost unable to speak. She struggled to open her mouth, though she was unsure what would come out of it when she did.

Before she could manage any words, Allie spoke again.

"No, never mind. I'm sorry I said any of that. I wouldn't even have brought it up again. It's just that you sort of asked. But it's none of my business. You're letting me sleep here again, so I need to shut up. I'm sorry. I have no right to judge you. Thank you for letting me sleep here tonight."

Bea took several seconds to straighten herself out inside.

Then she said, simply, "You're welcome."

No more words were spoken for a time. In fact, Bea assumed they were done speaking for the night.

When Allie spoke again, it made her jump.

"So why did you name your cat Phyllis?"

"Why not? What's wrong with the name Phyllis for a cat?"

"Well, it's unusual. But I didn't say there was anything wrong with it. It must have come from somewhere."

Bea sighed deeply.

"It was nothing. It's silly. It was just a TV show I used to like."

"What was the name of the show?"

*"Phyllis."*

"I never heard of it."

"It was long before you were born. It was a spin-off series starring a character from *The Mary Tyler Moore Show*."

"I know *Mary Tyler Moore*. But I never heard of *Phyllis*."

"It's not important. I don't even know why we're talking about it. It just made me laugh. I used to enjoy that half hour, when that show was on TV. Not a lot of things make me laugh. For that one half hour a week, I was happy." She paused, listening to those words as they reverberated throughout the van. They sounded hopelessly silly and sad. "I don't know if other people have that. Some foolish little thing like that, something that makes them feel everything's okay. That makes them feel happy."

"Sure," Allie said.

"Really?"

"Yeah. I think everybody has something that takes them away for a little while, and then they feel good."

A long pause. Bea felt disinclined to say more on the subject.

"Happy isn't all that easy," Allie said. "People talk about it like it is. People throw the word *happy* around like it's the most natural thing in the world. Like if nothing is dragging you down from it, you'll pop right up and be happy without even trying. But it was never that way for me."

"No," Bea said. "It was never that way for me, either."

———

When Bea opened her eyes again, it was morning. Fully light.

Allie was sitting up, petting the cat and staring into Bea's face.

"Why are you looking at me like that?" she asked the girl.

"I know where I want you to take me."

"Up the coast, you said."

"I need to change my mind. I mean, if I still get to."

"Remains to be seen. Where do you want to go?"

"My house."

Bea sat up, pulling the lever that raised her chair into its upright position.

"You have a house? Why on earth would you be here if you have a house you can go to?"

"I can't live in it. The IRS slapped padlocks on it. The neighbors would notice if anyone was living in it. They'd probably report me or something. But I could get in. It's my house and I know how to get in. I know which windows usually aren't locked and if they're locked for some reason I could even break a window and get in. I doubt the alarm is on. I don't see how it could be, and even if it is on for some reason, I know the code."

"And what do we gain by going there?"

Allie held her arms wide as if to indicate herself and her immediate surroundings.

"Not sure if you've noticed, but I've got nothing here. I don't even own a toothbrush or a change of underwear. I could get clothes. I could get cash. I have some cash in a piggy bank from when my grandparents used to give me birthday and Christmas money. And so long as you're going to a pawnshop, I have stuff we can pawn. I have a MacBook, and an iPhone 6, and an iPad. And even a little bit of jewelry."

"I don't know any of those things you just said. Except for the jewelry. And I know what an iPhone 6 looks like, but I still find it all confusing."

"Electronics. Expensive toys. Stuff that's worth money. That's all you need to know, right? Then we could eat. Then we'll know what to do for food and gas."

"We?"

Bea couldn't help being mildly affronted that this girl had called them a "we." As if she had just assumed she could stay on with Bea, when no such invitation had been extended.

Then again, if someone was inclined to attach herself to Bea for the scant shelter she owned, wouldn't it be nice if it was someone with food and gas money? That sounded most appealing indeed. Like a vast relief. A rest.

"Well . . . yeah," Allie said. "I mean, if you're willing to share your van, then I'm willing to share my money. That's only fair."

"Then . . . on to your house," Bea said.

# PART FOUR

ALLIE

# Chapter Twenty-One

## The True Value of Canned Garbanzo Beans

Allie rubbed the lumps on her head as they drove south again. Slowly, gingerly rubbed them. As though the touch of her hand could draw the pain away. As though anything could.

There was the lump above her left temple. That was where she had hit her head on the window when that awful man threw her into the backseat of his car. And there was the painful egg on the right, near the back, where this crazy old woman had thrown her against the side of the van by swerving. Because she'd thought Allie was carjacking her.

She could still feel the shopworn dregs of the trembling. Deep in her thighs, and in that low place in her gut that would first feel nausea if she had eaten something bad. It was a sickening location that felt so integrally part of Allie that maybe nothing that lived there could ever be fully expelled.

Such a close scrape with the worst outcomes the world had in store for a lost girl.

She wondered if her parents had been told yet that she had run away. Probably. She should call them. Let them know she was okay. But she had no idea how. She didn't even know where they were being held.

"What's with your head?" Bea asked her, interrupting those thoughts.

First, Allie said nothing. She just waited. She thought it went without saying. Apparently she was wrong.

"Bumped it."

"On what?"

"The car window when that guy was kidnapping me. And the side of your van when you thought I was a carjacker."

"Oh. Right. Sorry."

"I guess it was an honest mistake," Allie said.

The use of the word "honest" seemed to stop everything in its tracks.

They didn't speak for several miles. The cat climbed up into her lap, and Allie stroked her rough, dry fur. The purring felt good to Allie. It eased the trembling some.

"I owe you another apology," Allie said suddenly. But not to the cat.

She had been aware of her own thinking, of course. But she had not known she was about to say anything out loud.

"For what?"

"I think I've had some unfair thoughts about honesty."

For a minute that statement just sat there, and no one cared to comment. There was no sound but that of the tires on the road, and the cat purring. But sooner or later Allie would need to elaborate.

"The girl who got me in all this trouble . . . Well, not all of it, I guess. I was in trouble when I met her. But anyway, she's the one who brought me to that awful place. That house where I got sold for saying no to . . . her . . . whatever he is. I'm getting off track. There was this girl, and she said I was really super naïve. I kind of took offense to it. I thought it wasn't true, or anyway that I wasn't as bad as she was saying. But now I think she was right. I didn't know anything about the world until I got thrown out into it all of a sudden. So I had these ideas, but they were childish ideas, I guess. They'd never really been put to the test. Like a real-world test. You know what I mean?"

"I wish I could say I do," Bea said. "No offense, sometimes you just go on and on and I can't make any sense of it."

"Sorry. I'll try to be clearer. I lived all my life with these parents. My parents. They pretty much gave me everything I needed and most of what I wanted. So then here I am going around saying you shouldn't steal. You shouldn't take anything that doesn't belong to you. But maybe I have no right to say that, because I never needed anything. I was thinking about what you said. About how everybody needs to live. Like, if a person has no food to eat, and no way to honestly get it. He's going to take the food. You can't blame him for that. He can't be expected to voluntarily die just because the world doesn't care enough about him to make sure he at least has enough to eat. You don't try to shove thoughts about honesty at a person at a time like that, because the whole world is dishonest. The way it's set up. And it's not his fault."

A silence. Allie was unclear on how her speech was being received. Maybe she was just a spoiled girl and even admitting so hadn't let her off the hook. Maybe she was so sheltered that even her admission of being sheltered was that of a sheltered child, but in some way she was unable to see.

"So . . . ," Bea began. She sounded cautious. "Let's say you were starving. You were going to die any day of starvation. Would you go into a supermarket and steal a can of tuna?"

"I'm a vegan."

"Nobody's a vegan when they're starving."

"That's not true at all. When you don't eat meat for a long time your body can't just digest it again all of a sudden. I wouldn't steal a can of tuna just so I could throw it up all over the sidewalk. That would be a huge waste."

A sigh from the driver's seat.

"Okay, fine. So what do they have cans of at the supermarket? That you could eat?"

"Oh, I don't know. Maybe . . . garbanzo beans?"

"Fine. Would you steal a can?"

Allie sat with that for half a mile or so. She knew, but she wanted to be sure before saying it out loud. Everything was changing now. Life was revealing itself to her, and she was revealing herself to life. She had to be clear on who she was proving herself to be.

"Yes," she said firmly. "I would steal it."

"So everybody's principles are negotiable. Even yours."

"No. Not negotiable. I don't see it that way at all. It's more a matter of what's really right. I thought right and wrong were completely black and white, but they're not. It's not that I'd be starving, so I'd do the wrong thing. It's that right and wrong would be different than I thought, because we're talking about a person's life. My life is more important than a can of garbanzo beans. And not just because it's *my* life, either. Any life is important. Some things are just more important than others."

"But you're not starving now," Bea said. "And you're willing to go through your house and steal electronic items that rightfully belong to the IRS."

Allie felt herself bristle slightly inside.

"Those things are mine."

"Not really. Your parents bought them for you with money they should have paid to the government."

"Not every penny. They owe the government some money. Yeah. The IRS'll sell the boat, and maybe even the house. But then that'll probably be enough. They don't need to sell every little item we own. It's not that big a debt."

"But you really have no idea how much they owe."

"No," Allie said. "I guess I don't."

Another mile or two passed in silence. Allie took to rubbing the lumps on her head again. This conversation was making her stomach hurt.

"I'm not trying to discourage you," Bea said, and it made Allie jump. "I want nothing more than to be riding with someone who has cash. I'm all on board with that. So take the electronics, by all means. I'm only trying to discourage you from acting like you're better than I am."

Allie sighed. How long would she be riding with this woman? Surely not until she was eighteen. Somehow there had to be a plan. Something beyond this. But Allie didn't have one. So she turned her thoughts back to the conversation at hand.

"I'll try not to do that so much anymore. Tell you what. If I'm wrong, and my family owes the IRS the money from every single thing we own, then whenever I can, when I have enough money to do it, I'll pay the IRS for the stuff I took. I'll just send it in. You know. Anonymously."

"Oh, you'll do no such thing," Bea said, sounding irritated. "Everybody says things like that. But then life goes on. You'll forget."

Allie opened her mouth to say it wasn't true. That she would never forget. Never renege on that commitment. But Bea interrupted her thoughts before Allie managed to get any words out.

"Oh, never mind. Forget I mentioned it. *You* really *would* remember. I just realized that. How depressing."

They rode most of the rest of the way to Southern California in silence.

———

Just as the Ventura Freeway began to back up going through the San Fernando Valley, as traffic slowed to a crawl, Allie voiced something.

Something that felt big. Something that had been sitting in her head and chest for a long time, but without words.

It seemed Allie had missed the moment when the thoughts and feelings forged themselves into words. Instead she simply heard the words as they came out of her mouth and thought, *Right. There it is. That's what's been rattling around in there, all right.*

"I keep thinking about the girls who didn't get away."

"From that man, you mean?"

"I wish I only meant that. But I guess I mean from that man and all the other men like him."

"That's a lot for a girl your age to have to think about."

"How can I not, though? It could have been me. I got away because the bathroom door was heavy and it had metal on it. And because he was standing too close to it. And because it hit him just right so it rattled his brain and he couldn't get up right away. It was just luck. It wasn't that I'm smarter than those other girls, or braver. Just lucky. What really bothers me is that I knew there was such a thing. I knew girls got caught up in . . . what my teacher called 'human trafficking.' And I hated it. I thought it was terrible. But I didn't feel like I just *had* to try to do something about it. Until it almost happened to me. Why are we like that? Why do we not care enough about things until they happen to us?"

"I have no idea," Bea said. "Maybe because if we cared that much about everything, all the time, all at the same time like that, we'd die of exhaustion. We'd have no time or energy left to run our own lives."

"Maybe." But, truthfully, it sounded like a lame excuse.

"I don't know what you can do for them."

"Neither do I."

But at some point in her life, Allie now knew, she would have to find a better answer than that. Because it's so much harder to ignore something that almost happened to you.

"Then there are the girls like my friend Jasmine. Or I thought she was my friend, anyway. Nobody kidnapped her exactly. But she stays with that guy on purpose. He hits her and makes her work selling herself out on the street, and she keeps going back. She could have stayed in the group home, but she ran away and went back with him. Why?"

"Lots of women stay with men who abuse them."

"Yeah, but why?"

"I'm not the world's foremost expert on human nature. But I'd guess those women are looking for something. Something they never got. Something they figure they need. Maybe this man convinces them he has what they're looking for."

Allie shivered, remembering a moment when it had almost worked on her. *We'll get you the best meal of your life. Tell me what else you need to be happy, and I'll buy it for you.*

"And those men know exactly what they're doing when they take advantage," Allie said.

"I'm sure I wouldn't know about that."

But it didn't matter to Allie. She didn't need to have that thinking confirmed. It hadn't been a question in any way.

———

Allie stared up at her own house. Home. It filled her with an unexpected sense of dread. As if it had always been a place of great danger, but she hadn't known it. But she knew it now.

In fact, it didn't look like home anymore. It looked completely familiar. But it did not feel welcoming in any way.

"My goodness," Bea said. "You really did have everything, didn't you?"

It felt strange to hear the assessment of her home through Bea's eyes. Truthfully, she had gone to school with kids who had everything she'd had and much more. She had not felt the slightest bit advantaged at the time.

"Don't take this the wrong way," Allie said, "but you can't park here while I'm inside. You need to just drop me. And then . . . I don't know. Go around the block, I guess. I mean, you have to come back for me. But we have a neighborhood watch thing going on around here. And this van sort of . . . stands out."

A long silence. Allie could feel it crackle with subtext.

"You act like I don't know my station in the world," Bea said, her voice crisp and tight.

"I didn't mean it like that. I just don't want us getting reported. I don't want to get caught. I want to get some stuff and get out of here. That's all."

"Fine. I get it. Just go. Phyllis and I will give you five or ten minutes and then drive by."

But still she sounded more than a little affronted.

———

Allie let herself into the backyard via the side gate.

The pool sat uncovered, crispy-looking brown leaves floating on its surface. At one of its concrete sides, near the lounge chairs, three inflatable pool mattresses lay stacked one on top of the other.

"Perfect!" Allie hissed out loud.

She ran to them and grabbed one, opening the two inflation tubes and squeezing the air out.

*No more hard metal van floor under my hip,* she thought as she rolled it up tightly and left it by the gate.

She circled the back of the house, trying windows. The kitchen. The dining room. The den.

All locked.

Allie sighed. She had hoped to get in and get out without leaving any obvious signs of illegal entry. But what did it really matter now?

She let herself quietly into the garage. There she picked up a rubber mallet her father used for pounding vintage hubcaps onto the vintage cars he restored. Or had used to restore, anyway, before he'd learned that large boats were an even better hole into which to shovel your family's money. She grabbed a dirty towel off the open hamper in front of the washing machine.

She carried them back to the dining room's French doors.

The front door was padlocked, or so Allie had been told. She hadn't verified this detail with her own eyes. She assumed that anyone worth their salt—a person whose job is to lock people out of their own houses—would padlock the back door as well. But somehow the French doors to the dining room must have seemed more like windows. They'd been left as Allie had always known them.

She knew exactly which pane of glass she needed to knock out. Then she could reach through and unlock the doors from the inside.

Allie closed her eyes and held the mallet in position, ready to strike. Nothing happened. She felt as though she'd sent a signal to her arm to swing the mallet. Apparently it had not been received. She opened her eyes again and felt around inside that resistance. Just as she was not a person who stole smartphones, she was not a person who broke windows. It felt entirely outside her nature.

But this needed to be done.

She closed her eyes again and pushed harder against the sensation. The arm swung as directed. The sound of glass breaking, falling inward and smashing on the Spanish tiles of the dining room floor, made her jump. It sounded violent. Like some kind of sudden danger. Something Allie had never meant to invite.

She opened her eyes and regarded what she had done.

How long would the house sit empty, one pane of glass broken on these French doors? Would it rain in? Would leaves blow into the dining room?

More importantly, was there a compelling reason why she still cared?

She wrapped the towel around her arm to prevent cuts, then reached in and unlocked the door from the inside.

Allie stepped into the only home she had ever known. The place she had never imagined herself leaving until . . . how many days ago? She couldn't remember. She couldn't imagine. Seven? Ten? Twelve? And how was that possible? The whole world had changed since then. She was a different person and her life was a different life. How could it not have been at least months? Maybe more like years?

The memories the house reawakened seemed faded and ancient and dulled by absence.

The house itself felt different.

Allie set the towel and mallet on the tiles. She wandered through the dining room and along the hall toward the stairs, feeling the ways in which the house had changed. Like a person you always thought you could trust. But then, when you found out they lied to you, purposely and with malice, you had to go back and reframe everything you thought you knew about them. You had to rewrite an entire history.

Allie padded up the stairs, sensing something about houses that she hadn't known before: They are not entirely inanimate. They can be alive or dead. When they are alive, gas runs through pipelines to create heat. Water flows from faucets. Electricity creates light. Was this house alive or dead? Had someone turned off all its living functions before padlocking the doors? Or were the utility bills stacking up, shutoff warnings filling the mailbox to overflowing? Or . . . wait. Had enough time even gone by for the utility companies to notice a change?

She pushed the maze of thoughts out of her head again. She was a kid. It hit her fairly suddenly. She liked to think of herself as mostly grown. But as a fifteen-year-old, it was not her job to keep a house alive. It was not something she had ever learned, nor should have felt compelled to learn at her age. It was her parents' job. A job at which they had failed miserably.

It was okay for Allie to flounder in the details and give up trying to understand.

She swung the door of her room wide.

On a closet shelf she found two overnight bags that she and her mother had bought in South America. Intricately handwoven, functional art. One had been intended for her mother, but somehow Allie had inherited both. Her mother's South American bag had been one more small belonging above and beyond being needed, or even used.

She pulled them down and began to fill one with clothes.

Even a few days earlier Allie would have bemoaned the fact that these were her least favorite clothes. Her favorites had gone to New Beginnings with her, and were gone forever. She registered this fact, but did not react to it. After a few days of owning only the clothes she was wearing—after simply getting dirtier day after day, with no way to shower and no clean outfit to change into if she had—clothes were clothes, and any were welcome.

All of her life standards had transformed.

She stuffed the second woven bag with her piggy bank, laptop, iPad, Kindle, and phone, along with a coin collection she had inherited from her late grandfather and a one-ounce gold bar that had been a present from her one and only uncle, now deceased. She threw in the jewelry she deemed worth selling: a heavy woven necklace that she thought was real gold, and a diamond engagement ring that had been passed down through her father's side of the family.

She looked around the room, wondering if that was enough. Then she experienced a wave of dizziness, closed her eyes, and decided not to look around anymore.

Everything she saw in this room was a small component of Allie. Something that defined the person she had always thought herself to be. But it was all irrelevant now. Allie suspected the dizziness had come from this huge, destabilizing realization.

The thing to do was to stop looking around. Stop poking that emotional center to see what waves would emanate.

She needed to walk out again. The faster the better.

———

Allie stopped at the gate and picked up the rolled and deflated pool raft, which she tucked under her arm.

She charged through the gate, leaving it flapping open behind her. She trotted across the side lawn, weighed down by her sudden riches. She craned her neck to peer up and down the street, hoping to see the familiar white bakery van. The street was empty. Her stomach buzzed with nerves. She felt like a thief, which irritated her sense of the rightness of things. It was the second time that day she'd had to defend the right to her own belongings. This time she was forced to defend it to herself.

Just as she came out from beside the house and into the front yard, she felt the pool raft slip out from under her arm. She reached down to grab it. Then she straightened, bolting forward again at the same time, and ran into her next-door neighbor, Mrs. Deary.

Literally. Ran into her. Almost bowled her down.

"Oh," she said. "Mrs. Deary. I'm sorry."

"Alberta? What are you doing here?"

"Oh," Allie said again. Then a pause fell. And stayed for a beat too long. Allie knew they both must have heard and felt the hesitation. Lying was not in Allie's wheelhouse. "I didn't bring enough stuff to the group home. So my social worker brought me over here to get more."

Allie expected Mrs. Deary to look around in an attempt to locate this mythical social worker. She didn't. She was a small woman in a big, loose print housedress, like something from the fifties, with half-glasses stored on the crown of her head. She stared deeply into Allie's eyes as if reading a treasure map.

"I heard you ran away."

A cold river ran down Allie's throat and spread through her belly and gut. Down her thighs.

"Where did you hear that?" she asked, wondering if her voice was shaking. It felt as though it was.

"Somebody called me. Somebody from social services. They wanted to know if I'd seen you. If you'd come back to the house. They left me with a number to call in case I saw you."

The more words came out of Mrs. Deary's mouth, the more her forehead wrinkled with the intense gravity of the subject.

"That's all over now," Allie said, surprised that lying flowed so easily. "There was this girl there who threatened me, so I stayed away for a day. But I went back. They should have called you again and told you I was back."

"Yes." Mrs. Deary arched one eyebrow slightly. "They should have."

A movement caught Allie's eye. She turned to see the bakery van pulling around the corner. She dropped her bags and windmilled her arms to signal Bea. The pool raft hit the grass again.

"They have a *pool* at this group home?" Mrs. Deary asked.

"No, just lousy mattresses," Allie said, fast and desperate. "Here's my social worker now. Gotta go!"

She scooped up the dropped items and sprinted for the street.

"*That's* your social worker?" her neighbor called after her. "Why is she driving an old bakery van?"

"Her car broke down," Allie shot over her shoulder. "She just borrowed this. Normally she drives a Prius."

She pulled the passenger door of the van open and threw the bag of clothes and the pool raft around the seat and into the back. Then she climbed in with the bag of electronics carefully clutched in her lap.

"Drive," Allie said. "Drive."

"Who was that?" Bea asked, stepping on the gas.

"A problem," Allie said, staring at her neighbor in the side-view mirror.

Mrs. Deary stared back. She was standing in the middle of the street, watching the van drive away. As if memorizing the license number. But maybe Allie was reading that in. After all, you can't know what's happening inside a person while they stare. You can only imagine. And imagination can be a highly fear-based phenomenon.

"Neighbor?"

"Yeah."

"What's the problem?"

"She said she had a number that somebody at social services gave her. In case she saw me."

"Hmm. Think she'll call them?"

"I have no idea," Allie said, trying to breathe normally. Then, when she should have left well enough alone, she added, "But I have a bad feeling about it."

Bea swung the van around a corner and the troublesome neighbor disappeared from view.

"A Prius?" Allie asked out loud.

She tried to remember if Polyester Lady drove a Prius. Maybe that was where the idea had come from. No. As best Allie could remember, her actual social worker drove something American and big.

"What about a Prius?" Bea asked.

"I don't know. It's just weird. I started lying because . . . well, I had to. Or I guess I felt like I had to. And then the lies got kind of . . . specific. And I don't know where all those details came from."

"I won't even point out the lesson there."

"Thank you."

They drove for a mile or two in silence.

"I just didn't want to go to jail," Allie said. "Or . . . you know. Juvie. I think that sounds like the worst thing ever."

"I don't think so. I'm not sure it sounds bad at all. I've considered it. It wouldn't be hard to get into a place like that. Just walk into a police station and own up to some of the things I've done."

"Why? Why would you want that?"

"A roof over my head and three square meals a day."

"What about your cat? Phyllis?"

"I heard somewhere that the pound has to hold them for you until you get out."

"She's so old, though."

"I know. But still. When you think you can't provide for yourself and your cat . . . it changes your thinking. About . . . you know. What's safe. What's desirable. That bottom line of food and shelter starts to look like the only thing that matters. I guess it always *was* the only thing that mattered, only we didn't know it, because we thought a thing like this couldn't happen to us. Those were the good old days, huh?"

Allie opened her mouth to answer. All that came out was a sigh.

# Chapter Twenty-Two

## *Nobody Takes My Ancient, Peeling Lettering*

Allie circled the van, plotting and planning.

It sat parked in the dirt somewhere between the Cayucos pier and quaint little Highway 1. In other words, they had made it almost as far up the coast as they had the first time. Maybe twenty miles south of zebra territory. And they hadn't been stopped and arrested. But somehow Allie didn't expect that luck to hold.

"We could peel off a lot of the lettering," she said to Bea, who had recently stepped out to see what Allie was up to. "A lot of it has peeled off already, at least at the edges. Or we could get some white spray paint and paint over them."

"No," Bea said, simply.

"Why not?"

"Well, first of all, if that nosy neighbor of yours wrote down the license number, it won't help much."

"But we don't know if she did or not. And besides, even if she did. You have to be driving right behind a van to read its license plate. But if she just called in a description of the van, I mean . . . seriously, this thing is not hard to pick out of a crowd. It's fairly . . . unusual looking."

"And then there's the second reason."

"Which is?"

"I won't let you."

"Oh." Allie opened her mouth to say more, but then opted to leave it at that. She sensed she should stop talking, for reasons she did not poke or prod or otherwise deeply examine.

"This is my husband Herbert's van. Herbert is gone now. How much of him do you think I have left? What do you think I own as evidence that he once existed? Our little trailer is gone. I have a couple of cartons of things I left with a friend in Palm Desert. I have no idea when I'll see them again. Other than that, I have this van he used in his bakery business. It's really the only thing I have that's left over from our life together. And I did not invite you to paint over its lettering so no one will notice that you ran away from some kind of a home and you're traveling with me. So the bottom line is that you won't be making any changes to my van. Did I make myself sufficiently clear about that?"

Allie realized her jaw was hanging open too wide. She took a moment to adjust that. She could feel her face redden with shame.

"Yes. Of course. I'm really sorry. None of that ever occurred to me. I just figured because you don't have a bakery . . . I'm sorry. I guess I was being thoughtless. So . . . what do we do?"

"What do *we* do? I'm not sure there's any *we* about it. You just decide what you're going to do now. As I see it, you have two choices. Take a chance riding with me, or take a chance out there without me."

"Oh," Allie said again.

She felt more than a little bit stung. Truthfully, she'd thought ransacking her house and bringing valuables had secured her a place in Bea's van. She thought it made them a solid "we." The idea that she might have to go off on her own at this point had been put away, seemingly for good. It hurt to think of dredging it up again. It was another scrape with fear that Allie's gut felt she could not afford.

Allie looked around. Not that there was anything to see beyond what she'd seen already. An ocean. A little beach town lining the coast.

A pier. The route north. No police or Highway Patrol cars that she could see.

"If something goes wrong, though . . . ," Allie began. Hesitantly. "I hate to get you involved. You know. Get you in trouble."

"Why would I get in trouble? I've done nothing wrong."

"Aiding and abetting a runaway? That sort of thing?"

"Nonsense. I know nothing about any of it. I picked you up hitchhiking. I kept you around because you had gas money. You swore you were eighteen and I believed you. Why would I know any more about your background than that?"

Allie nodded. A bit limply.

Shoulders slumped, she walked back to the passenger door and climbed in.

Bea lifted herself up into the driver's seat a moment later.

"Probably not a bad decision," the old woman said. "And if it goes wrong, well, maybe you'll get to see my point about the three squares and the roof over your head in prison. Who knows? Maybe I'll claim I did know you were a runaway and get my three squares a day, too."

She started the engine and shifted into "Drive," aiming the van toward the highway north.

"Don't you worry about the privacy thing, though?" Allie asked.

"What privacy thing?"

"You don't think they'd give you a private cell, do you?"

"Hmm," Bea said. "I hadn't really thought of that. That would be hard, I think. As far as whether it would be harder than not knowing where to live or how to eat . . . I'm not sure. I think both are very important to me."

"Well, I have cash now." Allie pulled the piggy bank out of her South American bag and removed the plastic plug in the bottom that allowed access to the money. "So I think out in the world is our best bet for now."

Truthfully, she had forgotten about the bank. She would have counted the money a long time ago, the moment she'd first climbed back into the van, but the alarming brush with Mrs. Deary had knocked some obvious thoughts out of her head.

"Except this is no longer a private cell, either," Bea said.

"Oh. Right."

She counted in silence for a time while Bea drove.

"Three hundred and sixty dollars."

"That should pay me back for sharing my cell."

"And when that's gone we can start selling off my electronics. But after that . . . I mean, if we keep driving the way we've been doing . . . I don't know what we do when the money is gone."

"It only needs to last until the third of next month. Then I get my Social Security check."

Allie looked around as if the van might contain a post office or bank she had missed seeing.

"At what address?"

"It goes straight into my bank on direct deposit. Then I can use my new debit card for food and gas until the third of the following month, and so on."

"Oh," Allie said, drawing the word out long. "We might be in pretty good shape, then."

"There you go with the 'we' thing again. But we'll manage, yes."

"We should just keep going. You know. Before it all comes crashing down."

"Why should we do that?"

"I don't know. Why not? Probably better than what's behind us. Besides. It could be . . . you know. Interesting. It could be almost like an adventure."

She heard the old woman snort derisively.

*"Adventure?"*

"Sure. What's wrong with that?"

"After the experience you just had? I should think you'd want nothing but quiet safety from here on out."

Allie couldn't help noting that this was the first time Bea had referred to Allie's traumatic experience without hinting that it might have been made up and false. She wondered if that was a type of progress between them. Some hint of an ability to get along.

"Yeah, I see your point, but . . . there's nothing wrong with wanting to have *good* experiences. You know. After all that."

"No. Hardly. No adventure. I say a big hearty no to that."

"How can you not want to have an adventure?"

"Because life is plenty adventurous enough for me. Just the way it is. Every day. Thank you very much."

———

"Can you stop in Cambria?" Allie asked when she saw the sign for the town.

"I could, I suppose. But why?"

"I want to see if that nice lady at the market will let me use one of her electric outlets. I want to plug in my computer and do that thing where you restore it to factory specs. My father taught me you always do big computer jobs like that while you're plugged into power. I guess it drains the battery really fast."

"Eagle loggle google, pigs flying upside down," Bea said.

It occurred to Allie that the old woman might be having a stroke. *"What?"*

"Exactly. What you said made every bit as much sense to me as my sentence did to you. It's all nonsense when you talk about computer stuff. Or it is to me, anyway. Might as well be."

"It just means that you set it back to how it was before you put all your personal information on it. It erases all your data. You know. So you can sell it without anybody else having your personal stuff."

"Oh," Bea said. "I actually do know a little bit about that."

"Besides, the market has that fried chicken you like. I could bring you some."

"I guess a rest would do me good," Bea said, but Allie suspected it was the chicken that had won her over.

——

"Hey," Allie said.

The woman whose name she did not know, the store owner, looked up. A smile spread across her face, and Allie felt it like warmth through her gut. Maybe the search for that smile was why she had come. That longing for recognition. That hope that someone might actually recognize her and seem glad she was back. The store owner had a smile that looked strong and calm and seemed to arrive easily. She looked entirely at home in her own skin. Allie realized she had not met a lot of people who could make such a claim.

"I didn't know you were still in town," the woman said.

Allie wondered if she should ask the woman's name, but a sad flickering of reality in her gut reminded her their friendship was destined to be brief.

"Not still, exactly. Again. We made a little . . . surprise side trip."

"Those are the best kind."

Allie wandered into the shop with her laptop computer under her arm.

"I actually came to ask a favor. Can I plug my computer into your electricity?"

"Sure. You want to check your e-mail?"

"Not exactly. I have to restore this thing to the factory settings so I can sell it."

That stopped the conversation cold.

Allie sat awkwardly on the floor, cross-legged, painfully aware of how long it had been since she had showered, brushed her teeth, changed her clothes. She felt out of place suddenly. Physically and otherwise. No one spoke for a long time.

"Everything okay with you and your grandmother?" the woman asked, startling her.

"Yeah. Why? Why do you ask?"

"Um. Let's see. Maybe because you don't have access to power and you're about to sell your laptop?"

"Oh. Right. Well. We're camping. It's kind of an adventure. And yeah, we need all the gas money we can get. But it's fine. She gets her Social Security check on the third of every month. We'll manage."

In the silence that followed, Allie felt herself crash. Physically, mentally, emotionally. Psychically. The speed of the change alarmed her. The last of the relief surrounding her escape had drained away now, leaving a crushing sense of rock-bottom depression it its wake.

The store owner seemed to notice, but said nothing.

"I guess this'll take a minute," Allie said, staring at the screen. It seemed like a lot of trouble, the speaking thing.

"How long are you and your grandmother out on the road?"

"Hard to say."

"You have parents to go back to?"

"I have parents. Yeah." A long pause. Then, "They're in jail."

"I'm sorry. That's too bad. Lucky for you that you have your grandmother."

"Yeah," Allie said, still feeling the drag of the sudden depression. "I mean, yes and no. She's not the easiest person. She's not very . . . open. You know? She's kind of closed off to everything. But I need to have somebody, so . . . yeah. I guess I'm lucky."

"How long have you two been traveling together?"

"Just a couple of days."

"Maybe you can help her open up a little."

Allie lifted her head and looked into the older woman's eyes, which were frank, unguarded, and very blue. She hadn't considered that possibility.

"Yeah. Maybe."

Then she stared at her screen and waited, not having the energy to say or do much more.

"Where are you two staying tonight?" the woman asked after a time.

"Not sure."

"You want to stay the night at my house? I'd have to run it by my husband, but I can't imagine he'd object. You could take a hot shower and sleep in a real bed. I have a guest room with twins."

Hot shower. The words struck Allie as something grand. They wrapped around her sore gut and held on. As though the woman had said "nirvana" or "eternal happiness."

"Let me ask my grandmother."

———

Allie stuck her head into the van. It wasn't locked, which surprised her.

"Hey," she said to Bea, who lay sprawled on her easy chair, fully reclined, a book lying open on her chest.

"What?"

"You want to stay at this lady and her husband's house tonight?"

Bea lifted her head to level Allie with a withering gaze. "Absolutely not. Why on earth would I want that?"

"Because she has a shower."

"I do fine taking sponge baths in gas station restrooms. You really should cultivate the talent. It works well enough. Look, I took off in this van because I want my own space. Lately I have you in it, which seems to be a blessing and a curse in equal measure. But now you want to drag me somewhere completely unfamiliar and throw in a whole family of strangers. No thank you."

"I could totally use the shower."

"Fine. You go."

"Promise not to drive off without me?"

"Not really."

Allie sighed. The sense of depression, which had lifted ever so slightly at the thought of a bed and a shower, settled back into her belly with a painful thump. She backed out of the van and slammed the door behind her.

—

"Thanks anyway," Allie said, sitting down on the floor of the little store again, beside her computer. "But, like I said, she's not very open. It's too bad. I could have used that shower."

"The San Simeon State Park campground has showers. Is that where you're staying tonight?"

"Oh. I don't know. Where is it?"

"Just a couple miles north of here. You'll see the sign."

"Do you know how much it costs?"

"Not sure. It might've gone up lately. Might be twenty. Might be twenty-five."

"Yeah, okay. Thanks. Maybe we'll stay there."

But, inside, Allie's gut dipped lower. Because she knew Bea would never go for that. Too expensive when they could just park anywhere and sleep for free.

They sat in silence for a long time. A couple came in, paid for their gas, bought ice cream sandwiches and sodas, and left again.

Then, much to her surprise, Allie asked, "How do I help her?" The whole room seemed surprised by the question. For a moment, silence hung heavy. "I mean, how do you help somebody be more . . . you know . . . open?"

"Good question. In a very real sense, I guess you don't."

"Right. I thought that was too good to be true."

"But people can change. And sometimes they can change because of what they see in you. The way you are can inspire somebody. So I would say . . . just be a really good, clear example of what you hope both of you can be."

Allie sat with that a moment, waiting to see if her drooping and exhausted insides could take it in. Before she answered the question to her satisfaction, the restore process completed on her computer. She found herself staring at a screen just like the one she'd seen when her parents first gave her the computer two Christmases ago. It was another deep loss she could not afford. A year and a half of the recording of her online world, her communications. Allie felt as though a giant eraser was rubbing out her life. Or maybe her life was right here, right now, sitting on the hard boards of a little general store in a tiny town, and everything that had passed before had only been an illusion.

"Thanks for the electricity," Allie said. "And the advice."

"You want to take some fried chicken for you and your grand-mother? It's the end of the day and I can't hold it over anyway. You're welcome to it. I either have to eat it myself and feed it to my husband, or it gets thrown away. Some nights I have a homeless guy who comes around for it, but I haven't seen him for a while. I hope he's okay."

"That's a nice offer. Thanks. I'd like to take some for her. I'm a vegan."

It didn't feel as though it mattered, though, anyway, whether Allie ate. The depression had left her with no appetite.

"I have biscuits and coleslaw and three-bean salad."

"That would be good, thanks."

Because turning down free food seemed impossibly stupid, whether you were immediately hungry for it or not.

—

Just for a moment—just as Allie was walking out the door with her brown paper bags of food—it struck her that maybe she should try to stay. That the store owner would be a better bet than Bea. She lived in a real house, and felt at home in her own skin. She acted like it was good news to see Allie a second time.

Allie shook the idea away again.

She had no doubt this woman would help if Allie asked her to. But it would be the wrong kind of help. It would involve digging down to the truth. Notifying the proper authorities.

It would be that responsible kind of help that Allie could no longer afford.

—

"So . . . I was thinking . . . ," Allie said to Bea, who looked three-quarters asleep. The old woman had finished all five pieces of the fried chicken. It had been an amazing thing to witness. Meanwhile Allie had only stared limply at her biscuits and coleslaw and three-bean salad. "Maybe we could go up to that campground at San Simeon State Park. It costs about twenty dollars. But I have money. And I could take a shower there."

"I'm not moving," Bea said, and her lips barely moved as she said it. "I'm not driving another three feet. I can't drive as far as I did today. It's exhausting. My whole body is fairly buzzing with exhaustion. And my neck and shoulders hurt terribly. From now on four or five hours and that's it. Besides. *We* have money. It's not so much your money at this point. You committed it in return for the ride. So we make any decisions about how to spend it together."

Allie sighed.

She carefully moved the cat off her lap and began blowing up the flat bottom section of the pool raft. It made her feel painfully tired and out of breath.

By the time she had inflated it, Bea was snoring lightly.

Allie grabbed a towel and a washcloth from among Bea's things. She hadn't asked permission, but it seemed wrong to wake her up to ask. Besides, Allie's money had to be affording her some kind of perks. She carefully chose a clean outfit from her other handwoven South American bag.

Then she walked two blocks to the big gas station on the corner near the highway.

There, in their women's restroom, she attempted to cultivate the habit of the sponge bath. It was nothing like a shower, but it would have to do. Like so many aspects of her sudden new life, it seemed her only option was to adjust with as much good cheer as she could muster.

At the moment that cheer felt painfully small.

# Chapter Twenty-Three

## *Flattery Will Get You Everywhere*

They drove the high, winding, narrow ribbon of highway along the Big Sur coast. Allie gawked at the turquoise tinge of the ocean hundreds of feet below, with the jagged boulders at its edges, and the nearly vertical rock face that rose on the right, so close to the traffic lane that Allie occasionally thought it would scrape her side of the van.

Phyllis had been sitting on her lap, purring, but the constant twists and turns must have been making the cat carsick. She pinned her ears back along her head and slithered under the seat.

"Whoa!" Allie said, feeling and sounding like a kid. "Look at that bridge!"

A mile or so up the road the highway briefly morphed into a bridge with high steel arches of suspension underneath. To span what, Allie couldn't see.

"I can't look at that bridge!" Bea barked. It was the first Allie had realized Bea was not enjoying the scene with her. "I can't look at anything. I have to look at the road in front of us so I don't drive us right off the edge of a cliff to our untimely deaths."

Before Bea could even finish the sentence the road performed an amazingly tight hairpin curve, turning directly away from the ocean, then bending at a wild angle to face it again. Allie watched Bea's strained face for a moment. Then she looked around to take in the view.

That's when she saw it. A cop car. Well, a cop SUV. It was four cars back, but it was following.

"Uh-oh," Allie said.

"Uh-oh what? Don't say uh-oh unless you mean it! I'm seeing enough cause for panic without your help!"

As she spoke, Bea instinctively braked. The van slowed to a crawl. The car behind them honked.

"Don't stop!" Allie shouted.

"Well, you're telling me there's something wrong! I don't know what it is yet!"

"It's behind us. There's a cop back there."

Bea breathed in silence for a moment, and marginally accelerated. "What kind of cop? Sheriff? Highway Patrol?"

"I don't know. It's too far back to see what it says on the side. I just know it's black and white and has a light bar on top."

"Well, if it's too far away for us to read the writing on it, maybe the reverse is true."

"We need to find a place to pull off."

"There's no place to pull off!" Bea screeched. Then, seeming to achieve better control of her nerves—or at least her voice—she added, "In case you hadn't noticed."

Allie knew they had a potential problem, and that it would play out fast. Bea was driving far too slowly, holding up a line of cars behind them with her terror. Several posted signs had announced the law: slower traffic was required to use turnouts. Bea had driven right by the signs—and the turnouts—as if she hadn't noticed them. If they failed to turn out at the next opportunity, in full view of the cop, that was a citation-worthy infraction. If Allie carefully instructed Bea to turn out, and she did, the cars behind them would pass. Including the cop car. Whose cop driver would then get a good look at the van as he drove by.

Allie glanced desperately over her shoulder, but they had rounded a curve that obscured all but the car directly behind them.

She looked forward again and saw a dirt driveway. It was on the ocean side, guarded by a tall, wide, and ornate wrought iron gate. As luck would have it, the gate was standing open.

"Pull in here!" Allie shrieked.

Bea jumped, and the nose of the van swerved with her panic, but she did as she was told—even though it involved pulling across the southbound traffic lane at a blind curve. She just dove in and did it, and nobody came around the curve driving south.

The driveway led sharply downhill, and the van picked up speed and bounced violently on the rutted dirt.

"I'm not sure I have the suspension for—" Bea began. But the road got rougher, and Bea had to give all her attention to braking to a full stop.

Allie craned her neck to look back at the road. It was gone. The road was out of view from their current location. And, thankfully, they were out of view of the road.

They sat still a moment, breathing. Allowing the moment of panic to pass.

The vista of the ocean from their high perch was so overwhelming, so all-encompassing, that it took Allie a few seconds to notice there was a house just a few dozen yards down. It wasn't the house Allie might have expected in such a lavish location. It was fairly small and made of dark-brown, weathered wood. Funky. Almost poor-looking, except in light of its surroundings.

"I think we lost him," Allie said.

"Well, great." But it sounded sarcastic. "That's just great. Now we're on private property. I'm sure the owner will call the cops. Nice to know there's one so close by to answer the call."

"You worry too much. We'll just turn around and—"

A knock on the passenger window near her ear made Allie jump so hard and so suddenly that she felt as though she might leave her body behind.

A man stood outside the window. He looked to be in his fifties, with a porkpie hat and a creased face that looked both impassive and sad.

"Can I help you ladies?" the man asked through the glass.

"I'm no good at these things," Bea hissed. "I freeze up. This was your idea. You fix it."

Allie took a deep breath, smiled at the face outside the window, and opened the passenger door. She stepped out of the van and into the dirt. Into the ocean breeze. The place felt like heaven, like a place you might conjure up in a guided meditation, but Allie had no time to focus on that.

"I'm sorry," she said. "This is obviously private property. It was all my fault. It was totally my mistake. My grandmother was driving, and I looked over and I saw her start to nod off, and it scared me, because this is not the place you want to fall asleep while you're driving."

"Well, no place really is." His voice sounded flat. Deadpan. As if he could hardly muster the energy needed to participate in the conversation. "Granted, this place is worse than most. And there's nowhere to pull over for miles."

"Right! My point exactly. So I saw this chance to pull off the road and I told her to take it. But this is your house. Our mistake. Sorry. We'll just get out of your way."

The man rubbed his chin for a moment. As if Allie's simple offer to leave required mulling over. He had a soul patch—a tiny, beard-like rectangle of facial hair under his lower lip. Both it and his immense and shaggy eyebrows were blond, shot through with gray.

"She can take a nap here if she needs to. Don't want you two going off the road."

Allie breathed deeply. They were no longer in trouble. She could stop being afraid.

"That's very nice of you. Thanks."

"No problem. If you need anything, I'll be in the sculpture garden."

"Sculpture garden?"

The man pointed. Maybe words were too much trouble. He raised a hand laden with heavy silver rings and indicated a gate to the right of the house.

He walked away.

Allie jumped back into the van.

"Pull over there," she said to Bea, pointing. "Behind those bushes. Just on the off chance that cop comes back wondering where we went."

"Wait. What are we doing?"

"He said we could stay."

"*Stay?* What do you mean, *stay?* Stay how long? Why would he say that? He must be some kind of weirdo. Who tells some strangers off the highway they can stay?"

"Will you please relax? I told him you were falling asleep on the road. He said you could take a nap here before you try to drive on. He just doesn't want us driving off the edge of the cliff."

"Oh," Bea said. She sounded disappointed to have to admit the man was likely only being kind.

Bea looked again at the spot Allie had indicated, well concealed behind heavy brush. Then she shifted the van into gear and slowly, carefully drove there. It was shady in that spot, which Allie thought was extra nice, and the view of the ocean was astounding. Bea shifted into "Park" and shut off the engine. The silence was strangely complete. Just a light whistle of wind.

"Well," Bea said. "You're getting to be quite the experienced liar, aren't you?"

"Yeah," Allie said. "That's unfortunate. I was just thinking about that myself."

—

Allie listened to Bea snore for maybe five minutes. Maybe ten.

She didn't know why Bea needed a nap. It had been a made-up story about her falling asleep on the road. Besides, it was still morning. They'd driven barely a couple of hours since leaving Cambria. Still, there was no doubt that those two hours had taken a lot out of Bea.

Allie couldn't warm up to the idea of a nap.

She let herself out of the van and stood outside in the sun and wind for a moment, staring. Being hundreds of feet over the ocean made the view stretch out impossibly far, as though Allie could see to the edges of the earth. Or, at least, halfway to faraway lands.

She sighed, then headed for the gate the man had pointed out. It was heavily grown with ivy. Allie had to brush tendrils of green leaves out of the way to open the gate and move through it.

On the other side, Allie saw a zoo of rust-colored wrought iron animals. Life-size whales and dolphins surfaced out of the grass. Long-legged seabirds stood with wings spread, as if just touching down. Coyotes and mountain lions paced in between iron trees and oversize flowers.

In the middle of it all, the man stood wearing a welder's mask and working on a statue of a woman. More specifically, on her hair. She had amazing hair, that iron woman. Long and curly, separated into coiling strands by the wind. Or so the sculptor had made it seem.

For a few minutes she watched him adding strands to that astonishing head of iron hair.

Then he stopped, turned off his welding torch. Lifted the face shield of his mask. He noticed Allie there. Allie could see him notice her. See his roving gaze stop on her. He raised one hand faintly in recognition.

Allie walked closer.

"I hope it's okay that I'm here," she said. "You said if I *needed* anything. But I don't. I just got tired of watching my grandmother sleep. And I wanted to see the sculpture garden."

"No worries," he said, setting the torch in the grass.

Allie moved in another step or two. She didn't know this man. Bea was right about that. But the statue was drawing her in. And besides, she was strangely sure this man did not have the inclination—or the energy—to cause her trouble.

"I love her hair," Allie said. She waited, but the man did not reply. "Is she a real person? Inspired by one, I mean."

For a long set of moments, no words were spoken. Allie thought her question did not warrant a reply in her host's mind.

Then, barely above a whisper, he said, "My wife."

"Oh. Good. Got it. She must love that. I mean . . . does she? Does she like it? Does she think it looks like her?"

The man lifted the heavy mask off his head and set it in the grass. Then he turned to look at Allie. For the count of three or four, his gaze burned into hers, their eyes remaining locked. Then he looked off toward the ocean.

"She left me." Surprisingly, his voice rang out strong.

"Oh, I'm so sorry."

"That came out wrong," he said, still gazing out to the horizon. "I don't mean she left me as in she walked out on me. I mean she left all of this. Everybody and everything. She left the world."

Allie thought she followed his meaning, but didn't feel sure enough to speak.

"She died," he said a moment or two later. "It's still hard for me to say that."

"I'm so sorry. How long has it been?"

"Thirty-seven days."

"Wow. That's not much time to get used to a thing like that."

"No."

For a long minute or two he said no more. He was eyeing the statue now. Critically. Not as though he didn't like it. More as though it needed something else to be okay, but he couldn't pin down what. Then he shifted his eyes to Allie's face again.

"Where are my manners? Lemonade?"

"Thank you," Allie said. "That would be very nice."

The man disappeared into the house. Allie wasn't sure if she had been intended to follow. But she didn't feel comfortable going into a strange house with a strange man, so she chose to believe he had meant for her to wait.

She wandered among the sculptures, staring into the tiny, knowing eyes of the dolphins and whales. Their bodies had been formed with long, flowing strips of iron with plenty of air in between. Allie could see the ocean right through their massive forms, which seemed appropriate.

Allie walked up to the man's iron wife. She stood with her arms extended, open wide, as if to embrace the world. Her head was thrown back into the wind. She looked blissful. Allie wondered how it would feel to approach life that way. She wondered if it was even possible to do that while you were still alive. Maybe you had to wait until you'd left the earth and someone immortalized you in iron.

A movement caught Allie's eye, and she looked over to see a glass of lemonade extended in her direction.

"Thank you," she said, and took it. "Was she really like this?"

She expected him to ask for a definition of "this." He didn't.

"No. She was much more."

They stared at her in silence for a moment.

"Jackson," the man said.

"Allie."

"And this is Bernadette."

"I'm sorry for your loss."

"Not nearly as sorry as I am. But I had thirty-three good years with her, and that's not nothing. That's worth some gratitude."

Allie sipped the lemonade. It was surprisingly tart, but still good. It tasted like it had been made with honey instead of sugar. But she would deal with that.

"Is this what you do for a living?" she asked.

Jackson laughed. "Hardly. I'm retired." For a moment she thought he had no plans to say more. "I *wish* I was a retired sculptor. I'd like to go back and rewrite my history."

Allie watched his face in the silence. He looked as though he might be trying to do just that.

"But you can't undo the past. No, I was in finance. For a very long time. Decades. One day I woke up and realized none of it was real."

"None of . . . what? Finance? Finance seems pretty real."

"Well, it's not. Let me tell you. It's not. It's just a value we agree to put on things. It used to be numbers on a piece of paper. Now it's numbers in digital memory."

"But the numbers represent real money. Right?"

"There is no real money. Not anymore. The banks just make it up. We just create these numbers, more and more with every year that goes by. We use the numbers to keep some people up and other people down. Used to be there was a gold standard, but you're too young to remember that. The government used to own gold, and paper money represented it. But what does it represent now?"

"I don't know," Allie said, not sure whether or not she was listening to a reliable narrator. "What does it represent?"

"Whatever the people in power want it to. I had to get away and work with something real. I had to live in a place nature made, and use my hands to create something that isn't about to turn to dust."

He looked into Allie's eyes briefly, and made a conversational turn she could almost see coming. She didn't know where they were headed, but they were departing their current location. She had heard as much of his inner thoughts as he planned to reveal.

"So where are you and your grandmother headed?"

"Just . . . up the coast. We haven't really talked about how far we'll go."

"How much time do you have?"

"Well, that's the thing. We don't really know. How far *can* you go?"

"Just about to the Canadian border. And I would recommend it."

"That sounds like a nice adventure. But my grandmother doesn't have the nerves for this coast route."

"It's not quite this hairy all the way up. It is in a lot of places. Not straight through. I think she'll get used to it as she goes."

"Maybe," Allie said. But somehow she didn't think so. "So you can drive all the way to Canada on this road?"

"Yes and no. North of California it turns into the 101. It's not all on the coast. And you don't exactly drive to the Canadian border. Because it's in the middle of the Puget Sound. You can go up to this place called Cape Flattery. Nice up there. You have to walk out to it on this series of board-walks. Native land. That's the northwest tip of the U.S., right there. Or you can stop someplace like Port Angeles and take the ferry over to Canada."

"We don't have passports. I mean, not with us." Part of her felt she shouldn't speak for Bea. Another, bigger, part of her felt it was a pretty safe bet.

"To Cape Flattery, then. That's the best of the coast."

"That would be a great adventure. Thing is, my grandmother's not the adventurous type."

"Up to you to wake her up, then. Figuratively speaking." Then he turned abruptly toward the house. "You can just leave the glass on the table." With a flip of his head he indicated an iron table on his patio.

Then he was gone. Back inside his home.

Allie sipped the tart lemonade and wondered how many times Jackson and Bernadette had sat at that iron table. Maybe eating dinner, or drinking tea, or watching the sun set over the dark blue horizon.

Then she wondered what he would do without that, now that she was gone.

When that proved too sad, she wondered how she would talk Bea into driving up the coast all the way to Cape Flattery. By the time she arrived at the inevitable conclusion that she probably couldn't, that it was impossible, the strain had caught up with Allie, and a nap sounded like a good idea after all.

# Chapter Twenty-Four

## Spray Paint, and the Stretching of Worlds

Allie woke to a strange hissing sound. She blinked and looked around.

She was on the pool float in Bea's van, with Phyllis sleeping heavily on her chest. Bea hadn't bothered to draw the front curtains, probably because they were parked up against a thicket of impenetrable bushes. Which is how Allie knew they were still at Jackson's house.

She sat up, trying to avoid upsetting the cat in the process but failing. She rubbed her eyes.

She stepped out of the back door of the van to investigate that sound—and found herself face to face with Bea and an actively spraying can of spray paint.

"Whoa!" Bea said. "You almost got yourself painted white."

The hissing sound fell silent, leaving only a faint ocean noise and the breeze in the trees.

"Where did you get spray paint?"

Bea flipped her head in the direction of the house. "Courtesy of our host."

Allie turned around to look in the direction Bea's head was pointing.

Bea had almost entirely painted over the lettering on the passenger side of the van. She'd done a good job, too. No drips or sags. She must have put more than one coat on the letters themselves, because they did not show through.

"I'm confused," Allie said.

"Because I said there would be no altering of the van."

"Right. That."

"Well, I was doing quite a bit of thinking while you were asleep. Which . . . I have no idea why you slept all day, by the way. You did sleep last night, right?"

Allie looked around and noted that it was only a couple of hours before sundown. A bad time to head out again to drive this stretch of highway. At least, for very long. Besides, the paint job wasn't done yet.

"Pretty much. Yeah."

"Well, I got bored. So I talked to Jackson for a while. He just lost his wife to cancer thirty-seven days ago. Can you imagine that? How hard that must be? I remember thirty-seven days very well. Not the exact day, mind you. I just mean I remember when losing Herbert was all too fresh. But then he started talking to me about his marriage. Jackson, I mean, not Herbert. And then I did some serious thinking, and I realized it was never like that for Herbert and me. Oh, we got on okay. And he was important to me. How could he not be? He was the only husband I had. The only husband I'd ever had. And he was a lovely man in many ways. But he was a lousy, lousy businessman. Rotten. He always talked about the world like bad luck got that business down, and I talked about it the same way so as not to hurt his feelings, but he was just bad at it. I'm sorry to speak ill of the dead, but it's true."

Allie waited. She was beyond surprised to hear these words coming out of Bea's mouth. More like dumbfounded. So she waited in silence. If there were additional words, she hated to distract or discourage them.

"I have to say, it was the oddest feeling. Not Herbert. The conversation I just had with this Jackson fellow who does the metal sculptures. I realized as he was telling me all about his marriage that no one ever did before. Ever. I've had friends in my life, of course I have. But not huge crowds of them. And what friends I have had, well, I guess they were more the cautious type. Like me. So we never really talked about how successful our marriages were or were not, or how we felt about them. You didn't in my day. You just lived the marriage and left the talking part alone. But this man . . . he was just dying to talk about his wife, and I can't blame him. What else would he have on his mind after thirty-seven days?"

"While he was talking," Allie interjected carefully, "did he serve you large cups of coffee or something?" *Amphetamines, maybe?* she thought, but did not add.

"No, why?" Bea asked, missing the subtext entirely.

"No reason. Never mind."

"So, anyway. Where was I? All my life I thought my marriage was just like everybody else's. And now all of a sudden I'm not so sure. I threw my lot in with Herbert when I was just a girl. Never been married, never had a serious boyfriend. I just jumped on board with him, and I really had no idea where that train was going. How could I? That's just how we did it in my day. I'm not bemoaning the fact that he didn't make more money. Granted, a simple life insurance policy would have been nice, but I'm not judging him on the money. It's that I made him my whole world. And so my world was always too small. Then when he died, I didn't know what my world was anymore. I wasn't even sure I had one."

Bea dropped the can of white spray paint. She walked to the back of the van. Allie followed, transfixed. Bea reached down for the "If I'm driving slowly I'm delivering a wedding cake" bumper sticker, grabbed one peeling corner, and tried to rip it off. It ripped, all right, but not off. The corner only tore away and ended up in Bea's hand.

"Grab a table knife from inside and start working on this," she told Allie. "Will you?"

"Um. Sure." But for the moment she didn't move.

"So I made a decision. No more living in the past, because the past wasn't even a good example of my best choices in action. It's one thing to look back and see how I let my world get too small. But to hang on to that smallness now . . ."

"Wow," Allie said. "How long was I asleep? You made a lot of progress while I was away."

—

"About that adventure you were trying to talk me into . . . ," Bea said, leaning over Allie as she scraped off the last bits of bumper sticker. "I have no idea what one would even look like, because I'm new to this whole adventure thing. But I just might be game."

"Hmm," Allie said. And scraped. "We could drive all the way up the coast to Cape Flattery. Which is the northwest corner of the United States. It's about as far as you can drive without crossing the Puget Sound into Canada."

"Good. Let's do it."

Then Bea was gone, carrying masking tape and drop cloths and leftover spray paint back to the house.

Allie smiled to herself.

Truthfully, she wasn't sure if merely driving to someplace qualified as an adventure. Even if it was someplace a long way away. But it was wildly adventurous by Bea's standards, and for the moment it would definitely do.

—

Somehow Allie got elected to walk down to the house and tell Jackson they were leaving. Allie wasn't sure why. By all accounts it seemed as though Bea and Jackson had experienced a moment of connection.

Then again, maybe that was the why. Maybe that was the hang-up right there. Maybe Bea wanted to step back from that connection.

The late sun glared into her eyes as she walked downhill to his door.

She knocked, using a fancy iron door knocker shaped like a monkey hanging by its tail.

Jackson never answered.

In time Allie walked around to the ivy-covered gate and found him in the sculpture garden near the statue of Bernadette. Not welding. Not working in any way. Just appraising it in that manner that suggested he knew something was missing, but he still couldn't pin down the deficiency.

"We're taking off," she said, and he barely looked up. "I wanted to just let you know. And . . . you know. Thank you. For being so nice."

"I hope you're not going to try to go far tonight. You don't have much light left."

"No, just to Carmel or Monterey and then we'll stop and sleep."

"That should be fine. That won't even take you an hour."

*You've never seen Bea drive the coast route,* she thought. But she didn't say so. She inwardly agreed that just to Carmel or Monterey would likely be okay.

"Something about that talk you had really changed her," Allie said.

For the first time, Jackson took his eyes off the statue and raised his gaze to Allie's face. "I give up. What did I say?"

"Just all the stuff you said about your marriage. I don't know that it was any one thing specifically. It just got her thinking about her own life, I guess, and the choices she made, and what they all added up to. It's just funny, because you told me I was going to have to wake her up. Figuratively speaking. And then I went and took a nap, and you woke her up while I was asleep."

He smiled, but it was a sad-looking thing. As was everything he seemed to be able to access. "I still don't know how, but I'm glad. You take care of yourself. And your grandma."

"I will. Thanks. I wish . . ." But then for a minute she wasn't sure if she had what it would take to finish the thought. "I wish a lot of good things for you. Like being able to be really strong. And . . . healing. That's it. I wish you healing."

"I wish the same for you," Jackson said.

"Me? Why me? What am *I* healing from?"

"I have no idea," he said. "You tell *me*. I only know that your pain is written all over your face."

The face in question suddenly felt burning hot.

"Okay," Allie said. "Whatever. 'Bye."

Then she trotted back to the van before the conversation could get any more real.

———

First thing the following morning they sat in the van in front of a Monterey pawnshop, waiting for the guy to turn the "Closed" sign to "Open."

"You know how to wipe all the personal information off things," Bea said. "I know because you did it with your computer."

"Yeah . . . ," Allie said, the word stretching out with doubt and apprehension. "So?"

"So maybe do it with this phone."

Bea had the phone in her lap, one hand over it, as though it were a dirty little secret that someone passing by the van might see.

"No way. Absolutely not. That would be like . . ."

"I'm going to sell it either way. Whether you wipe it clean or the guy in the pawnshop does."

"That's not the point. The point is, I'm not going to be an accessory to your . . ."

"What? Crime? Were you going to say *crime*?"

"Well . . . what do you think? Is it legal to steal somebody's phone, or is it illegal? It's a pretty simple concept."

"So you think I'm a criminal."

"Do we really have to fight? We were just starting to get along some."

Bea sighed. "You can't come in with me, then. You'll have to sell your computer later, at a different pawnshop. Or later at this one. Because if you're right there and he thinks you're my granddaughter, then it's going to be hard to explain why you wiped all your information off the computer but refused to do the same for the phone."

"Fine. Whatever. You go in first. I really don't want to be any part of that phone being sold anyway."

They brooded in silence for a minute or two. Then the man flipped the sign to "Open."

"Wish me luck," Bea said.

Allie remained silent.

Bea shook her head too dramatically, eased out of the driver's seat, and walked stiffly to the pawnshop's door. Allie watched her go. Then, after Bea had disappeared into the shop, Allie read the signs in the window for the hundredth time. Including the one that said, "We Buy Gold." This time it struck her in a way it had not on the first ninety-nine reads.

She stepped into the back of the van and plowed through one of her woven bags until she found the one-ounce gold bar her uncle had given her on the day she was born. It didn't look like a bar exactly. More like a rectangular coin. She took it out of its miniature ziplock plastic bag and turned it over in her fingers. It felt vaguely heavy for its size, and was stamped with a lot of information that verified its authenticity. It was Swiss. That was stamped right in. It was "999.9 pure gold," which didn't quite make sense in Allie's head. It seemed to have its decimal point in the wrong place. But that's what it said. "Fine gold," it also said, though Allie didn't know if that was a verifiable thing with a definition.

It even had something like a serial number stamped in. She had no idea what it was worth. A few hundred dollars, maybe?

But the real value of the thing was clear: Bea didn't know she had it.

Allie had committed all of her electronics, any cash she owned, even a little bit of jewelry to the cause of traveling with Bea, and the food and gas involved in that travel. But she hadn't remembered the coin collection or the ounce of gold before going into the house or mentioned them after coming out. This could be something that was Allie's and Allie's alone—something to fall back on if things didn't go well with the old woman.

She slipped the gold back into its plastic bag and stuck it deep into the front pocket of her jeans.

"Next," she heard Bea say.

Allie jumped as if caught stealing. She looked up to see Bea sticking her head through the driver's side door.

"That was awfully fast," Allie said, trying to talk over her guilt.

"How long is it supposed to take? Anyway. It didn't work. You have to have a password or something to get the phone open."

"Oh. Right."

"You knew that?"

"Well . . . yeah."

"Why didn't you tell me?"

"I don't know. I didn't think of it. Why didn't you know? You said you've done this before."

"I did it once. And it worked fine."

"Maybe because you pawned it a lot faster? Or maybe you moved some keys on it or something. That would have kept it awake."

"Yes, I was playing with it as I walked along. Well, shoot. That seems like a waste. Anyway, thank goodness you have something to sell him."

"Don't you think I should wait a little? So he doesn't get it that we're together? Why don't we go have breakfast, and then we'll come back and

I'll sell the computer. Or . . . I don't know. We have plenty of money right now. Maybe we don't need to sell any of my stuff today. Maybe we should wait and see if we really need the money."

"The question is whether there will be *pawnshops* when we need the money," Bea said, easing her bulk into the driver's seat. "You know. Farther up the coast."

"Then I think what we really need," Allie said, "is a good map."

———

They sat at their table at a diner with a view of the bay. Allie had the map she'd bought spread out on more than half the table in front of them.

"We'll be going through Fort Bragg and Mendocino in Northern California," she said, tracing her finger along the coast. "Eureka and Arcata. And Crescent City. Oh, and of course San Francisco first, but that's coming up today, most likely, and I figured it went without saying. Not sure how big those other towns are. Hard to tell just by looking at the map. But I bet one of them would have a pawnshop. Monterey is not so huge and they had a bunch. Then Coos Bay in Oregon looks bigger. Tons of little towns along the coast, but they might be pretty small. Kind of hard to tell."

The waitress came by, a plump, perky-looking young woman in her early twenties with hair piled up on top of her head. She handed them each a menu.

"Travelers!" she said, as though she'd just struck gold. "I can always spot the travelers. We get a lot of 'em here, and I always like to ask people where they come from and where they're headed."

Silence.

Allie looked over at Bea's face. Bea seemed overwhelmed by the young woman's open cheeriness. Not in a good way.

"Coffee," Bea said flatly.

The waitress's face fell.

"I'm from Pacific Palisades," Allie said. "And my grandmother here is from the Coachella Valley. We're going to drive up the coast all the way to Cape Flattery in Washington. It's sort of an adventure."

"Well, it sounds like a darn good one," the waitress said, seeming relieved.

"I'll have tea," Allie added.

"Coming right up." She hurried away for two steps or so. Stopped. Turned back. "Of course you're going to see our aquarium while you're here, right? It's world famous."

"No," Bea said.

"Maybe," Allie added.

The woman frowned. Then she headed back toward the kitchen.

"That was rude," Allie said.

"I don't like people like that. Never have. What business is it of hers where I'm from or where I'm going?"

"She's just being friendly."

"There's such a thing as too friendly."

"I don't think so. I don't think there is. I think we're having an adventure, and we might as well accept that people will be part of it. We're going to meet people all along the way. Why not find out something about them? Why not tell them something about us? How can they use it against us? They can't. A few minutes later we'll be gone. It's just communication with other humans, and I don't know why everyone is so afraid of it."

The waitress swung by their table again and poured Bea a cup of coffee. She stood several steps back from the old woman and reached her arm out comically to pour, as if Bea were radioactive, or otherwise deadly. She set a small stainless steel pot of hot water in front of Allie, followed by a basket of assorted teas she had been carrying under her arm. She smiled at Allie and Allie smiled back. Then she was gone again.

Allie looked over at Bea to find the older woman searching her face in return. With some variety of grave scrutiny.

"What?" Allie asked, automatically defensive.

"What got into you?"

"Why did something have to get into me? I just think an adventure can include people. We could actually learn something about the people we meet and the other way around. You did that with Jackson, and it changed everything. It changed the whole way you look at the past."

"No, really," Bea said, her expression not budging. "What brought this on?"

Allie sighed. Geared herself up to tell the truth. After all, she had just been advocating doing so. And Bea was hardly a stranger anymore.

"When I was saying goodbye to Jackson . . . he . . . said something. About me. He said he could see my pain. He said it was written all over my face. I was kind of shocked, because I didn't figure people could see it. I figured I could keep it to myself if I wanted. So I left. I just walked away. And now I feel really bad about that. Why didn't I stand there and admit how things are hard for me right now? He told us about his pain. He was so open about it. And then he reached out for me to do the same thing in return. And I ran away. Why? Why is it so scary to let somebody see you like that?"

"Hmm," Bea said. "I have a bad notion you're suggesting we both try this."

"I thought you'd already started."

"Involuntarily. Tell you what. Feel free to do this wherever you go. I'll watch and see how it works out for you."

"Fine," Allie said. "You think you're kidding, but I'll take it."

———

Halfway through her oatmeal and fruit cup, which she had been eating in silence, Allie said, "I think we need to go to the aquarium."

"Nonsense."

"Why is it nonsense?"

"First of all, I don't think you know the meaning of the word 'need.' We *need* to breathe air and drink water and eat food. We'd need shelter from the elements if they were extreme, but here they're not. I'm sure it's expensive, that aquarium, and it's just entertainment. It's just a diversion. It's the last thing we need."

"But that's the old you talking. And you said you weren't going to keep making the decisions you made in the past."

Bea paused with a strip of crispy bacon halfway to her face. "I didn't say I would change every single thing about myself. Some of it is worth keeping. Especially frugality. Especially at a time like this."

Allie ate her oatmeal in silence for a few moments.

Then she said, "But I have money. And if this is what I want to spend it on . . ."

"You don't have money. *We* have money. You committed that money to our expenses. You can't just take it back and waste it."

They ate in a strained silence for several minutes longer. It was becoming increasingly important to Allie that she see that aquarium, and that she get Bea to do the same. It felt more crucial than she could really explain to herself. It seemed to set the tone for how this adventure was going to play out—whether it would be fabulous, like life paying her back for everything, or just another tense grind, full of sacrifice and boredom.

Finally she reached into her jeans pocket and curled her fingers around the one-ounce bar of gold. She pulled it out and set it on the table, covering it with her hand.

"What have you got there?" Bea asked.

Allie lifted one side of her hand so Bea could have a quick look. Then she stuck it back in her pocket, fast.

"Is that real? Where did you get it?"

"My uncle gave it to me on the day I was born. It was one of those things I was supposed to hang on to because it would just keep getting more valuable. I don't know what it's worth. But probably a couple hundred dollars at least."

"Is it an ounce?"

"Yes. An ounce."

"Then it's worth close to thirteen hundred dollars."

Allie could feel her eyes go wide.

"Are you sure?"

"Positive. The gold spot is nearly thirteen hundred."

"How do you know that?"

"Herbert used to have a little gold. Just a couple of ounces. For the same reason. You're supposed to hold it, because it usually increases in value. Over enough time, almost always. But he couldn't hold it. The business was in trouble and he had to sell it to pay some back taxes. Ever since then I've looked at gold prices in the paper, just so I can stay mad over what those two ounces would be worth now. I shouldn't have done it. It only irked me every time. But somehow I couldn't stop. So, that does help our situation quite a bit. That we have it."

"There you go with the 'we' thing again," Allie said.

Bea dropped her fork and sat back in the booth with an audible thump.

"Are you trying to say you're holding out on me?"

"Not exactly. I was going to. I hadn't promised that piece of gold because I didn't even remember I had it at the time. So, yeah. I was just going to keep it to myself in case things didn't work out and I ended up off on my own again."

"Mad money," Bea said.

"I don't know what that is."

"It's something girls carried on dates when I was young. Smart girls, anyway. The boy paid for everything. So theoretically the girl didn't need to bring any cash on a date. But what if you get out there and it turns out you've accepted a date with a loser who's all hands and no respect? We didn't have cell phones in those days. You needed to be able to walk away. Use a pay phone. Call a cab, maybe. So you squirreled away a little secret money. We called it mad money, for reasons that should be obvious."

"Right. Yeah. I was going to keep it as mad money."

"*Was* going to? Past tense? What are you going to do with it now?"

"I'm willing to throw it into the travel fund. I'll hold on to it, and not sell it unless I have to. But it'll be if *we* get into any trouble. If *we* need it. Under one condition: You don't always get to decide how much we spend and on what. You said we'd decide together, but it hasn't worked out that way at all. You say yes or no and expect me to accept it. I get to have some say in these decisions, too."

"You want to go to that darned aquarium."

"I want us both to go. Yeah."

"Let me see that thing again. Are you sure that's real?"

"Now why would my rich uncle give me fake gold as a present on the day I was born?"

She slid the bar out of her pocket and across the table, keeping it discreetly under her hand. Bea quietly accepted the transfer. Then the old woman pulled her reading glasses out of her pocket and studied the gold closely.

A moment later she slid it back across the table.

"On to the Monterey Bay Aquarium," she said.

# PART FIVE

BEA

# Chapter Twenty-Five

## How to Pet a Bat Ray

They stood in front of the giant kelp forest exhibit together, swaying slightly. Surprisingly, Bea was succeeding in ignoring the crowd around her. In fact, the other tourists seemed to have disappeared, so complete was her focus on the inside of the massive saltwater tank.

The glass walls of the thing soared more than twenty feet over Bea's head, looking like a real window onto a real kelp forest under the sea. Some sort of pump or other device caused the kelp to sway, the way the tide would in the open ocean. It had taken Bea several minutes to realize that both she and the girl were moving slightly in response.

Now and then a leopard shark swam lazily across her view, or a school of thousands of tiny silver fish flashed by in near-perfect unison. Larger fish, the kind Herbert used to catch on their trips to the coast, moved with purpose across her view, or just hung without swimming, swaying back and forth with the kelp.

Normally Bea hated to stand for any length of time. It made her feel hot and dizzy almost immediately, and drove her to look for a place to sit. But in this case the feeling had passed quickly, replaced by intense concentration. Bea was completely absorbed by what she was seeing.

"All right, I was wrong and I admit it," she said, nudging Allie slightly with her elbow.

"About what?"

"Coming here. This was worth . . . well, I was going to say twice what we paid for it, but I can't very well say that, can I? Because you wouldn't let me go along to buy the tickets, so I have no idea what we paid."

"Just as well. You were right that it was kind of expensive."

"But I was wrong when I said it's just a diversion. It's not. It's a way of learning about the world. And it seems especially meaningful what with our driving beside the ocean all these days. I was viewing it wrong. I was just looking at the surface of it, like that's all there was to it. Oh, I know better, of course, in my logical brain. I know it's deep and there are fish in it. But I never pictured that. I just never stopped to think about it. Now I'll look over at the water as we drive and understand there's a whole other world under it. It's like seeing part of the world you never thought about before. Never factored into your thinking. It makes the world seem bigger all of a sudden. I know I'm talking a lot. I hope I'm making sense."

"You are," Allie said. "But I think we should go look at something else now."

"But I like this so much."

"But how do you know you won't like *that* so much, too? The only way you'll know is if we go see."

"I hate it when you get all logical," Bea said.

———

"I am not touching one of those monsters," Bea told the girl.

"Well, I am."

Allie stood with one hand over the edge of the bat ray tank, a thigh-high open tank that allowed for petting. Though Bea could not imagine why. Petting zoos were one thing, but they were full of soft, cuddly mammals. With fur. Which is not to suggest that Bea would have enjoyed one.

"They sting," Bea pronounced, though really she had no way to know.

"No, they don't."

"You can get stung by a stingray. Why do you think they call them that?"

"These are not stingrays. They're bat rays. And they wouldn't have them in an open petting tank if they stung. And I'm petting one. So there."

Bea watched with mild alarm as the strange creatures lifted their front ends slightly out of the water, their winglike fins brushing upward against the sides of the tanks as though they planned to try to climb out. Then three or four glided by just under the surface of the water, looking like dark gray kites with stubby noses, and Allie dipped her hand in and allowed one of the creatures to slide against her palm.

"Whoa!"

"What does it feel like?"

"It's hard to explain. But it's soft. Almost . . . satiny. But wet. I couldn't describe it to you. You have to try."

"Oh, I think not."

"You really should do this, Bea."

"Why? Why should I do it? Give me one reason."

"Because this is probably the only chance you'll ever have to pet a bat ray. And because it's an amazing thing that they let you touch them. That they're not even afraid of us. And because it'll make your world bigger. And you keep saying you want that."

Bea wrinkled her nose. She could feel it.

"I said *one* reason."

"Get over here."

Bea moved closer to the tank and looked down. There was a bat ray just a foot or two away, gliding under the water in her direction. Somehow Bea knew the key would have to be an utter lack of preparation. Of anticipation. Once she allowed space for doubt, she would never overcome it. She would have to move faster than the doubt. She yanked the left sleeve of her sweater up to her elbow with her right hand, then stuck her left hand in the water and touched the bat ray as he swam by. It was satiny soft, just like the girl had said. But it was wet, living flesh, not fabric. It was unlike anything Bea had ever touched before.

She yanked her hand back before any part of the stinger could touch it.

"Oh my!"

"Now aren't you glad you did that?"

"I think maybe I am."

"I'm getting hungry. Are you getting hungry? We've been here for hours. We could get our hand stamped and come back in and see more after lunch."

"I could eat," Bea said.

———

"We can't always eat in restaurants," Bea said as they settled at their table. She picked up her menu. Looked at the right side first. Pricey. Everything was pricey. This was a tourist area, Cannery Row, and nothing came cheap. "It's just wasteful. Think how much food we could get at the supermarket for this kind of money."

Bea could see the disappointment written on the girl's face. Truthfully, Bea felt disappointed, too. The old Bea had returned, and issued an old Bea proclamation. It seemed both inevitable and sad.

"But we have no way to cook it."

"Not all food needs to be cooked. We might not be able to afford a hot meal three times a day."

"Okay. I get it. But we decided to have this one. So let's enjoy it."

"Good point," Bea said. "I'm sorry." Then she tried to stop talking. To leave it at that. But something about her simple apology—the very entrance of the word "sorry"—seemed to open a door that Bea was not strong enough to slam shut again. "Actually, I'm sorry for a lot of things."

Allie looked into her face. The girl seemed guarded. A little suspicious.

"Like what?"

"I guess I'm sorry I didn't believe you when you said you'd gone through that terrible experience. Which I now see you really had. And I'm sorry I was so quick to want to put you out of my van again. I was just being cautious, I guess. And about the money. Thank you for going back and getting your things from your house and using them for food and gas so we can get by until my next check. I wasn't being very appreciative about that. I was acting like you owed me all that and more. But it's generous. So I'm sorry I wasn't nicer about it. Money is a tricky subject for me. I'm always scared about it, and when I get scared I suppose I get rather . . . tight. And maybe not my very nicest self. I'll work on that."

"Wow," Allie said.

Bea expected her to say more. Instead a brief silence fell.

"Wow what?"

"I don't know. I just didn't expect all that from you."

"Don't be so surprised," Bea said, feeling herself bristle. "I can be nice."

"I didn't say you couldn't. I just—"

The waitress arrived, wanting to take their order. Which seemed strange to Bea, because she hadn't even taken a simple drink order first. *High prices and they push you through fast*, she thought.

Truthfully, Bea had barely glanced at the menu. But she knew what she wanted. It was a lunch choice that would be hard for Bea to order. Things being what they were. Bea being who she had always been. A day earlier it might have been impossible. But Bea felt she knew how to do it now: the same way you pet a bat ray. Without hesitation. Without creating a gap that doubt can wedge its way into, to create an even greater hesitation.

"I'll have the Dungeness crab," she said.

Allie's eyebrows looked strangely high in Bea's peripheral vision, but Bea did not openly turn her head to look.

"It was what I wanted," Bea said under her breath.

"I didn't say a word," Allie whispered back.

—

An hour or more after lunch they stood in a dim room of the aquarium filled with tank after tank of jellyfish. Bea found them mesmerizing.

She would never have imagined jellyfish as a thing of beauty. But these were brilliantly colored and patterned, veiled, glowing. They moved—pulsed, drifted—with astonishing grace. And something almost akin to serenity.

"I think we should find ourselves a good campground tonight," she told Allie. Quietly, because the room and its creatures inspired reverence. "With nice hot showers."

"Ooh," Allie breathed. Equally reverent. "That sounds great."

"Doesn't it? I haven't taken a hot shower since I left my home. What I really like is a nice deep bathtub. But I only had a skimpy little one in the trailer. I'll probably never take a hot bath again. But a hot shower will be the next best thing." Silence. Bea looked over to see the girl staring at her in the dim light. "What? Why are you looking at me like that?"

"You'll take a bath again. Why would you even say that? You don't know that you'll always be homeless."

"I don't see what's going to come along to change it."

"I'm not assuming I'll always be out in the world like this."

"You have parents."

"True. But when they get out of jail and I get to go home, you'll come take a bath at my house."

"Oh, I'm sure your parents would love that."

"After everything they've put me through, I doubt I'm going to put it like a question. I don't think I'd give them much choice."

But that's easy to say, Bea figured, when you're not looking said parents straight in the eye.

—

Bea sat on the front bumper of her van while the girl used the shower. Bea had showered first, and the feeling of cleanliness filled her with an exhilaration that would have seemed almost silly had she stopped to examine it.

They were at a state park campground, most of or all the way to Santa Cruz, camped just a few yards inland from a white sand beach that Bea had to admit was lovely. There was a pier. At the end of it a huge, ancient-looking ship sat broken apart and sunk in the shallow water. The setting sun made it look orange. The setting sun made everything look orange. And someone was flying a kite, all long tails, in front of that setting sun.

*It's a good thing this place makes me so happy,* Bea thought. *Because it was expensive.*

She pushed the thought away again. They had paid the camping fee. There was no going back now. Somehow she had to find a place inside herself that could relax and enjoy what they had purchased. Bea knew that would not be easy.

The people at the next campsite over had put chicken and sausage on the barbecue, and the smells had begun to drive Bea crazy. It would be hard to settle for the fruit and nuts they had bought at the supermarket.

*Squirrel food. I shouldn't have gone with only what the girl could eat, too. I should have bought some luncheon meat or cheese for myself.*

"That feels great," a voice said, and Bea jumped the proverbial mile. Of course it was only Allie.

"It does," Bea said. "For once you and I agree on something."

"What are you staring at?"

Bea realized it was not the ocean. Not the ship or the kite. The natural setting had lost her attention. Her focus had shifted to the meat cooking next door.

"Oh, just coveting dinner at the next site over."

She might have said it too loudly. A moment later Bea noticed the middle-aged couple responsible for the barbecue looking her way, disturbingly ready to break that conversational barrier.

"You don't have many of the comforts of home over there," the woman called.

Of course that was easy for her to say. She and her husband had one of those motor homes about the size of a Greyhound bus.

She was small, a compact woman with hair that looked beauty-parlor fresh. How one achieved such a thing on the road, Bea could not imagine. It made her feel self-conscious about her own thin gray hair, slicked back after her shower and left to dry on its own.

"We get by," Bea said.

"Any refrigeration?" the husband asked.

He was wearing a robe over swim trunks. Bea wondered if he really was brave enough to swim in that cold, wild ocean. People did, of course. Bea knew that. Still, she did not swim. And knowing what kind of creatures lived under there did not make her feel any more inclined toward a saltwater dip.

"No refrigeration," Allie said, answering for Bea, who was lost in thought.

"What do you eat?"

"Sometimes we eat out," Allie said. "Sometimes we buy stuff at the supermarket that doesn't need refrigeration."

"Short trip?" the wife asked.

"Not very," Allie said.

"We can throw some extra food on the barbecue," the husband called back. "You're more than welcome."

Bea felt her eyes go wide. "That's awfully generous."

She could feel two different emotions, two urges warring inside her: the part of her that wanted to keep to herself and build an invisible wall between her van and its neighbors, and the part of her that wanted barbecued chicken and sausage.

"My grandmother might like that," Allie said, moving a step closer. "I'm a vegan. I doubt there would be anything I could eat. But thanks."

"We have corn on the cob and salad and garlic bread," the wife said.

"We'll be right over," Allie replied.

——

"This is absolutely delicious," Bea said. "And we really appreciate the generosity."

"I'll say," Allie added, talking around a mouthful of roasted corn.

They sat at a picnic table with their hosts, watching the top of the sun touch the blue horizon and disappear. Turned out the bright orange of the sunset had only been warming up for its evening show.

The couple was tanned, Bea couldn't help noticing. Almost ridiculously tanned, as though they had nothing better to do than bask in the sun all day long. As though there were no such thing as skin cancer.

Three kids rode their bikes through the campground, ringing the bells on their handlebars and shrieking with laughter. Bea tried not to find it irritating.

She remembered suddenly that she was supposed to be communicating with the people they met on their trip. Not that she had exactly agreed to that challenge. But these people were feeding them a hot dinner. It seemed only right.

"Where do you folks live?" she asked. Just to dip her toe in that figurative human water.

Both the husband and wife pointed in the same direction.

"South of here?" Bea asked, not sure she understood.

"No, right there," the wife said. "Our rig."

"Oh, you *live* in that motor home."

It made Bea feel a little better. A little more kindly disposed toward them. They didn't have everything in the world that Bea didn't. They didn't have that huge RV *and* a big, fancy house. They had only what Bea saw in front of her. They lived on the road. Bea could relate to that.

"If you don't mind my asking . . . ," Bea began. Then she stalled. Who was she to ask them personal questions?

"We probably don't mind," the husband said.

"Was that a choice? Or out of necessity?"

"I guess everything is a choice at one level or another," the wife said. Then she looked up and around at the faces at the table. And seemed to note that more words would be needed to get her point across. "Andy's mother was sick. She was in her nineties, and she had Alzheimer's. We sold the house to live with her for her last few years. She didn't own a house. She lived in an apartment in Seattle. We hung on to the money from our home, but it wasn't enough to buy again. We'd had a mortgage to pay off. We didn't have a ton of equity."

"We *could* have bought another house," Andy added. Bea couldn't tell if he was every bit as anxious as his wife to share personal details, or if he was a little defensive regarding the picture she'd painted. "Potentially.

But it would have put us in so much debt. This rig we could buy free and clear, and that way we could afford to retire. I get a little pension."

Bea realized she had stopped chewing to listen to their story, which came as a surprise, because the food was too good to stop eating.

"Debt is the worst," Bea said. "Debt is a terrible, terrible thing. Somehow they've got us all primed to accept it. They've taught us it's part of the American dream or some such nonsense. But it keeps you in chains. The deeper in you get, the more money they make off your misfortune, and the deeper in you get. It's a big, vicious cycle where you give some faceless bank too much power over your life. And they don't care about you one bit. Don't for a moment think they do, because they don't. It was always so stressful for me. Like a sword hanging over my head. Like being chased by wolves all your life, and you can't stop running. No matter how tired you get, you have to stay ahead of them at all costs."

A long silence fell.

"So you're out of debt now?" the wife asked.

"I am. Completely." She could have added, "Because I lost my home and I live in my van now." She could also have added that she literally walked out on her debts. Left them unpaid. She didn't.

Change was one thing, but there was no point in letting it get out of hand.

—

"You did it!" Allie said after they had thanked their hosts profusely and let themselves back into the van in the dark.

The girl sounded inordinately excited, which seemed to argue painfully with Bea's fullness and sleepiness.

"What did I do?"

"You told them something about yourself. Something real. And, like . . . personal."

"How do you figure?"

Bea could remember only that she'd spied a perfect opportunity to admit her homelessness and firmly, consciously let it go by. Even though she was really no more homeless than they were. Just living on the road in considerably less luxury.

"You told them how awful it was for you to be in debt."

"Oh. That. Yes, I guess I did, didn't I?"

"I was so surprised! I thought you were going to sit back and watch me do it and see how it went for me."

"Yes," Bea said. "I guess I thought so, too."

# Chapter Twenty-Six

## *You'll Be in Heaven, and There Will Be Jellyfish*

Bea let a snort of air pass through her lips to vent her frustration.

They drove—if this inching along and stopping experience could be called driving in any proper sense of the word—through San Francisco, accidentally on the 101.

Allie had the map open in her lap. She'd said they'd have to go over the Golden Gate Bridge and several miles beyond before they'd get the chance to peel off onto Route 1 again and make their way west to the coast. She had promised Bea that after they did, their drive would turn remote again.

"This never ends," Bea said.

"It ends," Allie said, sounding more like the grown-up in the conversation.

"Well, it doesn't feel like it does. As far as I can see, there's nothing but these little short blocks. With a traffic light at every intersection. And the traffic keeps backing up and making us miss the lights. We haven't hit one green light since we came into the city. It's taken us longer to get this far down this route—except it's actually more of a city street—than it did to get up here from Santa Cruz."

"I don't know what to tell you, Bea. It ends. I'm looking at the map. I wish you were looking at it. After we get over the bridge and get back on Route 1, there's nothing. For miles and miles the coast is national recreation areas and state parks and national seashores. There's not much up there."

"Damn!" Bea spat as she missed another stoplight. Then, turning her attention to Allie, "That sounds good. Let me see that, please. It'll sustain me through *this*."

Allie handed her the map, and Bea pulled her reading glasses out of her shirt pocket and put them on. At first she couldn't even pin down where on the map she should be looking. Allie pointed, and Bea felt deeply soothed by the green shading of undeveloped coast just north of the city. Preserved land.

The feeling was forced out of her by a rudely honking horn. The light had changed.

Bea handed the map back and stomped on the gas pedal.

"I've begun to hate everything man-made," Bea said as she inched along.

"The van is man-made."

"I mean placewise. I like places where you can't even see that people have been there. I think that's a new thing about me. I always lived where there were freeways and stoplights and buildings. But I don't think I want to anymore."

The girl didn't answer.

"What about you?" Bea asked.

"I like going where there's nothing but cliffs over the ocean. But I think maybe when we're done seeing all that I could go back and live in a city again."

"It might be an age thing. I think we get to a certain age where enough of people and their ugly trappings is enough."

—

"What town is this?" Bea asked.

In the absence of knowing, Bea knew she liked it. Because it was small and quaint. Unobjectionable. And not a stoplight in the place.

"I don't know," Allie said. "I missed the sign."

"But you're the navigator. You have the map."

"Oh. Right."

The girl peered at the map for a moment or two.

"Might be Tomales."

"Well, I like it. Wherever it is. And I'm going to pull over and stop. Because I'm tired." Bea parked the van in one of the perpendicular spaces in front of a bakery café. "Think anyone will care if we're here all night?"

"No idea."

Bea turned off the engine. They sat listening to the metal tick as it cooled.

"Only trouble," Allie said, "is that if we only drive four or five or six hours a day, then here we are parked in a place and it's only afternoon. So what do we do?"

"I have no idea. I just know I'm not good for any more driving today. It's such hard driving. It was so twisty, especially that section just above the city. It makes my back and neck and shoulders ache."

"I wasn't blaming you for stopping. I'm just not sure what to do."

"That seems to be the worst part of this whole living-in-my-van experience. These long stretches of time to fill." A long silence. Neither one made a move to take off their seat belts or move out of the cab of the van. "It was worse before you came along, though."

Bea thought the girl might have a response to that, but apparently not.

"What I wonder now," Bea said, "looking back, is what I did all day in the trailer. I didn't have a job. Or much in the way of hobbies, come to think. I guess I read and watched TV. And the day went by. Probably if you'd asked me where it went I wouldn't have known what to say. Now I look back and all I can wonder is . . ."

But then she wasn't the least bit sure she wanted to finish the thought.

She looked over at Allie, who was clearly waiting.

"I guess I wonder why I didn't try to do more," Bea said, essentially the same way you pet a bat ray. "I had all these hours that added up to all these days, and I look back and it seems my goal was mostly to make them go away. But that's not a proper life. That's not really living. Why didn't I take up oil painting, or learn to play the flute or something?"

Allie waited, as if to see if Bea wanted to say more.

When she didn't, Allie said, "No idea. But we're living now."

"How very true," Bea said.

———

"I'm bored," Allie said, sitting up suddenly on her inflated bed. "Let's go for a walk."

"A *walk*?"

"Yeah. A walk. You know. It's one of those things people do when they're living."

"I'm an older woman, in case you hadn't noticed."

"So? Older people walk."

"This older person doesn't."

"Fine. Sit here in your recliner and read. I'm going out into the air."

The girl began to put her shoes back on. It made Bea feel restless. Truthfully, she wanted a change of scene, too. The inside of the van grew tiresome quickly these days.

Bea looked out the window for the fourth or fifth time at a restaurant and tavern on the next block. A thought broke through and became suddenly conscious.

"While you go for your walk I'm going to go to that tavern and have a drink."

Allie stopped tying her shoes and stared up into Bea's face. As if Bea had just said she was going to pick up men on a street corner. But the girl said nothing.

"What?" Bea asked, to challenge the look.

"I just didn't have you pegged as a drinker."

"I'm not. Hardly. I might have a beer maybe two or three times a year. I just decided this is one of those times."

—

Bea settled her tired bones at the bar and ordered that nice imported beer that came in the green bottles. The kind she and Herbert used to drink on Super Bowl Sunday. Bea had always hated football, but she had enjoyed its related rituals of good beer and mountains of empty-calorie snacks. That kind of indulgence had made her feel briefly content.

There was a restaurant on one side of the room, but it was neither lunch- nor dinnertime, and no one was eating. There was only one other woman in the place, a young curly-haired woman probably in her thirties playing darts with two older men. Three more men sat at the other end of the bar. Fortyish, all bearded. They had friendly faces that made Bea wish she was sitting with them.

She stared a moment too long, and one of them raised his mug to her, as if in a toast. Bea's face flushed, and her eyes darted back down to her beer bottle.

"Traveler?" he asked across the empty expanse of bar.

She nodded.

"Welcome to our little paradise," one of the other men said. He was wearing a panama straw hat over a thick and bushy head of hair.

"It *is* nice here," she said. "The only thing that would make it better is if you could see the ocean."

"Less than five miles that way," hat man said. "Well, you know which way. It would be west, wouldn't it?" He smiled at his own foolishness, and it made his cheeks dimple. "That's probably where you're staying tonight. Am I right?"

Bea felt her face flush again. She didn't want to tell them that she planned to park on the street to save the camping fee.

"How do you even know I'm stopping here? I could be driving on."

"We hope you're stopping," the third man said. "The coast route being what it is. We always like it best when people do their drinking at the end of the drive. Not so much in the middle."

"I won't be driving on," Bea said, taking the first long pull of beer.

She could feel it go down, quenching her thirst, loosening her muscles, and soothing the inside of her gut. That was probably more than a first swallow of beer can do in reality, but that was how it felt to Bea.

"Car or RV?" hat man asked.

"More like an RV. Little one."

"Okay. Then you're in luck. You go west at this corner," he said, pointing. "Road goes four, five miles and then at the end of it is the water, and a really big RV park. You can't miss it. Acres and acres. It's on a point of land right at the end of Tomales Bay. So you have open ocean to your right and still-water bay to your left. You can camp on the flat grass with just a walk over the dunes to the ocean, or you can go down to the seawall, which is on the bay. I'd go to the sea wall. You can put the nose or the tail of your rig right up to the wall, and if the tide is high I guarantee it'll be the closest you've ever camped to water. Some people think it's a little funky, that place. But if you're not a snob about such things, you'll be in heaven."

"I'm not a snob," Bea said, and took another long drink. The taste of the beer made her remember Herbert, this time in a positive light. "But I won't be camping there."

No one said a word. The bartender was washing and drying glasses, and the occasional light clink provided the only sound. Bea stole a glance at the men, who did not look back. The disappointment in the room felt palpable.

*It's just human communication.* Wasn't that what the girl had said? *And how can people use it against you? They can't. And I don't know why we're all so afraid of it.*

Or, at least, irritatingly precocious words to that effect.

"It sounds wonderful," Bea said. "But the truth is, I'm on a tight budget. I was just going to park here in town. You know. To save the camping fee."

Bea was careful to stare down at her beer bottle as she spoke. When she was done the silence reigned again. Bea did not dare look up to see how her admission had been received. She saw one of the men get up from his barstool, but she didn't look over. She could hear someone moving about the room, but did not turn her head to investigate.

For a moment Bea felt the urge to leave her half-drunk beer and run out the door. Her muscles disagreed, or never received the signal. Bea only sat.

A moment later hat man was standing at her left shoulder, but with his hat off. It was in his hand, upside down, extended in Bea's direction. Bea looked at his head and saw that all that bushy hair grew on the sides of his head only. He was bald as a bowling ball on top.

She looked into the hat to see a collection of bills. Several fives and one ten.

"What's this?" she asked.

"We took up a collection for you. We want you to stay in heaven tonight."

"I can't accept that."

"Why can't you? It's from all of us. It's a gift. We want you to go down to that point between the bay and the ocean. You'll like it. Trust us."

Bea stared at the money for a long beat or two, saying nothing. A moment later the bartender moved close and set another green bottle of imported beer in the hat.

"It's a narrow road, and a bit twisty," he said. "So go down there first and then pop that second one."

It felt impossible for Bea to say no now. Not even because of her pride. More because she'd begun to anticipate the heaven of the described experience.

"I don't know what to say."

Hat man only gestured in her direction with his hat.

"Thank you," Bea said.

She lifted the cold beer bottle by its neck and scooped the money out of the hat with her other hand. Then, much to her humiliation, tears rose in her eyes and spilled over for all to see. But no one stared, or said anything about her overreaction. Hat man just put his panama back on his bald head and sat down behind his mug again.

Bea pulled one more long sip of her beer and left the rest in the bottle. She slipped off her bar stool and hurried toward the door, carrying the money and the second bottle of beer.

"You all . . . ," she said. Then she stalled. She knew what she was thinking, but not quite how to say it, or even if she could. If she was brave enough for such a thing. "You just changed the whole way I think about strangers," she said.

Then she hurried out.

———

When she arrived back at the van, Allie was nowhere to be found.

Impatient, she decided to drive around and look for the girl.

Allie did not prove to be hard to find. Bea quickly spotted her around the corner.

Bea honked the horn and the girl jogged over and hopped in.

Bea accelerated and headed for the beach.

"I asked somebody," Allie said, "and they said you get to the ocean by taking this road. It's more than four miles, though. I thought I'd just walk a ways to someplace where I could see it. But it was a lot of ups and downs."

"Those are the worst," Bea said.

The girl reached out and fingered the sweaty neck of the cold, sealed beer, which Bea had set in the cup holder.

"So you took your drink to go."

"Something like that. Yeah."

"Where are we going?"

"The ocean."

"Oh. Good. I didn't think you'd want to do that. I thought you'd think it was a waste of gas."

"I'm changing my mind about what's wasteful and what's not," Bea said. "Seems all my life I had to make choices between what I considered wasting money and what I now see was wasting my life. If it keeps you from wasting your life, it can't very well be a waste, now can it?"

"Wow. You always make so much progress when I'm not around. I should go away more often."

———

Just past a beach parking lot with a backdrop of powerful waves crashing on the sand, Bea stopped at the gate of the RV park.

"I think you have to pay to go in there," Allie said.

"Yes, you do. Here." Bea handed her the money she had scooped out of a stranger's panama hat. It had been sitting in the other cup holder. "Tell them we want to be by the seawall."

"I'm missing something," Allie said, staring at the money but not taking it. "How do you know they have a seawall?"

"Some locals at the tavern told me."

"They must have made it sound great. Two nights in a row you agree to shell out for expensive campgrounds?"

"It sounded appealing, yes." While she waited, watching Allie look at the money but not take it, Bea berated herself for cowardice. And for being a liar, at least by omission. All Bea's life she had been lying by omission, she now realized. When you omit nearly everything you could be telling people, there isn't much truth left to go around. "Actually, there was more to it than that. I told them we couldn't afford it, and they took up a collection so we could come down here."

"Wow."

"Yes, it was very nice of them."

"I meant wow, you told them we couldn't afford it. But yeah. That was really nice. See? I told you most people are good."

"I could have done without the 'I told you so.'"

"Right. Sorry. The minute it came out of my mouth I knew it was wrong."

—

Between the dunes and the seawall, along a road of deeply rutted dirt, they drove past a row of trailers. It took Bea a moment to realize their occupants were not overnighters. These trailers were permanent. And probably what the man at the bar had been referring to when he used the word "funky."

The trailers themselves were tiny and ancient, huddled close together, even older than the one Bea had left behind. Most had fences hand built around them, often out of driftwood. Fishing nets and floats decorated the yards, along with a carved ship's masthead and even a full-size anchor. Imaginative, these residents were. Rich, they were not.

"Why aren't you driving?" Allie asked.

It startled Bea, who had been lost in thought and hadn't realized she had stopped.

"I was just looking at these trailers. I was just wondering . . . maybe I could afford to live in a place like this."

"But don't those trailers have refrigerators and little bathrooms?"

"Oh. Right. Of course. I forgot about that."

"And it might be expensive to stay here, even though it's not too fancy. Because it's right by the ocean. And everybody wants to be right by the ocean."

"True."

"And it might get cold in the winter."

"Okay, I've got it. You talked me out of it."

"I wasn't trying to talk you out of it. Just wanted you to think about those things."

"No. You're right. It was just a thought."

But it was a thought Bea hated to see fly away.

———

Bea pushed her easy chair closer to the back doors of the van, which stood wide open, providing a view over the seawall and Tomales Bay. She saw hills in the distance behind the water, a little fishing pier that seemed to be part of their campground, and the sun going down in a surprising location, reminding Bea that she had no idea which direction was which. But it didn't matter. The only thing that mattered was the way the late sun sparkled on the water.

"Aren't you afraid of letting Phyllis out?" Allie asked.

The girl was tying on her shoes again.

"Those first few days I was. I thought she might try to escape and run home. But I think she's used to the van now. I think she'll hunker down in here to feel safe. Anyway, I'm watching her."

"Come out for a walk with me. Just down onto the sand. We won't go far."

"Where do you see sand?"

"Right at the end of the seawall there's a place where you can get down onto the beach."

"Tell me all about it when you get back."

Allie sighed. Then she vaulted from the back of the van, over the low seawall, and onto wet sand on the other side. Phyllis spooked and ran under the passenger seat.

Bea sighed contentedly, breathing in the sea air. Drinking in the scene. Drinking her second beer while it was still cold.

What seemed like only a minute or two later, Allie was back, sticking her head in through the open doors.

"You have to see this."

"I'm too comfortable."

"No, really. I mean it. You have to see it."

Bea sighed, not so contentedly this time.

"All right, all right. But I hope it isn't very far."

"It's not. You can practically see the spot from here."

Bea set her beer down on the van floor and carefully stepped out, closing and locking the back doors behind her. She shuffled along beside the low wall, following the girl.

*This had better be good,* she was thinking. But she did not say so out loud.

"For one thing, I wanted you to see *him*," Allie said, pointing to a pelican. He was hunkered down in the parking lot, his neck entirely withdrawn into himself, his comically long, clumsy beak angled off his feathered chest and into the air. Bea could see every detail of his brown feathers. He was only a handful of feet away, and apparently not inclined to move away from them. Not in the least concerned about their presence.

"But it gets better," Allie added.

"I thought pelicans were white."

"Some are. But here on the coast we have Pacific browns. They're pretty common."

"How do you know all that?"

"I grew up near the beach."

"Oh. That's right. You did, didn't you?"

"Also I went to school. You know. Just because I'm young doesn't mean I don't know anything."

They moved through a gap in a fence at the end of the seawall. Bea reached out for Allie's arm to steady herself as they made their way down a short but steep hill of sand. Then they were walking on sand at the edge of the lightly lapping bay. Bea turned her head to look more closely at a tall dune on the land side, marked with perfect patterns—troughs and waves—that the wind had blown into its surface. In the setting sun it glowed orange.

It was all very beautiful, but also tiring. It was hard walking in loose sand, and Bea felt she'd had enough.

"I hope it's not much farther," she said, her voice marred by puffing breath.

"It's not. We're here. Look."

The girl stood at the edge of the water and pointed down. Bea followed the pointing finger and saw that dozens of jellyfish had washed up onto the beach. They were orangey, and looked a little like huge uncooked eggs with multiple yolks. But at the same time they were far more intricate and beautiful.

It formed a perfect loop in Bea's mind. On one end was the aquarium in Monterey, where they had been able to see—albeit in a simulated way—under the ocean waters. On the other was driving the coast while truly understanding that all that wonder really did exist just beyond their view.

She thought of the man with that hat and the bushy hair—wondered how he knew that this would be her perfect heaven. Or maybe he had been speaking more generically. Still, it felt prophetic now.

She looked up to see Allie staring into her face.

"You look happy," the girl said.

"I think I am."

"You think? You don't know?"

"It's an unfamiliar sensation. Give me some slack."

"Right. Sorry. So you're glad you walked down here, I hope."

"Yes," Bea said. "I'm glad."

They stood for a long time in silence. Bea alternated between watching the sun set behind the fishing pier and looking down at the way its golden light made the colors of the jellyfish glow.

"I think I had a false idea about heaven," Bea said.

"Heaven?"

"Not heaven like where some people think you go after you die. More like heaven on earth. I always thought it would be a place where nothing was going on and nothing was required of you. You know, perfectly restful. But now I think it might be a more action-oriented sort of deal." She paused to see if the girl had anything to add to the odd set of thoughts. "Well. We should go back before the sun goes down."

But for a good five or ten more minutes, Bea just stood and drank in that perfect moment.

# Chapter Twenty-Seven

*Definitely Friendly, but Definitely Not a Ghost*

Driving through the heart of Fort Bragg, a nice enough small town on a high cliff over the sea, Bea spotted the familiar pattern of black and white on an approaching southbound car. She was only just absorbing the color of its light bar, and what it meant to their situation, when Allie began to shout.

"Turn! Fast! Turn right here!"

Bea swung the wheel wildly. The tires squealed. She could only hope she had sufficient distance from the police car, or Highway Patrol car, or whatever it was. She could only hope its driver hadn't seen or heard that ridiculous turn.

"Turn again! Pull in here!"

"Stop barking orders at me! You're making me nervous."

Still, Bea turned, as she had been told to do, and rolled to a stop out of sight of the main drag—the coast highway through town. They waited in absolute silence.

Nothing happened. No police car drove down the side street looking for them.

Bea sighed and shifted the van into "Park." She rested her forehead on the steering wheel, breathing out as much of her alarm as she could manage.

"Maybe I should just get this over with," Allie said.

"I don't know what you're referring to. Get what over with?"

"You know."

"If I knew I wouldn't be asking."

"Maybe I should just turn myself in."

Bea opened her mouth to speak, but her throat felt tightly locked, and she wasn't sure if she would succeed. She reached out for the ignition key and turned off the engine. The silence felt stunning. The slight hum of cars on the highway formed a background to the moment, but all else held still.

Bea swallowed hard in preparation for attempting to speak.

"Please don't do that," she said to the girl.

"I'm just so tired of being scared like this. Always looking over my shoulder. And maybe they'd go easier on me if I turned myself in. Besides. We both know I have to. Sooner or later. I can't just ride around with you till I'm eighteen."

Bea's brain did not seem to be in working order, so she couldn't present cogent arguments in a crisp format as she might have wished. Instead she said, again, "Please don't." It sounded pathetic, like a puppy whimpering, begging for someone to make it feel more secure.

"I'll give you the gold bar before I go. If that's what you're worried about."

Bea shook her head. "It's not."

"What, then?"

"I don't want to go back to the way it was before I had you along. It was terrible. I hated it. I was alone and I was scared all the time. And now we're actually doing things that are . . . good. That make me feel good. And you don't even know for a fact that your nosy neighbor reported my license plate number. For all you know she was too far away to see it or didn't care enough to call. You might be making this huge decision for no reason at all. We haven't seen Cape Flattery yet. We're only halfway there, and you can't quit halfway through an adventure. It's just not right."

Bea waited. The silence stretched out. She didn't dare look at the girl. It would be too much like looking into a mirror and seeing the most vulnerable side of herself in the worst possible light.

"You never *act* like it's a good thing that I'm along," Allie said, her voice small. "You act like I'm a big pain in your ass."

"Well . . . you are, dear. But it was still much worse without you." Another long silence.

"Okay," Allie said. "I guess we should try to get all the way up to Cape Flattery before I make any big decisions."

Bea straightened up and filled her lungs with air.

"Yes. Excellent. Thank you. On to Cape Flattery."

She turned the key in the ignition. No sound. Well, one sound. Click.

She turned the key to "Off" again. She sat a moment, feeling the chill settle into her belly and her bones. Then she decided it had been an anomaly, or she had somehow turned the key in not quite the right way. This next time would be different, and all would be well again.

She cranked at the key a second time.

Click. Click. Click.

Not only did the engine not turn over, it didn't even try. Judging by its response, for all Bea knew a pickpocket might have stolen it right out from under the hood while she was begging the girl not to go.

Bea withdrew the key and set it in her lap.

"Uh-oh," she said.

"Now what?"

"I have no idea."

"I guess we call a tow," Allie said.

"With what? Do you still have that cell phone you took from your house?"

"Yeah, but I don't dare use it. You can track a person's location with a cell phone."

"That can't be true."

"Look. I'll get out and walk to the nearest business and borrow their phone."

"What do you think a tow costs, though?"

"No idea," Allie said. "I never called one. I'm barely old enough to drive, remember?"

She opened the door and stepped down out of the van. She stood on the sidewalk for a moment, digging into the pocket of her jeans. She pulled out what Bea thought she recognized as the one-ounce gold bar. To Bea's surprise, the girl pressed her lips to it, right through its plastic bag.

"Guess I can kiss this goodbye, though," Allie said.

Then she slammed the door and she was gone.

———

"So, is someone coming?" Bea asked before the girl could even jump back into the passenger seat.

"Yeah."

"How much is it going to cost?"

"I still don't know."

"You didn't ask?"

"I asked. Of course I asked. But it didn't help. He said there was a ninety-five-dollar hookup fee. And then it's five dollars a mile to tow it to a repair shop. After . . . I forgot. There are a few miles they throw in for free, but not many. I forgot the number. *They're* a repair shop, the tow truck people. So they can tow it into their own place. So they know where *they* are. But I had to put the guy on the phone with the lady in the store so she could tell them where *we* are. I didn't talk to him after that, so I have no idea how many miles it'll be."

"Oh. Okay. Well . . . we'll manage, I guess. You still have your computer. And the gold bar, and your phone, and . . . what did you call that other thing?"

"My iPad?"

"Yes. I have no idea what that is. But it's worth money, right?"

"Yeah, but we have another problem. There's no pawnshop. The lady let me look in her phone book. There's just a listing for a guy who buys gold and coins and stuff—"

"That's perfect. That's exactly what we need."

"—in Eureka. Unless we want to go inland, which I think we don't."

"Oh. How far away is Eureka?"

"I don't know in miles. But I could show you on the map." Allie pulled the map from the glove compartment and opened out its folds. "Here's us," she said, pointing to Fort Bragg. Then she slid her finger up the coast. Way up the coast. "And here's Eureka."

"Oh dear. Too far to walk, I'd say."

"Too far to walk in *a week*. And . . . Oh. That figures. Our tow is here."

"So fast?" Bea asked, her voice full of dread.

"Of course so fast. Because we need time to figure this out. If we'd wanted him to hurry, he would have been slow."

———

"Definitely your starter," the man said after Bea had attempted to crank the engine again at his request.

He was, quite surprisingly, Bea's age. Maybe even a little older. She would have guessed him to be eighty. Well past retirement age. He was clean shaven with neatly cut sideburns, but his snow-white hair flowed long and tumbled past his collar in the back. Bea felt it unfair that her hair had thinned while this gentleman's, not so much.

"So what do we do?" Bea asked him through her open driver's window.

"We put in a new starter and get you back out on the road."

"Okay, then. I guess that's what we'll do."

She climbed out of the van and watched him back his tow truck up to her front bumper. She felt the girl standing close to her shoulder, but did not turn to look, or acknowledge her presence. She just stood and watched the man do work that he was by all rights too old to do, and felt the sun bake down on her scalp and the wind toss her hair—such as it was—back and forth across her eyes.

"When do we tell him we don't have the cash to pay for this?" Allie whispered into Bea's ear.

"We might have the cash. How much of *your* cash is left?"

"Less than a hundred dollars. How much do you have?"

"Not much."

"So back to my original question . . ."

"Let's get the thing safely into the man's shop, and then we'll figure something out." Bea almost added, "I hope." She decided against it.

—

The man came out into the customer waiting area and found them. They had been sitting for the better part of an hour. Bea had drunk three cups of coffee and regretted the last two. Allie had been chewing on her thumbnail at regular intervals until Bea slapped her hand away.

The man settled himself onto the couch with them. Maybe to make them feel more comfortable. Maybe his old bones got tired over the course of a day's work. Hard to imagine they wouldn't.

He lifted a baseball cap from his flowing white hair and scratched his head briefly.

"I had my mechanic go over every inch of your van. Everything that could affect you over a long trip. Some good news, some bad. I wish the balance was better, but what can you do?"

"Let's hear the good news anyway," Bea said. "Even if it isn't much."

"He says there's a level at which the van has been cared for well. The oil is clean and topped up. All the fluid levels are good."

"My husband Herbert taught me a little about that."

"Well, you did a good job. The fan belt is frayed, though. It could go at any minute. And the hoses in your cooling system are very bad. Very old. The rubber is mushy and cracked, especially at the elbows. You can't imagine how much trouble that can cause. One of those babies gives way, you lose all your coolant, the engine overheats, and that could be the end of the old girl."

Bea blinked for a moment, a bit taken aback.

"What old girl?"

"Your van."

"Oh. I see. For a minute there I thought you meant me."

He threw his head back and laughed. It was a big sound, a genuine thing, emanating from deep in his chest. It made Bea like him some.

"I'm Casper," he said, reaching out a hand for her to shake.

"Like that little boy ghost who wanted to be everybody's friend," Bea said, shaking it. "I'm Bea, and this is my granddaughter, Allie."

Casper tipped his baseball cap at the girl. "Young lady," he said. Then, to Bea, "When I was born there was no such thing as Casper the Friendly Ghost. Not yet. Life was so much simpler back then."

"Sorry. You must be tired of hearing that. So, these hoses . . . is that a big, expensive thing?"

"Oh no. Not at all. Drives mechanics crazy that you can get them for pretty cheap, and it's quick to put them on, laborwise, but the whole engine can be lost if the owner doesn't tend to it. So we'll replace those all right. But there's another thing, and this'll set you back more. Those tires you've been driving on are downright dangerous."

Bea drew her head back in a pantomime of surprise. "That doesn't sound right. Herbert taught me how to do the penny test on the tread, and the tires passed that test before I left on my trip."

"That's not always the whole story, though. But don't take my word for it. Come see what I mean."

He pulled to his feet and reached an elbow out for Bea. As if Bea should take his arm and be lifted from the couch. Escorted into the shop. Bea wasn't quite sure how to interpret that. Was he being gallant? Or did he think her incapable of standing up and walking?

"I'll do fine," she said, and rose on her own.

She followed Casper into the shop area, where her poor disabled van sat next to a nice new BMW, looking sad and old. The girl shuffled along behind. Bea could hear her footsteps. It provided some comfort.

"The problem is your alignment," Casper said, speaking up to be heard over some sort of power tool. "Or lack of same. When's the last time you had a front end alignment?"

"I don't know. Herbert never taught me about that."

"Do you know when he last had it done?"

"Well, he's been dead several years, so none too recently."

"Oh. I'm sorry." Casper opened the passenger door of the van, reached through, and cranked the steering wheel to the left. "Now come look at this."

They bent at the waist for a time, staring at one of the front tires.

"See these scallops on the inside edge of the tread?" He pointed at a couple of spots where the rubber of the tire seemed to have been scooped out. "You're right down to the belt here. Very dangerous to drive on those. So you need to replace them, and of course we need to do an alignment so you don't ruin your new ones in short order."

"Oh dear. What about the back tires?"

"Not nearly as bad. But all four of them have cracks on the outside walls. I'd venture a guess and say they're older in years than mileage, but it works against you either way. You maybe could get away with just two for the front if money is a problem. But I'd replace all four if you possibly can."

"Oh, it's a problem. It's always a problem."

Bea straightened up. Probably too fast. And maybe—just maybe—that was the reason she almost passed out. Or maybe it was the sudden realization that once again her plan had been full of holes all along. Life was too complicated and too dangerous, and there was always something she hadn't anticipated. Why, she could have killed herself and that poor young girl, just driving along thinking she had everything under control.

And now she had to tell Casper the truth. That she did not exactly have the ability to pay him. Not without quite a bit of creative problem-solving. Not even for the tow, which was a service already rendered in good faith.

Or it might have been some combination of causes.

Whatever the reason, Bea's vision went white, especially at the edges, and she felt herself lose her balance and pitch to one side. Before she could slam down on the concrete shop floor, Casper was there. Holding her up.

"Let's get her back to that couch in the waiting room," he said to Allie.

They each took one of her arms. Or tried, anyway. Bea shook them off.

"I'm fine. My goodness. I'm not an invalid. I can walk. I just stood up too fast. Got a little woozy."

Still, they walked close on either side of her, which Bea felt was not such a bad deal. She just didn't care to admit it.

—

Bea had no idea how much later she opened her eyes, or even if she had slept. She was on her back on the couch in Casper's waiting room, her feet elevated. Allie was sitting on an uncomfortable-looking chair, staring at her.

"Was I asleep?"

"Guess so," the girl said. "It's been an hour or two."

"Help me up. I have to go tell Casper about our money problem."

"I already told him."

A pause fell while Bea absorbed that. While she reset her negative anticipation and relaxed back into the couch. She wanted to know how it had gone. At least, part of her did.

"I had a long talk with the guy," Allie continued. "He's pretty nice. He didn't take it badly at all. Not at all. He said we'd be surprised how many of the people who come through here haven't figured out how they're going to pay for their repairs."

"I thought everybody had credit cards. Except me."

"Mostly, yeah, but then they find out they're too maxed out to cover the bill."

"Hmm," Bea said. "That actually makes me feel better."

"He's interested in my MacBook. He might take it in trade for part of the repair. He says he has a loaner car that he lets people use sometimes. It's out right now. But it's supposed to be back at the end of the day. So maybe tomorrow we can drive up to Eureka and take care of that business with the gold."

"Tomorrow? I hate to be here so long. Where will we sleep?"

"I have no idea. But he can't get the new starter delivered till tomorrow morning anyway. So we're here tonight. That's just the way it is."

"Oh," Bea said. "Oh dear."

They stopped talking for quite a long time. Several minutes.

"Thank you for broaching that difficult topic with him," Bea said. She had to push the words to get them to leave her mouth. "And finding a way to work it out. That's quite a load off my mind, I must say."

"You're welcome."

Another brief silence.

"I'm trying to be better at letting you know what I like about having you along. Since I obviously communicate it clearly when you're a pain in the tail."

"Thank you," Allie said. "I appreciate that. What's *Casper the Friendly Ghost?*"

"It was just a silly kids' cartoon. It was before your time."

"Do you like him? The real Casper, I mean."

"He seems nice enough."

"He likes *you.* He asked about you a lot."

"Nonsense. Don't be silly."

"Why is it silly?"

"I'm an old woman."

"He's an old man."

"I won't hear any more about it. I'm sure you're wrong."

Truthfully, she wasn't positive.

———

Casper appeared around closing time. At least, his head did. It hovered in the slightly open doorway of the waiting area as though attached to nothing. His face looked hesitant. Tentative, like a man about to give a speech in front of thousands, balancing in the grip of stage fright.

Before he even opened his mouth, Bea knew the girl had been right. It was a strange sensation, that knowing. Scary and unwanted and buoying and a little bit heady all at the same time.

"I was wondering if I could have the pleasure of taking two lovely ladies out to dinner," he said. "Nothing fancy. There's a place down the street that makes great pizza and chicken wings. And they have the best salad bar in town."

Bea had been wondering how they were supposed to get anyplace where food could be purchased. The possibility of going to sleep hungry had played through her mind. Still she hesitated.

"We'd love to," Allie said. Then, turning to Bea, "Wouldn't we?"

"I think that would be lovely," Bea said. "Thank you."

———

"We could all get one giant pizza," Casper said, holding the menu up in front of his face. "How do you feel about pepperoni?"

"We can't all get one," Bea said. "Pepperoni is fine with me, but it's the girl. You know. Kids today. She doesn't eat anything that used to be an animal."

Then she sipped her iced tea, which she had sweetened just right, and felt suddenly fortunate. They were being fed, and the van was being repaired. It was not the end of the world after all. It was not even the end of the adventure.

"Or anything that *came* from an animal," Allie added. "So I can't order pizza. It's all covered with cheese. I have to just eat from the salad bar."

"They have vegan cheese on request," Casper said.

"You're kidding me!"

He reached over to Allie's menu and pointed it out.

"Whoa! I love this place!"

Bea's gaze flicked up to Casper's face and they smiled awkwardly, then looked away.

"Kids," Bea said.

"I know what you mean," he said. "But as kids go, she's a nice one."

"She'll do," Bea said, but it sounded affectionate. More so than she had planned. "I must admit it's nice to have a conversation with someone my own age for a change."

"I'm not your age," Casper said. "I'm quite a bit older, I'm sure."

Their waiter arrived, a young man who could not have been much over twenty. Clean cut and smiling.

"Evening, Casper," he said.

"A very *good* evening, Todd, I'll tell you that right now. The lady and I will split a large pepperoni and double cheese. And we all want trips to the salad bar. The young lady will order her pizza on her own."

"Small with vegan cheese," Allie piped up, sounding inordinately excited about it. "With mushrooms and onions and bell peppers and tomatoes and olives."

They folded up their menus and handed them over.

"Is it okay that I ordered so many toppings?" Allie asked.

"The plan was for you to order whatever strikes your fancy," Casper replied.

"I don't think you're older than me," Bea said when Todd had gone. "At least, not by much."

"I'll be eighty-one this month."

"Very much in the same ballpark."

"No way. I can't believe that."

"A lady doesn't give her exact age. So I'll just say I'm in my seventies and leave it at that." She sipped her tea for a moment in silence. "And I didn't exactly just arrive in them, either."

"So you remember eight-track tapes and black-and-white TVs and party lines on your telephone," Casper said.

"Oh, goodness yes. I remember when we felt oh so lucky to have them. Remember those little plastic inserts you snapped into your forty-fives so they'd play on the spindle of your phonograph?"

"As if it were yesterday," he said.

Bea looked up to see Allie wrinkling her nose. "I don't even know what a spindle or a forty-five is. I know what a phonograph is. Never saw one with my own eyes, though. I've seen pictures."

A silence fell. Bea wanted to extend the pleasant banter. It felt light and a little bit exciting, like flirting. But Casper had slipped into a more serious mood.

"Look," he said, and the one word pulled Bea back down. "I know the two of you have been using the van as a camper. That's easy enough to see from the way it's set up inside. I can't let you sleep in it while it's in the shop, though. It would be a problem with my insurance. I'm really not supposed to allow customers in the shop at all. If absolute worst comes to absolute worst, I can open the shop doors and push it out into the parking lot. But I hope you'll accept an offer to use my guest room tonight instead."

Bea opened her mouth to refuse him, but he cut her off with a hand like a stop sign.

"Before you answer, I just want you to know I'm a gentleman. You've been alive long enough to remember those, too. I know a lady when I see one, and I would never make such an offer in any sort of ungentlemanly way. The guest room has a lock on the door, if that makes you feel better. There's just one bed. A double. If you two wouldn't mind sharing."

Bea glanced over at the girl, whose eyes begged her to accept. They all but said it out loud, those eyes: "Please, please, please, Bea. A *bed*!"

Yes, a bed sounded like a lovely treat. Bea could scarcely remember her last experience with one.

"Thank you," she said. "If it's all very above board, we would love to take you up on that. Only thing is, I have to go by the shop after dinner. I have to feed my cat."

Casper's eyebrows jumped higher. His eyes widened. "You have a cat in there? I never saw one."

"I expect she's keeping a low profile. But the poor thing has to eat. And it would help to pick up a few items from the van. Toothbrush, change of clothes . . . Well, enough about that. I'm hungry. I say we hit that salad bar."

———

"Maybe we should bring the cat with us," Allie said.

They were all three sitting in Casper's car, just outside the shop, in the dark. Bea had been in to leave food for the cat, but Phyllis had not come out and made herself known. But she was all right. Bea had crouched down and peered under the passenger seat and seen the cat's eyes glowing back at her in the dim light. Phyllis was just upset. She'd get over it. She wasn't the only one who had to learn to be flexible these days.

"I honestly think she's better off in the van," Bea said. "It's more familiar. And besides, I couldn't get her out from under that seat if I tried."

"And I'm not such a big cat fan," Casper chimed in, as though he'd only just found his voice or his right to comment. "I'm allergic. But beyond that, I was just never much of a cat person. More into dogs."

"Do you *have* dogs?" Bea asked, suddenly alarmed at the idea of spending a night in a house with several massive, rough, ill-mannered beasts.

"No, I work too much. I'd like to have a dog. But maybe when I retire."

The comment sat a moment without much reaction. Then Bea burst into laughter. It was a big, hearty laugh, the kind that might not stop simply because you wanted it to. You had to let it play out. It had been gone for longer than Bea could remember, that kind of laughter.

"Casper, my goodness," she said when it had rolled through. "You're eighty-one years old. If you're not retired by now, when will you *ever* be?"

"When I absolutely, positively have no choice in the matter."

*And of course by then you'll be too old to take care of a dog,* Bea thought, but she didn't say it. The man's life was none of her concern. Just as well. She had never entirely trusted men who didn't like cats.

Bea turned her head to address Allie in the backseat. "The cat will be fine. It's been a long, difficult day. Let's get back to our host's house and have a shower and get some sleep."

———

They stepped into his living room together. Casper flipped on the light.

The first thing Bea saw were the animals, which were of the nonliving variety. A full-size adult bear, a victim of both a hunter and a taxidermist. Then she saw the head of some kind of horned elk mounted on the wall. Beside it, two long guns and a huge swordfish sat mounted on a wooden plaque over the fireplace.

*Oh dear,* Bea thought. *This will upset the child no end.*

She looked over at Allie, but the girl did not return her gaze. Bea waited for a rude comment, but none was made.

Casper noticed, though.

"Not everybody's cup of tea," he said. "But just so you know, I always get a clean shot. I shoot well to avoid their suffering. It's a point of pride with me."

"That's good to know," Bea said.

Still, it seemed a shame to kill a fish and not even eat it. It seemed a waste. Maybe he had eaten the rest of the elk, at least.

"Well, dibs on the first shower," Allie said. "Then I'm going straight to bed."

Bea thought she must be terribly upset about the dead animals. But a moment later Allie caught Bea's eye and gave her a sly wink.

Then the girl slipped into the guest room, leaving Bea alone with an actual man. As though there were nothing the slightest bit terrifying about that.

———

Bea sat out on the balcony of Casper's home, looking over the ocean and up at the stars, intermittently. Wishing Allie had stayed.

"A glass of wine?" Casper called in from the kitchen.

*That would be a lot of alcohol in just a couple of days,* Bea thought. *And a bit unlike me.*

"Sure," she said. "Why not?"

A moment later he appeared at her left shoulder, holding out a glass of something red, which she accepted.

"It'll help me sleep," she said.

Casper settled in the chair next to hers, and sipped from his own glass.

"Do you get up early in the morning?" he asked her.

"Depends. Why?"

"Something I want to show you and your granddaughter. Some*place*, actually. I want to go down there around sunrise, because too much later and it's absolutely overrun by tourists. To see it at its best you have to get up pretty early in the morning. That way you can have the place all to yourself. Or in this case *we* could have it all to *our*selves."

"I think that sounds worth getting up for. Allie is trying to teach me to be more adventurous."

"She's a delightful girl."

"She is," Bea said. In that moment she didn't even mind admitting it.

A long silence fell. As it progressed, it began to feel heavy. Awkward.

"You must think I'm a pathetic old man," Casper said after a painful length of time.

"No, why would I think that?"

"It must be so obvious that I'm lonely since my wife died."

"That's not pathetic, though. That's just human."

"Have you been lonely since your husband died?"

Bea pulled a deep breath, then let out a long sigh. She sipped her wine before answering. It made everything a little smoother. A little easier.

"Not so much as you would think. At first I was devastated by the loss, but I didn't turn out to be one of those people who jumps right back into being a couple again with somebody new. I keep my own company too well, I suppose."

"So you don't even think about that now? You wouldn't even consider it? Oh, I'm sorry, Bea. Don't even answer that. Don't say anything.

That came out completely wrong. We don't even know each other. We're one day away from being perfect strangers. Not even a whole day. And I was not—repeat, was *not*—putting the moves on a lady I only met this morning. I can't stress that too strongly. I guess I just thought it was nice getting to know you, and I suppose part of me wondered if you might be inclined to stay in these parts a little bit longer. You know. Just to see what's what with that."

Bea knew the answer was no. But she needed to say more, to explain why, so he wouldn't take it wrong and be hurt. So she sipped her wine and mulled her thoughts for a moment before responding.

She thought about the rifles and the dead animals in the living room, and the vote of no confidence in cats. They reminded her what it meant to allow someone into your life. You see something you like in a man, so you ask him in, but what comes in is all of him. Not only the parts you took a liking to, but the many parts that don't fit with you at all. That's always the way it worked.

But she knew she wouldn't tell him any of that.

"Oh, Casper," she said, uncomfortable and slightly giddy at the same time. "I'm so flattered I can hardly tell you. But I could stay here for years and not be ready for a thing like that. It's not you. You seem like a nice man. But relationships are so . . . I don't know. It's me, I guess. I'm just not easy with other people. Never really have been. Romances feel like so much trouble. So much constant compromising. I know for a lot of people it's worth it. But I don't think it is for me. When Herbert died, I was so lost. And then, after I realized I could get by on my own, life began to feel simple. It sounds terrible to say, but in some particular sense it was almost a relief."

She fell silent again, and stared up at the stars, pulling longer gulps from her glass. She did not look over at his face, because if he was hurt she didn't want to see.

"Well, you can't blame an old fool for trying."

"You're not a fool."

"Absolutely I am. I pride myself on it."

They sat without speaking for a few minutes, looking up at the stars. Bea was relieved they could be silent. She felt exhausted by communication. In time she heard the water shut off and heard Allie open the noisy shower stall door.

"That would be my cue," Bea said. "It's been a long day." She rose, but hovered a moment, knowing more was needed. "Thank you for everything," she said, and placed a hand lightly on his shoulder.

He turned his head to look at the hand. He smiled at it, but the smile was a tired, sad-looking little thing. It seemed to use up the last bit of energy Casper owned.

———

"I can't believe I got to take a real bath in a real tub," Bea said to the girl, who was already in bed. Bea stood in her pajamas, toweling her hair, wondering why she didn't feel sleepy.

"That's how it is at my house, too," Allie said. "Big bathtub on one side of the bathroom, shower stall on the other. Was this the kind of deep tub you said you wanted?"

"Yes and no. Smaller than the one in my dreams. Bigger than the one in my trailer."

She threw the towel over the back of a chair and climbed into bed with the girl. The sheets felt like flannel, which was so luxurious Bea found it almost hard to process. On top of them lay a heavy duvet that pressed down on Bea and made her feel secure and warm. It was a sensation almost unbearably like childhood.

"Were you terribly upset about the animals?" Bea whispered.

"You mean the dead bear and his friends? Not so much as you probably think."

"But you're so against killing animals."

"I wouldn't *do* it. And I wouldn't want to *see* it. But animals kill animals. You know. To eat. And I don't think that's so terrible. It's just the way nature planned it. So that elk, he lived free in the wild until the exact moment Casper shot him. Not so different from being brought down by a lion. What I can't stand is the way we raise animals for meat. The factory farms. We keep them in the most horrible conditions, and mistreat them so badly, and then, after all that, slaughter them in front of each other. That's the system I can't be any part of. A hunter . . . I don't know. I guess it's not the best sign in the world about the guy. But I'd be more upset about the fact that he doesn't like cats."

"Interesting," Bea said. She almost added, "You've thought this through more logically than I realized," but she withheld the words, realizing they hinted at an insult. "Still . . ." Then Bea performed an imitation of the stuffed bear. She raised her hands into claws and bared her teeth in a threatening grimace.

They both fell into fits of laughter.

"Nice to hear you so happy in there," Casper's voice said, floating into the room. "Goodnight. See you bright and early for our special trip."

"Goodnight, Casper," they both said, more or less in unison.

"Where are we going in the morning?" Allie asked.

"I don't know," Bea said. "It's a surprise."

# Chapter Twenty-Eight

### Beaches Made of Glass, and Other Fragile Things

They walked together, the three of them, across a bluff, heading for the ocean. Bea found herself wishing there were no walking involved, but she didn't care to admit it out loud. To confide in the girl was one thing, but not to an actual man.

"I hope I haven't oversold this," Casper said.

"You haven't told us anything about it at all," Bea replied, already slightly out of breath.

"But getting us up so early and taking you down here so you can see this thing I want you to see. Some people think it's just wonderful. They can't get enough of it. Others, I guess they miss what's so special."

"It doesn't matter," Allie said, sounding irritatingly fresh. "We like to see new things and find out for ourselves what we think."

"That's the right way to look at it," Casper said.

A moment later they ran out of bluff. They stood at the edge of the world, looking down at a cove. Bea had hoped for something she could view with enthusiasm, but it looked no different from any other beach. The sun was just ready to break in the east, and that was lovely, but nothing else struck her as extraordinary.

"I doubt I can get down there," Bea said, eyeing the steep dirt paths that twisted their way down the edge of the bluff.

"Oh, sure you can," Casper said. "I'll help you."

"No, I really don't think so, Casper. It looks dangerous to try. Whatever it is, I'll have to see it from here."

Meanwhile the girl had begun to scramble downhill.

"But you can't. You won't see it from up here. It's something that has to be viewed close up, or you'll never see it at all."

*I suppose I won't see it then,* Bea thought.

Bea heard a shriek that startled her, though it was clearly a cry of delight. Allie was down on the beach now, holding a double handful of what Bea assumed to be sand, peering at it closely.

"You have to come down here!" Allie called. "You have to see this!"

"I can't get down this steep bluff," Bea called back. "Tell me what's so wonderful about it."

"No. I won't. You have to see it with your own eyes."

Bea sighed.

"I think I'm about to break my neck," she said to Casper.

"I won't let you. Come on."

He took her arm. Over the next minute or two—though it felt like an hour—he helped her navigate the least steep of the steep paths. He did not let her fall.

Allie whooped joyfully as Bea's feet touched horizontal beach. She ran to Bea and poured a double handful of beach sand into her out-stretched hands.

"Now what's so special about this sand?" Bea asked, thinking she should have brought her reading glasses. But when it touched her palms it didn't feel like sand. It felt like small stones.

"It's not sand. There's no sand down here that I can see. It's all beach glass."

"How can it all be beach glass?"

"Look."

Bea stared closely at her hands. She was holding a pile of beach glass. Nothing but. It was worn smooth from the waves, every pebble. Some pebbles were clear, some brown, some green. There was even one bright spot of cobalt blue.

"How is that possible?" she asked no one. Bea lowered herself carefully to her knees in the sea of smooth glass pebbles. She put her palms down and looked at the beach surface from only inches away. It was all beach glass. Every pebble of it. "Herbert and I used to hunt for beach glass on our trips to the coast. If we found even two pieces, that was a banner day."

She looked up to see if anybody was listening, and saw both Casper and the girl standing close.

"Glad you're one of the ones who know enough to think it's wonderful," Casper said.

———

She sat on a driftwood log with Casper, watching the light of the beach change with the rising sun, watching the girl lie on her belly in the glass, sorting through its wonders. Even the sound was different, Bea noted. As each wave washed up onto the shore, the glass made a noise that sand cannot make, a light tinkling that had begun to sound like music to Bea.

"So, there has to be a story about how this is possible," Bea said.

"There is. You might like it or you might not. Years ago this used to be an official dump site. Locals brought their garbage here and dumped it into the ocean. Lots of glass bottles and jars and pottery in there. Some of the bulkier trash was burned off first. The more unsightly stuff was cleaned up later. But the glass stayed. The waves did their thing, and . . . here you have it. Most people hate that story because it's nasty to think of throwing trash into the ocean. I like it because I like the idea that something as terrible as that led to something as wonderful as this."

Bea breathed in an extra-deep pull of cool morning air. "I'll go your way with it."

"Bea, I don't want you driving all the way to Eureka and back again today. It's too long a drive. About six hours round-trip, and then you have to turn around and go right back up there anyway, because that's the way you're headed. And think how much of the money you'll put right back into gas."

"But then how do we pay you?"

"I'll just take that nice little notebook computer the girl offered me."

"Is it worth enough?"

"It is to me. You'll be trading it for more than a pawnshop would have given her for it. But I'll be getting it for less than it would have cost to buy a new one. And it's as good as new to me. So I say it's fine. I'll take you two back to my house, and you can just rest and relax while we mount the new tires and install the starter. We already did the belts and hoses and the alignment. Then you can move on." A weighted pause. "Unless you've changed your mind about moving on."

"I'm afraid I haven't."

But just in that moment Bea was struck with an idea. It made her stomach jump, and come to attention. It made her feel alive suddenly. Unusually alive. And it wasn't intended just for him, either. It wasn't a consolation prize. It was Bea's very own adventurous plan.

She looked to see if the girl was watching, but she had disappeared around the rocks to another cove entirely.

"I was just thinking, though," Bea said. "Maybe in the spirit of adventure . . ." Then she stalled and didn't say more for a few beats. She thought about bat rays, and how they had taught her not to leave spaces for doubt to settle. "Maybe just one . . . little . . . tiny . . . very tiny . . . kiss?"

Still she did not look at his face. She would not have dared.

"That would be an adventure," he said, his voice hushed.

She turned to face him and quickly closed her eyes. She felt his face move closer, and felt her own heart pounding. His lips touched hers for just the count of two. Maybe one and a half. She barely had the chance to register the feel of them, dry and warm. Then they were gone.

"Well," she said. "Maybe a little less tiny than that. But not . . . not like those disgusting things you see in the movies on TV with their mouths open, and all that slimy tongue stuff."

"No," he said, barely over a whisper. "Of course not."

Then it was happening again, soft and yielding, but tender. Not disgusting at all. It lasted for a few seconds, and grew a bit more intense, while remaining civil and not terribly frightening as kisses go. Still, Bea's heart pounded. And still she could hear the musical sound of the waves tinkling a million bits of glass.

She drew her head back and so did he.

"Well," she said. "That was a proper adventure."

"I'll say."

"And it's probably the last adventure I'll ever have. Because I'm going to break my neck going back up that bluff."

He laughed, which felt good to Bea. It was a lifting of tension that she'd been needing. More than she had even known.

—

The young man from Casper's shop came by the house at ten thirty a.m. to get them. He was driving Bea's van.

"Well, look at that," she said, stepping out into Casper's front yard to greet it. As though the van were a long-lost relative who had changed for the better over the years. "Those tires are so new! They still have those little rubber hairlike things on them from their manufacturing. What do you call those?"

"Hairs," the young man said. He seemed uninterested in the humor of the moment, or in bantering. He handed Bea the keys. "Johnny over there followed me from the shop." He pointing to a compact car idling at the curb. "He'll give me a lift back. So you folks can just take off from here."

"Oh, but I have to at least go by the shop and say goodbye to Casper."

"He's not there. He took the day off."

"Really? Why would he do that? He's not sick, is he?"

"Nah, he's fine. Sometimes when he has a lot on his mind he takes a day off and goes crabbing. Oh. I almost forgot. He told me to give you this." He pulled a small, slightly rumpled envelope from his back pocket and handed it to Bea. "And I'm supposed to pick up a computer?"

"Right. Right. I'll just get that."

Bea stuck her head back into this near-stranger's house. This near-stranger whom she had recently kissed. It made her head spin to think about it, literally. It made her a little dizzy. So unlike her. And yet in another way, maybe . . . not. Maybe not anymore.

"Allie?" she called. "Bring out that computer of yours so we can pay for this repair, okay? Then we'd better get back on the road."

While she was waiting for that transaction to play out, Bea opened the envelope. In it was a small scrap of paper torn from a notepad, printed with the words "Casper's Automotive," along with a drawing of a tow hitch.

"Bea," it said in a scratchy pen scrawl. "I'm no good at goodbyes. Never have been. You know where I am if you change your mind. Thanks for this morning. It meant the world to me."

No signature. But then again, it wasn't as though Bea needed to know who it was from.

———

"So, I have a question," Allie said as they drove. "When we get to Eureka, do we sell the gold or don't we?"

"I think we probably should," Bea said. "We have a lot of coast in front of us, and the gas will go fast. Do you mind it?"

"I guess not."

Allie was staring at the map while Bea drove.

The ocean had disappeared as the coast route bent east, away from the views Bea had come to love. The problem was, it just kept bending. And bending. And bending. They had been traveling through forest land for some time now, with hairpin turn after hairpin turn. Bea's shoulders already ached, but she had vowed to make miles today. An unheard-of number of miles, at least for her.

Because you just never know what will happen between any given "here" and any given "there."

———

Before the girl walked into the office of the man who bought gold, Bea couldn't help noting that she stopped in the back of the van and dug around in one of her fabric bags. Bea was fairly certain Allie had been keeping the ounce of gold in her jeans pocket. And besides, when the girl pulled something out of the bag, it was far bulkier. Maybe the size of a small notebook, but with a leatherlike cover that wrapped around itself and snapped.

Allie stuck the mystery item under her arm and disappeared.

*You're still holding out on me,* Bea thought. But she didn't say it. She just sat and nursed a feeling in her belly that hurt. Unfortunately, it was not indignation, nor anything else clean and satisfying. Nothing in the anger category at all.

If compelled to tell the truth, Bea would have had to admit that it hurt her feelings. Somehow she'd thought her relationship with the girl had grown more trusting than all that.

———

"Okay, you'll be happy," Allie said as she jumped back into the van.

Bea started the engine and began to drive again, not even waiting to hear what would bring such happiness. Because she wanted miles. She wanted to get closer to Cape Flattery, and the goal.

"How much did he give you? I know it can't be more than what we talked about. He has to resell it at some profit. He's in the business. So he'll always give you a little less than the spot price."

"I got more than sixteen hundred dollars!"

Bea's head spun a little as she absorbed that number. It was such a familiar figure—almost exactly what had been stolen from her bank account.

"And . . . ," the girl continued. She dug into her jeans pocket. "I got you this."

Allie held something out in Bea's direction. Something small, that must have fit neatly into her hand, because all Bea could see was the hand. Bea held her own hand out, palm up, and the girl dropped something into it. A coin. Maybe the size of a quarter, or a little smaller.

Bea glanced in her rearview mirror. No one was coming up behind. She pulled slightly right and slowed to a crawl. She looked down into her palm. In it was a small gold American Eagle coin.

"I got us each one," Allie said. Bea raised her eyes to see the girl's face lit up in a genuine grin. "They're a quarter ounce of gold each. You know. In case of emergency. We'll each have one."

"Explain the math to me," Bea said, glancing in her rearview mirror and realizing she had better drive again. "You go in with an ounce of gold. You come out with two quarter ounces of gold and over sixteen hundred dollars. How does that happen?"

"He buys coins, too. So I sold him my grandfather's coin collection. I had no idea what it was worth. But now we know, right? It was worth plenty!"

Bea drove in silence for several minutes, shifting the landscape of emotion in her belly. Or maybe it was shifting her.

"You're a very thoughtful girl," she said, eventually.

After a moment or two of no reply, Bea stole a glance at the girl's face. Allie looked about ten percent gratified and ninety percent astonished.

———

They stood side by side at a Laundromat somewhere in Oregon. In some small town on the Oregon coast, after dark, after a beast of a long day on the road, folding their clean, dry laundry. It felt like a luxury, the warmth and cleanliness of the only clothes Bea owned. She wondered if it was a good thing or a bad thing to feel so much appreciation for something so small.

She leaned closer to the girl, her body language rife with conspiracy. She had a secret, Bea. And even though there was only one other woman in the Laundromat, and that person stood nowhere near, it was a secret that required discretion.

"I kissed Casper," she whispered.

At first, nothing. No response. As though the girl hadn't heard.

Then Allie squealed out a few words at a volume that made Bea jump. "Get outa town!"

It even made the other woman, who was reading a magazine near the door, jump. And she was a good twenty paces away.

"I don't know what that means," Bea said.

"It means . . . well . . . it's kind of hard to translate."

"And here I thought we were speaking approximately the same language."

"It sort of means . . . you're kidding!"

"I'm not kidding. And I won't get out of town. Or however you answer that thing you just said."

Bea braved a look at the girl's face. It was wide open, unguarded. Exuberant, almost.

"*You* kissed *him*?" Allie asked, still a little too loudly.

"Yes. If you must know, yes. I'm not saying he didn't kiss me back. But it was my idea."

"What kind of kiss are we talking about here?"

Bea held a finger to her lips in warning. "I didn't say I was willing to share details," she hissed.

"Like a *French* kiss?" With an almost reverent emphasis on the key word.

"Of course not. Don't be disgusting."

"You don't mean like a polite little peck on the cheek, do you?"

"If it was a polite little peck on the cheek, I wouldn't even be telling you about it like it was something worth telling. That's only the sort of kiss you get from your aunt."

"That's what I was going to say if you'd said yes. Only I would have said grandfather, because I never had an aunt. So . . . it was on the lips. But not just a quick little thing, right?"

Bea felt her face flush. "Please," she whispered. "You're embarrassing me."

A long silence. Bea was almost done folding her clothes, and felt unsure of what to do with herself and her life when the folding was over.

"All right . . . *Bea!*" the girl shouted.

She punched Bea on the arm. Fairly hard.

"Ow!" Bea said, but still under her breath. "Why did you hit me?" She rubbed the spot that had just been assaulted.

"Oh, I'm sorry. Was that too hard? It was just meant to be a friendly little thing. I do that with my friends all the time. It's not supposed to hurt."

The girl began to rub the spot Bea had just finished rubbing.

"I suppose it's because they're younger than I am," Bea said.

A split second later she looked up to see the only other woman in the place standing directly in front of them, smiling. She was fortyish, with auburn hair spilling perfectly across her shoulders, and an old denim shirt.

"I just had to tell you this," the woman said. "I hope you don't mind. It's so nice to see a grandmother and granddaughter who get along so well. Talking and laughing together. My kids barely speak to their grandparents."

A long, stunned silence.

Then the girl said, "Um. Thank you?"

The woman turned and wandered outside.

"That was interesting," Bea said.

"That was . . . bizarre," the girl replied. "But nice."

"Yes. Yes, I suppose. Nice." Then, after a long pause, "Do you miss them?"

"Who?"

"Your friends."

"Oh. That. I did. At first. Now I just feel like . . . I just think we wouldn't have anything in common anymore. After everything I've gone through, how would we even fit together now? I think about them sometimes, and it's like I knew them a couple of decades ago. Not a couple or three weeks. I guess that's what happens when you get thrown out into life like this. It grows you up fast."

"I'll drink to that," Bea said.

———

They lay quietly in the van together, Bea in her easy chair, the girl stretched out across that thing you floated around on in a pool. If you had a pool. They were camping in the Laundromat parking lot. Lying there in the dark, as if sleeping. But Bea knew that neither one of them was asleep. Bea could hear the roar of the surf, which felt comforting.

"Psst," the girl hissed quietly.

"Yes," Bea said. "I am indeed awake."

"Why did we drive so far today?"

"I just want to get where we're going."

"But you said you get too tired. You said four or five hours, tops. We drove for almost nine hours."

"I want to make it to Cape Flattery."

"But there's no hurry."

"Isn't there? Really? In one day yesterday we had what we thought might turn into a brush with the police, you decided you might surrender yourself to them, and we had a mechanical breakdown. I want to get there before anything else goes wrong."

"Oh," the girl said, simply.

They lay in silence for several minutes.

Then Allie said, "We can go back there, you know."

"Back where?"

"Fort Bragg. Casper."

"I just told you I'm anxious to get to our destination."

"On the way back, I mean. We can go back through there. You know. If you want to see him again."

"I don't."

"Oh. Well, then . . . why did you kiss him? If you were going away right after and you never wanted to see him again?"

"You just answered your own question," Bea said.

"I don't get it."

"Oh, honey. Casper is a nice enough person. But the last thing I want to do is tie myself up with another man. My goodness. That's how most of the last fifty years of my life disappeared, even though I didn't know it before now. And believe me, that's all it takes. One little kiss and then you've thrown your lot in with someone, and your whole life has to be built around him. And all the parts of you that don't fit with him have to go into hiding, and all the ones that do have to come to the surface and act like they're the whole of you. The entire reason I did what I did is because we both knew I'd be gone in a few hours. It's the first time in my life I ever got to do a thing like that and not stay around to pay the price. You'll understand when you get older."

"I doubt it," Allie said. "But I'm happy for you all the same."

"Besides," Bea said. "Must love cats."

"Right. Must love cats. I'm with you on that."

# Chapter Twenty-Nine

### Don't Cross Your Boardwalks Before . . .

"Can we stop at *this* lighthouse?" the girl whined. "I really want to see one."

"What's this sudden obsession with lighthouses?" Bea asked, continuing to drive. Not even slowing.

"It's not sudden. I've always liked them. But I never got to go in one."

"How do you know they even let people go inside that one?"

"Because there's a big sign telling people to pull in and park."

"That hardly proves your case."

The girl sighed deeply. She had the cat on her lap, and was scratching between Phyllis's shoulder blades.

"Doesn't matter anyway *now*," she said, all teenage mopey. "It's passed."

A long pause, during which Bea assumed she was meant to feel guilty. She decided against it.

"You know," Allie said, "there's such a thing as too much hurry."

"Maybe not in our situation."

"Oregon is almost gone. We drove it in mostly one day. We hardly saw the Oregon coast."

"I saw it. Where were you? All you had to do was turn your head left."

"But if you don't even have time to stop and see a lighthouse . . ."

"I'll tell you what. After we see Cape Flattery . . . which was your idea, as you'll recall. After we see all the coast we have ahead of us . . ."

But she stopped, and never finished her thought.

They had talked very little, if at all, about what they would do after Cape Flattery, and it wasn't the slightest bit sorted out in Bea's head. In fact, she wasn't sure she could remember why it felt important to go there in the first place. Except that it felt important to go somewhere, and that seemed the farthest place imaginable.

———

Maybe an hour later Bea spotted a place to pull over and enjoy the view. It had room for five or six cars, with a low stone wall to keep you from rolling right over the edge and falling a hundred feet to the sea. No one was parked there.

Better yet, there was a lighthouse less than an eighth of a mile or so up the coast, and this would be a good spot from which to view it.

Bea made a sharp left and pulled in. She shifted into "Park" and shut off the motor. The lack of constant engine noise felt stunning. It felt like silence, though Bea could clearly hear dozens of seals barking, and the crashing of surf. She could feel a ghost of the vibration of the steering wheel in her arms and shoulders. It felt like buzzing.

"We stopped," Allie said. "I don't believe it."

"I have to go to the bathroom," Bea said, which was true enough, though not the reason she had pulled over.

"There's no bathroom here," Allie said.

"I'll just have to make do."

The girl stepped out of the van and looked around.

"Not much privacy," she said through the open passenger door.

"You go out and look at the lighthouse from here, and I'll stay inside and use the bucket. And then I'll just . . . quietly empty it outside."

"Okay," Allie said, clearly wanting no more details. "Whatever."

—

It was several minutes before Bea stepped out of the van, what with drawing all the curtains and then opening them all again.

The girl was leaning over the waist-high stone wall, barking at the seals. Imitating their raucous clatter.

Bea set the bucket in the dirt and walked to her.

She looked down the dizzying cliff to see the seals crowding the rocks at the water's edge. The wind swept her hair back and made her narrow her eyes.

"What do they have to be so noisy about?" she asked the girl.

"Just excited about life, I guess."

"You know . . ." But then Bea stalled.

"What?"

"We never really talk about what we'll do after Cape Flattery."

"Hmm," Allie said. "Drive home, I guess."

"Home being exactly where?"

"Oh. Good point. Maybe we'll want to stay up there."

"Too cold. It's nearly Canada. Don't forget we have no heat and no air-conditioning unless we're driving. We have to choose our weather carefully."

"We could go inland and down a different route and see a whole different set of things."

"Again," Bea said, "it's all about the weather."

"Right. Hot inland."

"And only getting more so." Bea watched the way the sunlight sparkled on a swath of ocean all the way out to the horizon. Like a path to somewhere. Somewhere not of this world. Somewhere Bea was not yet ready to go. "We could come back down the coast. And this time we could go slow and see the lighthouses."

"That sounds like a pretty good plan," the girl said.

"I only bring it up because I sometimes think about Cape Flattery and . . . how do I say this? I feel like maybe it's an artificial goal."

"No, it's real. I found it on the map."

Bea sighed, a bit too dramatically. "That's not what I meant. I meant maybe *the goal* is artificial. We're acting as if all we have to do is get there, and then this adventure will be complete, and we will have accomplished something. But we'll still be us. We'll still be out here. Needing to figure out what to do."

"Well," Allie said. "Yeah, but . . . cross that boardwalk when we come to it."

"I believe the expression is 'bridge.' 'Cross that *bridge* when we come to it.'"

"I was trying to make a little joke. Because Jackson said you walk on these boardwalks out to the cape."

Before Bea could comment on the little joke—before she could even register dread over whether the cape would be too far a walk, over too many boardwalks—a vehicle pulled in. One of those bus-size motor homes. It completely ruined the privacy of the moment.

Bea quickly and discreetly emptied her bucket, and they drove on.

—

Driving across a very long bridge over what appeared to be a bay, Bea began to feel uneasy. Her stomach registered the fear, like a roller coaster ride. Oh, she knew in her head that people drove over the bridge every day and the structure held. Still, she could see water beneath them in her peripheral vision, on both sides. It felt as though there was nothing underneath the van. It felt like falling. Or, in any case, being about to.

So Bea talked to cover over the feeling.

"What is this?" she asked the girl, who was staring at the map.

"What is what?"

"This bay, or whatever body of water we're crossing."

"It's not a bay. It's the Columbia River."

"Awfully wide for a river."

"Well, it's the mouth of the river. It's wider at the mouth. You know, if we weren't in such a hurry, there's a really pretty drive you can take along the Columbia River Gorge. It has these high waterfalls right at the road, and nice places to hike."

"It says that on the map?"

"No. A kid I went to school with did a report on it once after his family's vacation."

"Maybe on the way back," Bea said.

"Right," Allie replied, folding up the map. "Everything on the way back. Here's the thing about us driving over the Columbia River. By the time we get off this bridge we'll have crossed the state line. We'll be in Washington."

"Good," Bea said.

They drove in silence for a moment or two, and the panicky feeling of falling began to set in again.

"Here's the thing for *me* about driving over this river," Bea said. "I get scared. I get scared on long automotive bridges because it feels like there's nothing underneath me."

"Here's what you do. You raise your eyes to the other end of the bridge. The way we're going. And you just keep them lifted like that. You never take your eyes off the other end of the bridge."

"Oh," Bea said after trying it for a time. "That actually helps."

"Don't sound so surprised."

"I had a thought about what we could do after Cape Flattery." She paused, but the girl only left space for Bea to continue. "I thought we could wind our way back down, more slowly, and this time drive the coast from Pacific Palisades to Mexico. Then we can honestly say we've seen the whole West Coast of the United States. Maybe we could even pop into Canada on our way up and Mexico at the end."

"We can't go to Canada or Mexico."

"Why can't we?"

"We don't have passports. I mean, I don't have mine along. And I'm guessing you don't have one at all."

"You don't need them for just Canada and Mexico."

"Oh, yes you do."

"Now this is a subject I happen to know something about," Bea said forcefully, her gaze still glued to the far end of the bridge. "I grew up in Buffalo, New York. Just a short drive from the Peace Bridge into Ontario. And you do *not* need a passport to cross the border. My family took that drive more times than I could count."

"I hate to be the one to tell you, Bea. But things change."

"When did they change that?"

"After the whole September eleventh thing. It's a Homeland Security–type change. You know, after we get off this bridge we should find a place to stop for the night. I think we're only about six hours or so from where we're going. And we'll be right on the water. But then in the morning when we drive again, we'll be inland a whole lot of the time. Probably it'll be hotter."

Their drive across the bridge ended. Finally, blessedly ended. Bea let out a huge breath she hadn't known she'd been holding.

"That's really a shame," she said.

"Stopping to sleep is not a bad thing, Bea."

"I meant the way terrorism changes everything. It wasn't that way when I was younger. The world was a safer place."

"When you were younger there was *World War Two!*" Allie exclaimed.

"Oh," Bea said. "True. I guess that is a point."

"Maybe a place with a shower? I could use a shower again. It's been two days since Casper's house."

"I could go for that myself," Bea said.

———

"Bea," Allie whispered in the darkened van. "Hey, Bea. Are you asleep?"

"I was. Almost. Now not so much."

Bea opened her eyes, but they had not adjusted to the lack of light. So the effect was more or less the same. She had showered and changed into clean pajamas before bed. The comfort was something that actually broke through enough for Bea to feel, despite the fact that she was not consciously thinking about it.

The little campground near Willapa Bay was surprisingly free of artificial lights, which Bea felt might be a good thing. She wondered if she should stick her head out and look at the stars.

"Sorry," the girl said after a time.

"Might as well say what you have on your mind."

"That money I got for the gold. And the coins. He gave it to me in an envelope. I had it in my pocket at first, but I just want you to know I put it in the glove compartment. Way at the bottom, just in case somebody steals the van or breaks into it."

"Wouldn't it be safer with you?"

"I was just thinking . . ."

But for a strange length of time Allie didn't say what she was thinking.

"Finish," Bea said, perhaps too abruptly.

"I was thinking that if we got separated, I'd want you to have it. You know. For gas and food and all. And so you'll be all right."

The words made Bea's face feel tingly and red.

"Why would we get separated?"

"If the police picked me up and dragged me back to L.A. That sort of thing."

"That won't happen now. We're almost to Cape Flattery."

But even as she said it, Bea knew that made no difference. They would always be somewhere. They had to be somewhere. And the police could always be in the same place.

"Well, whenever it happens. If it does. I just want you to know where that money is. I wrote my full name and my date of birth on the envelope. You know."

"Not really," Bea said. "I don't think I do know."

"If we got separated . . . you don't even know my whole name. I just wanted to make sure you could . . . un-separate us again. You know. If you wanted to."

"Oh," Bea said. "Thank you."

She felt she should say more, but her thoughts would not seem to untangle. And, suddenly, sleep was no longer in the picture.

Bea stepped out of the van in her pajamas and bare feet and looked up at the riot of stars for a few minutes. Inside herself, without words, Bea was fighting back against a strong, uneasy feeling that their adventure was about to come to a crashing end.

———

Bea figured she had been driving in the dark for at least an hour, maybe more like two. The girl shifted and seemed, from the sound of it, to be waking up.

Bea heard a muffled sentence, but couldn't make out Allie's sleepy words.

"What did you say?" Bea asked over her shoulder.

A minute later the girl flopped into the passenger seat, wrapped in a blanket. Her hair fell over her face, a disheveled mess. Bea could see her blinking too much by the soft light of the dashboard instruments.

"I said, 'Why are we moving?'"

"I couldn't sleep. So I figured I'd drive."

"What time is it?"

"No idea. It's too dark to see my watch."

"What time was it when you started driving?"

"About three."

They drove in silence for a time, the only sounds the familiar hum of the engine and the occasional whoosh of another car going by headed south.

"So . . . ," Allie began, "not to criticize or anything . . . but it sort of seems like this hurry thing of yours is getting to be . . . maybe a little bit . . . obsessive?"

Bea paused, feeling she had to shape her thoughts before presenting them.

"I keep having this feeling," Bea said after a time, "that something will happen. Something . . ." She knew there was more to say, but she never said it.

"That's just a leftover feeling from Fort Bragg."

"Maybe," Bea said, though she didn't think so.

"But it doesn't feel that way." It wasn't a question.

"No."

Allie sat back and looked out the window.

"Any idea where we are?" the girl asked after a time. "Oh, wait. Never mind. There's the turnoff for Lake Quinault. I know where that is from the map. You know it's rain forest around here?"

"I thought rain forests were only in places like South America."

"Most of them, I guess. But there's still some in Olympic National Forest. Which is more or less where we are."

"How do you *know* all this?" Bea asked, her voice a high whine of emotion she had not seen coming. "Everywhere we go, you seem to know something about the place. You're like an encyclopedia with legs and a mouth."

"So I paid attention in school. I had no idea that was a bad thing."

"It isn't," Bea said with a sigh. "It's very good. And I'm glad to know the things you tell me. I guess it just makes me feel like I know nothing."

A mile or two of silence.

"You can go back to sleep," Bea said. "I promise to drive carefully while you're not in your seat belt."

Allie scratched her nose. Then she rose without comment and disappeared into the back of the van.

A few moments later Bea heard the girl's voice drift back up.

"You have these feelings a lot?"

"The inadequacy thing, you mean?"

"No, I mean that something bad is going to happen."

"If you mean, do I worry a lot, yes. I always have. But an actual sense that I can feel something coming? Not once before in my life," Bea said. "It's actually quite unlike me."

She waited for an answer from the girl, but none ever came.

———

They were driving along the water at Neah Bay—a place Herbert would have called "spitting distance" from their Cape Flattery destination—when Allie called for her to stop the van. Bea pulled over as best she could, but she had to drive a little farther to find any place to get off the road.

"Back up!" Allie shouted. It sounded happy, not alarmed or alarming. "Back up, Bea!"

"I can't back up. There's no place to park back there."

"Fine. We'll walk back."

"To what?"

"Come on. You need to see this."

They stepped out into the cool, damp morning. Into this little town on the Makah Reservation. Just at the very edge of Neah Bay, a shallow inlet along the Strait of Juan de Fuca. Bea blinked, feeling the world had changed overnight. This was nothing like the coast they had been driving all these days. This was new.

She followed the girl until they stood under a tree just a few dozen yards from the beach. Allie was looking up, so Bea looked up, too.

"What are we looking at?"

"Ever seen three bald eagles in a tree?"

"I've never seen one bald eagle in a tree. I've never seen a bald eagle. They don't have those in the Coachella Valley."

"Well, you've seen three now," Allie said.

Bea followed the girl's pointing hand.

Halfway up the tree, spaced a few feet apart, perched three enormous birds. Identical, like triplets. Dark brown feathers. Brilliant white heads. Light-colored eyes, staring down at Bea with stern concentration. They looked almost angry. Forceful. Their beaks and talons formed a sharp color contrast of yellow.

"Wish I had a camera," Allie said.

"Yes, that might have been a nice thing to take on our adventure, but we didn't think of it."

"I have my iPhone. But it's silly to take photos on it when I'm just about to pawn it."

Bea felt her eyes go wide.

"Those telephone-computer things are also *cameras*?"

The girl only sighed and shook her head. They began the walk back to the van together.

"We have to stop and get a permit," Allie said.

"What kind of permit?"

"This is Makah Indian land. They get to charge us to be on it if they like. You need to buy a recreation permit to park here and see the sights."

Bea stopped walking abruptly. It took Allie a minute to notice.

"See, there you go again. How do you *know* all this? Don't tell me they taught you that in school."

"No, it was on the sign. There was a sign about it when we drove onto the reservation."

"Oh," Bea said, and began to shuffle along again. "I guess I wasn't paying good enough attention."

—

"Here's the thing," Allie said, jumping back into the van. "I got the permit. And it wasn't expensive. Only ten dollars. But the boardwalk trail to the cape is three-quarters of a mile."

"Round-trip?"

"No. Each way. A mile and a half round-trip."

Bea felt something sag and nearly collapse inside her.

"Oh dear. I was afraid of this. I can't even remember the last time I walked a mile and a half."

They sat in silence for a moment. Not driving on. Not doing anything.

"So what are you going to do?" Allie asked.

"What *can* I do? I'm going to walk it."

Bea could feel a ball of tension slip out of both of them and fade.

"Good for you, Bea."

"I'll be damned if I'm going to come all this way and let three-quarters of a mile stymie me."

"I don't know what 'stymie' means."

"Good. Finally. Something I know and you don't."

—

They walked together on the path that led to the cape. Through evergreen forest, sunlight dappling the path here and there. Over the damp, often tilted, rough-cut wood that formed their boardwalk. It wasn't milled lumber. It was more natural than all that. Bea could feel the humidity in the air, and hear the distant sounds of ocean waves on rock.

"I need to stop and rest a moment," she said.

There was no place to sit, so Bea leaned on her own thighs and puffed. A moment later the girl moved closer to Bea's side and encouraged Bea, without words, to lean on her.

Bea did.

"I've been thinking," Allie said. "Now that we have this big adventure behind us . . . I think I need to figure out a way to get in touch with my parents in jail and let them know I'm okay."

"Oh," Bea said. "I hadn't thought about that."

"I've thought about it enough for both of us. The first few days I was just so mad at them. It's like I figured it served them right. But it's been so long now. They must be getting pretty panicky. I'm not sure I want to punish them *that* much."

"So you figure they know you ran away?"

"Well . . . yeah. They must. I mean, their kid gets turned over to the county. I should think the county has to let them know if they . . . you know. Lose her."

They began to walk again. Slowly. The morning was getting warmer, which didn't help Bea's energy level one bit.

"Do you have any idea how to contact them?"

"None," Allie said. "If I knew how to call them, I would have done it days ago."

"You think we've oversold this to ourselves?"

Bea knew it was a sharp conversational turn. But she had no idea how to help with the problem of the girl's parents.

"The cape, you mean?"

"Yes. That."

"I think we'll find out in about a quarter of a mile," Allie said.

—

By the time they arrived at a viewing platform at the very northwest tip of the country, Bea was finding it hard to keep her head lifted. It felt easier somehow to bend over herself, as if sheltering her straining lungs.

"There's a bench," she heard Allie say.

Bea stopped, pulled in a few ragged breaths, and looked up.

In front of her, under the shade of several trees, lay a rustic wooden deck with small tree trunk poles forming a railing. More poles rose to meet it vertically, so no little children could fall through. And yes, there was a plank bench. Beyond that, Bea could see the jagged edges of more cape on the other side of a small cove. Inside the cove Bea could make out sea stacks—huge boulders extending up from the water, big enough to be their own tiny, very tall islands. Trees even grew on top of them.

"There are steps up involved," Bea said, still breathy. "Only a couple, but still."

"But I think it will be worth it," Allie said. "Come on. I'll pull."

A moment later Bea stood with her feet on the plank decking and her hands on the round rail. She looked down to see caves worn into the sheer stone cliffs topped with dense evergreen, the water frothing white at the edges of jagged maps of rock. She could hear echoing roars as waves rolled into the caves and met the end of their travels. Bea could relate to reaching the end of one's travels.

"I've never seen a piece of coast that was so . . . complex," Bea said.

"You mean like the way it's all ragged?"

"Yes. Like that. It's so intricate. Lacy, almost. I guess the ocean has carved all this over the years."

They watched and listened in silence. The sun at the railing of the platform was making Bea too hot, but she didn't want to go sit down. She wanted to keep looking off the corner of the world. Her world, anyway.

"So . . . ," Allie began. "Did we oversell it?"

"No," Bea said firmly. "No, it would be impossible to oversell it. I think it's the loveliest place I've ever seen. And I have you to thank for it, for keeping after an old fool until she finally broke down and tried something new."

# PART SIX

ALLIE

# Chapter Thirty

## *Travel Advice from Ducks*

"I want to stop at Ruby Beach," Allie said.

There was a new sense of conviction in her tone. A sureness. Finally she was stepping up to take better charge of this adventure.

They were driving south on the 101, inland by default, and Ruby Beach would mark the spot where they arrived on the Washington coast again at long last.

"And you really can't say no," Allie added, "because all the way up I asked you to stop a million places, and you always said, 'On the way back. On the way back. On the way back.' And now we're on the way back."

"Fine," Bea said, her eyes still glued to the road. "Ruby Beach it is."

It seemed almost too easy. Allie thought maybe it was a sign that the trip would be easier from here on out.

—

When Allie arrived back in the parking lot from her exploratory trip on foot to the beach, Bea was hanging her upper body out the open driver's side window.

"There's a walk involved," Bea said, "isn't there?"

"It's short. And you have to see it, Bea. It's the most beautiful beach ever. And there's no one here. We have the place all to ourselves."

"Tell me what's so different about this beach from every other beach we've seen all along the way. Tell me now, before I get down on my tired old legs and my sore old feet and haul all the way out there after that long hike I took at the cape."

"I can't describe it, Bea. You have to see it with your own eyes. Tell you what. If you get out there, and I'm wrong, and it wasn't worth it, you don't have to stop at a single lighthouse on the way back."

The older woman seemed to digest that offer for a moment. Then she powered up her window and stepped down from the van.

"That makes me a winner either way, I suppose," Bea said.

———

They stood together at the end of the path, breathing. Surveying their surroundings.

The air was misty with moisture. Fog-like low clouds blew, parting occasionally to show a steely blue-gray sky marked with higher, more distinct white clouds. The mouth of a creek emptying into the ocean ran through rocks and sand near where they stood. Its water was wide, flat, and shallow. It seemed to hold perfectly still, reflecting the cloudy sky.

There were sea stacks here too, just off the driftwood-littered beach. One was huge and wide, like a high, sheer-sided island. Others rose ragged and pointy, severe haystacks of rock.

"What are those stones for?" Bea asked.

Allie turned her eyes to a log, a massive fallen tree trunk of drift-wood. On it, someone—or many someones—had stacked dozens upon dozens of small rock towers, little pyramids of stones. Round, smooth, flat stones, like river rocks—the largest on the bottom of each pile, decreasing in size as they rose. Some only three stones high, some six or seven.

"They're like ducks," Allie said.

The mood of reverence broke, and Bea regarded her with a comical skepticism.

"They are nothing like ducks, little one. What about those stacked rocks reminds you of a duck?"

"That's not what I meant. Not real ducks. I mean ducks, like cairns. People use them as trail markers. If it's not clear which way to go, hikers stack rocks to mark the trail. To point the way."

Still Bea was staring at her, eyes squinted with doubt. Or maybe that was just the wind.

"They taught you this in school, too?"

"No, my dad and I used to hike. Sometimes. On the weekends, or when we were on vacation. But that was a long time ago."

*Back when we had less money and more fun,* Allie thought. But she didn't say it.

"Hmm," Bea said. "So if one of these little stacks means 'go this way,' then what do a hundred of them mean?"

"I'm not sure. Maybe that we're here? That all roads lead here?"

"No idea," Bea said. "But we'll still need to stop at some lighthouses on the way down. Because this is one stunning beach. Damn it."

———

They had almost reached the parking lot when Allie heard it. A sound that froze her blood and made her heart pound in her ears: the static of a transmission over a police radio.

She stopped. Bea stopped, but maybe only because Allie had.

"What's wrong?" Bea asked.

"Did you hear that?"

"No. Hear what?"

So maybe it was only Allie's paranoid imagination. Or maybe Bea's ears weren't what they had used to be.

Allie took a handful of cautious steps. Bea followed behind, seeming to catch the fear as if by contagion.

The van was where they had left it in the parking lot. Parked in front of it and blocking its exit sat a white Washington State Patrol car. Allie's heart pounded harder, then skipped a beat. She couldn't see a patrolman, but she could hear him talking on his radio.

She was eighty percent sure she heard him say, "But no sign of the girl."

She reached a hand around and touched Bea's collarbone, pushing her back into an area mostly obscured by trees.

"It's a little late for that," Bea hissed. "He knows we're here, now doesn't he?"

Allie's brain scrambled for footing like a spooked wild animal. "He doesn't know just from looking at the van that I'm still traveling with you."

"So what are our options?"

Allie looked into Bea's face as she spoke. The old woman looked every bit as scared as Allie felt.

"We could go back to the beach on foot and find another way out of here."

"I can't walk anymore! It's too much. And I can't just leave the van behind. It has everything I own in it. And what about Phyllis?"

"Oh. Right. Phyllis." A pause, while Allie tried to organize her thoughts. "Okay. You go back to the van alone. Tell them I was riding with you down in Southern California, but you let me out days ago, and you haven't seen me since, and you have no idea where I am."

"And what will you do?"

"Take off on foot."

For a moment, no one spoke. No one moved. Allie wasn't sure either one of them was breathing.

"Okay." Bea took a step toward the lot.

Allie grabbed her sleeve.

"No, wait, Bea. Don't."

They stood still together in the middle of the panic. The moment seemed to drag on. To stretch out. All panic and time, and not much more.

"Don't lie to them for me," Allie whispered. "Because if I get caught they'll know you lied and that could get you in trouble. Lying to an officer. Could be an obstructing justice kind of thing."

"So what do we *do*?" Bea asked, sounding quite desperate.

In that moment, Allie knew exactly what she should do.

When had she stopped being Honest Allie? her brain asked within a muddle, a swarm of uninvited thoughts. The Allie people teased and criticized for her unbending ways? And now here she was telling someone to lie for her while she made a desperate dash to evade her own consequences.

*So this is how it happens,* she thought. *You're in trouble, so you lie and run because you think you have to. Because you think you don't have any other choice. But there must always be two choices. At least two. Right?*

"I need to do what I should've done all along."

She marched through the parking lot and straight up to the uniformed officer, who was now standing by Bea's driver's side door. He looked up, his dark brown eyes meeting her own. He seemed surprised to see her.

"And you would be Alberta Keyes," he said. "Am I right about that?"

"Yes, sir."

"You've got quite a few people sick with worry down in Southern California, young lady."

"Yes, sir. I know. I'm sorry."

"It's not me you need to apologize to. But anyway, there's time for that later. Let's start by getting you back where you belong."

As Allie slid into the back of his patrol car, without having to be put there by force or even supervision, she was aware of a painfully familiar feeling. The paralyzing grip of fear had returned.

It was surprising, if only because Allie hadn't realized it had been gone.

———

They rode in the back of his car together, Allie and Bea. Going where, Allie didn't know. She hadn't been able to bring herself to ask.

"You really need to leave her out of this," Allie said to the back of the patrolman's head. "She had nothing to do with any of it. She didn't know I wasn't eighteen. She didn't know I was a runaway. She just gave me a ride, that's all, and there's nothing illegal about that."

"Right," he said, meeting her eyes for a split second in the rearview mirror. "So you told me the first ten times. And I told you, also ten times, that the police just want to ask her some questions."

"And then she can go?"

"Depends on the answers to the questions."

"If you do charge me with something," Bea said, "what will happen to my van? And my cat?"

"Oh," he said. As if just waking up. "The cat is *in the van?* So that's what you were trying to tell me."

"Yes," Bea said. "The cat is in the van. That's what I was trying to tell you."

"If things don't go your way, ma'am, the vehicle will be impounded. If there's a live animal inside, it'll be given over to the department of animal services, who'll hold the pet until you're able to reclaim it. But you ladies are getting ahead of yourselves. Alberta, we need to get you back to California. As to your friend here, we just want to ask her some questions."

They drove in silence for several minutes. North, Allie guessed by the angle of the sun. The ocean had disappeared from view again. Allie stared out the window and tried to think no thoughts at all.

*"Alberta?"* Bea asked after a time. "I always figured Allie was short for Allison."

"I wish. My parents named me after my grandfather. Albert."

"Oh," Bea said.

A few more miles of silence fell.

Allie reached into the front pocket of her jeans, grasped her quarter-ounce gold coin, and quietly slid it out. She reached over for Bea's hand, and when Bea opened her hand in surprise, Allie pressed the coin into her palm.

She wondered if Bea could feel her hand shaking.

Bea mouthed the words "Thank you," and Allie nodded.

——

Twenty minutes, or an hour, or two hours later—time was a hard entity to pin down in Allie's brain—they arrived in a coastal town of fairly good size, somewhere along the Puget Sound. A town they had not seen in their travels. It might even have been a small city, but Allie had no map now, and no idea what city it was.

Bea stirred next to her, and Allie knew they both felt it. That sense of *over-ness.* Allie thought about the hundred rock cairns on the log at Ruby Beach and wondered if all those "ducks" really did signify the end of the road.

"Well," Bea said, "that was a nice adventure while it lasted."

"Yeah," Allie replied. "It really was. While it lasted."

——

For what might have been half an hour, Allie sat alone in an empty room. It was a strangely plain room. Tan walls. A table with one chair on either side. A ceiling fan that made an irritating amount of noise. No windows. No clock.

Allie wondered if the lack of clock was done on purpose, to make time feel stretched and surreal. To put pressure on whatever unlucky fool had to sit here and wait, not even knowing for what.

Meanwhile Allie felt nothing, as far as she knew. There was no resistance inside her. That much felt clear. It was bad, what was happening, but Allie's whole being was in a state of utter surrender. As if her heart and gut had fallen down a very deep hole. No part of her was actively trying to get out, or even prevent more falling. It was just over.

In time the door opened.

The woman who walked in wore plain clothes, but her pants and suit jacket were a police-uniform shade of blue. She had long brown hair tied back in a ponytail. Allie thought she might have been forty. There was a calmness about her. In her face, in her movements. It didn't feel like a satisfied calm. Allie would not have assumed she was a happy woman. But she presented herself as unruffled and low key.

She sat down on the other side of the table and began to make notes on a clipboard.

"You're Alberta Keyes," she said after a few seconds.

"Yeah. I think we nailed that."

The woman's eyes flickered up to Allie's, but she did not otherwise react.

"Officer McNew," she said. "I want you to tell me everything you can about what happened."

"Why I ran away, you mean?"

"And what kind of danger you were in after you left the group home."

"How did you know I was in danger?"

"I was just talking to your friend. She's your biggest fan and supporter; I hope you know that."

"It wasn't her fault at all. Please don't charge her with anything. Please. She didn't know I was a runaway. Or that I was underage. She might even say she did, because she thinks she might like jail, because she's homeless. But I don't think she'd like it. I don't think she knows what she'd be getting herself into."

The woman leaned back and chewed on the end of her plastic pen. It was the first sign that everything was not placid all the way through her being.

"You've been incarcerated?"

"No, ma'am."

"Then you don't know what she'd be getting herself into, either."

"I feel like I was just starting to know, though. Getting pulled out of my house and stuck in that home with that crazy roommate. And then being kidnapped. I know how it feels when somebody else controls you and there's nothing you can do about it. And I don't want that for Bea. She doesn't deserve that."

"Neither did you."

In that moment, just that suddenly, Allie's tears let go. She hadn't felt them coming. Hadn't known they were in there, waiting to be cried.

"Please just put me in juvie and leave her alone," she sobbed.

The officer got up from the table and left the room. Allie cried in solitude for a moment, wondering what the sudden exit meant. Then the woman was back, extending four tissues in Allie's direction.

"Thank you," Allie said.

"I doubt your friend is in any trouble. Lot of people will pick up a runaway or homeless teen. It's not always for nefarious purposes. Usually they just want the poor kid off the street. We would've liked it a lot better if she'd called someone in law enforcement, or brought you back. But she had no bad intent. We'd likely charge her if she'd lied about your whereabouts. You know. To throw us off the track and keep us from finding you."

*Which I almost had her do,* Allie thought. But she said nothing.

"Or if she contributed to your delinquency in some way."

That seemed to hang in the air a moment. The gravity of the soft prod for information felt self-evident.

"Like what?"

"Gave you alcohol or something along those lines. But she didn't, right?"

Allie sniffled. Then, much to her surprise, she laughed. Just a short bark of a laugh. "I think I might have contributed to *her* delinquency. But not so much the other way around."

Officer McNew smiled a crooked smile. "I thought as much. But I needed to hear it from your own mouth. I'll go ask somebody to drive her back to her vehicle. You want something to drink?"

"Yes, ma'am. Thank you."

"Soda?"

"No, thanks. I don't want all that sugar."

"Diet soda?"

"Oh, definitely no," Allie said, shuddering slightly. "That's just about the only thing that's worse."

"We have coffee, but I'm not sure I'd recommend it. It could moonlight as paint stripper."

"Maybe just water," Allie said.

The officer walked out, leaving Allie alone again with the noisy ceiling fan. And all that stretchy time.

—

When Allie finally had been wrung dry of words, the officer sat back, stretching her writing hand to counteract cramps.

She read over what she'd written, or at least scanned over it.

"Think you could find that house in Sherman Oaks again?"

"I doubt it. I was asleep when he drove me there. It was dark when I got driven out, and I was all in a panic. I don't even know for a fact it was Sherman Oaks. Just that Jasmine said that's where Victor lives."

"And I suppose license numbers would be asking too much."

"Sorry," Allie said, resisting an urge to knock herself in the head with her own fist. "I feel so stupid. Here I've been thinking I want to do something to help other girls who get themselves in that position, and I could've helped a lot by just memorizing a license plate, but I didn't do it."

"There are ways you can help," McNew said. "But that's for later."

"Like what?"

"Sometimes girls go around and give talks at schools."

"Wouldn't that be better coming from some girl who didn't get away?"

"Not necessarily. Let them use their imagination about what would've happened to you. That's scary enough."

"Yeah. Well. Not much touring you can do from juvie."

"Why do you keep assuming we're going to incarcerate you?"

"Jasmine told me when you run away from the system they put you in juvie."

"Seems Jasmine told you all kinds of things."

"Oh," Allie said, feeling and sounding even more defeated. "That's a good point, I guess."

She sipped her water in silence.

"Sounds like Jasmine was a chronic runner. Also that she got involved in criminal activities every time she was out. It's case by case. If we thought it was the only way to keep you off the streets and safe, yes. We would lock you up. But with extenuating circumstances . . . Well, I should warn you it won't be my decision. Some judge in California will likely make the call. But based on what you've told me, you could get a second chance to stay put."

McNew leaned back. Threw her pen on the table. As if things were getting far more serious, and fast.

"Look. Alberta. I was your age once. Hard to believe, but it's true. I know it seems like the whole adult world is out to get you. Like nobody cares until you mess up, and then they're all over your case. But the people in the system are trying to help you. It's an imperfect system, and everybody knows it, but the idea is to make sure you're okay. Now . . .

having said that, I think you won't be too surprised if I tell you we have to take you to a juvenile detention facility for tonight."

Allie felt her stomach turn slightly, but she said nothing.

"You have to be somewhere. And we have to know where you are. And we have to know for a fact that you'll be there in the morning so we can figure out how we're going to get you back to L.A. Understood?"

Because it was a direct question, and the officer seemed to be waiting for an answer, Allie said, "Yes, ma'am."

McNew glanced at her watch. "It's late. I have to call over there and see if they've served dinner already. If so, I'll order us something. Sandwiches? Pizza?"

"That'll be hard," Allie said. "There's an awful lot I don't eat."

"Let me call and find out, anyway."

McNew rose to her feet, hands braced on her thighs.

"I hope they've already eaten," Allie said quickly. Before the officer could get away. "Because I just about guarantee you, if you take me there for dinner, I'll starve. Dinner will be a slice of plain bread."

For a moment, the woman only stared down at Allie. As if measuring something. Then she broke for the door.

"I'll see what we have in the way of take-out menus," she said.

———

"Here's what I don't get," McNew said. She was eating spaghetti and meatballs from a round, corrugated foil container. "So you got away from the girl at the home who you thought might hurt you. And then you got away from the trafficker. Why not just call the police and get yourself resituated?"

Allie had been using disposable chopsticks to hold a piece of Japanese vegetable roll, but she set it all down again. As if the question had made her lose her appetite, which was partly true.

"Jasmine said I'd go to juvie."

"Juvie might have been better than the street."

"But I wasn't *on* the street. I was with Bea. I knew I was okay with her. If I'd turned myself in, I'd be leaving a situation where I knew I was okay and going into this totally scary new world. Do you have any idea how many times I'd just done that? I couldn't bring myself to do it again. I was sort of shell-shocked. I just couldn't take one more big jump into the unknown."

"Got it," McNew said, her mouth full of spaghetti. She swallowed. Wiped her mouth with a sauce-streaked paper napkin. Set the napkin down. "So, I've been going back and forth on whether to tell you this. If it would help or hurt. But I guess here goes. I had a talk with a couple of your social workers. The one assigned to you personally and the one associated with the home. The day after you took off . . . and I mean literally when the sun came up in the morning . . . they had an opening in a foster home, and they were going to take you there."

Allie set her face in her hands and tried to decide what she felt. All this could have been avoided. All the terror and the danger. So did she wish she had stuck it out another day at New Beginnings, even if it meant she would never have met Bea and Phyllis? Never seen almost the entire West Coast of the United States on their great adventure?

Before she could sort it all out, McNew asked, "How does that make you feel?"

"Stupid."

"That wasn't what I was going for. I just wanted you to think twice next time. Maybe give things another few days to play out."

"Yeah. I see your point."

Still, Allie decided, she would not want to go back to a world in which the big coastal trip had never happened. Weird as it had been at times, disagreeable as Bea could be, that trip was very high on a list of episodes Allie would never want to see subtracted from her life.

It might even have held the winning spot.

—

An unsmiling uniformed woman led her to the tiny cell that would be Allie's lodging for the night. It looked a lot like prison. In fact, it fairly screamed prison. Then again, she thought, it *was* prison.

Cream-colored concrete block walls. A concrete floor painted dark green. A bed that consisted of not much more than a thin pad of mattress on a built-in shelf. A stainless steel toilet with a miniature sink built right into the top of the tank.

There was a window. But it was high over the bed, small, and surrounded by a strong metal frame that divided the opening with two horizontal bars.

*All this trouble,* Allie thought, *everything that's happened—it was all because I didn't want to go to juvie for the night. And now here I am.*

"You've eaten?" the woman asked.

"Yes, ma'am. Thank you."

The woman handed her a small bundle. A thin pillow, one folded blanket, a threadbare, overbleached white towel and washcloth. Toothbrush with a tiny tube of toothpaste. Cheap plastic comb.

"Someone will come get you in the morning when it's time."

"Any idea what happens to me then?"

"I think someone's going to take you to Sea-Tac."

"Sea-Tac?"

"The airport. Seattle Tacoma. You'll probably fly back to L.A. With a law enforcement escort, of course. But they may still be working out the details. Lights-out in an hour."

"Oh. Okay. How do I turn out the lights?"

The woman laughed. Allie had no idea why.

"You don't. When it's lights-out, the lights will go out."

"Oh. Okay."

The woman walked out, closing the door behind her. It closed with a frightening whump. It sounded sturdy and airtight. It made Allie think the woman had left her with not enough oxygen to breathe. Allie felt suddenly claustrophobic in the small cell.

She lay on the bed for a few minutes, sure she wouldn't sleep. Marveling at the fact that, once again, she owned nothing more than the clothes on her back.

A moment later she got up and stood on the bed, peering out the high, small window. She hadn't quite discussed it with herself in her brain, but in her heart she knew what she was hoping to see.

Maybe Bea had driven back to that police station. Maybe she had followed Allie here. Maybe she was packing Allie's scant belongings in those two wonderfully familiar South American bags, just waiting for the chance to deliver them. To be Allie's support team. To prove she still cared. Maybe she hadn't just driven on and left Allie and her troubles behind.

The window overlooked the parking lot, and Allie saw two official-looking government vehicles—something like unmarked police cars—and a couple of passenger cars that might have belonged to employees.

No vans as far as her eyes could see.

# Chapter Thirty-One

### A Close, Personal Relationship between Woman and Cash

"So when can I go to the foster home?"

The Polyester Lady only stared at Allie, then back down at her files. She never answered the question.

They sat in an office in the second juvenile detention facility Allie had occupied in little more than two days. This time in Southern California.

"I'm starving here," Allie continued, to break the weird silence. "I didn't eat on the plane because they didn't have anything I could eat. Then I got here in time for dinner last night, and all I could have was some iceberg lettuce and a slice of dry white bread. What's the point of eating white bread? It has no nutrition."

Polyester Lady looked up from her folder of . . . Allie had no idea, really. There was always paperwork in this woman's polyester world, but Allie had little idea what any of it meant, or what purpose it served. She stared at Allie again, unblinking. Seeming not to comprehend.

"Did you tell them about your dietary restrictions?"

"I told the girls who were serving the food. I'm not sure yet who else to tell. They told me if I'm hungry I should eat what they serve."

"Well . . ." As though it were an idea of some merit.

"Oh, no. Not you, too."

"What's this foster home you were asking about?"

"Some policewoman in Washington told me you had a foster home for me. She said you were going to take me there the morning after I ran away. Was that true?"

Polyester Lady took off her reading glasses and set them down on her file. Like an actor in a TV movie, portraying sudden grave concern.

"Yes. It was true. The key word being 'was.' That vacancy has been filled. We couldn't just hold it for you when there are other children in need. We had no idea where you were or whether we'd ever see you again."

"I'm sorry," Allie said.

Allie grasped for the first time that her social worker was angry with her. Also that Polyester was hurt in some personal way Allie never would have anticipated.

"I think we can get you another one. Things are not as scary-tight as they were when I first met you. But you'll be here in detention until we get you in front of a judge. A judge needs to make the determination that you're not a flight risk, and that he sees no need to sentence you to more detention."

"Oh," Allie said. She was looking up, watching dust motes fly in a beam of morning sun shining through a high, small, dirty window. Maybe because everything below was so abnormally awful. "When do I do the judge thing?"

"When we have a date, I'll let you know."

Polyester Lady stood to leave. Halfway through her dramatic bustle to the door, Allie stopped her with a question.

"Wait. Don't go away for a minute. Did you hear anything from Bea?"

"I have no idea who that is."

"Did anybody call and ask about where I am, or how I'm doing?"

"I've talked to your parents. But nobody else. But you should ask the staff. In case somebody called here."

"I did," Allie said, followed by a sigh. "Nobody called here."

———

"I'm starving," Allie said to her roommate, a minute or two after lights-out.

Her cell was much the same as the one in Washington, except the floor was painted brown, and it housed two uncomfortable slab beds instead of one.

"They give you vegetarian if you ask for it," the girl said.

Her name was Manuela, and she was a year or two older than Allie. She seemed wise to the ways of this place, yet cautiously nonaggressive at the same time. Which Allie found to be a great relief. No, more than a relief. A blessing of a magnitude that brought tears to her eyes when she dwelled on it. It was the first break Allie had gotten in what seemed like a very long time.

"I tried that. They gave me this mushy pasta covered with some kind of dairy. Like milk and cheese but mostly milk. I couldn't eat that."

"If somebody visits you they can bring you food."

"Oh," Allie said. "Wish I had someone to visit me."

They lay in the dark for a moment in silence. Allie figured Manuela would be just as happy to go to sleep, but she also knew that if she said more, her roommate would listen. Allie was so full of longing and loneliness and uneasiness that her seams felt ready to burst. So she said more.

"I thought maybe that old woman I was riding with might come. I wrote down my full name and date of birth. I figured if she cared enough to want to find me, she could make some phone calls and figure out where I am."

"So now you figure she don't care enough?"

"I don't know. I don't want to decide that yet. It's only been like three days. Maybe she couldn't even drive down from Washington this fast. But I was hoping at least she'd call. Even if they didn't let her talk to me. I was hoping she'd call to find out where I am. But nobody called."

A brief silence. Allie thought that might be it for their talk.

"You were close with her?"

"I don't know. I guess I thought so."

"How long'd you ride with her?"

"I'm not sure exactly. I lost track of days. Probably eight or nine days. After a while it was hard to keep it all straight."

"That's not much time."

That seemed to be Manuela in a nutshell. Just the facts. Just the least she could get away with saying.

"It felt like a lot, though. Like we got to know each other a lot."

"So, like . . . she just one of them people you latch onto real fast? Like, all loving? That sorta thing?"

Allie laughed out loud. "Oh, no. Not at all. At first she kept wanting to put me out of the van. We didn't really get along."

"When'd you start getting along?"

"Well . . . Let me think. I figured out how to get some money for gas and food. Then she seemed much happier to have me."

"Uh-huh," Manuela said. Just that. Uh-huh.

"What does that mean?"

"Whatever you want it to mean, I guess."

"I really think toward the end we were getting along great, though."

"Let me ask you one thing. This gas money you had. Who got it now?"

"She does."

Another silence. Probably more than a minute. Allie wanted to say something more, some defense of her bond with the older woman, but she was afraid her roommate had fallen asleep. Or that it would only sound pathetic. Not necessarily in that order.

"Well, you hang on to what hope you want," Manuela said after a time. "You will anyway. Don't matter what I say. But if she don't call in the next couple days, at least you oughta think how maybe this big bond was really more between her and your money."

Allie opened her mouth to argue. To say, "No, Bea's not like that." But Bea *was* like that. Bea stole cell phones and pawned them. Money was everything to Bea. To some degree this was through no fault of her own—everyone has to eat, as the older woman had pointed out. Still, it was true. With Bea it was all about the money.

Allie closed her mouth again and tried to sleep. But between the hunger and the knot of fear and disappointment in her sore belly, she knew sleep was unlikely anytime soon.

———

Allie stood in the lunch line the following day, up on her tiptoes to try to see what was being served. It didn't look promising. Some kind of goop of brown gravy, with that white rice that's had all its rice nutrition wrung out of it. And when does anybody ever put anything in brown gravy unless it's meat?

The line shifted suddenly, and she found herself face to face with an older girl who may well have been an inmate. But she was on the other side of the stainless steel food island, serving.

"I can't eat any of this," Allie said desperately. She could have eaten the rice, but the prospect felt dismal. "I'll starve. I'm getting hungrier and hungrier, and I don't know what to do."

Before the serving girl could answer, Allie heard her name called. Just her last name.

"Keyes?"

She looked around to see a uniformed female guard at the entrance to the cafeteria, or mess hall, or whatever you called this horrible room in this horrible institution.

"Keyes?" The woman barked again.

Allie's hand shot into the air. Almost gratefully. As if the woman had offered to take her away from all this and buy her the best meal of her life. Only when it was up, waving, did Allie think—or, really, feel in her gut—that maybe having your name called in this place was not a happy event.

"I'm here," she said, a little weak from the not knowing.

"You want to come with me, please?"

A collective ooh ran through the girls, a taunting recognition that Allie was in some kind of trouble. And that each of them was relieved it was Allie being called and not her.

Her heartbeat pounding in her ears, Allie followed the woman out of the cafeteria.

"What? Did I do something? Am I in trouble?"

"You have a phone call," the woman said simply.

Allie's heart jumped, rose to a peak of expectation so suddenly it felt painful, a pressure in her chest.

Bea had found her. Bea was calling.

*I knew she would,* Allie thought. *I knew she cared. That she couldn't just drive away and leave me behind.*

She followed the guard down a long, dim, ugly hall—everything here was depressingly ugly to Allie—and around a corner. Allie saw a bank of six pay phones mounted on the wall. One was off the hook, its receiver dangling.

The guard pointed Allie to it and stood fairly close, her back against the wall.

Allie grabbed up the receiver.

"Bea?"

"Oh, honey. Oh, Allie. I was so scared!"

Not Bea.

"Mom," Allie said.

"Yes, it's your mom. And I'm so glad you're safe I could just cry, and I might, but I'm also so mad at you I could just . . . Lucky for you I'm not there in person, young lady! I don't think I've ever slapped you before, but I'd really like to right now. What the hell were you thinking, Allie? It's not like you to use such abysmal judgment. Anything could have happened to you out there!"

"Tell me about it," Allie said quietly.

"*Washington State?* What in God's name were you doing in *Washington State?* Every time I think about it I get so mad I could just—"

"Mom," Allie said sharply, and a blessed silence fell. "Stop talking now."

Amazingly, it worked. Her mom did as she had been told.

"Look, Mom. I didn't run away for no reason. I was in a really, really terrible position. And you're the one who put me in that position. When you hear the story you're going to feel incredibly guilty, so save yourself some guilt and don't yell at me anymore until you know what happened."

A silence on the line.

Then her mother said, "I'm listening."

"I didn't mean now. It's a long story. I was thinking, like, next time we're in the same room together. No way either one of us'll get that much phone time. How did you even manage to call here, anyway? I thought inmates could only make collect calls."

"Don't use that word in reference to me." Her mother's voice sounded tight and uncomfortable.

"What word?"

"That *I* word."

"Inmate? Why not? We're both inmates right now. If I can face it so can you."

Another long, awkward silence. Allie glanced up at the guard, who did not look back.

"I got special permission to call," her mom said. "I convinced them it qualified as an emergency. I was so scared, Allie."

"I know. I'm sorry. I wanted to call but I didn't even know where you were or how to get in touch with you. I'm sorry I scared you."

"You could have tried. Did you even try?"

"I was about to. When they picked me up."

"Don't you think that's a little late?"

Allie's rage rose to the surface, and she knew she would let it out now. It had to get out. Allie had no choice, no way to control it.

"I was pretty pissed at you, too, Mom. How could you do this to me? Do you have any idea what kind of hell my life turned into when they dragged you out of our house? I know it was Dad's idea. I know that because I know him. And I know you. He's the one who got greedy. But you went along with him. Why did you go along with it? Why didn't you just say no? Tell him to get another accountant and leave you out of it? Then he'd be in jail, and I'd be home with you right now. But no, you have to do whatever he says. And I'm just so mad at you for that!"

Allie heard something like a sigh on the other end of the line. Or it could have been a soft sob.

"I know, honey. I'm mad at me, too."

Allie stood a moment in that dingy hall, feeling her rage drain away. It had to. It had to go now. Because her mother was no longer a brick wall at which to direct that rage. She had gone back to being a wounded human, with feelings. Allie couldn't bring herself to hurt her anymore.

"Can I ask you a question?" Allie asked her mom.

A silence, during which Allie could picture her mother squeezing her eyes closed. Because that's what her mom did when she sensed something coming. Something she knew she didn't want.

"I suppose."

"Do we still have a house? When this is over, and you get out, and Dad gets out, do we even still have a house to go back to?"

"Yes. It's not strictly official. Yet. Technically the investigation is still open. Still ongoing. The IRS found a bunch of unreported income, and they seized the boat and most of what we had in the bank to cover it. Technically they're still looking for hidden income. But I happen to know there's no more for them to find. So we should still have a house."

"Oh," Allie said. "Good. That's good." *And surprising,* she thought. She didn't say it.

Neither one of them spoke for a strange and uncomfortable length of time.

"Mom?" Allie asked after what seemed like minutes. "Are you still there?"

"Yes, I'm here. But I don't have much more time. I'm getting signals."

"I'm sorry I yelled at you," Allie said, tears suddenly brimming over and running down her face.

"Likewise. Honey, I have to go now. We'll talk soon."

"Right. Soon."

Then the line was silent, dead, and Allie was holding the receiver at arm's length, staring at it.

She hung up and followed the guard back into the cafeteria, head hanging, doing her best to think nothing at all. More importantly, to feel nothing at all.

She sat at a table, on the very end, one bench seat away from any other girls. The guard came and looked over her shoulder.

"Why aren't you eating? Not hungry?"

"I'm starving to death, actually. But I'm a vegan. And there's nothing here I can eat."

The woman shook her head and wandered off.

*So that's it,* Allie thought. *I'm starving and no one cares.*

What might have been three minutes later, or maybe five, just as the other girls began to clear their trays and shuffle out of the room, a tray appeared in front of Allie's face. She turned to see the older girl who had tried to serve Allie lunch just before her difficult phone call.

On the tray was a plate with a peanut butter and jelly sandwich on white bread, potato chips, and carrot sticks. Next to the plate Allie saw a glass of what looked like apple juice.

Allie hated white bread, and she avoided jelly because it was mostly refined sugar. And the addition of the potato chips and fruit juice made for a very high-sugar, high-carb meal. But none of that mattered now. Because she could eat this food. She could actually eat it.

"Thank you!" she said. "I can *eat* this!"

The girl smiled, at one corner of her mouth only, and set the tray on the table in front of Allie.

"Thank you!" Allie called again as she walked away.

Then she scarfed down every bite of the food. Every crumb.

Every last carb.

# Chapter Thirty-Two

*Actually . . . They're Alpacas*

Polyester Lady showed up with a dress in a paper bag.

"I want you to put this on for court," she said.

She pulled it out and showed it to Allie, who immediately felt most of the blood drain from her face.

"Oh," Allie said. "So that's why you asked me my size."

"I think it helps to dress up a little for the judge."

"It's so pink, though."

*And it has polka dots,* she thought, but did not add. Truthfully, it was the most outrageously horrible dress Allie could ever remember seeing. But was she really going to go in front of a judge in jeans and a T-shirt—probably not even clean—or a prison-issued jumpsuit? Just because the dress was not her style?

"It won't hurt you to look a little girly and innocent just for one day."

"I guess not."

Actually, Allie figured it would hurt plenty. But it wouldn't kill her.

—

Polyester jiggled Allie's elbow, which Allie took to mean her turn had arrived. She had been trying to listen to the proceedings—to the judge ruling on other cases involving other minors—but her brain would not hold still.

Then Allie was on her feet and walking toward the judge's bench, her social worker at her right elbow. They stepped into a spill of sunlight from the one courtroom window. It made Allie wince and narrow her eyes, which she didn't figure helped the girly, innocent look much. Apparently the dress would have to pull off the job alone.

"State your name for the court," someone said.

It wasn't the judge who spoke. She had been looking at the judge and his lips hadn't moved. A bailiff, maybe? Allie turned her head to search for the owner of the voice, but the sun glared into her eyes, and she had to blink them closed.

"Me?" she whispered to Polyester Lady.

"Yes, you. Now."

"Alberta Keyes," Allie said loudly.

The judge had his gaze trained down, reading something on the desk in front of him. They stood in silence for what felt like several minutes, allowing him his time to read.

Allie's heart pounded almost painfully, and when he looked into her eyes it skipped a beat.

"So. Miss Keyes. I'm getting the impression you feel you had extenuating circumstances that caused you to run away."

"Yes, sir. My roommate at the group home was sort of . . . vicious. She was going to hurt me. A lot."

"Didn't you consider reporting this to the home supervisor, or your social worker?"

"I told the supervisor, and she asked if I wanted to report her to the police, and I did. Why do you think she wanted to hurt me so much?"

"Ms. Manheim?" the judge asked, raising his gaze to Allie's social worker.

*So that's her name,* Allie thought. *How did I miss that?*

"I really think, Your Honor, that if Alberta is placed in a proper foster home she won't run away again. She had some pretty frightening experiences out there, and I think she understands now what can happen. She used bad judgment in a stressful situation—I'll be the first to admit that—but she's a smart enough girl to learn from her mistakes. That's my opinion, anyway. And I want to add, Your Honor, that I share some of the blame for this mess. I couldn't find her an emergency foster. I should have taken her to juvenile detention until I could. Or at least until I could check her into a group home more properly. But she was scared to go to detention, even for one night. She begged me to take her to the group home instead. So I did, thinking I was giving her a break. But I think I was wrong to do it. I think my judgment was off in this case. Because she was in the beginnings of this trouble before I could even come back the next day and check on her. I'd hate to see her suffer for my mistake any more than she already has."

The judge sat back and scratched his mostly bald head, then smoothed his traces of hair, as if there were enough of it to be messy. He looked around the courtroom.

"Anybody else connected to Miss Keyes here today to speak on her behalf?"

"No, Your Honor," Ms. Manheim said. "Both her parents are—"

"*I'd* like to say something."

Allie's head whipped around to find the source of the familiar voice. And there she was. She wore a pink top as if in solidarity. Her thin white hair looked freshly washed and combed.

"Bea!" Allie shouted.

The judge banged his gavel once, then pointed it at Allie in a warning.

"Sorry," Allie mumbled.

"And you are?" the judge asked Bea.

Meanwhile Bea was making her way up the aisle, looking sore and stiff.

"I didn't say you should approach the bench," the judge added.

Bea looked up and stopped. She was just a few inches from Allie's left elbow now. Allie wanted to lean over and ask how she knew about the hearing, how she found Allie in this place, but she didn't want to be gavel-warned again.

"Who are you, now?" the judge asked Bea.

"Beatrice Ann Kraczinsky. And yes, I have something I want to say. This little girl is so honest, when I met her I couldn't even stand her she was so honest. I kept trying to put her out of my van for being so straitlaced, and if you lock her up, then the world just doesn't make a darned bit of sense anymore. If you lock her up, you have to lock up everybody else in the world, too, because she's more honest than all of them. It's like a joke that anybody would blame any of this on her. There she was minding her own business and trying to grow up, but her parents broke the law, both at the same time. You're supposed to put her in a foster home if that happens, but I guess you got busy and didn't have one. So you put her in this place where somebody was trying to kill her, and now you say it's illegal to try to get away from being killed. You can't make that illegal. People have to stay safe, and you can't tell them they're breaking the law if they—"

"Wait," the judge interjected. "Slow down, please, Ms. Kraczinsky. What is your relationship to Miss Keyes?"

"Oh. That. Well. I'm sort of her grandmother."

"Can you explain to me how you can be 'sort of' someone's grandmother?"

"Sure I will. It's like when your family has this Uncle Fred, and then later you find out he's really no blood relation to your family at all. But meanwhile he was just as good an uncle as all your other uncles. Maybe better."

"So if you're so close to this girl and her family, why didn't *you* take her in?"

"Oh. I actually . . . hadn't quite met her yet. At the time."

"I see. At least, I think I see. It's a confusing load of information. I hope you realize, Ms. Kraczinsky, that the point of this proceeding is not to decide whether to punish Miss Keyes. We're trying to decide whether she'll be safe in a foster home, or whether she's still a flight risk."

"She's safe," Bea said, her voice argumentative and hard. "That's what I'm trying to tell you. She's smart. She's not stupid, that girl. You're talking about her like she can't even think for herself, but she has a good brain. Keep her where she's okay, she'll stay put."

"Thank you, Ms.—"

Bea opened her mouth to talk again, but the judge banged his gavel. Twice. Allie jumped.

"Thank you, Ms. Kraczinsky. I think I have all I need."

Silence. Nothing and no one moved.

"You may take your seat now," the judge said, pressing the bridge of his nose as though his head hurt.

Bea moved out of Allie's peripheral vision. Allie didn't watch her go because she was too focused on the judge. On what he would say and do next.

The judge leveled Allie's social worker with a serious stare.

"You have a suitable placement for Miss Keyes this time?"

"We have a foster home lined up, yes."

"All right. Miss Keyes, I'm going to exercise my discretion and sentence you to time served. The few days you've spent in detention, waiting for this hearing, is all you'll be asked to serve. But this ruling comes with a warning."

Allie found herself staring at his pointed finger. It reminded her of the Greek gods they'd studied in school. Hadn't one had the power to shoot lightning bolts from the end of a finger?

"If you let me down, and end up here in my courtroom again after another unauthorized foray into the world, my ruling will be very different, and you'll be sorry you crossed me."

For one shivery moment Allie thought about the man she'd ditched at the gas station in San Luis Obispo. The way he'd told her she'd be one sorry little girl if she ran. So many people using so many different forms of power to control her.

"Yes, Your Honor."

Polyester Lady took her elbow and turned her, leading her away from the bench and toward the courtroom door.

Allie looked everywhere for Bea. But Bea was already gone.

———

"We have to stop and get your things from the detention facility," Allie's social worker told her on the drive.

Allie had forgotten the woman's name again. The courtroom experience had felt dreamlike and foggy to Allie. Her world had seemed unfocused at the edges—probably a result of fear—and no part of that morning had tended to stick.

"I didn't imagine the part where Bea showed up there," Allie said. "Right?"

"Oh, no. You didn't imagine it. She was there all right."

"You don't say that like it's a good thing."

A sigh. A half mile of silence.

"Look," Polyester said. "We got through that. We got you no more detention. Let's just look forward."

"What I have at that juvie place is nothing. One set of clothes. Not even ones I like. A cheap toothbrush they gave me. Let's just go to this foster home."

"No, they have more of your things than that. I got a message on my voice mail. Two bags. Nice-looking soft bags, woven or embroidered with . . . llamas, I think they said. They have clothes in them, and one has an iPad and a phone, and what looks like some gold jewelry. Somebody dropped them off this morning."

Allie opened her mouth, but was too overcome with emotion to speak for a moment. Manuela had been wrong. Bea had brought Allie's things back. Hadn't hocked the iPad or the phone. Hadn't stolen the gold necklace.

"You okay?" Polyester Lady asked.

"Actually," Allie said, "they're alpacas. Yeah, we have to go get that stuff, then. That's a lot of my stuff."

"Should I even ask how you got all those things? Because just about everything you brought to New Beginnings you left behind there."

"No. You definitely shouldn't ask."

They drove most of the rest of the way in silence. Allie was thinking that, actually, Manuela had been half-wrong. Bea hadn't stolen Allie's stuff. But she also hadn't stayed around.

"Thank you for taking part of the blame," Allie said. Right around the time she saw the detention facility looming.

"What I said in court, you mean?"

"Yeah. That. You could have said you did everything right and I messed up. You didn't have to put it on yourself."

"Sometimes we have to own our decisions. Good or bad."

"Right," Allie said. "I'm getting that. I thought I got that all along, my whole life. But it turns out I just didn't have many hard decisions at the time."

———

They pulled up in front of a house in Reseda in the San Fernando Valley. It was a big house, but plain. Grayish blue. It could have used a new coat of paint. But Allie had been told she somehow would be welcomed inside the place, so what did paint really matter?

Polyester Lady got out and opened her trunk while Allie pulled her two South American bags from the backseat.

"What's all that?" Allie asked.

Her social worker was pulling two full-ish garbage bags out of her trunk and setting them on the curb in front of Allie's new foster home.

"This is everything you left at New Beginnings."

"Oh. Good. I kind of figured I'd never see that stuff again."

Allie looked up to see a woman standing at the now-open door of the home and felt gripped with a whole new variety of fear. This woman in the doorway was Allie's foster mom, and she was a complete and utter stranger. She could be kind. She could be deranged. She could be anything. But she was already the most important person in this next chapter of Allie's life.

—

Allie sat in what was suddenly her new kitchen, drinking a glass of iced tea. When the woman looked away for any reason, Allie studied her. She seemed young. Or young*ish*, anyway. Late thirties. She had short dark hair. Creases on her forehead, maybe from the gravity of life.

Allie wanted to ask what motivated her to take in kids she'd never met before, but couldn't think of a proper way to phrase such a question.

"Where are all these other kids you said live here?"

"It's a school day," the woman said. She had been introduced as Julie Watley, but Allie had no idea what it was proper to call her. "Tomorrow you'll go, too."

"But it's so close to summer vacation. Just a few days, right?"

"Nine days, actually, for the high school. But you have to go. I'm sorry, but attendance in school is mandatory for the foster care system."

"Okay," Allie said. "Not a problem."

She wanted to say thank you. She felt overwhelmed—almost crushed—by the weight of her gratitude to this woman. For taking her. For the simple act of wanting her. But she couldn't seem to wrap the feeling into words.

"What do I call you?" Allie asked after a time, to break the silence.

"'Julie' is fine. So, listen. Tomorrow I'll take you to school because I have to register you. But after that . . . I have kids in three different levels of school, and I can't drive everybody everywhere, so I take the youngest ones to elementary. So you'll have a bus pass, and I'm trusting you to get there on your own. I know that might seem like a burden . . ."

"No," Allie said. "It's fine."

"Oh." Julie seemed surprised. "Good. Thank you for that positive attitude. A lot of the kids I've taken in over the years are used to being driven everywhere, and they're insulted at the idea."

"I just appreciate how you're letting me live here."

Julie looked up into Allie's face. Almost right into her eyes, but Allie cut her own gaze away in embarrassment. "You hungry?" Julie asked, without addressing the weightier topics of gratitude and desperation.

"Starving. I've barely been getting food because there's so much I don't eat."

"Right. Ms. Manheim told me about that. I have some Cuban black beans and rice if that sounds good. I hope brown rice is okay."

"It's . . . perfect," Allie said, feeling the beginning of prickly tears. "Thank you."

———

Allie lay in her single bed in the dark, most definitely not asleep. She had no idea if her new roommate, who was only ten, was sleeping or not. Based on sounds and breathing, Allie guessed not.

"What happened to the girl who had this bed before me?" Allie asked. Her voice was just a whisper. If the little girl was sleeping, Allie didn't want to wake her.

"She got to go home."

"Oh," Allie said. "That's good. I hope I get to go home sometime soon."

"I hope you do, too."

"That's sweet. Thank you."

"If you go home I get this room to myself again."

"Oh. Okay. Less sweet. But I get it. Sorry you have to share."

"It's not your fault," the little girl said. "I know you wouldn't be here if you had anyplace else to be."

"You can say that again."

"I know you wouldn't be here if you had anyplace else to be," the girl repeated.

Allie had no idea if it was her idea of a joke, or if she didn't understand the rhetorical nature of the phrase "You can say that again." Or maybe the younger girl simply had no sense of irony whatsoever.

—

On her second morning in the new place, Allie trudged in the direction of the bus stop. She wore her favorite jeans and her best summer-weather shirt, untucked just the way she liked it. She carried an empty backpack—at least, empty except for a brown-bag lunch Allie actually could eat. Julie had said the pack would be filled with books by the end of the day.

It all seemed like a waste to Allie. Eight more days. By the time she felt even halfway caught up with schoolwork, she'd be on summer vacation.

"Need a ride?"

Allie whipped her head around to see a familiar white van pull up to the curb near her left shoulder. She stopped in her tracks, stunned by the sudden familiarity of . . . well, everything.

"Bea. What are you doing here?"

"I don't have to be here if you don't want." With that, the passenger window began to power up again.

"No, I want you here. Really. I was just asking." The window stopped rising. "I just meant, like . . . how did you find me?"

"I followed you guys from the courthouse."

Allie stood a moment, taking in the changes. Then she walked two steps to the van and hopped in.

Just like old times.

———

"She missed me," Allie said, indicating the cat purring in her lap. "Ow! Phyllis! Ow!"

"Of course she did. Look out for the claws, though, when she's been missing you."

"Now you tell me. Why don't you clip them?"

"If you'd ever tried to clip that cat's claws, you wouldn't ask."

Allie took Julie's hand-drawn map of the route to school out of her pocket and studied it closely. "I think you turn left at this next light. Why did you leave so fast?"

"Which time?"

"After court."

"Oh. That. I was humiliated. That judge acted like he didn't want to hear a word I was saying. He kept gaveling at me and telling me to stop talking."

"He did that to me, too. I think it's just how he is. Bea, turn! This is our turn!"

"Oh," Bea said.

The tires squealed as she swung left.

"*I* wanted to hear what you said, though. Thanks for showing up in court."

"Good. I care more about you than I do that damned judge. So if *you* wanted to hear what I had to say, that'll do."

———

When she dropped Allie off at school, Allie didn't ask if Bea was sticking around. If she was planning to come back. If Allie should take the bus home, or if Bea was going to be there with a ride.

Or if Bea had just come around to say goodbye.

It wasn't that she forgot to ask, either. More that she couldn't bear to know.

———

Bea was there after school.

And the following morning.

And that afternoon.

And the morning after that.

Day after day she showed up and offered a ride, but they never discussed the ride after that. Life proceeded on a strict ride-by-ride basis.

# Chapter Thirty-Three

*The Epilogue-Like Part, Two Months Later, with Bathtubs*

"I have a surprise for you," Allie said, the moment she hopped into Bea's van.

"Before or after I drop you off at the shelter?"

Allie had been volunteering three hours a day at a homeless shelter since school had let out for the summer. It hadn't exactly been her idea. Volunteerism was encouraged in her foster home. But it hadn't been a bad idea, either. Plus Bea had driven her there and back every time, which Allie thought was worth the price of admission in itself.

"Neither one," Allie said. "We're not even going there today. My last day there was yesterday."

"Oh. You didn't tell me. So where are we going?"

"*My house*. And you get to take a bath in a nice, deep tub. Just like you always wanted. Just like I promised you that day in Monterey."

"Wait," Bea said. But, paradoxically, she pulled away from the curb as she said it. "How are we supposed to get into your house?"

"Through the door. My mom is home!" Allie heard her own voice rise to an odd squeal as she said it. "My social worker was supposed to drive me there officially this afternoon. But Julie said this was okay.

My mom got some kind of early release. My mom and dad found out it might take a year or more to get me back, even after they got out of jail. So my dad changed his story and put the whole thing on himself. Said my mom didn't even know about the tax stuff. She's been home a few days, but she had to get this hotshot lawyer. She had to have him to cut through some legal process to get custody again. Normally that can take months. Even years. You know. If a kid got pulled from a home because of abuse. But in this case it was pretty fast, because . . . you know. Money. And because legally she's sort of . . . innocent now, all of a sudden. Like, wrongly convicted. I don't know. It was all very strange."

Allie stopped to pull a breath after all those words.

"So," Bea said after a time, "you kept this from me because . . . ?"

"I only just found out that it worked. That the judge ruled in her favor. Besides. If I'd told you, it wouldn't have been a surprise."

"Right. Silly me. What about your dad?"

"He's in for probably another two years at least."

"Sorry to hear that. So . . . I hate to even ask this, but it seems to need asking. How does your mom feel about me coming in and taking a bath?"

"I guess we're about to find out."

Bea stepped on the brake too hard, and Allie lurched forward and hit the tether of her seat belt.

"You haven't even told her about me?"

"Relax, Bea. Trust me on this. I have everything under control."

———

Before Allie could even open her mouth, her mom grabbed her in a bear hug. She seemed not to have noticed the older woman standing behind Allie on the porch. She seemed disinclined to let Allie go again.

In time her mom pulled back, her hands holding Allie's face, and regarded her daughter closely. Allie studied her mother's face in return.

Her hair was cut strikingly short now, which felt like a shock. She seemed to have more lines in her forehead and around her eyes. And her eyes themselves looked different, though Allie could not have summed up in words exactly how they had changed.

And it was like a wonderful dream to see her again. And there were emotions surrounding it, big ones, but they all seemed to be hiding behind a wall where Allie couldn't quite get to them. Maybe it would just take time.

"Mom," Allie said, "this is Bea."

Her mom raised her eyes and looked past Allie. Her face fell.

"Bea is going to come in and take a bath," Allie added. "Okay?"

A silence, which only lasted a second or two, but felt heavy and wrong.

Allie reached back and took hold of Bea's elbow. Together they marched into the foyer.

"Actually," Allie said, "there's more. Bea's going to be living with us now. In the guest room. Bea, go out to the van and get the cat."

"Wait," Allie's mother said. "Wait, wait, wait. You can't bring a cat into this house."

"Why can't we?"

"Your father is allergic."

"My father is in prison for two more years at least."

"Right. And then he'll be back. And he's allergic to cats."

"Mom. The cat is eighteen years old."

"Oh." And with that, her mom seemed to run out of steam.

Meanwhile Bea stood behind Allie on the Persian rug of the foyer, uncharacteristically silent.

"So, it's all set. Bea and the cat will be living in the guest room."

"Honey. Can I talk to you privately?"

"No. No, Mom. Anything you can say to me you can say in front of my grandmother."

"Allie. Honey. I'm your mom. I *know* all your grandparents. Remember? If someone is your relative, I would know."

"It doesn't matter. It doesn't make any difference, Mom. I don't care that she's not actually related to us. Look, I know I'm telling you how it's going to be. Not exactly asking. But you fell out on me, Mom. I'm sorry, but I needed somebody and you weren't there. And Bea was there. And she didn't let me down, and I'm not letting her down now. So, Bea. Go get the cat."

They all three stood a moment in that stunning silence.

Then Allie's mom spoke up.

"Okay," she said. "For right now at least . . . I guess . . . go get the cat."

———

Allie lay on the guest room bed instead of her own, poking at the feeling of the familiarity of home. She almost might never have been gone. The whole last few months could have been a dream. But no, it couldn't have been, because Allie was not the person who had lived here before. And in most respects that was good.

"So is that everything you ever wanted in a tub?" she asked when Bea stepped out of the guest bathroom.

"All that and more," Bea said, toweling her hair dry. "In every way the bathtub of my dreams. Where's your mom?"

"Downstairs in the living room. Crying. And being shocked. While you were taking your bath I told her the whole story. Everything that happened to me."

"Oh," Bea said. She set down the towel and perched on the edge of the guest bed, where Allie lay sprawled, petting the cat. "So . . . you honestly think she's going to let me live here?"

"I think so. I'm not really giving her much choice. Not that I can force her, but . . . it's just not something I'm going to back down on.

And she feels so guilty. She owes me one. And she knows it. I think it's going to be okay."

Bea sat still a minute. Then she began swiveling her head. Looking all around the room. Even up at the ceiling.

"I didn't really take all this in before. Because I didn't believe I get to stay here. I'm still not sure. She'll find a way to get me out."

"Over my dead body," Allie said.

———

Just before bedtime Allie's mom came in and sat on the bed beside her.

Her mom opened her mouth to speak, then burst into tears again. For a moment she just sat and cried, and nothing was said.

Then she seemed to pull herself together some. At least enough to manage words.

"I am so, so sorry for what happened to you out there, Allie. And what could have happened. I know it's not good enough to sit here and say it. But somehow I'm going to make it up to you. You watch. I'm not sure entirely how. But I will."

"All you have to do is let Bea stay, and then we're good."

Unfortunately, her mom had no reply. So maybe Bea had been right after all.

Allie talked over the awkwardness of the moment.

"So, Mom. Two things I need to ask you. About my plans and all. When school starts again, I might be going around to some different schools in L.A. and doing some . . . talks. So other girls maybe don't end up in that same kind of trouble. I don't know how that'll fit with my schoolwork. I don't know a lot of things. I actually haven't worked it out yet. Haven't gotten like . . . official permission or anything. But I want to do it. And a cop told me I could do it. So I'll do it. I just have to figure out the details."

"I think that's fine, honey. I like the idea. And I'll help in any way I can. But what's the other thing?"

"Oh, Right. Bea and I need to take a little trip sometime. It's just like this loose end we want to tie up. We're going to drive down the coast to the Mexican border. I mean . . . with your permission. Of course."

Allie watched for a reaction. Her mom rocked back a little on the bed, but not much more. In the dim light from the hall, Allie couldn't see the details of her mother's expression.

"I don't like the sound of that."

"Why not?"

"Sometimes people go to Mexico for weird reasons."

"We're not going to Mexico. Just down to the border. We want to be able to say we saw the whole West Coast of the United States. We drove all the way up to the Puget Sound. And now if we just go from here to Mexico we will have seen the whole thing."

"I don't know, Allie. I have misgivings."

"What kind of misgivings?"

"Like what if she has some illegal business in Mexico?"

"I told you. We're not crossing the border."

"But what if you get all the way down there, and it turns out you are but you didn't know it?"

"She doesn't even have a passport, Mom."

For several moments, Allie lay on her bed in silence, trying to read her mother's face in the dim light. Trying to find a way to turn this conversation in a better direction.

"If you're so worried," Allie said, "come with us."

"Oh. I didn't know I was invited."

Another silence, during which Allie felt a softening of the energy between them. A lifting of tension.

"That would be nice, actually," her mother added. "It might be kind of fun. Yeah. Let's do that. Maybe next week. Meanwhile I have to ask you a question. And it's important. So think before you answer. And please be honest with me. That story you told me . . . Where you were about to end up . . . That woman in the guest room, the one you've decided is your new grandmother . . . I mean, I know she gave you a ride and all. But did she have a *big* part in things not happening that way? As big as you made it sound?"

"Oh, definitely," Allie said, not stopping to think as she had been instructed. "A huge part. She drove me out of there before the guy could get up and find me. And then she looked after me. Jeez, without Bea . . . I hate to think."

Allie thought she saw her mother sit up a little straighter, but it might have been her imagination.

"Okay. Okay then, honey. Then she's welcome here."

She kissed Allie on top of her head and slipped out of the room.

—

Allie waited a minute or two, then climbed out of bed and padded barefoot down the hall to the guest room. She knocked lightly on the door, opened it, and stuck her head into the darkened space.

"Bea," she whispered. "You awake?"

"Yes. Why?"

"Welcome home," Allie said. At a stronger volume.

Then she put herself back to bed.

# *ALLIE AND BEA* BOOK CLUB

# QUESTIONS

1. At the beginning of the book Bea is called by a man who claims he is from the IRS. What painful choice is Bea forced to make after succumbing to this scam? Do you think she chose wisely?

2. After Bea takes to the road and starts living in her van, she quickly realizes she does not have the money to make it past the next few days. She makes the choice to steal a cell phone and pawn it. Are there some circumstances where breaking the law is justified? Is this one of them?

3. Allie and Bea perceive the world quite differently. In what ways do these views shift throughout the novel and become less black and white?

4. Allie's childhood offered her everything money could buy, and yet circumstances left her just as homeless as Bea. In what ways did her parents' drive for wealth lead to her situation?

5. Allie's choice to be a vegan is based on her principles and beliefs, and she firmly adheres to them throughout most of the book. Do you agree with her choices despite her circumstances? Why do you think she stands so strongly by these ideals?

6. How does the kindness of strangers play a crucial part in both the outer and inner journeys of the main characters?

7. Allie suggests that they "just keep going" and turn their homeless plight into an adventure. How does this decision shape their overall outlook on life and help them both grow? Do you think putting a positive spin on a difficult situation can ultimately affect the outcome?

8. Despite Allie and Bea both being let down multiple times in their past by others, in what ways do they ultimately come through for each other?

# ABOUT THE AUTHOR

Photo © 2014 Hunter Kilpatrick

Catherine Ryan Hyde is the author of thirty-two published books. Her bestselling 1999 novel, *Pay It Forward*, adapted into a major Warner Bros. motion picture starring Kevin Spacey and Helen Hunt, made the American Library Association's Best Books for Young Adults list and was translated into more than two dozen languages for distribution in more than thirty countries. Her novels *Becoming Chloe* and *Jumpstart the World* were included on the ALA's Rainbow List; *Jumpstart the World* was also a finalist for two Lambda Literary Awards and won Rainbow Awards in two categories. *The Language of Hoofbeats* won a Rainbow Award. More than fifty of her short stories have been published in many journals, including the *Antioch Review*, *Michigan Quarterly Review*, the *Virginia Quarterly Review*, *Ploughshares*, *Glimmer Train*, and the *Sun*, and in the anthologies *Santa Barbara Stories* and *California Shorts* as well as the bestselling anthology *Dog Is My Co-Pilot*. Her short fiction received honorable mention in the Raymond Carver Short Story Contest, a second-place win for the Tobias Wolff Award, and nominations for *Best American Short Stories*, the O. Henry Award, and the Pushcart Prize.

Three have also been cited in *Best American Short Stories*.

Hyde is the founder and former president of the Pay It Forward Foundation. As a professional public speaker, she has addressed the National Conference on Education, twice spoken at Cornell University, met with AmeriCorps members at the White House, and shared a dais with Bill Clinton.